Rare Vintage

Rare Vintage

By

Dee Rismiller

Desert Palm Press
www.desertpalmpress.com

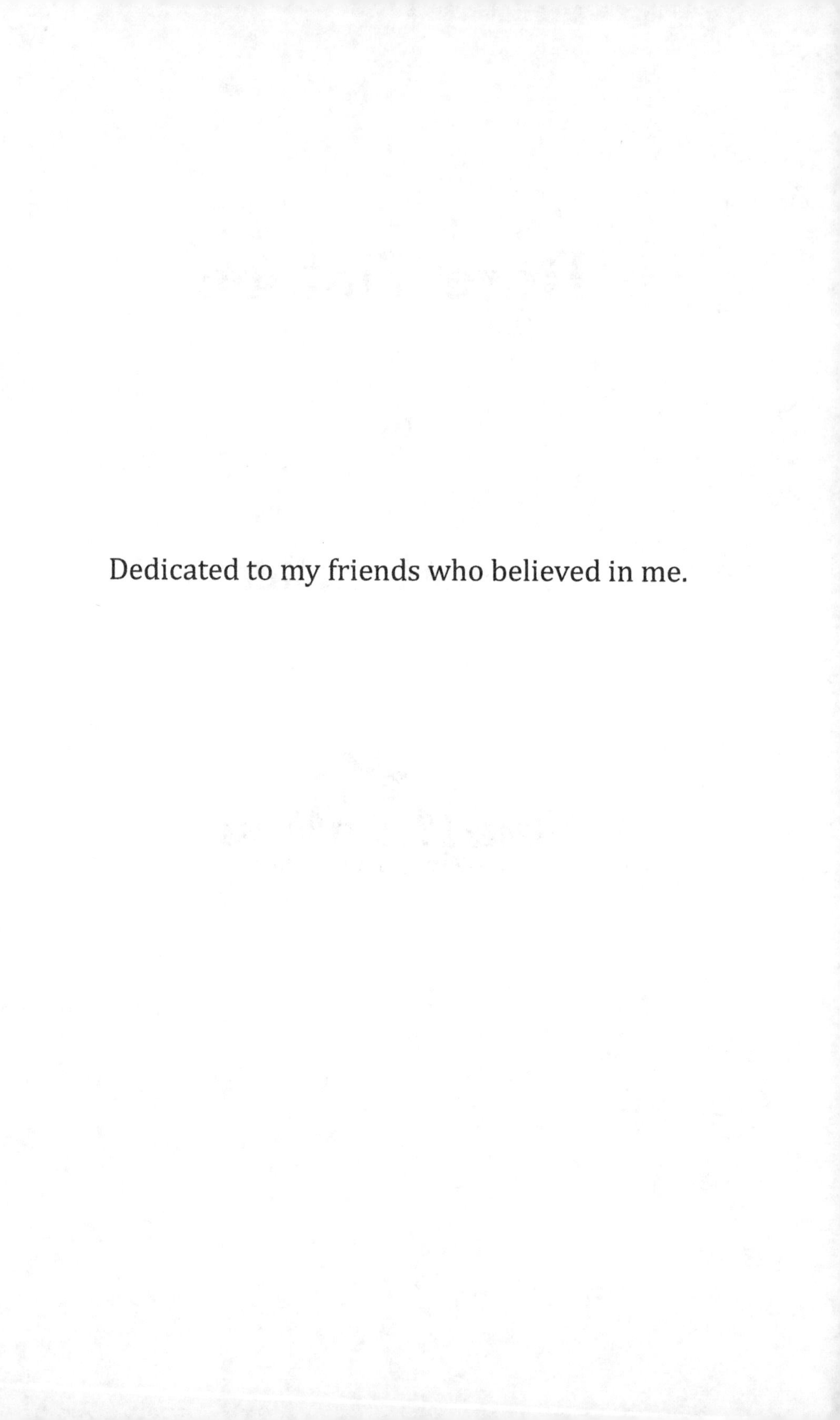

Dedicated to my friends who believed in me.

Prologue

February 14, 2025
Friday

ERIN'S FEET AND BACK were killing her. Doing two back-to-back autopsies inevitably strained muscles that she would just as soon forget she had, but completing three was near torture. Erin never doubted her calling to join the FBI, to track down criminals and put them behind bars where they belonged. There were days, though, when she sometimes regretted having gone to medical school, days like this one. Well, she didn't *really* regret it. She just wearied of performing autopsy after autopsy on innocent victims and still being no closer to identifying the UNSUB (unknown subject) responsible for their deaths.

With a heavy sigh, she didn't sit down so much as collapse into the chair. She brought her right foot up to prop it on her left knee by pulling on the fabric of her scrub pants until it was within reach. Once she had her foot in place on her knee, she pushed off her shoe and started to massage the knots out of the arch of her foot. She would need a long, hot soak in the tub when she got home.

"Good night, Dr. Little."

"Good night, Tom," she called out to the attendant who had placed the last of the three slain women she had just examined into the cooler.

Tiredly, she slipped her shoe back on and turned her chair to face the computer. Erin typed up her initial notes on the final autopsy and printed them out. She grabbed the copies of the audiotapes she had made during the autopsies to transcribe in detail later and entered the locker room. It was a hellacious way to spend Valentine's Day, not that she had any plans to celebrate the day with anyone, but doing autopsies on young women was just...Erin shook her head and let out a heavy sigh as she started the shower.

After a hot shower, she changed into clean clothes and headed out to return to the Hoover building in Washington, DC, where the taskforce was set up. For security purposes, the bodies were being kept and examined at Quantico.

Exhausted, Erin dropped into the chair beside her partner, Special Agent Derek Holton.

"How did the autopsies go?" he asked, unable to mask the hopefulness in his voice.

She let out a soft sigh. "Nothing new: no fibers, no DNA, nothing." Like everyone working the case, she felt exhausted and drained.

Erin's reputation as a top forensic pathologist and an excellent investigator had led to them being assigned to the taskforce that was formed to identify and stop the serial killer the press had labeled "The Slasher."

Holton had been her partner for less than a year. He'd joined the Army right out of high school. After three years in the war and two Purple Hearts, he was released from the military and attended college on the GI Bill. During undergraduate school, his talent for reading people came to the fore, and he majored in psychology. While obtaining his degree, Holton had worked diligently to physically rehabilitate his left leg—injured by shrapnel from an IED and responsible for cutting his time in the Army short. Holton had joined the police force the same day he graduated from college. Only a year later, the FBI accepted him into the program. After graduating from Quantico, he was assigned to the Washington, DC field office and became her junior partner for her to mentor.

She took in her partner's unusually scruffy appearance. He usually kept his six-foot frame a little too stiff, as if his suit was his dress uniform and he was about to stand inspection. But right now, his jacket was tossed over the back of his chair, his sleeves were unevenly rolled up, shadows were apparent under his blue eyes, he was leaning on his elbows on the desk, and he needed a shave. This was his first experience with a taskforce. Just like every other agent, he was doing whatever was asked of him and giving it all he had.

Suddenly, there was a quiet commotion in the bullpen near the elevators. Assistant Director Benjamin Taylor, the man leading the taskforce, had left his office and gone to the lobby. A loud ding announced the elevator's arrival, and soon after, a hushed conversation took place in the open doorway. Taylor had been an offensive lineman in college and carried his bulk with grace and athleticism even into his late forties. His six-and-a-half foot large frame blocked everyone's view of the people in the lobby to whom he spoke, but when he turned and escorted his guests to his office, the whispered comments started. His guests consisted of the director and a dark-haired woman.

"I'll be damned."

Erin looked at her partner. "What? You can't be surprised the director would drop in after all the heat the Bureau has been taking in the press."

"No, not him—*her*. I can't believe it's her."

Erin looked at the back of the woman as she disappeared into Taylor's office before he closed the door. "What do you mean, Holton? Do you know her? Who is she?"

"I never thought she'd ever come back to the Bureau."

She tried to make sense of Holton's almost reverent tone of voice and his wide-eyed expression. "Who is she, Holton?" she asked.

"Jessica Morgan!"

When she didn't react to the name, Derek's expression changed to incredulity. "Come on, Little. You must have heard of Special Agent Jessica Morgan. She's only the best profiler the FBI has ever had. She's the one that took down Neil Croskey. And she was the only one who correctly profiled Devon Conrad."

She suppressed a smile at her partner's enthusiasm. His desire to train as a profiler and join one of the Bureau's Behavior Analysis Unit teams was no secret. She glanced at Taylor's closed office door. Erin, of course, knew that Neil Croskey and Devon Conrad were both particularly vicious serial killers, even if she hadn't been involved with those cases and didn't know the details. She was also aware that Devon Conrad had brutally murdered an FBI agent before he was eventually caught.

"I'd love the chance to compare notes with her on this case."

Rolling her shoulders, Erin stood up. "Well, it's late, and we both need to get some sleep so we're ready for tomorrow. Come on, Holton, let's get out of here."

With a wistful glance at the assistant director's office, Holton stood and walked with Erin to the elevator.

Chapter One

AFTER THE DIRECTOR LEFT, Assistant Director Taylor took Jess to an empty office. "It's not much, Agent Morgan, but it's yours for as long as you want."

"Thank you."

"Copies of the files are in the box there," he said, pointing out the obvious box on the desk. "The director ordered them prepared for your arrival. I didn't know what time you would get in, so…"

"I'll get started." Jess slipped off her coat and hung it on the back of the chair.

"Uh, okay. Are you sure you don't want to get checked into your hotel? I mean, get some rest and start fresh in the morning?" he asked.

She shook her head. "I'm fine," she said. "I'd rather get started. Thank you, Assistant Director," Jess said as she sat down and opened the box.

"Ben."

She looked up at him.

"You can call me Ben," the AD said with a smile.

She pulled a file out of the box and turned back to the desk without comment.

"Well, if you need anything—files, coffeemaker, pencil sharpener—just let me know."

Jess wondered why AD Taylor was still standing in her office. She looked over her shoulder at him and saw him simply staring at the box of files. "I work better with paper files than I do digital files."

He nodded.

"Thank you. I'll let you know if I need anything else," she said, dismissing him.

Taylor nodded again and left.

Jess read the extensive file on each murder that made up the string of killings done by "The Slasher." She did not read any of the profiles or conclusions other agents had prepared. She was there to do her workup on the UNSUB. The Slasher was, no doubt, a clever and very brutal killer. He enjoyed killing. He also enjoyed sending the local police and the FBI on wild goose chases. Only a cursory glance at the crime scene photos was enough to tell her this was bad. Of course the director only called her in for the nasty ones.

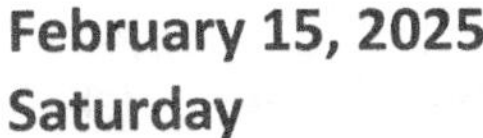

February 15, 2025
Saturday

More than eighteen hours after she'd started, Jess was still in her office. She had taken several crime scene photos from the files and taped them up on the walls, along with several sheets of handwritten notes she'd created while reading the files. She moved slowly, from one gory photo to the next, studying each in detail.

She was on the hunt. Only time would tell how long it would take to find her prey.

After completing her final circuit around the room, Jess stood in front of the only window and stared out, looking at nothing. For nearly an hour, Jess stood motionless, allowing her mind to clear, to sort, to make connections. Finally, she took a deep breath, turned, and left her office. She walked through the open door of AD Taylor's office.

Taylor looked up. "What can I do for you?"

"How many of the bodies do we have?"

"Here? The last three. Local law enforcement or the Bureau field offices handled the previous ones. The first four have been buried. Because they were all in different jurisdictions, it took a while before we connected all the dots and realized what was going on."

Jess walked over to the window and looked out. "Who's the best pathologist you've got?"

"SSA Little."

"Little. She did the posts on the last three victims," she said, recalling the name and signature on the autopsy reports.

"Yes."

"How long until you can get the other bodies here?"

"Within a day—at least for some of them."

"Do it," she said decisively. Without another word, she turned from the window and left Taylor's office.

February 16, 2025
Sunday

When Erin walked into the autopsy bay after changing into her scrubs, she was surprised to find one of the women she'd autopsied two days earlier pulled out of its drawer and someone in scrubs looking at her. "Can I help you?" she asked.

The person turned around and faced her. "Hi. I'm SSA Jessica Morgan," the brunette said with a small smile as she offered her hand in greeting.

"SSA Erin Little," she replied as they shook hands. She quickly sized up the other agent: average five-foot-six height and apparent athletic build. Though attractive, there was nothing particularly striking in Morgan's features save her gray eyes.

"...you all right?"

"Wha-what?" Erin was surprised to find she was still holding the other agent's hand and staring into her sparkling gray eyes. She felt embarrassed as she awkwardly let go and averted her gaze. She almost felt short of breath and had to shift her feet under herself to regain her balance.

"Are you all right, Agent Little?"

"I'm fine. I'm fine."

Morgan seemed to sense it best not to question the veracity of her statement and let it go unchallenged. "I want to thank you for looking at the other bodies for me."

"Not a problem. I just hope we find something. I haven't been able to yet."

"I know. But I'm hoping the UNSUB was less thorough in covering his tracks in the earlier cases. I was told that if anything was missed in the autopsies of the earlier victims, you would be the best person to find something."

Erin couldn't help but feel a sense of professional pride, pride hard-won.

Morgan looked back down at the body for a couple of moments. "She was beautiful and too young to end up here," she said reverently. After another moment, she pulled the sheet over the body again and pushed the drawer back in.

"Who do you want to start with?" Erin asked.

"Let's start with Karen Rivers."

Even though it was a re-examination of the body, it was still time-consuming. Erin had to be careful not to make any assumptions as to whether the previous pathologist had missed anything. It was well past lunchtime when she finished the first autopsy. As she reached for the drawer that contained the next body, Morgan suggested they break for lunch.

"I don't need a break. I'm fine," said Erin.

Agent Morgan looked at her. "I know your back and legs must be killing you. Mine ache, and I'm not the one cutting. Let's break for lunch and come back fresh."

Erin hesitated but nodded in agreement when she realized Morgan was being genuine and wasn't patronizing her. They went into the locker room to change into their street clothes.

"Do you like Italian, Agent Morgan?"

"Italian?"

"There's a nice little Italian restaurant not far from here. Would you care to join me for lunch?"

"Do you mean Benetti's?"

"Yes."

Morgan paused as she dressed, obviously giving the invitation some consideration. "All right. But would you mind if I met you there? There's something I need to do first. It'll only take a few minutes."

"Sure thing. I'll see you there."

They went their separate ways when they left the locker room.

Erin had only been seated for about five minutes when SSA Morgan arrived. A waiter quickly took their orders, leaving them with just their thoughts.

Finally, Erin broke the silence. "You seem very comfortable in the autopsy bay. Most agents aren't."

"I wouldn't exactly say I'm comfortable, but it is part of the work." She paused for a beat. "It's hard to figure out what the killer's thought processes are if you don't look at their 'art.'"

Erin nodded, understanding what the other agent meant. "How long have you been with the Bureau?"

"About nine years, but not all in one shot. I resigned for a while and then returned. And yourself, Agent Little?"

"I'm coming up on ten years."

"How long have you been with the BAU?"

"Oh, I'm not currently with the BAU, although I have been with them in the past. I'm currently assigned to the DC field office, where I've been for about a year. I've also been an instructor at the Academy. What about you?"

"My first six years with the Bureau, I was with the BAU. I was assigned right out of the academy."

Erin was impressed. Typically, there was a three-year minimum requirement of field work before an agent was even considered for assignment to the BAU. But in truth, the positions were so competitive that agents selected for the unit usually had significantly more experience than a mere three years.

"A lot of the agents were unhappy with my presence in the unit," Morgan said, as if she'd sensed Erin's thoughts.

"Well, my partner says you made quite a name for yourself while with the BAU." Erin watched a dark eyebrow rise.

"Who's your partner? Maybe I know him."

Letting out a soft chuckle, Erin said, "I doubt it. Special Agent Derek Holton has been an agent for less than a year. He's a rookie."

The eyebrow crawled a little higher on Morgan's forehead. "Oh?"

"He's…" Erin paused as she tried to find the right words. "Holton is a nice guy: ex-army and goal-oriented. He knows what he wants." She smiled with amusement. "And he wants to join the BAU and become as good at profiling as you are. I think he's professionally enamored with you." Seeing a light blush beginning to color the other woman's cheeks, Erin changed the topic. "What field office are you assigned to now?"

"I'm not."

"I don't understand."

"I'm not assigned to a field office. I'm a traveling troubleshooter. I work on a case-by-case basis. For all I know, I'll be in Wisconsin or Utah next week."

"Sounds like a lot of travel."

Morgan nodded. "They're trying to get me to return to Quantico."

"To teach at the Academy?"

She again nodded.

"Are you considering it?"

"I've guest-lectured, but full time? I don't know if it's what I want. It's very different from being in the field. You know. You've taught."

Erin nodded. "Yes, it is. I did enjoy it though."

They continued making small talk during their meal, but before they were done, Morgan's phone interrupted them.

"Morgan…All right. Don't let anyone touch a thing and keep everyone out of the house." She hung up and looked at Erin. "There's another victim, and I need to get to the crime scene. I'd like for you to come along."

Erin nodded. "Absolutely." She knew there were often clues that could be found when a body was initially inspected *in situ*, rather than waiting until it had been manhandled and sent to the morgue.

They quickly dropped money onto the table to cover their meals and left the restaurant.

Both women ducked as they exited the helicopter when it landed in Richmond, Virginia. AD Taylor was waiting for them at the front door of the modest house in an unpretentious neighborhood. "No one has been inside since the responding officer found her. Nothing has been processed."

Morgan nodded. "Thank you. Keep everyone outside until SSA Little and I are done."

He nodded. "You got it."

Erin and Morgan donned shoe protectors to prevent contaminating the scene with their footprints and entered the house. Erin heard Agent Morgan stifle a slight hiss as she inhaled. She couldn't blame her; the stench of death was a singular odor.

They both carefully approached the body, slipping on gloves. After Erin had taken pictures, Morgan tenderly moved a lock of hair to expose the woman's entire face. Morgan whispered something that sounded a lot like "I'm sorry," before standing and stepping away from the body. She slowly moved around the room, taking careful visual inventory of everything.

Erin began a gentle and deliberate inspection of the body.

"How long?" Morgan asked.

"She's been dead three to five hours. I'll know better once we get her back to Quantico." She stopped and peered closely at something on the woman's shoulder near her neck, stuck in some blood. "A hair." She quickly took pictures of it and then carefully removed it with tweezers, bagging it. "This isn't the victim's." She looked up and met Morgan's inquisitive eyes. She might have just found their first piece of tangible forensic evidence.

Erin resumed her inspection of the body while Morgan continued to take in the surroundings. After a while, Erin announced she was done inspecting the body, but she quickly realized she was talking to an empty room. She found Morgan in the victim's bedroom, looking around.

"I can get started on the autopsy as soon as I get the body back to Quantico, Agent Morgan. I'll take the body back now and meet up with you later," she offered.

Morgan looked at her. "I'd rather sit in on the autopsy, if you don't mind." She paused, a look of consternation drawing her features together. "Something doesn't feel right."

"All right. Do you want me to take the body back now and wait for you there?"

Morgan took a deep breath and looked around the room once more. "No, I'm done here."

They exited the house together. The body was loaded on the helicopter, and they flew back to Quantico.

Once they were back in the autopsy bay, they worked together to remove the victim's clothes, photographing and documenting each step along the way. Erin examined the body under a magnifying glass, inspecting every inch of skin. It took four hours to complete the painstakingly meticulous autopsy.

They rode back to the Hoover building together, where the taskforce was busy gathering information about the latest victim.

"Little," Holton called out to her as they entered the bullpen.

Walking over to him, Erin almost laughed at the eagerness she saw in his eyes. "Supervisory Special Agent Morgan, may I introduce you to my partner, Special Agent Derek Holton. Agent Holton, SSA Jessica Morgan."

Holton looked like a beagle puppy eager to please as he shook Morgan's hand. "I'm so glad to meet you, Agent Morgan! I've read about every case of yours that I've been able to access. Did you know you still hold the record for the best solve rate in the BAU? I'd love to learn how you do what you do. If you have some time, I'd love to sit down and discuss some of your past cases. I mean, how are you so often right with your profiles when others are wrong? Especially in cases like Neil Croskey and Devon Gaines Con—"

Upon seeing Morgan's expression of amusement disappear and shadows pass behind her eyes, Erin stepped in and physically rescued Morgan's hand from Holton's grip. "That's enough, Derek," she admonished, cutting him off.

Holton had the good graces to blush. "I'm so sorry, Agent Morgan. I didn't mean...sorry." He looked at Erin. "So how are you doing?" he asked.

She nodded. "Fine. We just finished with the latest victim's autopsy."

"So that makes fourteen," he said with obvious disappointment.

"I'm not so sure about that," Morgan said softly.

Holton and Erin both looked at her in surprise.

"What makes you say that?" Erin asked.

Morgan let out a breath and shook her head slightly. "Not much more than a feeling at this point."

AD Taylor entered and called everyone together. He went over the information that had been gathered so far about the latest victim and how her murder was consistent with the killer they were tracking. He also reviewed the current profile they were using.

Erin watched as, after the meeting, Morgan went into her office without a word, closing the door behind herself.

Chapter Two

February 18, 2025
Tuesday

FORTY-EIGHT HOURS LATER, ERIN was exhausted from re-examining the bodies of the earlier victims that had been shipped to Quantico. She also knew she wasn't the only one feeling the investigation's stress and strain. AD Taylor had called a meeting for that afternoon. Everyone on the taskforce, regardless of what shift they worked, was required to be in attendance.

She sat at her desk and checked her email while waiting for the appointed time to arrive. Holton came and sat on the edge of her desk with a coffee cup in hand.

"You know, Little, I've been thinking."

"That's a dangerous thing," she quipped. "And you better have another coffee if you're going plop your butt on my desk."

"This one is yours," he said with a bright smile, holding the cup out to her. "Just the way you like it—black, two sugars."

She accepted the proffered cup and carefully sipped the steaming liquid. She suppressed a moan of pleasure. "Adequate," she told him. It would not do to let Holton know he'd done well. He was still a rookie. After a couple more sips of the delicious coffee, Erin looked up at Holton. "Okay, so what have you been thinking about?"

"The blood."

"What do you mean?"

Before Holton could answer, AD Taylor entered the bullpen and started the meeting. In truth, it wasn't much of a meeting. It was simply a rehashing of everything the taskforce had investigated and a review of their working theories. Unfortunately, there was nothing new of significance to report or share with the taskforce.

After everyone was dismissed, Erin turned to her partner. "You were saying something about the blood?"

"Well, I was just wondering."

"About what?"

"There's a lot of blood missing from the bodies. Where is it?"

"Holton, the knife wounds explain the blood missing from the bodies."

"Not all of it is at the crime scenes. The missing blood didn't just evaporate into thin air."

"Maybe the UNSUB is a vampire and drank it." She smirked.

His eyes widened, full of alarm.

If he was too tired to recognize her jest for the joke that it was, he was overdue for some sleep. "Until we solve the case, we're not going to know for certain."

"I guess you're right."

"Come on, Holton, you're obviously sleep-deprived. Go home, Get some sleep. It's okay to think about and wonder about these things, but don't let the minutiae prevent you from getting sleep and taking care of yourself. You're no good to anyone if you're walking around half asleep anyway."

"Little—"

"Go. Get some sleep. We'll talk tomorrow." She pushed him toward the elevators.

"You're right. See you tomorrow, Little."

Erin started to follow but stopped. She felt the pull to go back to the bullpen, so she turned back. Regardless of the time of day, some agents were always present when a taskforce was formed to work a case such as The Slasher. The mood in the bullpen was subdued due to the lack of progress and growing body count. But that wasn't why she was there.

She stopped and looked at the closed door to one particular office. She hadn't seen the mysterious agent since they had finished the autopsy on the most recent victim, Andrea Bishop. Something about the enigmatic agent intrigued Erin, something she couldn't put her finger on. A good investigator didn't rush to conclusions without evidence, and Erin was nothing if not a good investigator. Nor was she a coward.

Erin took a deep breath, marched to the closed door, and knocked.

"Come in," came from inside.

She opened the door and saw Agent Morgan sitting at the worktable in the room. The walls were covered with grim crime-scene photos. The desk and worktable were overflowing with stacks of file folders, reports, and even more photos.

The fact that Morgan had obviously been holed up in the office for over forty-eight hours didn't diminish the woman's attractiveness. Though a bit creased, her suit still snugly fit the toned form of the agent. Her dark, shoulder-length hair had lost none of its shininess. And her captivating gray eyes were still alert and bright, though a tenseness surrounded her mouth and eyes. Even so, she smiled warmly at Erin when she looked up.

"Ah, Agent Little, you have great timing."

"Oh?"

"I need your expert opinion on something."

"What can I help you with?"

"I've got some autopsy reports I'd like you to look over for me, if you don't mind."

"All right." Erin slipped off her jacket and set her briefcase down on the end of the worktable. She opened it, took out a folder, and gave it to Morgan. "Here are my findings regarding the last re-examinations of the earlier victims. Unfortunately, there's nothing new to report. Sorry."

"Not your fault." Morgan handed her a file folder.

"Is there something specific I'm looking for in these reports?"

Morgan shook her head. "I don't want to bias you. In the meantime, can I get you something to drink? I can offer you bottled water or hot tea," she said with a gesture to the small square refrigerator in the corner next to the desk and the coffeemaker sitting on top of it.

"Tea would be fine."

While Erin began to read the autopsy reports, Jess prepared two mugs of hot tea. Both women sipped their drinks while they reviewed their respective reports.

It wasn't long before she saw why Jess had asked her to review the autopsy reports. After an initial, quick review, Erin felt her heart drop to the pit of her stomach. She then went back through the reports slowly and carefully to make sure. She set the last report down and closed the folder on the table. "Oh god," she whispered. She looked up and met Morgan's eyes.

"So I'm not crazy?" Morgan asked quietly.

Erin shook her head. She saw Morgan close her eyes as she grimaced and lowered her head for a few seconds.

Morgan stood up and attached several more pictures to the wall. She had labeled each with names, dates, and places. They both stared at the line of victims, now significantly longer than the fourteen they'd had two days before. They shared a look. It was obvious they both felt sick to their stomachs.

Erin's voice was a little shaky when she spoke. "Why didn't anyone know about these before?"

Morgan sat back down and ran a hand through her hair. "The Violent Criminal Apprehension Program is only as good as the information entered into it. The problem is that some one-horse towns and rural areas just don't utilize it. I've been on the phone nonstop getting these."

Erin shook her head. "It never ceases to amaze me when we run into a sheriff or a police chief that doesn't even think about looking at, much less utilizing ViCAP. It's been available to all law enforcement since 2008." She sighed and looked at the new pictures on the wall. "So The Slasher has been active longer than we thought."

Morgan nodded. "Yeah. I'll need your help to look at his earliest victims."

"Of course. You have it," she said.

Morgan nodded again. "Thank you." She let out a sigh. "Get a good night's sleep, Agent Little. We'll be on the road tomorrow. If I know the director, he'll light some fires, and the exhumation orders will be signed first thing in the morning." She stood up but wavered so badly that she tried to grab the table's edge to steady herself but missed.

Jumping up, Erin grabbed Morgan, keeping her upright. "Whoa, whoa." She was surprised at how light the other woman felt. "Easy does it," Erin said as she helped Jess back into the chair.

"I'm okay."

Erin lifted Morgan's chin and looked in her eyes. She held up the index finger of her right hand. "Follow my finger."

Morgan impatiently followed her finger and then sat back in the chair. "I'm fine, Agent Little. I just stood up too fast."

"Let me be the judge of that since I'm the doctor."

Morgan frowned. "I've got an M.D. as well, and I know I'm fine. My blood sugar is just a little low. I need to eat something, that's all."

Erin stood up straight. "When was the last time you ate?"

"Lunch," she answered.

Erin didn't miss the slight blush that colored the other agent's cheeks. She quirked an eyebrow. "Lunch? Do you mean the lunch we had together over two days ago?" Not bothering to hide her disapproval, Erin hauled SSA Morgan to her feet, helped her into her suit jacket, and physically took her by the hand to lead her out of the building and to a restaurant.

The women returned the menus to the waitress once they had placed their orders.

Jess sipped her water and gave the platinum blonde sitting across from her a slight smirk. "So do you always manhandle fellow agents and forcibly abscond with them to restaurants, Agent Little?" It wasn't until Little had forcefully dragged Jess from her office that she realized the short woman—Little couldn't be more five-foot-three without her high heels—packed more strength in her petite form than Jess would have ever guessed.

"Do you always ignore common sense and not eat or sleep for days at a time, Agent Morgan?"

"Not on purpose. But enough time has been lost on this case," she pointed out. "And enough lives," she said softly.

"I understand that. But you won't do anyone any good if you run yourself into the ground."

"I'm pretty resilient."

"Mm-hmm. Says the woman who nearly did a nosedive into a table not fifteen minutes ago."

"I know my blood sugar is down. I would have gotten something to eat and been fine." Jess took in the sternly arched eyebrow. "But a hearty meal is a good idea," she finally conceded with a small smile.

"Well, at least you have some sense."

"You know, Agent Little, if you're going to give me such a hard time, you may as well call me Jess."

"Only if you call me Erin." Little's smile brightened her eyes.

"Deal."

"Oh, I meant to tell you about the hair we found on the last victim."
Jess nodded. "It doesn't belong to our UNSUB."

"Right. It belonged to an earlier victim. How did you know?"

"That it belonged to an earlier victim? I didn't. That it wasn't his?" She shrugged. "He likes playing games with us. So far, every piece of forensic evidence that we've found has turned into a red herring. He's taunting us, thumbing his nose at us. He's saying, 'Look at how good I am. Not only can I do what I want, kill who I want, but I can send you on a wild goose chase too.'"

"It's scary when they're this good."

"Yes, it is. But it will also be his downfall. Eventually, he'll get tired of the game as it is. He'll get tired of manipulating us so easily. After all, what fun is the chase if there's no chance of being caught? So he'll eventually leave a clue that will be genuine."

"You mean he wants to be caught?"

"No. He only wants a *chance* he'll be caught so he can show how superior he is when he isn't. Our job is to be better than him anyway. To catch him before he takes more innocent lives."

"Let me ask you something. What do you think he's doing with the blood? Granted, the crime scenes are bloody, but not enough to account for all of it. There are at least a couple of pints unaccounted for. Is he taking it to use in some ritual or something?"

"I think he's taking it just because he can." Jess let out a quiet huff. "Then again, he could be washing his hair with it. There's no telling. Either way, we have to find him and stop him."

The waitress arrived with their food. They managed to restrain themselves from discussing the case while they ate. After dinner, Little dropped Jess off at her hotel.

Even though Jess had managed to maintain an acceptable semblance of small talk during dinner with Little, she had been reviewing each case file in her head. The profile of the UNSUB was still not falling into place for her. Something was missing. She knew she needed some solid hours of sleep, and then she would begin fresh in the morning. She also had to write a summary of the new cases for everyone on the taskforce and prepare her presentation.

A call to the director to let him know about the additional victims was the last thing Jess did before finally crawling into bed and getting some much-needed sleep.

Chapter Three

February 19, 2025
Wednesday

ERIN ARRIVED AT WORK early after a good night's sleep. She was surprised not to see her partner at his desk. Having grown up an Army brat, she was used to the mindset of "on time is late" that Holton still maintained from his time in the military. It was one of many things her father had instilled in her and her two brothers, Brian and Danny. It never really worked with her older sister. Lauren had been the eldest Little child, an artist, and a very unique individual. In another time, she might have been a flower child. Getting Lauren anywhere at a specific time was like herding cats.

Before Erin could travel too far down memory lane to the pain of Lauren's death, Holton arrived with coffee in hand.

"Black, two sugars. Just how you like it, Agent Little," he said with an almost too cheerful smile.

"Thanks." She took a sip and set the cup on her desk without looking. "I'll be right back."

She slipped off her coat, hung it up, and walked across the bullpen to the open door of Morgan's office. She wasn't surprised to see the office already occupied. She tapped on the open door.

Morgan looked up and smiled. "Agent Little. Good morning."

She returned the smile. "Good morning. And I thought we agreed on first names."

"We did, we did. But I have a hard time turning off the formality when off duty, much less *on* duty. I'll work on it though."

"To tell you the truth, so do I," Erin replied with a smile. She then crossed her arms and adopted a mock stern expression. "Now, what time did you come in, Agent Morgan?"

"About five o'clock. I got over six hours of uninterrupted sleep," Morgan replied proudly. "And before you ask—yes, I ate breakfast."

Erin smiled again. "Very good. You have potential after all." She was surprised but pleased by the woman's soft chuckle. "What are you working on?" Erin asked as she approached Morgan's desk.

"I'm putting the final touches on the presentation I have to give this morning to bring the taskforce up to date on our findings. I spoke to the director last night. After the meeting this morning, you and I will head out and look at the earlier victims. Hopefully, we'll find something. Nobody is perfect right out of the gate. He had to have made a mistake somewhere."

"With almost thirty victims, he's certainly had enough practice to become perfect," Erin said with disgust.

"I know," Morgan replied with a sigh.

They were silent for a few moments, both lost in their thoughts. AD Ben Taylor appeared in the doorway. "I need to speak with you, Agent Morgan."

Erin excused herself and returned to her desk. By the time Taylor and Morgan were done talking, the rest of the agents on the taskforce were present, and it was time for the briefing.

Morgan stood up front and flipped over three free-standing whiteboards at one end of the bullpen. On them were pictures of twenty-seven women— fourteen the taskforce already knew about, plus the additional thirteen she had dug up through her research.

"Ladies and gentlemen, our job has gotten even more difficult. What you see here are the pictures of the victims of our UNSUB. Almost twice as many as we thought." She paused to let the murmuring and grumbling settle down. "I shouldn't have to tell you that we obviously don't want this getting out to the press, but let's make this clear: *no one* says a word to the press about this. The only authorized contact with the press is through our press liaison SSA Mackenzie Chadwick. I know you've all been working very hard investigating any and all possible leads in this case. Now we have thirteen new victims to investigate. We have them, their families, their friends, their acquaintances, everything. Leave no stone unturned. Be thorough, but do your best not to let on in any way that your investigation has anything to do with The Slasher case. I've prepared a brief for everyone that you can take with you. Assistant Director Taylor will give you your assignments." She started handing out the briefs she'd written up for everyone.

Taylor tapped Morgan on the shoulder. "Come into my office, Morgan."

"All right." She handed the rest of the briefs to another agent and followed Taylor.

Erin watched as Taylor stopped and looked around before entering his office. She looked down at her paperwork quickly, not wanting anyone to notice that she had taken an interest. "Little," he called out. When she looked up, he waved her over. "Come here."

Taylor ushered both Erin and Morgan into his office and closed the door.

"Have a seat," he said as he sat behind his desk. "I spoke with the director this morning. He's informed me that you will be looking at the earlier victims and has arranged the necessary exhumations. He also said that you two are to be partnered for the duration of this case." He paused and looked at both women, as if waiting for them to say something if they wanted to. "Okay. If there's anything you need, just let me know," he said dismissively.

"Thank you," said Morgan.

"Thanks," said Erin.

The two women stood up and exited his office.

Morgan turned to Erin. "I've got our tickets. Our flight doesn't leave for a couple of hours. Do you need to go home and pack?"

Erin shook her head. "I keep a go-bag in my car, just in case."

"I need to take care of a couple of things, and then we can go."

"All right."

Morgan entered her office while Erin returned to where Holton was sitting, finishing a cheese Danish. Holton stood, wiping away any stray crumbs as she approached.

"Are you ready to go? We have to interview the family of this Carol Evans," he said, snapping his fingers against the sheet of paper in his hand. "And it's almost a three-hour drive there. I'm all ready to go."

"I'm not going with you, Holton."

"What? What do you mean?"

Before she could answer, another agent joined them. He was fiftyish and had the obvious beginnings of a beer belly. "Special Agent Holton? I'm Special Agent William Coleman. I'll be your partner since SSA Little is being reassigned."

"What? What's going on, Little?" Holton was unhappy. He gave her such a puppy dog look with his blue eyes that she almost felt sorry for him.

"It's only temporary. It's just for the duration of this case."

"So where are you going? Why are you being reassigned?"

"I've been assigned as Agent Morgan's partner." She nodded toward the whiteboards. "We're going to be taking a look at the bodies of the earlier victims."

"Well, why can't the three of us work together?"

Knowing how much Holton admired Morgan, she personally wouldn't have minded having him along. He would have learned a lot from Morgan just through observation. However, she didn't make the assignments. "It's not my decision, Holton. The director himself reassigned me, so I'm not about to say no. You've been an agent long enough to know we do what we're told."

He gave a reluctant nod. "So you get to work with Agent Morgan." Holton gave her a small half-smile. "I don't know whether to be jealous of you or her. You're the best partner anyone could have, but I'd love the chance to pick her brain."

"Come on, kid. Let's go. We've got a long drive ahead of us," Agent Coleman grumbled impatiently.

"I guess I'll see you later," Holton said as he followed Coleman, obviously still unhappy about their separate assignments.

On the flight down to Savannah, Georgia, both agents quietly rested. Experience had taught them, like soldiers, to catch rest when possible. They never really knew what would happen, especially in a case like the one they were working on.

Even so, Jess' mind was seldom entirely at rest. She was reviewing the files in her head, working on her profile. She knew there was a piece of the puzzle she was not seeing, that wasn't yet falling into place. With so many victims, it was both a hindrance and a help. More victims meant a more complete picture of the UNSUB's actions, but so many victims also meant more information to correlate and more places for that crucial piece of the puzzle to hide or get lost.

Once they landed in Savannah, the two agents rented a car and drove south to a small town called Midway. The town's police chief, Bud Calhoun, didn't exactly welcome them with open arms, especially since the body that had been exhumed that morning was the daughter of his cousin. However, they were not about to let a small-town cop with a big attitude prevent them from doing their job.

After leaving the police station, they went to the funeral home where the body was waiting for them. The mortician wasn't any more welcoming, but he left the women alone to do their work.

Jess watched as Erin started. After a few minutes, she moved away from the table and sat on a stool, opening the case file onto the counter to begin studying the crime scene photos. After about thirty minutes, she closed the file and returned to the table.

"If I talk to the victim's mother, Mrs. Leila Browning, will you be all right here alone, Erin?"

"Of course. I'll be here for a couple of hours. They don't have everything I need, so I'll have to send most of the samples to the lab at Quantico."

"All right. I'll be back in a while." Jess left, taking their rental car.

⬬

The house she parked in front of was a modest two-story with a covered porch that spanned its width, a swing and two chairs sat on one side of the porch. It was easy to imagine the victim growing up on this tree-shaded street, playing within the picket fence-enclosed yard, her mother watching over her from the porch swing and sipping tea. Jess shook the image from her head. Preconceived ideas about the victim were no help in her job. She opened the car door and got out with a soft sigh. She knew the image had been a hope, really, a hope that Dawn Browning's life had been a happy one before it had been so brutally ended.

Jess walked through the open gate and ascended the three steps to the porch. She pressed the doorbell and waited.

"Hello?"

The woman who answered the door was dressed in jeans and a light-blue oxford shirt that was untucked. She wore minimal makeup, but even heavy makeup would not have disguised the fact she'd been crying. Her eyes and nose were red and puffy, her cheeks damply streaked where she'd obviously tried to wipe away the evidence of her tears moments before opening the door.

"Mrs. Leila Browning?"

"Yes?"

Showing her credentials, Jess said, "Mrs. Browning, I'm Supervisory Special Agent Jessica Morgan with the FBI. May I come in and speak with you about your daughter?"

Mrs. Browning silently nodded and opened the screen door for her. Gesturing toward the couch, she said, "Have a seat. Would you like a cup of coffee?"

"No, thank you."

Taking a seat on the other end of the couch, Mrs. Browning said, "I don't understand, Agent Morgan. Why is the FBI interested in my daughter's case? It's been months. Why did they have to dig up my baby?"

22

"I am very sorry for any distress this has caused you, Mrs. Browning. But we have reason to believe Dawn's death is related to another case we're investigating," Jess said gently.

"That doesn't make any sense. Chief Calhoun arrested the man who killed Dawn. He's in prison."

"I understand." Jess could tell the woman was close to breaking down, and pushing her wouldn't be helpful. "Your daughter lived here at home with you, didn't she?"

Mrs. Browning nodded.

"Would it be possible for me to see her room?"

"It's upstairs, first door on the left. I can't..." Mrs. Browning's tears finally started, and her voice trailed off.

Jess quickly grabbed some tissues from the box on the coffee table and handed them to the other woman. "I understand. It's okay, Mrs. Browning. You stay here," she said softly.

Once upstairs, Jess opened the first door on the left. It was immediately apparent that Mrs. Browning had kept Dawn's room just as it had been on the day her daughter had died. Jess was confident that Dawn Browning had been a victim of The Slasher, but what she was looking for in her bedroom was a sense of who Dawn had been and why The Slasher had chosen her, if indeed there was a reason beyond random chance.

When she was done looking around, she returned downstairs to the living room and sat on the couch next to Mrs. Browning. Handing the grieving woman some more tissues, she squeezed one of the woman's hands. "I really am sorry our investigation is causing you additional pain, Mrs. Browning."

Wiping her eyes and drying her face, Mrs. Browning raised her head and looked Jess in the eyes. "Just promise me it won't be for nothing. Promise me that disturbing my baby will make a difference and that you'll catch whoever you're after."

In that moment, she wanted nothing more in the world than to make that promise to Mrs. Browning. However, experience had taught Jess promises like that should not be made because they couldn't always be kept.

"I promise." She made it anyway. She wouldn't stop until she made good on it.

Chapter Four

ON THE WAY BACK to the funeral home, Jess stopped at a small diner where she picked up a cup of tea and a cup of coffee. She had been gone a little over an hour by the time she pulled into the parking lot.

As soon as she entered the building, she heard Chief Calhoun's raised voice. She rushed into the prep room and found the police chief yelling at and advancing on Agent Little. Without thought, Jess set the drinks on the counter, marched up behind the man, and grabbed him by the back of the neck and his gun belt. Before he could react, she quickly shoved him out into the corridor, where she spun the overweight man around and slammed him up against the wall. Jess held him with her left hand around his throat with just enough force to keep him in place but not choke him.

Calhoun's left hand went for his gun, but she stopped it with a vise-like grip on his wrist. He tried to remove her hand from his throat with his right hand but soon found he couldn't budge it. He continued to struggle until he looked into her eyes. She gave him a feral sneer, flashing her sharp fangs. His struggles came to a halt as she watched the color completely drain from his face until he was white as a sheet.

"Now that I have your attention, explain why you threatened my partner."

"Uh...I...um..." On the verge of hyperventilating, he began to tremble.

"Jess, are you all right?" Erin asked from behind Jess, as she joined them in the hallway.

Without losing eye contact with Bud, she answered, "Just fine. Bud and I are just clearing up any misunderstandings. Isn't that right, Bud?" She tightened her hold on his wrist to encourage him to answer.

"Ye-yes."

"Bud was just telling me how bad he felt about his behavior and wanted to apologize to you, Agent Little." She tightened her grip more, right to the threshold of breaking his bones. Jess knew she was inflicting quite a bit of pain, but she did not handle threats to her partner well. Never had.

"Tha-That's right. I'm sorry, ma'am. I-I was out of line. The loss of Dawn has been really hard on our fa-family, but that doesn't excuse my be-behavior. I'm very so-sorry."

Smelling the distinct odor of urine, Jess finally loosened her grip. Despite his size and bluster, Bud was an utter coward. She could see in his eyes how he was already convincing himself that he couldn't possibly have seen her fangs, much less her eyes changing color. Nope, he did not see anything unusual, he was telling himself, and their encounter did not really happen.

"We appreciate your apology, Bud. Agent Little and I both understand what grief can do to a person. Please keep in mind that we are not the bad guys here. We are only after the truth. We are only trying to stop other innocent young women like Dawn from being killed." She completely let go of him. "Thank you for your time, Bud. If we need anything, we'll let you know," she said, dismissing him.

Cradling his left wrist, Calhoun nodded and left, trot-walking as quickly as he could down the hallway.

Jess closed her eyes and took a deep breath before turning around and facing Erin. "Are you all right?" Her eyes traveled down to see Little's weapon in her hand.

"I'm fine," Little answered, as they entered the prep room together.

"I'm sorry I wasn't here. I didn't expect the chief to come and harass you."

"It's not your fault." Little set her weapon on the instrument tray next to the body she'd been working on. "I can't believe I left my weapon in the bathroom with my street clothes."

"Do you normally keep your weapon on you when you perform an autopsy?" she asked with half a smile.

Erin sighed. "No."

"Then don't beat yourself up over it." Jess retrieved the drinks from the counter. "Here. I stopped on the way back and got you a coffee," she said, handing one to Erin. "Black, two sugars," she said.

"Oh, bless you."

She chuckled at the heartfelt response.

"Mmmm," Erin sighed after taking a sip.

"So did you find anything?" she asked as she took the lid off her hot tea.

"Nothing new. The knife wounds are consistent with the others. I won't have the test results until Quantico runs them and gets back to me. I'll send the samples overnight."

"Are you done here?"

"Not quite. I should finish up in about twenty minutes."

"All right."

When they were finished at the funeral home, they got into their rental and drove approximately a hundred and twenty miles north to their next destination, the small town of Bamberg, South Carolina. They had stopped for dinner at a small diner before checking into their motel.

The clerk at the motel's front desk handed Morgan a FedEx envelope. "This arrived for you, Agent Morgan."

"Thank you."

As they walked to their rooms, Jess opened the FedEx packet. She took out a white envelope from which she removed a credit card. With a smile, she held out the card to Erin. "It came addressed to me, but it's for you."

Little took the card. "I don't understand."

"It's a card on my expense account. Just use the card for anything you would normally put on an expense report to get reimbursed for, such as copies, car rental, meals, or whatever."

"You have a Bureau credit card account?"

Jess smiled. "It beats the hell out of always filling out expense reports. Especially with how much I travel." She stopped in front of the door to her room. "This is me," she said, unlocking the door. "I'll see you in the morning, Erin. Good night."

"Good night, Jess," Erin replied, moving to the adjacent door and unlocking it.

February 20, 2025
Thursday

In the morning, Erin and Jess drove to the sheriff's office, where Sheriff Greg Munson met them. Their presence was much more welcome than it had been in Midway. Erin could see Jess' eyes light up when they were told the crime scene was still intact. It wasn't often that an older crime scene was intact.

"Why don't you go and investigate the crime scene, Jess, while I go to the hospital and take a look at the body?"

Morgan gently pulled her aside. "Are you sure?" she asked quietly. "After what happened yesterday, I'm hesitant to split us up."

"It's okay. Sheriff Munson is no Bud Calhoun." She gave Jess a slight smirk. "And I won't leave my weapon in the bathroom."

Jess gave her a small smile in return. "All right. Go ahead and take the car. I'll walk to the victim's house to check out the scene."

"Okay. I'll see you later."

After a shower, Erin let out a sigh and put on her street clothes. Doing autopsies day after day on young women killed by The Slasher was quickly getting to her. She was frustrated because she couldn't find anything that might be considered a lead. Whoever the UNSUB was, he didn't seem to make any mistakes. She finished dressing. When she slipped on her watch, she realized it had been over three hours since she'd parted ways with her partner. Erin had expected Jess to show up long before she finished the autopsy and was quite surprised that she hadn't.

Erin walked out of the hospital and got into their rental car. She tried calling Jess on the way, but when she got her voicemail, Erin decided to return to the sheriff's office in Branchville.

"Agent Little, how did things go?" Sheriff Munson asked as soon as she entered.

"Just fine, Sheriff. Has Agent Morgan been by?"

"No. I haven't seen her since she left to look at the Jensen house."

A niggling shot of worry skittered across her senses. "Can you give me directions to the Jensen house?"

"Certainly. Just turn left out of the parking lot, then right at the third intersection onto Chestnut. It's 1947 Chestnut."

"Thank you." Erin turned to go.

"Agent Little?"

"Yes?"

"Would you please make sure your partner returns the file she borrowed?"

"Sure thing, Sheriff."

"Thanks."

Sheriff Munson had offered Jess a ride to the crime scene, but she politely declined, looking forward to the chance to stretch her legs on the walk. She hadn't been running for several days because of work, and the crisp winter air smelled and felt good. Once she arrived at 10947 Chestnut Street, she stood for a few seconds, looking at the front of the house. Nothing about the house's exterior gave a clue about the horrible scene inside it. Even the yellow police tape was gone. The house had simply been locked up and left undisturbed. No one had wanted anything to do with it.

Jess opened the accordion file the sheriff had loaned her and withdrew the key as she walked up the front steps of the porch. She pulled open the screen door and inserted the key into the deadbolt, easily turning it. Stepping into the house, she immediately smelled the staleness of the air. Beneath the staleness was death. Despite the morning hour, the house was dark. All the shades and curtains were drawn shut. She tried the light switch near the front door, but the electricity was disconnected. It didn't matter. She didn't need it. Her eyes shifted so she could see in the dark.

Even if she hadn't read the file, Jess would have found the room where Annie Jensen's body had been discovered. The smell of death still held its grip on this place. Death's presence wasn't in the living room in the front of the house where most guests would be entertained, but rather in the smaller, more intimate den in the back of the house off the kitchen. As she passed through the kitchen, she took note of the single plate and glass in the drainer by the sink—dinner for one.

She stopped just inside the doorway of the den. Jess had read the case file at the sheriff's office but resisted looking at the photos since the crime scene was available. Consequently, she was hit with the full force of the scene before her.

"Bloody hell," she whispered.

She sat in a chair in the corner of the room and stared, her mind racing.

Erin walked up the steps of the porch. She opened the screen door and turned the knob of the front door, finding it unlocked. She stepped into the darkness. Nothing happened when she flipped the light switch near the door, so she retrieved a small flashlight from her coat pocket. With the flashlight in one hand and her weapon in the other, she cautiously proceeded into the house's interior.

"Jess?"

No answer.

Erin carefully made her way through the house. "Agent Morgan?" she tried again, but still received no answer. Finally, she came to the kitchen. Something in the corner of her eye made her spin to her right and go through the doorway into the den. Her flashlight landed on her partner sitting in a chair in the corner of the den.

"I'd prefer it if you didn't shoot me," Morgan said without looking at her.

Lowering her weapon, Erin placed it back in her holster at the small of her back. "Why didn't you answer when I called your name?"

"Sorry."

Erin moved toward Morgan slowly. Something was off. Her voice was flat, expressionless. "Have you been sitting here all morning, Jess?"

Morgan simply nodded.

"Why?"

"Annie Jensen was killed here," she said with a slight nod at the scene in front of her.

"I know, Jess. That's why we're here."

"No, you don't understand. Annie was killed *here*, not brought here after she was killed. This is a primary crime scene. All the crime scenes we've had until now have been secondary crime scenes. He's been killing them somewhere else and then bringing their bodies back to where they're discovered."

Erin turned her flashlight to illuminate the crime scene. "Oh my god. So that means—"

"There are more crime scenes to be found. And it means I've underestimated this bastard. He's been active longer than we think, and there are more victims we don't know about." Jess finally tore her eyes from the scene and looked at Erin. "We're nowhere near the beginning of his killings. These bodies aren't going to give us what we need."

"So what do you want to do?"

"We have to go back to Headquarters. We get people looking for the primary crime scenes and work them as they're found." She paused for a beat. "And we go through however many more case files it takes to find his beginning. Somewhere, he made a mistake."

Jess was silent during the drive to the Columbia, SC, airport and on the flight to Washington, DC, but Erin didn't find it an uncomfortable silence. She knew the other agent was lost in thought, assimilating the new information they'd discovered and working on the profile of the UNSUB. Besides, it allowed her to watch Jess, something she found herself doing more and more.

When they landed, Jess and Erin went their separate ways. Jess told Erin that she was going to her hotel and would see her in the morning. Erin went home. As she turned the key to unlock the door to her building, Holton came bounding up the walk from the parking lot.

"Little!"

"Holton? What are you doing here?" she asked, shocked to see him.

"I was in the neighborhood and thought I'd take a chance that you might be in."

She arched an eyebrow. She and Jess had only been out of town for one night. By all rights, they should have been gone for several days, considering the number of bodies they had to examine.

Holton must have seen the skepticism on her face because he ducked his head and blushed. "Okay, you got me. I wasn't just in the neighborhood. I happened to be in AD Taylor's office when he got a phone call from someone telling him Agent Morgan would be addressing the taskforce in the morning. I thought I'd drop by and see what things were like on your part of the case."

"I see." She finally gave him a half-smile. "All right, come on in." She led him into the building and then her apartment. "Have you eaten dinner yet?" she asked once they were inside.

"No."

"Go ahead and order a pizza. I'll be just a couple of minutes."

"Okay."

Erin went into her bedroom and quickly changed into jeans and a sweatshirt. Returning, she started a load of laundry in the small utility room off the kitchen. "Do you need something to drink?" she called out as she entered the kitchen.

"No. I already grabbed a beer," replied Holton.

Erin got a beer from the refrigerator and joined her partner in the living room. Dropping into a chair, Erin looked at Holton where he sat on her couch. "It's been a while since we've done pizza and beer," she said with a smile.

He nodded. "A good way to celebrate the end of a hard case." He picked at the label on his beer bottle. "But I have a feeling it's going to be awhile before anyone celebrates the end of The Slasher case." He sounded discouraged.

"I'm afraid you're more right than you know."

"What do you mean? What did you find out?"

"The other day, you mentioned wondering about missing blood."

"Yeah. There's not enough blood at the crime scenes and in the bodies to account for all the blood loss."

Erin nodded. "Because all we have are secondary crime scenes."

"Then where are the primary crime scenes?" He paused. "But wait, that doesn't make sense. How is he able to move and place the bodies into the secondary crime scenes without leaving any trace evidence?"

"I don't know. But from what I saw of the primary scene we found in South Carolina, this guy is not only good, he is continually improving."

"Then how do we catch him?"

"The same way we do anyone else—hard work." She gave him a smirk. "And we hope SSA Morgan is as good as you say she is."

His eyes lit up. "So what's it like working with her?"

"She's a professional, and like other agents I've worked with."

Before Holton could pepper her with more questions, the doorbell rang, announcing the arrival of their pizza. They had a relaxing evening of pizza and beer, even if they only talked about work.

Chapter Five

February 21, 2025
Friday

IN THE MORNING, JESS was sitting at the worktable in her office when Erin stopped in.

"I see you got an early start this morning," Erin quipped.

"Actually, I've only been here about twenty minutes." Jess leaned back in her chair and let out a sigh.

"How is your profile coming along?"

"It's done. Or at least it's as done as it can be based on what we know at this point. I'll be presenting it to the taskforce this morning."

There was a knock on the open office door. Jess and Erin both looked up and saw Director Cavanaugh.

"Good morning, sir," said Erin.

"Morning, sir," said Jess.

The director smiled and entered. "Good morning, Agent Little, Agent Morgan. Are you ready to give your profile, Jessica?"

"Yes. And you're not going to like everything I have to say."

He frowned. "It's that bad?"

She nodded. "I'm afraid so."

The director looked at Erin. "I don't mean to be rude, Agent Little, but could you give us a minute?"

"Certainly, sir." Erin left.

The director closed the door. "So now that you've got your profile, are you ready for your next assignment?"

Jess shook her head. "No. We've just scratched the surface on this one, Lou."

"What are you talking about? You found the additional victims—"

She got up and walked to the window. She crossed her arms and leaned back against the windowsill, turning her head just enough to look outside and keep the director in her peripheral vision. "This is a lot worse than anyone thought. Look, I don't know what will lead to us catching this guy: finding a mistake he made when he was first starting out, or he tires of his current game of toying with us and deliberately leaves us a clue. Either way, his body count is going to continue to grow. I need to see this case to the end, Lou."

He gave her a measured look. "Why is this one so important to you?"

"I underestimated this son of a bitch," she replied evenly.

"So you're not perfect. Nobody is." He paused. "It's more than that. I can tell. What is it, Jessica? Tell me."

She stood upright and fully faced the window. She answered him quietly. "I made a promise."

"A promise? To whom? And what exactly did you promise them?"

"It doesn't matter. What matters is that I made a promise, and I'm going to keep it. And that means I will work this case until we catch this guy." Jess watched the director's reflection in the window as he ran a hand over his face. They'd had a similar discussion once before.

"I brought you back to the Bureau, Jessica, but I can also end our arrangement and let you go. I care about you too much to stand by and watch you get sucked down into the rabbit hole. And I know what you're like when you make promises you shouldn't make. I don't want a repeat of what happened when Toni—"

She whipped around to glare at him. Cutting him off, she said with a growl in her voice, "Leave Toni out of it."

"Toni is never out of it," he said evenly.

She brushed past him, opening her office door and marching out, refusing to listen to him anymore, even as he said, "Toni hasn't been out of it for six years!"

Erin had been waiting near Jess' office after the director had excused her, so she couldn't help but overhear their raised voices just before Jess barreled out and almost ran into her. Jess mumbled an apology as she marched to the front of the room and prepared a whiteboard for her presentation. Neither did she miss the apparent look of concern Director Cavanaugh leveled at Jess' back as he exited the office and paused before heading to AD Taylor's office. She wondered who Tony was and what he had to do with the case and Jess.

It only took Jess a couple of minutes to finish with the whiteboard before indicating she was ready. The director and Taylor came out and sat off to the side while all the agents, including Erin, took a seat.

"After the discovery of the additional victims a couple of days ago, SSA Little and I were given the task of exhuming and re-examining these earlier victims' bodies as well as reviewing the casework. Some of you might have heard about the discovery that brought us back here so quickly."

Jess tacked up some photos of the crime scene in Annie Jensen's home on the whiteboard.

"What we found was an intact crime scene where Annie Jensen's body was found." She paused just long enough to let her words sink in. "As you can see, this crime scene is not the same as the ones we've seen to date with this UNSUB."

"Then how can you be so sure it is even the same killer?" someone interrupted.

Jess took the question in stride. "It's him. The MO and signature are the same. The reason the crime scene is different is that this," she said, pointing to the pictures, "is a primary crime scene, and the ones we've seen to date are secondary crime scenes."

"Wait a minute. You just said his MO was the same. Moving the body is a change," another agent said.

Jess shook her head. "That's just the UNSUB getting better, refining his MO." She drew a breath and continued before anyone else could interrupt. "The UNSUB we're looking for is a white male, thirty to thirty-five. He's charming, a chameleon, fitting in anywhere he chooses to, whether in a small, rural town or a fast-paced city. He's intelligent and educated. He probably has a graduate or postgraduate degree. He has money, enough that he doesn't have to work if he chooses not to. He's most likely self-employed if he does work, allowing him the time and mobility to stalk, seduce, and kill his prey. On the off chance he has a job, it's one with little supervision or accountability, for those same reasons." She paused for half a beat. "And I believe the UNSUB has had training in law enforcement of some kind."

"You're saying he's a cop?"

"No. But I do believe he's had the training. Whether or not he's ever actually worked as a cop, we won't know until we name him. If he has, it's in his past." Jess took a deep breath. "Now, for the bad news. Our UNSUB has been active far longer than any of us thought. The twenty-seven victims we've found so far are just the tip of the iceberg. Part of the job now, besides trying to stop any future killings, is also to identify more of his past victims."

The director stood up and addressed the group. "All right, people, I realize that eventually the press will catch wind of the scope of this, but I want to delay that as long as possible. So no leaks. *No one* talks to the press," he said sternly. "Dismissed."

Jess ignored the director when he moved as if to speak to her. Erin watched the director give a slight shake of his head as he watched Jess deliberately walk away from him and into her office. Erin got up and went to Jess' office, stopping in the open doorway. She watched the other agent as she sat at the worktable, stern expression in place, her laptop open, presumably searching for more cases that tied into their case. After a few moments, Erin entered and joined Jess at the worktable, opening her laptop and pulling up a file to peruse.

Erin glanced up, taking in the still stern expression. "So who is Tony?" she asked as nonchalantly as possible.

"Toni has nothing to do with this case," Jess said curtly.

"But the director said—"

"Drop it," Jess said harshly with a scathing look that took Erin aback. Whoever Tony was, he was a sore subject for Jess. She decided to let it go.

Jess and Erin worked on their computers all day, going through files and databases to find more cases that could be attributed to The Slasher. Since they worked past dinnertime, they ordered pizza. Erin called it a night at 9:30.

"I'm starting to go cross-eyed. I'm going to head home."

"See you tomorrow, Erin."

"You should go, too, Jess."

"I will. I just want to work for a few more minutes. I'll see you in the morning."

"All right. Good night."

"Good night."

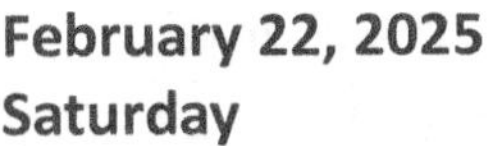

February 22, 2025
Saturday

The next morning, Erin was surprised not to find Jess in her office when she arrived. She removed her jacket and hung it on the back of a chair before turning on her laptop. Before it was done booting up, Jess came in—still in the same clothes from the day before.

She arched an eyebrow. "I thought you said you were going to go get some sleep last night."

Jess blushed. "I was going to, but I got on the trail of something."

"Oh? What?"

"We have this UNSUB who kills his victims and then places their bodies in their own homes. We've been unable to find the primary crime scenes for the later murders."

"Right."

"But with Annie Jensen, we saw that he simply killed her in her home. He went from the easier scenario in his earlier murders to a more complicated one: one where he's increasing the risk of getting caught."

"Right."

Jess and Erin sifted through files and reports all day. Jess alternated between rubbing her eyes and pinching the bridge of her nose to ward off a headache already taking root when she vaguely heard Erin say something about enough being enough. She didn't pay much attention to her, truth be told. Jess rubbed her eyes again with the heels of her hands and then stared back down at the file she was reading.

A warm hand on her shoulder surprised her, making her heart skip a beat and race as she nearly flew off her chair. Her head whipped around and up to see Erin standing beside her, concern clear in her eyes.

"You need to get out of here, and that reaction just proves it. Come on."

"You go, Erin. I just want to check a few more files."

"Right. I've heard that one before. Jess, you've been here two days without a break. You're tired, and you need to eat. You've been going nonstop for days. You need to get out of here."

"I need to find this bastard."

"I know, but you're not the only one looking for him. It's not all on your shoulders."

"I couldn't have said it better," a male voice said from the doorway.

Both women looked up to see the director standing there.

"Jessica, you're no good to me or the victims if you run yourself into the ground. You have to take care of yourself. I know how hard you push yourself. Go. Get out of here. Take tomorrow off and come back fresh." He held up a finger to quiet her as she started to object. "That's an order. Remember what I said about the rabbit hole." He looked directly at Erin. "Agent Little, I trust you'll see that Agent Morgan follows those orders. I don't want to see either of you back here before Monday morning."

"Yes, sir."

The director turned and left.

Jess dropped her head backward and looked up at the ceiling as she sighed heavily. "You're right. He's right. I know it." She closed her eyes.

She could hear the smile in Little's voice when she spoke.

"How long has it been since you've had a home-cooked meal?"

"Almost as long as it's been since I've had an orgasm." Jess' eyes immediately popped open, and her head snapped upright. "Oh, shit. I said that out loud, didn't I?" She felt her cheeks burn with embarrassment. "I'm more tired than I thought. I'm sorry, Erin."

She stood up. Turning to get her jacket from the back of her chair, she saw Little holding one hand to her lips, her face pink and her body shaking from her silent laughter. If Little was laughing at her, Jess hadn't offended her. She relaxed and gave Little a smirk. "I'm so glad you're amused," she said in a beleaguered tone.

Erin smiled. "Come on, let's go. I can at least do something about one of those," she said with a chuckle. When Jess reached for her briefcase, Erin stopped her. "Nope. No work, Jess."

Jess looked at her for a couple of moments, silently debating.

A blonde eyebrow arched.

She smirked. "All right. But don't think that look is always going to work."

"I don't know what you're talking about," Erin replied, as she lightly pushed her toward the door.

"You know, you're a bossy woman, Erin."

"Keep moving."

"See?"

Chapter Six

AFTER STOPPING AT JESS' hotel so she could take a quick shower and change clothes, they arrived at Erin's apartment.

"Make yourself at home, Jess. I'll be a minute." Erin went into her bedroom and changed into her standard off-duty uniform of jeans and a sweatshirt. After a short debate, she donned warm socks but didn't bother with shoes. She then went into the kitchen to start working on dinner.

"Is there anything I can do to help, Erin?" Jess turned on the CD player, and soft jazz began to play.

"Nope. I already made the lasagna. I just need to put it in the oven to cook."

When she finished in the kitchen, Erin brought a bottle of wine, a corkscrew, and a couple of wine glasses to the living room. She uncorked the wine and poured them each a glass. She sat back as she handed Jess her wine.

"How long has it been?" She paused a beat. "Since you had a home-cooked meal?" she asked with a smirk, amusement twinkling in her eyes.

Jess rolled her eyes. "Cute. Let's just say it's been a while."

"Fair enough. So where do you call home?"

"When?"

"Ah. Army brat?"

"No, but I was born in California, lived in Vancouver, British Columbia, until I was four, England until I was twelve, Massachusetts until I was fifteen, and then back and forth between the US and England until I was twenty-one."

"What about now? Where do you call home?"

"Now? Well, for the last three years, home has been whatever hotel I'm checked into."

Erin's eyes widened. "You're kidding."

"Nope. Besides what's in my suitcases, all my stuff is in storage." Jess shrugged her shoulders. "There's no use having a house or an apartment to maintain when I'm never there. I'm always on the road, working one case or another."

"Do you always work cases like this one?"

She nodded. "Murders, rapes, molestations, kidnappings. Whatever the director needs me for."

"I can't imagine it. Working the worst of the worst day in and day out. Why do you do it?"

"Someone has to." Jess let out a sigh. "And I'm good at it," she said softly.

Erin didn't miss the weariness in the woman's voice. "When was the last time you had a day off?"

"Does traveling between cases count?"

"No."

"Then it's been several months, almost a year."

"You're more than overdue for some time off."

Jess nodded. "Yeah." She paused long enough to take a sip of wine. "Enough about me. What about you, Erin? Where did you grow up?"

"All over. I was an Army brat. My dad retired as a brigadier general."

"Where do your parents live?"

"My mom lives in Baltimore, but my dad's gone."

"I'm sorry."

"It's okay. It's been a few years."

"Do you have any siblings?"

"Two younger brothers and an older sister who is gone. You?"

"I was an only child."

"What about your parents? Are they in England or here in the States?"

"Both my parents are gone."

"I'm sorry."

Jess shrugged. "It was a long time ago, and I barely knew them."

"What do you mean?" Erin asked.

"I was sent to boarding school when I was four, and I stopped going home for the summers when I was six after my mother died. I didn't see my father again until his funeral when I was fourteen."

Appalled, Erin didn't know what to say. The ringing of her home phone saved her from saying the wrong thing. "Excuse me." She got up to answer it. "Hello."

"Hey, Little, how have you been?"

"Fine. What's up, Holton?"

"Um, well, I was wondering how the case was going. I mean, I don't get to see you every day now that we're not partners, so we don't get to talk about...stuff."

"You know how the case is going, Holton. You're still on the taskforce. You get the same briefings as everyone."

"Oh, okay." He sounded wounded, so she decided to throw him a bone. "So what is Agent Coleman like to work with?"

"He's nothing like you, Little. That's for sure. All he wants to talk about is the Dallas Cowboys."

"I thought you liked football."

"Yeah, but not the Cowboys. I'm from Philadelphia. I'm an Eagles fan!"

Erin chuckled. "Well, you're posted at the Washington field office. I should think you're used to dealing with disappointment since you're in Commander territory." She heard a grunt of disapproval on the other end of the line. "Good night, Holton."

"Good night, Little."

Erin hung up and turned the volume down on her answering machine. She no sooner turned to rejoin Jess on the couch than her phone rang again. She just let the machine get it.

"So that was your partner, huh?"

"Yes. I think he's feeling abandoned and neglected since being reassigned to a new partner for the duration of the case."

"If it's a problem, I can get you reassigned back together."

Erin shook her head. "It's just that he's a rookie, and I'm his first partner. Learning how to work with someone else will be good for him. It's the FBI. You never know where you'll be assigned, who you'll be assigned to work with, or what kind of case you'll be working. You have to be flexible. Things change."

"Very true." Jess smiled. "But I also remember how much I relied on my first partner. John was the best, and he became like family, like a big brother. I checked your file, Erin. Holton is damn lucky to have you to mentor him."

Erin couldn't keep from blushing at the compliment. "Thank you."

"I'm also lucky to have you as a partner during this case." Jess averted her gaze and appeared nervous as she ran a finger around the lip of her wineglass. "And I owe you an apology for yesterday. I was out of line to snap at you when you asked about Toni."

"It's okay. He's obviously a sensitive subject for you."

"She. SSA Toni Jeffers." Jess' eyes followed her finger as it continued its circuit around the lip of the wineglass.

"Toni Jeffers…" Erin frowned momentarily. "Why does that name sound familiar to me?"

"Toni was an agent in the BAU who was killed six years ago by a suspect I profiled—Devon Gaines Conrad."

"Oh yeah. I remember when Conrad was caught, an agent had been killed. But I was an instructor at the academy then, so I wasn't involved in any way. I didn't know the agent who had been killed or how it had happened."

"He came looking for me, but he found her instead." Jess' finger finally stopped tracing the lip of her wineglass, but her gaze was still lost in the red depths of the wine within it.

"I don't understand."

"Toni was older, wiser, gutsier, and everything I wanted to be as an agent. At first, I was just so damn flattered that she was interested in me. But she was also a heartbreaker. Everyone knew she could have anyone she wanted, and she never made anyone any promises. So I resisted." Jess paused as she took a sip of wine. Her voice sounded haunted when she continued, her words bridging the past with the present. "No one could resist Toni indefinitely, including me. So I eventually went out with her."

A small smile played across Jess' lips. "I had surprised Toni because she had to work to convince me to go on a second date, something she'd never had to do before. Then she surprised me and everyone else: the woman who'd never promised anyone anything promised me everything—her heart, her love, and her fidelity." Her smile faded. "She kept her promise right up until she was murdered. I promised Toni that I'd catch the bastard who'd murdered her. And we did. We caught Conrad..." Her voice trailed off. She inhaled slowly before continuing. "And as soon as we did, I turned in my badge and gun and quit."

"What did you do? Where did you go?"

"Initially, I went back to England, to my grandfather's house, and had myself a grand, little pity party."

Erin nodded with understanding, remembering how much she had wanted to just curl up in a ball and cry after her sister had been killed.

"Then a friend from boarding school came to visit. She wasn't even a particularly close friend. I hadn't kept in touch with nor heard from her in nearly a decade. Anyway, this friend came by and convinced me to get out of the house and do something, anything, to distract myself. So I went to medical school."

Erin worked to keep from reacting outwardly. After all, she'd never met anyone who attended medical school as a *distraction*.

"Shortly before graduation, Lou—Director Cavanaugh—came to me and asked me to return to the Bureau as his troubleshooter." Jess finally looked at Erin. "And here I am."

Erin felt her own heart clench at the loss Jess had experienced. "I'm so sorry, Jess, for what you've been through. I know what it's like to lose someone you love. My sister, Lauren, was killed in a car accident while driving my car because the brake lines had been cut. It was supposed to be me in the car, so I understand."

The oven timer sounded, interrupting them. They held each other's eyes for a couple of long moments, and then, with a nod, got up and went into the kitchen together.

A few hours and a couple of bottles of wine later, both women were in a state of quiet lassitude, barely able to keep their eyes open. It was a battle they both lost.

After an hour or so of slumber, Erin slowly awoke to some semblance of consciousness. The alcohol in her system, the easy camaraderie of the evening, and the physical comfort of her body all combined and contributed to the languidness. She listened to the steady breathing of the other person sleeping next to her. Without opening her eyes, she calmly wondered who it could be. A part of her said she should be alarmed and that she should get the hell out of wherever she was. She never allowed herself to sleep with her lovers—she could not lower her guard enough to do that. She always left after sex or made them leave. She never let anyone get that close to her. She couldn't be that vulnerable. Not even the fellow instructor she'd dated for several months at the FBI Academy. Of course he'd always had his wife to go home to.

Erin did not want to leave. She was comfortable and felt safe and peaceful. She took a slow, deep breath and let it out with a soft sigh. The head so near her own rolled even closer, lips brushing against her hair, breath teasing her ear.

"Shhh...It's okay. You're safe. Just a dream."

She recognized the voice. It was Jess. "Mmmm..." she replied.

"You okay?"

"Mm-hmm. You?" she responded, continuing their mumbled conversation.

"Mm-hmm."

Erin finally lifted her head and looked around through squinted eyes. Both she and Jess had fallen asleep on the couch, heads on the center cushion, legs dangling over the arms of the sofa. "Little crowded here," she said as she lay her head back down.

"S'kay. Not a lotta room on the couch." Jess yawned.

"Could move to the bedroom...more room."

"Means we gotta move."

"Mm-hmm."

"Hmm...'kay."

Neither moved.

"Guess we should sit up firs'," Jess said, still mumbling. She yawned again. "On three."

"M'kay."

"One...two...three..."

Neither woman so much as moved a muscle.

Jess broke the silence after half a minute. "Nigh'..."

"Nigh'..." Erin mumbled back in response.

Both women were asleep only a moment later.

Chapter Seven

WHEN ERIN WOKE UP, she was surprised to find herself alone. That thought brought her to an immediate stop. Why the hell wouldn't she be alone? Jess! She opened her eyes as fractured memories came flooding into her mind. She saw a thermal travel mug with a note taped on it. Slowly, she sat up and pulled the folded note with her name on it off the side of the mug.

> Erin,
> Made you some coffee. Thanks for
> the hospitality. Enjoy your day off.
> Jess

She sat up and took the lid off the mug. The coffee was still hot and tasted good, with just the right amount of sugar. It helped to clear some of the cobwebs. She remembered everything about the evening before, especially how much she liked talking and spending time with Jess. She found the woman pleasant, funny, and charming on a personal level; respectful, courteous, and intelligent on a professional level. It had been quite a while since she'd had someone in her life who was a true equal personally and professionally.

Erin looked at the clock. She would have been at work for at least an hour by now. Since being assigned to the taskforce, she was not used to having an entire day off. Technically, the director gave her an order to ensure Jess relaxed and didn't work today. She was certain Jess would be glued to her laptop if she didn't intervene. Finishing her coffee, Erin put her mug in the kitchen sink and went to dress for the day.

Jess was working on her laptop at the desk when there was a knock on her hotel room door. She took the pen from between her teeth and stuck it behind her ear as she stood up and walked to the door. Looking through the peephole, she couldn't help the small smile that graced her lips when she saw Erin. She opened the door, but Erin marched into the room past her before she could even say hello.

"Well, come in, Erin," she said to the woman's back and closed the door. Jess followed her and found Erin looking at her computer.

"Ah ha! Just as I suspected," declared Erin.

"What?"

"You got up, came straight back here, and got to work. You're supposed to take today off, Jess. That's what the director ordered you to do. He told me to ensure you followed those orders." Closing the laptop, Erin turned and looked Jess up and down, apparently not approving of her sweats and t-shirt. "Get changed. We're going out."

Jess was amused, but she crossed her arms and arched an eyebrow. "Actually, I came back here, went for a workout in the gym, took a shower, and *then* got to work. And just who are you to come in here and order me around, Agent Little?"

The blonde smirked. "Well, for the duration of this case, I'm your partner." Her smirk morphed into a smile. "And after last night, I'd like to think, your friend."

Jess held her stern expression for a second longer before finally giving the other woman an amused smirk and a nod. "All right. Just give me a couple of minutes to get ready." She opened a suitcase, grabbed a change of clothes, and stepped into the bathroom. She stepped back out after changing into jeans and a flannel shirt. "Where are we going?"

"The National Gallery of Art."

"Mmmm. I've been there. They have some stunning pieces of art."

"But have you been to their skating rink?"

"The ice skating rink in their sculpture garden? No, I can't say that I have."

Erin grinned. "You won't be able to say that after today."

"Ice skating? Do you have any idea how cold it is out there?"

"It kind of has to be cold for there to be ice to skate on," Erin replied, still grinning.

"I'm more of the tropical beach type." Morgan smirked. "Or at least a hot tub."

"Well, today you're going ice skating." Erin pushed her toward the door.

"Didn't I already say something about you being a bossy woman?"

They both chuckled as Morgan put on her coat, and they left.

Though Jess wasn't very experienced at ice skating, with her athleticism and natural grace, she could skate pretty smoothly without falling. However, Erin surprised her with how well she skated. She was a regular speed demon and quite agile. Erin credited it to having grown up with three siblings, two of whom were brothers who knew how to play hockey.

"What can I say? I was a total tomboy."

"You? With your ever-present three-inch heels?"

Erin sped up and made a quick turn in front of Jess, facing her and skating backward. "I'm not wearing heels today."

"True. And was it your sister and brothers who also taught you to be so bossy?" Jess joked.

"Nope. They teach that in medical school. You should know that since you went. But maybe you missed that class."

Jess laughed. "It's my professional opinion as a psychologist that it has more to do with you being a pathologist."

"What?"

"Well, all your patients are dead, so when you give them orders, they never talk back or argue. You've gotten used to it, and it's left you with a sense of expectation, entitlement even. You feel that everyone should do as you say and shut up about it."

It was Erin's turn to laugh. "Or it could just be that when I tell you to do something, I'm right!" She swiftly spun around and took off, leaving Jess behind as she shook her head.

After spending most of the afternoon at the ice rink, the two women finally returned to Erin's car.

"Since you were such a good sport about the ice skating, you get to pick where we have dinner," Erin announced. "What are you in the mood for?"

"How about Japanese?"

"Sushi?"

"No. Hibachi."

"Sounds good. There's a place not far from here." Erin put the car into drive.

"By the way."

"What?"

"I know you pushed me into that snowbank on purpose," Jess said. "And I'll get you back for it."

Both women were smiling as they continued on their way.

It was still early when they finished dinner and decided to return to Erin's apartment. They stopped on the way to pick up a nice bottle of wine. However, when they got out of the car to go in, they left the wine in the car, forgotten in the midst of their conversation. Just as they neared the door to the apartment building, Erin remembered.

"Oh! The wine!"

"Give me the keys to the car, and I'll get it. You go on in," Jess volunteered. She accepted the car keys and headed back to the parking lot. She was only about halfway to the car when she was suddenly and very unexpectedly smacked in the back of the head with a projectile. Jess stopped dead in her tracks. Cold, wet snow began to fall in clumps from her hair, and icy cold drips ran down her neck and back. She reached up, unbelievingly, and brushed the clinging splatters from the back of her head. She slowly turned around and just stared at the blonde. "Did you just throw a snowball at me?"

Erin's expression was a mixture of feigned innocence and smug guilt. She was already preparing another snowball.

Jess held up an index finger and slowly wagged it at her partner. "You don't want to do that."

"Oh, I'm pretty sure I do," Erin replied with an evil glint in her eye.

Just as Jess opened her mouth to reply, Erin let loose with her second snowball of the evening, nailing Jess in the ear as she turned away.

"You are so going to pay for that!" Jess shoved the car keys in her jeans pocket and began chasing Erin, scooping up some snow as she ran and forming a snowball. She had excellent aim and splattered the back of Erin's coat collar and neck.

An all-out war had begun.

Both women were wet and freezing when they finally went inside.

"We need to get out of these wet clothes. Come on." Erin led Jess to her bedroom, where she pulled out an oversized sweatshirt and a pair of sweats. "The sweats belonged to my sister, so they should fit you. And here are some socks," she said as she added some athletic socks to the pile. "Just leave your clothes in the bathroom, and I'll put them in the dryer after you change."

"Thanks."

Jess headed into the bathroom to get out of her wet clothes. When she came out, Erin had already changed and started a fire in the fireplace.

Erin looked over her shoulder. "Better?"

"Much."

"Well, come and sit in front of the fire and get warmed up." Erin dropped a blanket around Jess' shoulders as she sat on the floor in front of the couch. "I'll be right back."

Jess let herself relax in front of the fire as she listened to Erin moving through the apartment, loading the dryer with their snow-soaked clothes, then in the kitchen making hot chocolate—using real chocolate, according to her sense of smell. Erin shortly returned with two mugs of hot chocolate. Jess accepted the one offered to her as Erin sat on the floor next to her, wrapping a blanket around her shoulders.

"Hot chocolate and a gas fire. It's the best I can do since I don't have a hot tub or a tropical beach handy."

Jess chuckled. "It'll do." She took a sip of her hot chocolate and sighed. "I can't remember the last time I did something just because it was fun or silly." She looked at her companion. "Thank you."

"You're welcome."

"Are you always so impulsive and carefree?"

Erin almost choked on the sip she'd just taken. She managed to swallow it without making a mess. "Hell no! The last time I did something impulsive was two years ago. I got drunk, got a tattoo, and almost got married to an Elvis impersonator."

"What?"

"It's a long story." She paused. "And one I'm not likely to tell unless severely inebriated. Suffice it to say, if you hang around Quantico long enough, you'll hear a few nicknames I've been christened with: Dr. Ghoul, Cast-Iron Bitch, and Ice Queen being the most popular." She sighed. "And then there's always Agent Tiny or the standard Mrs. Whoever-I'm-Partnered-With at the time. I *know* that with a name like Little and being short, I will hear the jokes. I've heard them all my life. I just wish someone would come up with something *original*."

"Cast-Iron Bitch and Ice Queen? I don't see it. I only met you a week ago, but I'd never say you were cold, merely professionally dispassionate, something you have to be to do what we do. As for Mrs. Whoever, despite this being 2025 and the progress that has been made, the Bureau is still very much an old boys' club. Unfortunately, that kind of crap is everywhere. There was a lot of speculation about John and me, even after Toni and I were a couple and living together. And don't even get me started on the names and crude behavior I put up with because of that." She paused as she took another sip of her hot chocolate. "So what prompted today's impulsiveness?" Jess was surprised to see Erin's cheeks suddenly color with embarrassment. "What is it?" she asked.

"It's my birthday," was the soft reply.

Erin wouldn't look at her, so Jess bumped her shoulder against her companion's. "Hey." She waited until their eyes met. "Happy birthday."

"Thanks."

"Not that I'm complaining, but why not spend your birthday with your family?"

"My brothers are both stationed in California, and I talked to Mom earlier today. But the truth is, I spent the day exactly how I wanted to, Jess. And I did so for the first time in a long time, longer than I care to admit." That there was a hidden depth to her words was not lost on either woman.

Jess watched Erin avert her eyes as her cheeks colored more. She could see a lot of emotion rising to the surface in a woman who, like her, usually kept herself under tight control. Even as Erin's eyes watered, Jess allowed Erin the silence and tacit understanding to regain her equilibrium. But then a single tear defied Erin's will.

Jess reached up and tenderly wiped the tear away. "I understand." She slipped her arm around Erin's shoulders and gently pulled the woman closer. Erin seemed to resist instinctively at first but then gave in. Jess felt Erin bury her face into Jess' shoulder, and when silent tears began wetting her neck, Jess brought her other arm up to complete the embrace.

After a few minutes, Erin pulled back, wiping the tears from her face. "Sorry."

"Don't be. I get the feeling you've been holding those in for a while." She paused. "I also think there's a lot more that needs to be let go," Jess said gently.

Erin shook her head and sniffled as she wiped her face again. "Not tonight."

Jess nodded in understanding. "But keep in mind that if you don't let them out, they can build up until you drown."

"How much for the session, Dr. Morgan?" Erin quipped defensively.

Jess let out a soft sigh. "I've simply been speaking from personal experience, as one friend to another." She paused for a moment. "But if you would prefer, I can do the psychologist bit."

"No. I wouldn't prefer that," Erin said quietly.

"Good. Because I'd much rather be your friend than your therapist." Jess bumped her shoulder against Erin's. "It's all right. I'd prefer you to be my friend rather than my pathologist, so it's only fair," she said with a small smile. She got the response she was hoping for when Erin smiled.

"I should hope so!"

The buzzer from the dryer sounded, startling both women.

"Well, on that heart-stopping note, I think I shall use your bathroom," Jess said, standing up.

"Down the hall, on the right," Erin told her as she also stood.

"I remember."

"I'll check to see if your clothes are dry."

After Jess finished in the bathroom, she opened the door and found Erin waiting with her clothes, fresh from the dryer.

"Here you go."

"Thanks. I'll just be a minute." She retreated and changed into her nicely warmed clothes. When she came back out, Erin was in the kitchen.

"Did you want some more hot chocolate, Jess?"

"I think I'll call it a night."

"It's still rather early."

"I know. But I think you might have been a good influence on me today."

"Oh?"

"Yeah. I might try to get a good night's sleep for a change since it's back to the grindstone tomorrow morning," she said with a small smile.

"You mean you're not returning now so you can work this evening?" Erin challenged.

"Nope. I'm going to make a couple of phone calls to some friends and then get some sleep."

"In that case, I approve." Erin smiled. "Let me get my keys so I can drive you back to your hotel."

Jess was waiting by the door when Erin grabbed her keys and got her shoes and coat on. She stopped Erin as she reached for the doorknob. "Erin, I want you to know I really did have a good time today." She lowered her eyes, embarrassed. "And it's been a long time since that happened." She looked up into dark brown eyes. "I know today was your birthday, but you're the one that gave me a gift today. Thank you," she finished softly.

Erin suddenly hugged Jess. "And you made this one of my best birthdays in a really long time, so thank you too."

Chapter Eight

ERIN RETURNED HOME AFTER taking Jess to her hotel. She turned on some music, put in a load of laundry, and sat down to take care of some correspondence. Despite the brief incident of tears earlier, she really was feeling good and had a wonderful day.

She had just gotten her laundry from the dryer and started folding it when she heard a knock at her door. She looked through the peephole and saw Holton. She opened the door, but before she could say hello or even ask why he was there, he brushed past her with a pizza box balanced on one hand and a six-pack of beer in the other hand.

"Happy birthday, partner! I bring food and drink," he said with a grin as he headed into her kitchen. He proceeded to prepare two plates of food and opened two beers. Going into the living room, he set everything down on the coffee table and turned to her. "Come and get it, Little," he said, with a big smile.

Little continued to fold some of her laundry. "Have at it, Holton. I'm not hungry."

"But I got your favorite: pepperoni and anchovies."

"No, that's your favorite. I hate anchovies. Besides, I already ate, Holton. Agent Morgan and I already had dinner. A very nice dinner."

"Oh. Well, that's nice. How is Agent Morgan? Do you like working with her? Can you believe how she found those other victims on this case? Do you think she'll be coming back to the BAU? If so, do you think she'll be in the field, or will she be taking over command of one of the units?"

"I've already told you that Agent Morgan is very professional, so working with her is just fine. You're still on the taskforce, so you're kept in the loop on any new developments in the case, including anything she and I may turn up. It's only been four days since you and I have temporarily been assigned to work with new partners, yet you've dropped by my apartment twice in that amount of time without notice or invitation—something you've never done before in the ten months we've been partners. What's going on, Holton?"

Holton visibly deflated as he sat in a chair next to the couch. "I don't mean to be a pain," he said. He took a breath as he appeared to gather his thoughts. "I know I'm just a rookie, but you've always treated me like I've at least got a brain cell or two."

As he spoke, Erin took a seat on the couch. "I take it Agent Coleman has a different mentoring style than I do."

"I don't think you can call it mentoring. To him, I'm just the coffee boy. All I'm allowed to say is 'yes, sir' and 'no, sir.' I can forget about asking questions other than what he wants for lunch."

"I'm sorry, Holton. Some agents, like Coleman, are old school. Remember, it's only temporary. You will survive it. No matter who you have as a partner, you can learn something if you keep your eyes and ears open. I know how smart you are, so you can find a way to make it work with Coleman."

He nodded. After a few moments of silence, he spoke again. "Did you really eat dinner already?"

"Yes, I did."

"Okay. Well, I didn't mean to intrude on you, and since you don't like anchovies, I'll take the pizza and leave you alone." He picked up the plates of pizza as he stood. "I hope you had a good birthday, Little."

"Thank you, Holton. I did."

He put the pizza slices back in the box and said goodbye as he let himself out.

February 24, 2025
Monday

Erin and Jess both arrived at work early Monday morning. Once again, they buried themselves in the case files Jess had requested based on the search parameters she'd set to find early victims of The Slasher. However, after only an hour of sorting faxes, files, and printouts into piles of "no way" and "maybe," Jess tossed a folder down in frustration. She got up, walked to the window, and gazed out.

When Erin finished what she was reading, she looked up. "What's wrong, Jess?"

Jess rubbed her face with her hands before turning to face Erin. "We can sit here and read these damn files for weeks, but it's not going to tell us what we need to know. We don't even have crime scene pictures for most of these." She sighed. "How are you doing with the autopsy reports?" she asked in a calmer tone.

"Well, there are some similarities, certainly. But without the bodies, or good pictures of the knife wounds and their placement, it's hard to be sure."

"That settles it. We'll go look at them."

"All right. But you must know that doing, or redoing, autopsies on bodies this old…"

"Yeah, I know. But we can at least access the original files and photos and check out some of the crime scene locations." Jess walked over to her desk and picked up the phone to start arranging for their trip.

They were on a flight to San Diego, California, that afternoon.

March 1, 2025
Saturday

The two agents spent the next four and a half days visiting various cities on the West Coast, liaising with the local police and sheriff departments, evaluating case files, and inspecting crime scene locations. Then they got a phone call.

"Morgan," Jess answered her phone, stepping away from Erin and the detective working with them.

"Agent Morgan, it's Ben Taylor."

"Yes?"

"We've got another one. It's in Wilmington, Delaware."

She closed her eyes and sighed. "It's been thirteen days since the last one. He's still not sticking to any pattern in frequency."

"That's not all."

"What is it?"

"There's a note." He paused. "It's addressed to you."

"What?"

Jess saw Erin glance over at her, concern showing in her expression.

"It was mailed to the office. The envelope was addressed to 'The Slasher Taskforce Leader,' but the note inside was addressed to you by name."

"What does it say?"

"'You look for me high and low. How far are you willing to go? Are you ready for The Slasher? To find me, you must be brasher.'"

"I assume you had forensics check the note and envelope."

"Yes. Too many hands on the envelope for prints to do any good. And no prints at all on the note. Both the envelope and paper are too common to trace. Sorry, Agent Morgan."

"All right. We'll get a flight to Philadelphia as soon as possible. Obviously, you can't leave the body at the scene in the meantime, so make sure they take a lot of photos of the scene and the body *in situ* before they move it."

"I already have them working on it. I'm also emailing you a scan of the letter."

"Good. And please send the note to the Philadelphia field office. I want to see more than just a scan of it. I'll call you with our flight information so someone can pick us up."

"You got it. Talk to you later, Agent Morgan."

"Goodbye." Morgan put her phone away and rubbed her temples.

Erin finished up with the detective and approached Jess. "What's going on, Jess?"

"We've got another one."

"Damn."

"Yeah. We've got to catch the next flight to Philadelphia. Let's go."

Jess was lost in thought on the flight from Portland, OR, to Philadelphia, PA. The note threw her for more than one reason. Most obviously because it had been addressed to her personally. She hadn't been on the press radar, so there hadn't been any TV or newspaper reports that mentioned her. So how did The Slasher even know she was working the case? And after what had happened with Toni, having a serial killer know who she was, that she was hunting him, brought up some bad memories.

Then there was the note itself. It simply made no sense. The wording was banal and felt forced. Not something she expected from the mind of the killer she had profiled. Sending a note at all just did not appear to fit with the person who committed so many murders without leaving any useful forensic evidence. The kind of person who would plant a hair from an earlier victim on another victim just wasn't the kind to write such a note. It lacked intellectual elegance.

It was nine o'clock at night when they landed in Philadelphia. Special Agent Erik Bowman was waiting for them as they exited the plane.

"SSA Morgan, SSA Little?" asked the young man who approached them. He looked barely old enough to shave and was clearly fresh out of the Bureau academy.

"Yes?" said Jess.

"I'm Special Agent Bowman. You can call me Erik. I have a car to drive you to Wilmington."

"Good. Let's go."

When they got to the car, Bowman scurried to put the senior agents' bags in the trunk. Erin and Jess exchanged an amused look. He even opened the passenger side car doors for them. Jess got into the back seat, leaving the front for Erin. Bowman hurried around to the driver's side. He started the car, allowing it to warm up, and pulled a legal-size envelope from a valise to pass back to Jess.

"Assistant Director Taylor sent this for you, Agent Morgan."

"Thank you." Jess opened the envelope and took out the contents. She looked at the note that had been addressed and sent to her and stared at the block-printed message, trying to make sense of it.

"Jess? Jess," Erin prodded.

"Huh? What?"

"Agent Bowman asked if you wanted to go by the field office before heading to the crime scene."

"No, no," she answered distractedly.

Bowman put the car in gear, and they were on their way. For the entire forty-five-minute drive, Jess sat in the dark of the back seat, staring at the note. Her thoughts raced, bouncing between the current case and the past.

Erin had to prompt Jess out of her mental wanderings again when they arrived at the crime scene. Sensing something was wrong other than a new victim, Erin kept a concerned eye on her partner as they entered the house. Because she was watching Jess, Erin caught the involuntary breath she sucked in with a slight hiss. And something strange momentarily happened with her eyes. Didn't it?

"Are you all right, Jess?"

"I'm fine. Let's get to it." Jess moved past Erin, pulling on her gloves.

Erin arched an eyebrow as her partner passed, but she didn't voice her doubts. They had a job to do.

Due to the late hour, they decided Erin would do the autopsy in the morning. Even though it was after midnight when they checked into a hotel, it felt earlier since they had started their day on the West Coast. Erin changed clothes and then knocked on their adjoining door.

"It's unlocked," came from the other side.

Erin opened the door. She stood in the doorway, leaning against the jamb, with her arms crossed. Jess was sitting in one of the chairs, facing the window. Her feet were propped up on the table, crossed at the ankles. Erin waited silently for several long seconds. Finally, she spoke.

"Are you going to tell me what's going on, Jess?"

"What do you mean?"

Erin shook her head and uncrossed her arms. She walked over and sat on the edge of the bed, close to Jess' chair, but still to her back. "Look, I've only known you for a couple of weeks, but we've spent a hell of a lot of time together, on and off duty. You've not been yourself since this morning. What's wrong?"

Jess took a deep breath and slowly let it out. "Maybe I've been doing this too long."

"Why do you say that?"

"Because I'm confused."

"About what?"

Jess didn't say anything, but after a moment, she got up and retrieved the envelope from her briefcase. She handed it to Erin, who opened the envelope and pulled out the note while Jess began to pace slowly. She read the note and frowned.

"How did he know you were working the case?"

"I don't know. But that's not what I'm confused about."

Erin reached out and gently grabbed Jess' arm as her pacing brought her near. "Sit down here and talk to me, Jess."

Jess sat down next to Erin on the bed with a sigh.

"What are you confused about?"

"The note itself. It just doesn't make any sense to me. The profile I did—he just wouldn't do this. And if he did write us a note for some reason, it sure as hell would be more elegant. This," she pointed to the letter, "doesn't fit." She sighed again and shook her head. "Unless I'm way off with my profile. In which case, I don't know where to go from here."

"Well, we start with the body tomorrow morning."

"I'm not holding my breath that we'll find anything new."

"Then we continue what we're doing."

"But that's just it. I don't know if what we're doing is the right thing to be doing. If my profile is wrong, then..."

"Then what, Jess? Then you're wrong?"

Jess gave Erin a look. "Don't you get it? If I'm wrong, then people die."

"That's a risk we all accept when we put on the badge. Lives depend on the decisions we make and the actions we take. Jess, you're an excellent profiler and investigator, but everybody makes mistakes. We're human. All anyone can do is do their best."

Jess still looked full of doubt.

"Come on. Let's go." Erin stood and pulled Jess up by the hand as well.

"Go?"

"To get something to eat."

"At one o'clock in the morning?"

"You skipped lunch and didn't eat on the plane either."

"I think I'll just go to bed."

She arched an eyebrow to show her disbelief. "As tightly wound up as you are? I don't think so. You need to eat something and relax a bit." She gently pushed Jess toward the door. "Let's go."

"What did I tell you about being bossy?"

"And what did I tell you about me being right?" Erin retorted.

Jess shook her head and opened the door with a soft chuckle.

Chapter Nine

March 2, 2025
Sunday

FIRST THING IN THE morning, Erin and Jess went to the morgue. Needing to focus her mind on something other than the note and crime scene photos, Jess also changed into scrubs to assist Erin.

Per the FBI's request, the body had been bagged at the scene and then left alone. The two agents removed the body bag from the cooler, and Erin unzipped the bag. After carefully removing the body from the bag, they began their examination, starting with her clothes.

When Jess took one of the hands in her own to scrape under the nails, she paused. She lifted the hand and sniffed the wrist. She then reached across the body and did the same with the other wrist. Erin raised an eyebrow at her in question.

"Erin, could you toss me the evidence bag with her shirt, please?"

Erin grabbed the bag and tossed it to her.

Jess took the shirt out and sniffed the material at the collar. She handed the shirt to her partner. "Do you smell that?"

Erin sniffed the collar, but the scent wasn't as clear to her less-sensitive senses. "Perfume of some kind?"

"Mm-hmm. It's Estée by Estée Lauder, a fragrance spray, around seventy-five dollars a bottle, depending on where she bought it. I knew someone who wouldn't wear anything else." Jess bent down and sniffed again, this time at the victim's breastbone and knees. "And she was looking forward to a romantic night." She took hold of a wrist and brought it up, bending the elbow and sniffing the victim's wrist once again. "And her date brought her a gift."

Erin looked confused. "What?"

"Take a sniff," Jess instructed.

Erin bent down and sniffed the proffered wrist. She frowned. "It smells different."

Jess nodded. "Clive Christian's No. 1. About five hundred and fifty to eight hundred dollars for a one-and-a-half-ounce bottle." She gently placed the arm back on the table. "I'll have someone try to run a check on purchases. No telling when or where he bought it, but it's worth a try."

Erin nodded in agreement.

After finishing up the autopsy, Jess and Erin went to lunch, during which they decided their next move was to return to Washington. They finished lunch, and went back to their hotel to check out. Then, they caught a flight from Philadelphia to Washington. Back at headquarters, they each worked on consolidating and polishing their respective reports.

At the end of the day, they went their separate ways, Erin home to her apartment, and Jess "home" to her hotel room. However, a surprise waited for Jess in her room.

When Jess opened the door to her room, she intuitively knew something was wrong. She didn't need to look to know someone had been in her room. She could smell it.

She smelled the blood.

Jess dropped her bag and pulled her weapon from her holster. Not bothering to turn the light on, she inched into the room, all her senses on high alert. Only after satisfying herself that no one was present, Jess put her weapon away. She stood and stared at the words on the wall, words written in blood.

Roses are red, violets are blue.
You don't see me, but I see you!

Jess took out her phone and called AD Taylor.

"Taylor."

"It's Morgan. I need a forensics team to come to my hotel room."

"Why? What's happened?"

"Someone's been here and left a message on my room wall *in blood*," she said, emphasizing the last two words.

"Damn." He paused. "All right. I'll get a team out to you ASAP. I'll be there myself in just a few minutes."

"All right. See you soon." As soon as she hung up with Taylor, she called down to the hotel's front desk and requested that the on-duty manager come up. She then stepped back out of her room and waited in the hallway.

The manager, Noah Levine, arrived quickly, and Jess explained that someone had been in her room. She wanted a list of all the employees who had access and had handled cleaning the rooms on her floor that day. They were still talking when AD Taylor arrived with some agents and technicians in tow.

An agent was sent down with Mr. Levine to get the employee names and to talk to on-duty personnel. Jess let the others into her room. The technicians got to work taking pictures, dusting for prints, and taking blood samples. Taylor asked Jess if anything else in the room was disturbed or missing.

She went in and looked around. It didn't look like anything was missing, but her things had been rifled through. Jess and Taylor went back into the hallway.

"I don't like that this guy knows you're working the case and now knows where you're staying. He's making this personal."

"You think I do? It's my things he went through!" she snapped uncharacteristically. She lowered her head and pinched the bridge of her nose. "Sorry." She took a deep breath and let it out. Jess looked at Taylor again. "But on the upside, this could be a blessing in disguise."

"How the hell do you figure that?"

"If he's fixated on me, maybe he won't go after another woman. Or maybe he'll get sloppy." She gestured toward the room door. "This goes beyond leaving misleading clues and sending us on wild goose chases. Leaving a message written in blood on my wall is a blatant 'fuck you.' It's not at all subtle or nuanced. He could finally be so damn arrogant and full of himself that he'll make some mistakes."

"Or he could come after you."

"Possibly," she conceded.

At that moment, Erin arrived. As soon as Taylor got off the phone with Morgan, he called her, catching her still in her car. Heavy traffic delayed her arrival at the hotel. "Are you all right, Jess?"

Jess turned to her partner and nodded. "Yeah. Just had a nice little present waiting for me when I arrived." She nodded at the open door to the room. "Go on and take a look."

Erin stepped into the room and stopped when she saw the writing on the wall. Jess watched as Erin shook her head and stepped back out with a grim expression as the people processed the room. It was going to be a long night.

It had taken some arguing, but finally, Erin, with the help of AD Taylor, convinced Jess to go home with her for the night. Jess had been quiet on the way to Erin's apartment, and she was wound tighter than a spring as her thoughts raced. She knew it had to be apparent to her partner how tense she was.

Once they arrived at Erin's, they went inside. Erin told Jess to make herself at home as she went into her bedroom to change clothes. Having already changed her clothes in the bathroom, Jess watched as Erin checked her answering machine after returning from the bedroom.

"I don't feel like cooking tonight, but we can have something delivered. What do you feel like having for dinner?" Erin asked.

"It doesn't matter. Whatever you want is fine by me."

Erin grabbed the menu from a Chinese place and joined Jess on the couch. They made their selections, and Erin called it in. Thirty minutes later, they were eating. After a silent dinner, they cleaned up, and Erin opened a bottle of wine.

"Okay, Jess, what are you thinking? What's going on with this guy?"

Letting out a long sigh, Jess paused before answering. "As I told Taylor, he's gone beyond leaving misleading clues. That message was a 'fuck you'."

"Not very subtle."

"No. Hopefully, it means he'll be making some mistakes."

"He knows who you are and where you were staying."

"As far as him knowing I'm working the case, enough people know that it could have gotten out without anyone realizing it. Something as simple as my name coming up in a conversation about the case. It's even possible where I was staying got out the same way. Or someone could have hacked into a computer somewhere."

"Possibly." Erin paused. "But what I really want to know is how he knew you would be there *tonight*? I mean, he had to have done it today after housecleaning had already been through, or else they would have seen it. It makes no point to take the risk of it being seen if you wouldn't be back tonight. Otherwise, the hotel could have cleaned it up without you ever knowing it had happened."

"They would have called the police," Jess pointed out.

Erin raised an eyebrow. "That would have been the proper thing to do, but you and I both know that's not always what's done. There's a real possibility that someone at the hotel could have decided to cover it up to avoid any bad publicity. We didn't decide to come back to DC until we were at lunch today. We could have gone back out west. So I ask you: how did he know you would be here?"

Jess wasn't surprised Erin picked up on that little tidbit. She was, after all, an excellent investigator. But no one else had thought to ask that particular question. She looked into those soft brown eyes. "I don't know, Erin."

They wouldn't find any answers that night, so as they drank some more wine, they changed the subject to anything other than work. Which was easier said than done. However, they eventually succeeded, and both women managed to relax, especially with the help of the wine and pleasant companionship. Finally, they were both having trouble staying awake.

Erin grabbed Jess' hand and stood up. "Come on. No sleeping on the couch this time."

Jess opened her eyes. "Sorry," she said and yawned.

Erin urged her up from the couch and guided her to the bedroom. Once she settled onto one side of the bed, Erin crawled onto the other side. They were both soon asleep.

She'd had a long day and was looking forward to getting home. What she wanted more than anything was to take a hot shower and crawl into bed with her lover. She needed to feel Toni's arms around her. She had told Toni she would be home by six o'clock, but then they got a possible lead on the killer they were after. And Jessica was the best interviewer of witnesses and suspects. Even the jerks who resented her presence in the unit came to her for the tough interrogations.

Anyway, after the interview with the reluctant witness, she could finally call it a night at eleven o'clock. Jessica had to stop and get gas on the way home. When she went inside to pay for it, she bought a small stuffed bear on impulse. She smiled at the little five-inch bear, started the car, and pulled away. Toni had a secret collection of the cute stuffed animals she'd kill to keep a secret from her fellow FBI agents. It didn't fit with her tough-as-nails, no-nonsense image. Jessica's smile widened. Settling down with one person for the last three and a half years didn't fit Toni's reputation either. It was the last thing anyone thought Toni would ever do. But that's how long Jessica and Toni had been together.

Jessica parked the car and picked up the little bear with a smile. "Come on, buddy. Let's go make Toni smile."

She rode the elevator up to their floor and had her keys out before she got to the door. With a heartfelt smile, she unlocked the door, stepped inside, turned on the hallway light, and stopped. There was blood on the wall and floor. Her heart dropped like a stone. "Toni? Toni!" she called. She rushed into the living room. "Toni!"

Jessica dropped to her knees and pulled the lifeless, bloody body of her lover into her arms. The stuffed bear was forgotten in a pool of blood. "No!"

"No!" Jess cried out and sat up in bed. Tears rolled down her face, and her whole body trembled.

Erin sat up next to her and put her arm around her shoulders. It took every bit of self-control that Jess had to fight the instinct to roughly push Erin's arm away.

"Shhh, it was just a dream. It's okay, Jess," Erin said, her voice filled with understanding, even if she didn't know what Jess had dreamed about.

She slumped, leaning into Erin and accepting the offered succor. Jess broke down and cried. Erin wrapped her other arm around Jess and held her close.

After a few minutes, Jess quieted. She wiped her face as she pulled out of Erin's embrace. "Excuse me." She got out of bed, left the bedroom, and went into the bathroom.

After washing her face, Jess stared in the mirror and saw the shadows in her eyes. She closed her eyes and took a deep breath. She stood for a few seconds before turning off the light and returning to the bedroom. She silently slipped back into bed, lying on her back. After several moments, she finally spoke. "Sorry."

Erin shifted to lay on her side, facing Jess. She put her hand on Jess' shoulder. "You don't have anything to apologize for, Jess." She paused. "Do you want to talk about it?"

"Not really."
"I'm your friend, and I'm here if you ever do."
"Thank you."

Chapter Ten

JESS WOKE UP SOMETIME later during the night. She was lying on her right side, and Erin was spooning her from behind. While it felt good to be held—certainly, her body was reacting to the warmth of Erin's breath on the back of her neck and the press of her breasts against her back—she didn't think it would be the best way for new, temporary FBI partners to find themselves come morning. Besides, she needed to go to the bathroom. Jess carefully started removing Erin's left arm from around her waist.

Still sleeping, Erin tightened her arm around Jess and murmured in her sleep. "It's okay. Just a dream…"

Jess couldn't help but feel warmed by the caring Erin showed her. Still, she needed to change their situation. She mentally shrugged and went for the direct approach. As she moved Erin's arm again, she softly said, "I've got to go the bathroom."

It worked. As she got out of bed, Erin rolled onto her other side and faced the opposite direction. Jess went to the bathroom and silently slipped back into bed when she returned without disturbing Erin. She had no trouble falling back asleep.

Once Jess' breathing evened out and Erin was sure Jess was asleep, she opened her eyes and stared into the darkness. She didn't want to embarrass herself or Jess, so she had pretended to be still asleep when Jess woke up and wanted to move. It was just easier that way. She had been surprised to wake and find herself curled around the sleeping form of her partner; she was anything but a cuddler. However, she liked the way Jess felt in her arms. She really wouldn't mind waking up like that on a regular basis. That thought brought her up short.

She took a deep breath and slowly let it out, as she rolled onto her back. She thought back over the last couple of weeks and how she'd felt drawn to the enigmatic agent. Erin enjoyed their working relationship. She liked working with an equal—it was so different from what she was used to. Of course her most recent partner was Holton. Having a rookie partner had her doubting his skill and knowledge—did he really have what it took to back her up in a life-and-death situation should one arise? If she had to teach someone how to do the job, she'd rather be an instructor at the academy than in the field, risking life and limb. Even though Erin and Jess were still getting to know each other, they had an easy camaraderie and respect that came from their level of experience and professionalism on the job.

Erin even liked spending time with Jess away from work. That was something she usually didn't do with a partner. For the most part, Erin always tried to keep her work life and her personal life separate. Holton had been to her apartment only four times, and two of those times had been in the last ten days, not to mention that those two recent times were *uninvited*. She didn't invite people from work to her apartment very often. On the few occasions she and Holton had pizza and beer to celebrate the closing of a difficult case, it had always been at the pizza joint down the road from the field office.

Erin had gone out of her way to spend time with Jess off duty. She found Jess to be funny, charming, vulnerable, intelligent, compassionate, and beautiful. It was no wonder she was so attracted to Jess.

"Oh shit," she whispered almost silently.

March 3, 2025
Monday

Erin got up early the next morning. She'd come to a decision and decided to act on it as soon as possible rather than procrastinate. She was typing up a letter on her laptop when a freshly showered and dressed Jess joined her.

"Good morning, Jess. I'm afraid I don't have much to offer in the way of breakfast since I haven't had the chance to go grocery shopping. I do have some coffee, though, if you aren't averse to drinking that instead of your preferred tea."

"I'm not hungry anyway, and I'll pass on the coffee." She met Erin's eyes and smiled. "I never did acquire the taste for coffee. I guess I'm too Continental for it." She took her smartphone out and quickly sorted the emails and texts she'd received.

"I hate to ask, Jess, but could I drop you off at Headquarters this morning? I have a meeting I need to attend. I can meet up with you afterward."

"Sure thing. I've got to meet with the director first thing anyway."

"Great. Thank you."

Erin went to the Washington field office after dropping Jess off at the Hoover Building. She sat across the desk from Special Agent in Charge Ken Takashima, the man in charge of the Washington field office.

"Thank you for seeing me on such short notice, sir."

"What can I do for you?"

Little handed SAC Takashima her letter. "I wanted to give you this."

He took the short letter and quickly read it. "Are you sure about this?"

"Yes, sir, I am."

"You do realize that I can't act on this until after your current assignment to the taskforce is over."

"Yes, sir. I know."

"I respect your work, Agent Little. While I will miss your skills and insights in the field, I have no doubt you will make an outstanding contribution to the Academy. I will forward your request for transfer with my endorsement."

"Thank you, sir."

"May I ask, Agent Little, would it make a difference if I assigned you a new partner?"

"No, sir, it wouldn't. It's not about Holton. This is about me."

"Very well."

Jess took the elevator up to the director's office. When she arrived, the director's personal assistant, Stacy Drexler, greeted her. The fiftyish woman with salt and pepper hair came around her desk and hugged Jess.

"It's so good to see you, Jessica."

"Thanks, Stacy," she replied, feeling embarrassed.

"I just heard this morning what that creep did to your hotel room yesterday," Stacy said as she reluctantly let go of Jess. "I can't believe it. I told the director we should put you in one of the Bureau's safe houses while you're here."

"No, no, no, Stacy! I'd much rather the UNSUB focus on me than on his next innocent victim. I can't hide away. As long as he's playing games with me, he's not out there hunting someone else."

Stacy just shook her head. She opened her mouth to say something else, but the director's office door opened. "Jessica, in here. Stacy, no interruptions, please."

"Yes, sir," replied Stacy.

Jess followed Lou into his office, closing the door behind them, and sat in one of the two chairs facing the director's desk.

"Good morning, Lou," she said.

"Good morning, Jessica." He didn't beat around bush, letting her know why he'd summoned her to his office. "Now tell me why the hell I had to find out about what happened in your hotel room last night by reading about it in a goddamn report," he demanded, frowning. "Don't you think it's important for me to know that some killer is stalking you?"

"There's no evidence that he's stalking me, Lou. He just broke into my hotel room."

"And wrote a note in blood on your wall."

"I know. I was there."

He shot her a look. "All right. Tell me what you're thinking. What's going on with this guy?"

"To be honest, I'm not sure. The notes don't match up with my profile. But I do think it's better to have him focused on me than stalking another innocent, young woman."

"You did say at some point he may want to step up the games he's playing with us. Maybe this is it."

"Maybe. This just feels different somehow. Our UNSUB is..." She trailed off as she sought the right words. "He's been perfect, many times, even while having a taskforce actively looking for him. Logically, he could go on, just as he has been, making no mistakes and not getting caught. These inelegant taunts seem childish and gauche. Everything our UNSUB has not been up to this point." Jess took a deep breath and let it out with a sigh. "But as you well know, no profile can predict everything about a person. There are no guarantees. And no one is infallible at guessing what's in a person's psyche. It's not an exact science."

"I know. But you are right about people more than anyone I know, so I trust your judgment. However, I am still the director. And if things get out of hand or become too dangerous for some of my agents, I will do something about it."

"I'll be fine, Lou," she reassured him.

"All right. Now get out of my office and get back to work, Agent Morgan. I have a Bureau to run."

"Yes, sir," she said with an amused smirk.

When Erin arrived, Jess was reading a file at one end of the worktable in her office. She looked up and quirked an eyebrow. "What's got you so chipper this morning?"

"You know that feeling you get when you finally do something you've put off too long? And you wonder why you didn't do it sooner?"

Jess smiled. "Yeah. Accomplishment mixed with relief with a touch of amazement."

"That's it exactly," Erin replied with a pleased smile. "What did the director want?"

"He wanted to know about last night and my thoughts regarding it." She picked up a folder and tossed it toward Erin at the other end of the worktable. "Forensics report."

Erin opened the folder and scanned the report. "No prints, not even yours or any hotel employees. He wiped everything down." She paused. "Bovine blood. So he didn't use blood from any of the victims."

"No. I'm not sure what the significance of cow's blood is, other than it's easy to obtain."

"What are you working on?"

"I'm going through the interviews of the friends and family of each victim."

"What are you looking for?"

"Anything." Jess sighed. "Anything that could be a lead that others might have overlooked or dismissed as unimportant."

Following Jess' lead, Erin reached toward the pile of case files on the table and grabbed one to read.

The women spent all day reading the case files. Erin put each one that she read into a pile. Jess did the same. Then they switched piles. It was well past dinner time when they finished working their way through them.

Jess tossed the last file down on the table with disgust and frustration. She closed her eyes and rubbed them with the heels of her hands. "Well, that was a damn waste of time."

Erin stood up. "Come on, Jess. Time to get out of here."

"I've got to be missing something," Jess exclaimed, frustrated.

"Let's go get something to eat, get a good night's sleep, and come at this fresh in the morning."

Jess looked at her partner, debating her next move: do as Erin suggested, or stay and try to find something in the files. Her eyes were burning and her head hurt. She and Erin had already reviewed all the case files, so she nodded. "All right," she said and sighed.

Jess followed Erin in her rental car. They stopped to pick up some barbecue chicken for dinner and then headed to Erin's apartment.

Jess was holding the bag of food as Erin unlocked her door. As soon as the door opened a few inches, Jess knew something was wrong. She smelled it—the blood. She didn't hesitate. Without even having to think about it, she grabbed Erin's arm and pulled her away from the door, moving her aside and pressing her against the wall.

Clearly shocked and about to ask what was going on, Erin appeared to catch on that something was wrong when Jess, with her weapon already drawn, pressed a finger to her lips, indicating quiet, and slipped into the darkness of Erin's apartment.

Jess' eyes changed so that she could see in the blackness of the apartment. She didn't see anything of note until she entered the living room. The blood was still wet, meaning he had been there *very* recently. She whipped around at a faint sound that came from the direction of Erin's bedroom. The window was closed in the bedroom except for a half-inch gap. She looked out and saw someone running away from the building. The bastard had used the fire escape and window to get in and out.

"Call for backup and don't touch anything," she yelled to Erin as she opened the window and stepped out onto the fire escape. A leap over the railing and she landed on the snow-covered ground two stories below. She took off running in the direction she'd seen the suspect run.

Erin, unable to see in the pitch dark of the apartment, had slowly and carefully made her way to the kitchen, where she silently slid a drawer open and retrieved a flashlight. She had no idea where Jess was or how she could possibly move around her apartment in the dark. She had just turned on the flashlight when she heard Jess' yell from her bedroom. She rushed to the bedroom doorway. The only evidence of anyone's presence was the open window. She looked out the third-story window and saw what she thought was Jess running away from the building.

"How the hell did she get down so fast?" she murmured. Erin pulled out her phone and called for backup, reporting that her partner was in foot pursuit. She then quickly checked the rest of the apartment, ensuring no one else was present. In the living room, Erin turned on a light and saw the blood on her wall.

Sorry I missed you!

Erin dialed her cell again, this time calling AD Taylor.

Chapter Eleven

JESS RAN, TRACKING HER quarry by following the slight sounds of his footfalls. Just as she closed in, about to finally get a look at him, he got into a car and drove off. Her run had brought her out on the other side of the woods and onto another street. The car was already around the corner and accelerating away. She let out a yell of anger and frustration. She wanted to hit something, but it wouldn't accomplish anything. She holstered her weapon and headed back.

Backup had arrived by the time she arrived at Erin's building. She told the agents at the front door of the building what she had seen and where she had chased the suspect. Unfortunately, without a description of the suspect or his car, there wasn't much that could be done. Before going up to Erin's apartment, Jess made a call on her cell phone.

"Cavanaugh."

"Lou, it's me."

"What's wrong?"

"He was just at Erin's, Agent Little's apartment."

"Who is he? Did you see him?"

"No, I didn't get a good look at him. I chased him, but he had a car waiting."

"Why would he break into Agent Little's apartment if he's playing games with you?"

"He left another note in blood. Lou, it said, 'Sorry I missed you.'"

"Jesus Christ. He *is* fucking with you. This is getting complicated, Jessica."

"I know!"

"And someone needs to read Agent Little in on all the details and specifics of the Conrad case."

"No. What you need to do is pull her off this case."

"Why?"

"Dammit, you *know* why."

"It makes more sense to put more people on this case than to take people off it. Especially talented people already familiar with it."

"Then put her somewhere safe and put a detail on her."

"You know, I'm looking at her service file right now. SSA Erin Little doesn't strike me as the type who would take very kindly to having a protection detail assigned to her."

Jess was getting angry with Lou's seeming lack of understanding and willingness to protect Erin. And it had just been that morning when he'd told her he'd do what was necessary to protect his agents if things got too dangerous. "I don't care what she thinks, Lou. Under the circumstances, some prudence is more than called for. I won't just sit by and do nothing and see another talented agent killed for no good reason."

"I'm not about to do nothing either, so calm down, Jessica. But now you know how I feel about making sure you're all right working this case."

"Yeah, well, I'm fine, Lou. And I'm ready to catch this guy."

"Be safe."

"All right. Bye." Jess hung up and took the stairs up to the third floor of the apartment building.

When Jess entered Erin's apartment, she found AD Taylor already there. A couple of techs were taking samples and dusting for prints.

"Agent Morgan, are you all right?" Taylor asked.

"Yes. But he got away. He had a car waiting."

"Did you get a look at him?"

"No."

Taylor's phone rang. He answered it and stepped into the kitchen for some privacy.

Jess turned to her partner, where she was staring at the blood on her wall. "I'm sorry, Erin. I couldn't catch him."

"It's not your fault." She looked at Jess. "How the hell did you know?"

"Know what?"

"Out in the hallway, when we first got here. How the hell did you know this was here?"

"I smelled it, the blood."

"All I could smell was the barbecue." She shook her head. "If I hadn't called in our order on the way, we wouldn't have gotten here when we did. We would have arrived later. He would have come and gone without us seeing him. And why—"

"Pack a bag, Agent Little," Taylor interrupted when he reentered from the kitchen.

"Why?"

"Because you're not going to stay here. You and Agent Morgan will stay at a safe house."

"There's no re—"

"Orders from the director," he stressed. "You don't have a choice."

Although Erin wasn't happy about it, she went into her bedroom and started to pack.

Jess turned to Taylor. "I'm the one who called the director. I'm also the one who insisted Erin be taken somewhere safe. But there's no reason for me—"

"His orders were very explicit. You are *both* going, Agent Morgan. Agents are already at your hotel getting your things and checking you out."

AD Taylor had arranged for Jess' rental car to be returned, so when she and Erin were escorted downstairs, they were ushered into a Bureau SUV with darkened windows. As their vehicle pulled away, so did two others that were identical in appearance. The vehicles would head out in three different directions to throw off anyone who might want to follow.

Erin wasn't pleased about the situation, but it was apparent to her that it upset Jess even more. However, she didn't press Jess to talk about it in the car, not with the other agents present. Erin simply watched her partner.

Once they arrived at the safe house, Erin and Jess were taken inside. Jess' things from her hotel room were already present. Agents were unobtrusively stationed outside around the house. Erin and Jess would at least have the house to themselves without other agents underfoot.

Erin dropped her bag in one of the bedrooms. After changing clothes, she went to the kitchen. She was looking in the refrigerator for something to drink when Jess joined her. "There's not much to choose from. There's milk, Coke, and orange juice. What's your pleasure?"

"Vodka."

Erin turned and looked at her partner. "Not that I wouldn't mind a drink myself, but that's not one of the choices."

Jess smirked and set a bottle on the table.

A blonde eyebrow arched. "Where—"

"My stuff from the hotel."

"I thought wine was your drink of choice."

"It is if I want to enjoy a drink. Vodka is for getting drunk."

"And you intend to get drunk?"

"I'm seriously considering it."

"Well, they say it's best not to drink alone, so pour one for me," Erin said as she turned and put their delayed meal in the microwave. Once the barbecue chicken was done heating up, she set the plate on the table and joined Jess.

After finishing their meal and a few shots, Erin pinned her partner with a pointed look. "All right, Jess, spill."

"What?"

"Something is bothering you, and I know it's more than just the case. What is it?"

Jess sighed. "The note on your wall."

"What about it?"

"The timing, for one thing. You said it yourself. He would have been in and out without a trace if you hadn't called in our dinner order. We got to your place before he expected us to."

Erin thought about it for a few moments. "Are you saying what I think you're saying?"

"He knew we stopped, but he expected us to take longer than we did."

"He followed us to the restaurant," Erin realized.

Jess simply nodded and poured herself another shot. She offered to pour Erin another, but Erin shook her head. She was trying to put some of the pieces together. After a few moments, she spoke again.

"Why would he write 'Sorry I missed you' if he never intended to be there when we arrived?"

"Because the bastard is baiting me."

"What do you mean, Jess?"

"'Sorry I missed you.'" Jess downed the shot she'd poured. "It's the exact same thing Devon Gaines Conrad wrote on my apartment wall...in Toni's blood."

Jess' revelation stunned Erin. It certainly explained Jess' wanting to get drunk. But it also raised questions. Not the least of which was: What was the connection between Devon Conrad and the current case?

"So what do you want to do?" she asked softly.

"You mean besides getting drunk?" Jess paused, shaking her head. "It's not a matter of what I *want* to do, but what *needs* to be done." She rubbed her face with her hands before continuing. "We need to see Conrad and find out what he can tell us about our friend." Jess got up, headed into her bedroom, and closed the door.

March 4, 2025
Tuesday

When Erin entered the kitchen the next morning, she found Jess already up and sipping some tea.

"How do you feel?"

"If you're asking if I have a hangover, I'm fine. If you're asking if I'm looking forward to today, absolutely not." Jess let out a soft sigh. "I found some tea in the cupboard, so I made a pot. There's some instant coffee if you prefer."

Erin made a face at the mention of instant. "Tea sounds fine." She gave Jess' shoulder a gentle squeeze as she passed her. Erin poured herself a cup of tea and sat down.

"I already called North Branch," said Jess, referring to the hyper-max prison in Maryland. "We have an appointment to see Conrad. Warden Garrett said he has a file of correspondence Conrad's received since he's been in prison and recordings of his phone calls."

"When do you want to leave?"

"Whenever you're ready. A helicopter's waiting at Quantico to fly us out there."

"I only need a couple of minutes."

"No rush."

Warden Garrett had sent someone to escort Erin and Jess when their helicopter landed. Upon entering the prison, they had to surrender their weapons and lock them in small lockers. A guard took them to the warden's office.

The warden stood as they entered his office. "Agent Morgan, Agent Little, welcome to North Branch. I'm Warden Garrett." They shook hands. "I have a room set up with the items you requested. Copies of all incoming and outgoing correspondence and recordings of Devon Conrad's phone calls."

"Thank you for all your assistance, Warden. It's greatly appreciated," Jess said.

"It's not a problem, Agent Morgan. There's not nearly as much as one might think. Since Conrad was transferred here last year, he's been in solitary. And I understand he was in solitary at Keen Mountain. If you're ready to meet him, I'll have him moved to an interview room."

"Actually, I'd prefer to go through the correspondence first. Just in case there's anything that we need to ask him about."

"Certainly. Sgt. Morris will take you to check that out. Just let him know when you're ready to have Conrad moved for visitation. And if you need anything else, don't hesitate to let me know."

"What about a log of his visitors?"

"He hasn't had any visitors since he's been here."

"All right. Thank you, Warden."

Sgt. Morris took Erin and Jess to the room where they could review Conrad's contacts with the outside world.

Both agents slipped off their coats and jackets as they sat at the worktable. Jess opened the box and took out a tape player, a few cassettes, and some file folders. Just as the warden had indicated, it was less than she expected. She paused, looking at everything.

"What do you want to start with?" Erin asked gently.

"Let's start with the letters." She opened a file folder labeled "incoming."

They worked their way through all the incoming and outgoing letters. There wasn't anything unusual in any of the letters. Then, Erin put a tape in the player and started it. As soon as Conrad's voice sounded on the tape, Jess stood up and walked away from the table. She leaned against a wall with her arms crossed and her head down. Erin kept an eye on her. Even though Jess didn't move while the tape played, Erin could practically feel the tension rolling off her. Jess remained as still as a statue while Erin played the rest of the recordings. Finally, she finished.

"That's it, Jess. That was the last tape."

Jess didn't respond.

Erin got up and walked over to her. She placed a hand on Jess' shoulder. "Are you all right?" When Jess finally lifted her head, Erin could see the answer in her gray eyes.

"I'm sorry…" Jess swallowed and took a steadying breath. "I don't think I can…"

"It's all right, Jess. You don't have to. I'll talk to him."

"I'm sorry."

"It's okay. You wait here, Jess."

Erin returned to the table, put on her jacket, and opened the door. She told Sgt. Morris that she was ready to see Conrad. When he questioned her about Jess, she told him it didn't take both to interview Conrad and that Jess was staying with the correspondence.

Chapter Twelve

ERIN WATCHED A SECURITY monitor as guards brought Devon Gaines Conrad into the private visitation room. Conrad was six-foot-two and had the physique of someone who had nothing to do but exercise while locked up in a cell twenty-three of twenty-four hours a day. Blonde stubble, white teeth, neatly trimmed hair, and a square jaw combined to give him a rugged, if not handsome, appearance that would have seemed appropriate for a classic lumberjack or construction worker. But his green eyes betrayed the overall effect. There was no missing the malevolence behind them.

The guards locked his shackled legs to an eyebolt in the concrete floor and locked the chain of his handcuffs to a bolt in the table, which in turn was also bolted to the floor. One guard stationed himself in the corner of the room, and the other came to let Erin know it was all right to enter.

Erin entered the interview room and sat at the opposite end of the table. "Mr. Conrad, I'm Supervisory Special Agent Little with the FBI, and I have some questions to ask you."

"I've got nothing to say to you, Agent Tiny."

"You agreed to this meeting."

"I only agreed to this meeting because the delectable Agent Morgan requested it. So where is my Jessica?"

There was something very sleazy and perverse in how he pronounced Jess' name. It made Erin's skin crawl.

—

Jess was sitting at the table glancing over the letters Conrad had received once more when the door opened. It was Sgt. Morris.

"Agent Morgan?"

"Yes?"

"Conrad is refusing to speak to your partner. He says he'll only discuss the matter with you."

She closed her eyes, took a deep breath, and let it out. She really didn't want to talk to the man who murdered her lover. But she couldn't put herself before the victims of the current case. Preventing more deaths was the goal.

Morris, noting the tight expression on her face, broke the silence. "I'll tell them to put Conrad back in his cell."

Jess opened her eyes. "No. I'll talk to him."

Erin moved to stand next to Jess, where she was watching Conrad on the security monitor. She placed a warm hand on Jess' back. "You don't have to do this, Jess."

"Yes, I do. We have to find out what he knows."

"We didn't find anything in the letters or phone calls. Chances are he doesn't know anything."

"There's still a chance he does. And that message on your wall is too much of a coincidence not to be connected somehow." Jess schooled her features into an impassive mask and went to the door. The guard let her into the room, leaving Erin to watch.

"Hello, Devon."

"Well, well, well. If it isn't Agent Morgan." He gave her a feral sneer. "Or should I say, Doctor? After all, you quit the Bureau, didn't you?" He grinned with satisfaction. "Couldn't take it after I took that bitch from you."

"How do you like your new accommodations?"

"You should have heard her, Jessica. She squealed like a little pig, and then she begged for more. She died cursing your name."

Jess simply stared at him, refusing to rise to the bait.

"It's really a shame you weren't there to join us. Sorry I missed you."

"Me too," she replied flatly, thinking of what she'd have done to him if she had been home that night. "As a matter of fact, that's why I'm here."

"Do tell."

"It seems someone else is sorry he missed me. Even copied your message to me in blood on a wall."

"Hmm, I must have a fan."

"Perhaps. But he doesn't have your flair. He used cow's blood."

"Then he's a pussy."

"By any chance, Devon, do you happen to know who your fan is?"

"Maybe...maybe not. What if I do? What will it get me?"

"Nothing. You're here because while your lawyer goes through the appeals process, you still haven't learned how to play nice with others, Devon. There's no way you're getting out of super-max. And, once your appeals are exhausted, they're going to strap you down, stick a needle in your arm, and kill you. Nothing is going to change that, Devon."

"But you'll be there. I'll haunt you even after my death."

"Dream on, lover boy. I won't waste another second of my time or thoughts on you once I walk out that door. If there's anything you have to say to me, this is your one and only shot, so make it good. If you know anything, tell me. This little moment of my time is all you'll ever get."

She sat for several seconds in dead silence, returning his stare without flinching.

Finally, Jess stood up. "All right, I'm out of here."

"Wait!"

She paused and looked at him. "What?"

"I do have something to tell you."

She waited a few seconds for him to speak, but he didn't. "What is it, Devon?"

"I'll tell you, but not with anyone else listening," he said with a nod at the guard in the corner of the room and another at the camera in the room.

"You know that's not how things go, Conrad. It's not going to happen," the guard responded.

"Why don't we see what Jessica has to say about it?" Conrad looked at Jess, waiting.

Jess crossed her arms, still keeping her face impassive. Without looking away from Conrad, she addressed the guard. "It's all right. You can go."

"I can't do that, ma'am."

She looked up and glared at the guard. "Yes, you can. Now get out." Her tone left no doubt that she expected her order to be followed.

The look in her eyes was enough to get the guard to back down. He silently stepped out of the room. Jess then looked directly into the camera. "Turn the camera off, Agent Little."

Erin watched with concern as the guard left the room. She told herself that Conrad was chained to the table and the floor. He couldn't hurt Jess. But then Jess looked directly into the camera, as if looking right into her eyes, and told her to turn off the camera. Erin hesitated momentarily but reached for the switch as she watched Jess close the distance between herself and Conrad. She was only a couple of feet from him. "Be careful, Jess," Erin whispered to herself.

"Don't do it, Agent Little," said Sgt. Morris.

"I trust my partner's judgment." She flipped the switch, turning the camera off.

A couple of minutes later, Erin turned as Jess entered the observation room. "Are you—"

"Let's get out of here, Agent Little, and head back to Quantico."

"All right."

Jess was silent as they checked out of the prison, returned to where the helicopter was waiting, and flew back. She didn't say a word until the pilot informed them that they would land at Reagan National Airport instead of Quantico.

"Why?" Jess asked the pilot.

"I don't know, ma'am. Just the orders I received."

When the helicopter landed, AD Taylor was waiting for them. "Sorry about diverting you from Quantico, but I was caught up in meetings all day and couldn't make it to Quantico. How did it go with Conrad?" he asked.

Jess shook her head. "He didn't know anything."

At the behest of the director, AD Taylor tried to talk Jess into having a driver, which was a not-very-well veiled attempt to assign her a bodyguard. She, of course, declined, but she did agree to drive one of the Bureau's armored SUVs, mainly due to her not wanting anything to happen to her partner.

Once Erin and Jess were alone in the Bureau SUV and Erin was driving them away from the airport, Erin broke the silence in the vehicle. "Conrad didn't have anything to say?"

Jess let out a sigh. "He had plenty to say. Just nothing about our case."

Her phone cut off whatever Erin was going to say. While she talked on her phone, Jess closed her eyes and thought about Conrad and their talk.

After Erin turned off the camera, Conrad finally told Jess what he had to say. Which was nothing helpful—simply his foul and sick fantasies. She let him have his say, keeping her

face expressionless. Conrad sat grinning up at her, so pleased with himself. She finally moved to stand behind him. She put her hands on his shoulders, bent down, and whispered in his ear.

"You are so lucky you're locked up in here, Devon."
"Why?"
"Because you're safe."
He turned his head to look at her and froze. What he saw obviously scared him. Jess' features had completely shifted—eyes fathomless black, canines elongated and sharply pointed. But beyond the actual physical changes, the aura of power and control shook him to the core. He tried to stand, but her hands on his shoulders dug into his trapezius muscles and painfully held him in place.

"In here, you're safe from me." She let go of his shoulders and walked out the door. She heard him yell before the door shut behind her.

"Guard! Guard! Get me out of here!"

"What do you say, Jess?"
Erin's voice suddenly pulled Jess back to the present. "Hmm?"
"About dinner?"
"Whatever you want."
Erin put her phone back to her ear. "Sure, Mom. See you soon."

"Mom, this is Jess Morgan. Jess, this is my mother, Eleanor Little."
"Ellie, please," she said as they shook hands.
"It's nice to meet you, Ellie."
"Well, come on in and make yourselves comfortable. Dinner will be ready in just a little bit."
The three sat down in the living room.
"Erin tells me you're an FBI agent like she is."
"Yes, ma'am."
"What do you do? Or are you not allowed to say?"

Jess smiled. "I'm a psychologist, a profiler."

"And what does that mean you do?"

Erin arched an eyebrow. Her mother knew what a profiler was and what they did. She had been in the FBI for almost ten years and had discussed her work in the BAU and working with profilers before.

"My job is to analyze a crime, the victim, the circumstances, the physical evidence, etc., and then based on all of that, come up with a psychological profile of the suspect," Jess answered.

"That sounds like difficult work."

"It can be."

"Jess is the best, Mom. She works cases all over the country and reports directly to the director."

"So what's brought you here?" Ellie asked.

"A case."

"We can't really talk about it, Mom."

"Sorry, I didn't mean to pry," Ellie said. A buzzer sounded in the kitchen. "The roast is done. I need to get it out of the oven."

"I'll help you," Erin volunteered.

"Could I use your bathroom, Ellie?"

"Sure, Jess. It's down the hall on the left."

"Thank you."

Erin went into the kitchen with her mother. She set the table as Ellie got the roast out of the oven.

"Derek called me last night."

Erin looked at her mother. "Why on earth would he call you?"

"He wanted to know if you were staying here and if not, where you might be." Ellie took in the expression on her daughter's face. "Erin, what's going on? Why doesn't your partner know where you're staying?"

Erin shook her head. "We've each been assigned temporary partners for the duration of the case we're working. He's partnered with someone else, just like I'm partnered with Jess. There's no reason whatsoever for him to be bothering you."

"But why doesn't he know where you're staying? What is that about?"

"It's nothing to worry about, Mom. Jess and I are just on the road a lot."

Having returned from the bathroom, Jess stepped into the kitchen to join Erin and Ellie.

"Isn't that right, Jess?" Erin asked.

Due to her superior hearing, Jess had heard Erin sidestep the answer to her mother's question about Holton not knowing where she'd been staying, so she played along. "I'll say. I'm not sure how many states we've been in, but I think we've hit all the time zones," she said with a small smile.

"I don't know what's worse, having you posted nearby in Washington but traveling all the time with your job, or having both of your brothers stationed across the country but at least having them stay put for a while."

"Well, my situation may be changing."

"Oh?"

"When this case is over...I've put in a transfer request, Mom."

"Where to?"

"Back to Quantico, to the Academy. At least until I figure some things out."

"But I thought you liked it at the Washington office."

"I do. But I need a change."

"The Academy always needs experienced agents to pass on their priceless knowledge to the up-and-coming new agents," Jess said with a teasing smile. The director used the same line on her recently.

"Everything's ready. Let's have a seat," announced Ellie.

Dinner was good, and all three women seemed to relax and enjoy the meal and conversation. Ellie had drawn Jess out, asking probing questions. Jess wasn't used to the way a parent could keep asking questions and not stop until told to do so, and Jess wasn't about to be rude and tell her partner's mother to stop. She answered all of Ellie's questions, being too polite to do otherwise.

Chapter Thirteen

"ELLIE, I WANT TO thank you for the delicious meal and excellent conversation. It's been a very enjoyable evening. I'm glad I got the chance to meet you."

Ellie smiled. "It's been my pleasure, Jess. You should make my daughter bring you again."

"Take care, Mom. I'll be in touch," Erin said as they hugged.

"Be safe. Both of you." Ellie then surprised Jess by pulling her into a firm hug.

Erin saw her partner's shocked expression and stifled a quiet chuckle. As she and Jess walked to the SUV, she smiled. "That means she likes you."

"I got that," Jess replied, still a little surprised.

"Sorry about the inquisition during dinner. Mom could teach a class or two on how to interrogate someone," Erin said, putting the SUV in drive and pulling away.

Jess laughed. "It's all right. I like her, and she's obviously proud of you." She smiled. "I also see where you get your strength and determination from."

Erin smiled. "My mother would call it stubbornness and say I got it from my father." She glanced at Jess. "Where do you get yours from?"

"What? Strength and determination? Or stubbornness?" Jess asked with a smirk.

"Either? Both?"

"I would say my grandfather." She took a deep breath and slowly let it out. "He was the only relative that ever really gave a damn, He made a real difference in my life. He was an infinitely patient, but demanding, teacher."

"What did he teach?"

"Oh, he wasn't a teacher by profession. I just mean he taught me a lot. 'With power and privilege comes responsibility.' He taught me what each of those things—power, privilege, responsibility—are, and how they directly related to me. His were the most important lessons, the most valuable. There's no telling how I would have ended up without his understanding and support."

Erin didn't miss the reverent tone in Jess' voice. "He was very special to you."

Jess nodded. "Yes, he was. I miss him."

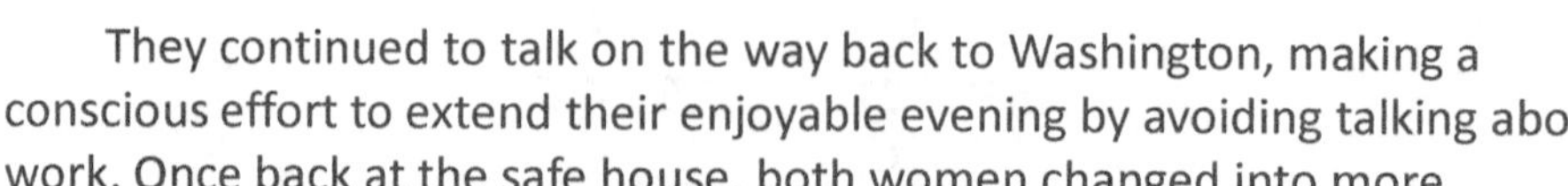

They continued to talk on the way back to Washington, making a conscious effort to extend their enjoyable evening by avoiding talking about work. Once back at the safe house, both women changed into more comfortable clothes before deciding to watch some television.

Erin watched Jess more than she did the TV. She could tell that Jess was much more relaxed than she had been after their visit with Conrad. She smiled as she thought about how her mother had gotten her partner to open up. And Jess had completely charmed her mother. It was ironic that a person without experience dealing with her own parents could so easily, and without guile, thoroughly charm and entertain someone else's mother. Somehow, it pleased Erin that her mother had taken such a strong liking to the other woman.

"Jess?"

"What?"

"Are you all right? I mean, I know today was difficult for you."

Jess looked at her and nodded. "Surprisingly, I'm fine. I was just thinking about today, about Conrad."

"He tried to get to you."

"Yeah. You know, I'd put him out of my mind, for the most part, for some time now. At least until this case. It was hard to listen to his voice today, and then to meet with him face-to-face, but something's different since I talked to him." She paused before she continued, trying to express what she was thinking and feeling. "I know I told him I wouldn't waste another second thinking about him, which was not exactly true. But at some point, while I was talking with him, he lost some of his power over me." She let out a rueful huff. "Or rather, I took some of that power back from him, since people only have that kind of power when we allow it." She took a slow breath. Her eyes focused back on Erin. "It's surprising." She smiled. "And then having dinner with your mother and spending time with her was great. It was just what I needed. What I want to know, Erin, is how you seem to know what I need?" she finished with an arched eyebrow.

Erin smiled. "Great minds think alike?" she offered humorously. "I don't know. It's not like I know with certainty. Maybe it's instinct."

Morgan chuckled. "Then I say you should trust your instincts."

"I think you're right. I've been ignoring my instincts about some things for a while now. I've just recently started listening to them again."

"Good. I've watched you work—you have good instincts."

The unexpected compliment almost embarrassed Erin. She smiled demurely. "Thank you. I appreciate that."

Jess shrugged. "I just call them as I see them."

They continued talking until it was finally time to get some sleep. They walked together down the hallway, stopping at Erin's bedroom.

"Thanks again, Erin. For everything."

"You're welcome."

They hugged each other. On impulse, Erin turned her head and kissed Jess' cheek. When they pulled back, their eyes met and held. Before she could stop herself, Erin brought her hand up and tenderly cupped Jess' cheek, caressing the spot she'd kissed with her thumb. Then she leaned in and pressed her lips to Jess'. Her heart trip-hammered when the soft lips against hers responded. It was a gentle melding of lips and breath as they stood there, loosely embracing. It was so much better than she'd imagined or dreamed. All too soon, it ended. Their eyes once again met.

"Good night," Jess said softly.

"Good night," Erin said. And then she was standing in her doorway alone. She closed the bedroom door and leaned her head against it, her eyes closed. "Oh god..." she whispered. She took a deep breath and let it out slowly. Her pulse was still racing as she turned and moved to sit on the side of her bed. She lowered her head and took a couple of deep breaths, replaying the scene in her mind. Soon, her body started to feel phantom caresses. Her eyes snapped open, and she lay back on the bed. She grabbed one of the pillows and curled up around it.

When their lips parted and their eyes met, Jess knew she was in trouble. They both said good night, and then she retreated. She walked away from Erin's bedroom resolutely. Once in her bedroom, Jess leaned against the closed door and sighed. "Bloody hell." No one had stirred her like Erin did in years.

That the woman with platinum blonde hair and soft brown eyes was beautiful had never been a question. But Jess had long ago set such considerations aside. She was, in fact, quite pleased with their working relationship. She hadn't worked so well with a partner since Casper. Of course she had refused to work with a partner since she had rejoined the Bureau at the director's request. She'd made working on her own a prerequisite for her return. Jess would usually come in to work a case, cooperating with the agents assigned to it, but she never actually partnered up with any of them. Until this case.

Erin had turned out to be one of the best agents Jess had ever worked with. She was, without doubt, the best pathologist she'd ever seen. Somehow, Erin had gotten Jess to drop some of her shields, and she'd gotten closer than Jess was used to. And now, one kiss, one exquisitely soft kiss, and her heart was racing as if she'd run a marathon.

Jess took a deep breath, let it out, and went to bed.

March 5, 2025
Wednesday

In the dark, a hand snaked out and grabbed the offending noisemaker.

"Morgan," she answered laconically. Listening to the voice on the other end, Jess was suddenly wide awake. She sat up and turned on the light on the nightstand. She found a pen and something to write on and wrote down directions. "Got it. See you soon," she said and hung up her cell. She rubbed her face with her hands and then stood up. "Damn."

Jess hadn't slept well. She tossed and turned because she couldn't quiet her mind or her imagination. Every time she closed her eyes, she saw Erin's beautiful brown eyes. Jess had hardly even looked at another woman since Toni. Oh, she'd bedded a couple, but they had never really touched her heart. She never gave them a second thought afterward. However, Erin...well, Erin was different. For reasons she couldn't fathom, Jess had let Erin get close. She had spent time with the woman away from work. She cared about Erin. Their kiss replayed in her mind. It had been exquisite, so soft and gentle, yet no less arousing for its tenderness. Jess could have stood there kissing Erin for hours. She shook her head to clear it. It wasn't the time to think about such things. Unfortunately, they had a job to do.

She walked down the hall to Erin's door and knocked. "Erin?"

"Yes?"

"Get dressed. We've got another one."

"Okay."

Jess returned to her room to dress.

Both women were quickly ready to go.

"Where to?" Erin asked as she started the Bureau SUV.

"Annapolis. AD Taylor said to take the Rowe exit off 50, then left onto Melvin Avenue, following that until it ends. Then we're to take a left onto Wardour."

"I know it. That's almost at the Naval Academy."

Neither one of them spoke as Erin drove. Erin was mentally berating herself for doing something so stupid and unprofessional as kissing Jess. She had been enjoying working with the talented agent and laying the foundation of a new friendship. But she had to go and ruin it by kissing Jess. She dared a glance at the other woman, who was staring out the side window. Maybe she didn't ruin anything. After all, Jess had gently kissed her back. Erin tightened her grip on the steering wheel and concentrated on the task at hand. It was not the time to think about Jess' soft, warm lips. It was time to try to catch a killer.

They made good time and arrived at the house in question in just over thirty minutes. The sky was beginning to lighten, though sunrise was still yet to come.

"Nice neighborhood," Jess observed.

"Very. These houses are all seven figures."

They got out of the SUV and approached the house's front door. A couple of police officers were standing outside the entrance. Jess and Erin flashed their badges, and one of the officers opened the door for them. Once inside, they were directed to a room on the second floor. They removed their overcoats, slipped on gloves, and entered the bedroom.

Erin left the house with the body of Andrea Hicks, taking it to Quantico. Jess stayed behind and spoke with the distraught parents of The Slasher's newest victim.

"Can you tell me if Andrea was seeing anyone?" asked Jess.

"Andrea was too busy with her studies to date," Mr. Nicks replied.

"Actually, she did tell me she'd met someone," Mrs. Nicks said.

"When?" her husband asked, sounding upset.

Mrs. Nicks wiped her cheeks. "She said they met about a month ago. I think she said his name was Joe or John. I'm not sure."

"What did she tell you about him, Mrs. Nicks?"

"Not much. Just that they'd met and she liked him."

"Did she meet him in school? Is he a student?"

"Oh, no. She did say he had his own business on the internet or something like that. She didn't say much about him."

"Why didn't I know about this guy?" Mr. Nicks exclaimed.

"Jeff, I don't think it was serious. And besides, Andrea is—" She paused for a beat before continuing, "was twenty-two years old, a grown woman." Mrs. Nicks broke down and couldn't continue.

Mr. Nicks took his wife and went to a friend's house.

After going through the Nicks' home and the victim's personal effects, Jess left the house and drove to the home of the victim's sister and brother-in-law, Linda and Gary Everson. Mr. Everson was out of town for work, but Linda was the one Jess wanted to talk to anyway.

"I'm very sorry for your loss, Mrs. Everson. I appreciate you meeting with me."

"Call me Linda. I just can't believe Andrea's dead."

"Your mother said Andrea mentioned someone she'd met, someone named Joe or John. Did she say anything to you about this guy?"

"Do you think he's the one who killed her?"

"I don't know, but we need to talk to all of Andrea's acquaintances, friends, and family. The more we know about her, the better chance we have of finding who killed her."

"His name was Joel. I don't know his last name."

"What did she tell you about him?"

"Not much. She said he had some online business. And that she really liked him."

"Did she say what the name of the business was?"

"No. I'm sorry I don't know more."

"It's all right, Linda. I checked your sister's things but didn't find her cellphone. Do you know where it might be?"

"Oh. Yeah. She left it here by accident yesterday. She watched my daughter for an hour or so while I ran some errands. I'll get it for you."

"Please."

Linda got up and left the room. She returned moments later with the phone. "Here you go."
"Thank you."

Chapter Fourteen

ERIN LOOKED UP WHEN Jess entered the autopsy bay. "Hey. I'm just finishing up."

"Anything new?"

"Unfortunately, no. What about you? How did it go with the parents?"

"Neither of them had any idea who would want to hurt Andrea. The mother did say that Andrea mentioned a new guy, someone she'd met about a month ago."

Erin finished the last stitch, pulled her gloves off with a snap, and stepped away from the table. "Did you get his name?"

"Mrs. Nicks thought it might be Joe or John. But I spoke to Andrea's sister, who said his name was Joel. She didn't know his last name though. Still, I will have someone check the name against the purchase list for Clive Christian's No. 1 perfume. It's a long shot, but..." She shrugged her shoulders. "I also got Andrea's phone. It's locked, so I'm going to have the techs dump everything on it, and we can start talking to all her contacts. Maybe she confided in a friend about this new guy. Supposedly, he has some internet business." She sighed. "It's not a lot to go on at this point."

"It's somewhere to start," Erin pointed out. "And it's more than we've had with some of the other victims."

"I know. I'll take the phone to the techs as soon as we return to the bullpen," said Jess.

"All right. I just need a quick shower and a change of clothes. I won't be long."

"All right."

Jess and Erin spent the day going through the list of contacts from Andrea's phone and calling her friends, trying to find someone she may have talked to about her love life and this new man, Joel, she was seeing. Unfortunately, their interviews with her friends didn't yield any new information. No one had met this mysterious new man in Andrea's life. No one had seen him, knew anything about his business, or even how Andrea met him.

Well after dinner, they finally decided to stop for the day.

Jess sighed as she settled behind the SUV's steering wheel. "It's been a long day today. What do you say we go out for dinner?" she asked Erin. "No takeout, no pizza. A real dinner, my treat."

Erin smiled. "All right. What did you have in mind?"

"How do you feel about steak?"

"Sounds good."

"Great."

They were seated at a table by one of the windows. After the waiter had taken their orders, Erin kept staring out the window.

"Something interesting out there?" Jess asked.

Erin frowned. Concern colored her voice when she replied. "I'm not sure, but I think someone's been following us."

"If you're referring to the dark green Taurus, you're right."

Erin snapped her eyes back to Jess. "What—"

"Security detail. The director assigned a team to you."

There was no mistaking the anger flashing in Erin's brown eyes. "What the hell for?" she ground out slowly.

Jess took a slow breath as she nervously fingered her fork. "Because I asked him to."

Erin started to say something, but Jess continued, cutting her off.

"You have to understand. The last time a serial killer made things personal, Toni was killed because of me." She looked up, finally meeting Erin's gaze. "Your apartment was broken into and the same message written on your wall that was written on mine in Toni's blood. This UNSUB knows who you are, Erin. He knows where you live. I cannot take the risk that he'll go after you. I'm *not* going to let someone else get killed because of me." She swallowed the lump that had formed in her throat. "I couldn't bear it," she finished shakily.

When Jess finished, Erin reached across the table, placed her hand over Jess', and squeezed it. The anger was gone from her eyes. "It's okay, Jess. I understand. If our places were reversed, I'd do the same thing."

Erin looked like she might have wanted to say something else, but the waiter arrived with their salads.

Dinner was pleasant and very filling. Erin and Jess felt quite relaxed and satiated as they enjoyed an after-dinner drink.

It was rather late when they arrived back at the safe house. They took turns showering and getting ready for bed. Jess was in the kitchen getting some ice water when Erin exited the bathroom and entered the kitchen, still drying her hair with a towel.

"Would you like some ice water?" Jess asked.

"Please."

Jess dropped some ice into a second glass and filled it with water. She turned and handed the glass to Erin, who draped the towel around her neck and took the glass from her. Erin felt Jess' eyes on her as she closed her own eyes and took a long drink.

Erin felt Jess reach out and gently brush aside a few strands of hair that had caught on Erin's eyelashes. She opened her eyes, locking with Jess'. Suddenly, the air seemed thin, and both women felt a little lightheaded. Neither one consciously moved, yet they were inexorably drawn together. Lips softly met, and breath was shared.

Jess slid her left hand into damp hair and cupped the back of Erin's head. Jess sucked in a silent gasp as Erin slid her tongue along Jess' lower lip. Erin softly sighed as she was granted entrance. Their tongues met and danced. Their kiss deepened yet remained gentle. Erin thoroughly explored Jess' mouth and also welcomed Jess' exploration. Jess' right arm tightened around her waist as Erin squeezed her arms around Jess, clinging to her to keep herself steady on weakened knees.

After several minutes, their kisses transformed into soft brushes of lips and quiet sighs. Their lips finally parted. Foreheads rested against each other's and hearts pounded as lungs tried to replenish oxygen levels.

"Jess..." Erin said. "Come to bed with me."

Jess' eyes flew open, and her heart stopped. She was speechless, but Erin responded to the trepidation written all over her face.

"To sleep. I simply want to be near you tonight."

Jess gave a mute nod in response.

Erin stepped out of Jess' arms, took her hand and, turning off lights on the way, led her to her bedroom.

Jess lay on her back in bed, and Erin snuggled up to her on her side. They shared a pillow and held each other as they drifted to sleep.

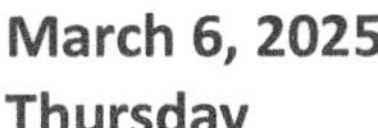

March 6, 2025
Thursday

When Jess woke in the morning, she was on her right side, with Erin spooning her from behind. One arm was under her neck, and Erin's left arm was wrapped around Jess' waist. Jess could feel her bedmate's steady heartbeat and slow breaths against her back and neck. She closed her eyes and enjoyed being held so closely and firmly.

Jess could tell Erin awoke from the change in her respiration and the increase in her heartbeat.

"Good morning," Jess said softly.

"Mmmm, good morning."

Jess couldn't help pressing back into Erin, and Erin tightened her embrace.

They both started a little bit when the alarm clock went off. Without speaking, they both got out of bed. Jess wordlessly left Erin's bedroom and retreated to her own. It took her little time to dress and prepare for the day. In addition to her briefcase, Jess grabbed a small duffel bag before heading out to the living room.

"You planning on going somewhere?" Erin asked when she saw the duffel bag.

"I thought I'd use the gym at headquarters. I haven't been running in weeks and haven't had a workout in nearly two weeks. I feel off if I go too long without working out," she answered.

"Do you mind if I join you?"

"Not at all."

Erin went back into her bedroom to retrieve some workout clothes.

At the headquarters gym, both women got in a good workout. Jess ended hers with a five-mile run. If the weather had been better, she would have run outside rather than doing laps in the gym, but Jess was happy for the workout nonetheless. It felt good to slip into an easy rhythm, letting her muscles work and her mind go blank. Well, not totally blank.

Jess was confused. She knew she was more than just attracted to Erin. However, she lived a very nomadic life, working all over the country, never staying in one place more than a few days or a few weeks at the most. It was a lifestyle that suited her: no ties, no complications, no personal attachments.

But Erin was different.

Erin was smart, beautiful, talented, and bossy. Jess had to stifle a chuckle. Did she really want to complicate her life by letting someone like Erin into it? The night spent in Erin's arms was her best night's sleep in six years. What was it about the platinum blonde that allowed her to get past Jess' walls so damn quickly? Not even Toni had been able to do that. She didn't know whether she wanted Erin to get "in" any closer or not.

When she finished running, Jess headed to the showers. She consciously decided to shower and dress on the far side of the locker room from Erin.

On their way from the gym to the bullpen, Jess received a call letting her know that the footage from the security cameras from the houses on Andrea Nicks' street was ready to be reviewed. They stopped by and picked up the disc. Jess turned on her computer in in her office and slid the disc in. Erin pulled her chair up next to Jess' so they both could watch the footage.

"I was hoping that someone's security camera caught an unaccounted-for vehicle."

"You mean Joel's?"

Jess nodded. "Or The Slasher, if they're not one and the same."

"That's if either ever drove to Andrea's house," Erin pointed out.

"Well, he had to get in and out of the house with her body, so he had to transport it there somehow."

"Don't forget those houses all had private docks as well. He could have just as easily used a boat instead of a car."

Jess sighed. "I know, Erin. A couple of the houses had cameras on the docks as well. I know we won't be able to see everything, but we still have to try."

"Of course we do, Jess," Erin gently replied.

They spent several hours carefully watching the security footage, taking note of all the vehicles they spotted and comparing them to the registered vehicles of the area's residents. All the cars were accounted for, and no boats were recorded coming or going from the docks covered by security cameras. So much for catching Joel and/or The Slasher coming or leaving the area.

Before they left for the day, AD Taylor made an announcement in the bullpen. "Listen up, everyone. I'm calling in everyone on the taskforce to a meeting tomorrow. I want everyone here, regardless of what shift you're assigned. So everyone be here at one o'clock tomorrow." Taylor went back into his office.

"I wonder what that's all about," Erin mused.

"He probably just wants everyone to check in and report on where they are in the investigation. Maybe pool some ideas."

Chapter Fifteen

AT THE SAFE HOUSE, Erin changed out of her work clothes. When she came out of her bedroom, she found Jess, also casually dressed, settled on the couch with her laptop. Erin went into the kitchen to see what was available to fix for dinner.

"There aren't a lot of choices, but there is enough stuff here that I can make some dinner," Erin said as she entered the living room. "I can make us some spaghetti if you like, Jess."

"Hmm? Oh. Whatever you want is fine with me."

"Or we can do takeout."

"That's fine…" Jess replied absently.

Erin reached out and put her hand on Jess' shoulder. "Jess."

Jess looked up at her. "What?"

"Tell me, if I didn't fix something or order some takeout, would you even notice missing dinner?" she asked.

"Probably not."

Erin shook her head and gave her partner a small, affectionate smile. "You really should take better care of yourself."

Jess shrugged. "I just don't think about eating sometimes when I'm working."

"And you're always working. You don't even take a day off unless the director orders you to."

"It's not like I can afford just to take time off when I'm working a case," Jess said a little curtly. "Too much rides on my work, too many lives!"

With sudden insight, Erin realized the motivation behind Jess' relentless drive. She sat in the corner of the couch next to Jess, facing her with one leg tucked under. "Jess, please."

With a soft sigh, Jess closed her laptop and set it on the coffee table. She sat quietly, waiting, apparently knowing Erin had more to say.

"Jess, you can't take personal responsibility for every crime. It's not your fault that people are victimized every day. You didn't create the killers, the rapists, and the molesters. They are not your fault. And neither is Toni's death. It's not your fault Conrad killed Toni."

Jess swallowed a couple of times as her eyes welled up and shined with unshed tears. "There were threats…I should have quit the case."

She did not know the answer to her next question, but given her observations of her new partner, Erin was more than confident that it was worth the risk of asking anyway. "Did Toni know about the threats?"

Jess took a slow breath before responding. "Yes," she said softly.

"Who were the threats against, you or her?"

"Me."

"And what did she have to say about them?" Erin asked gently.

"She said not to let the bastard win, to catch him and put him behind bars."

Erin let Jess think about that for several seconds. Finally, she broke the silence, speaking softly but clearly. "Jess, no matter how many perpetrators you put away or how many lives you save, it can't change what happened."

"Don't you think I know that?" A couple of tears finally escaped and rolled down Jess' cheeks.

"Intellectually, yes. Yet you keep assuming a burden that's not yours to bear to find absolution for something that's not your fault." She paused. "Somehow, I don't think that's what Toni would have wanted."

Erin watched Jess close her eyes and a few more tears rolled down her cheeks. She reached out and put her arms around Jess. Jess turned her face into Erin's shoulder, finally letting the tears go. Erin leaned back into the corner of the couch, pulling Jess with her, holding her close.

"Let it go. It's not your fault." She dropped a kiss on Jess' head as she continued to hold the quietly crying woman.

Jess drifted to sleep after a few minutes. Erin gently ran her fingers through silky, dark hair. After about five minutes, she felt the woman in her arms begin to stir. She let go of Jess as she sat up.

"Sorry about that."

"Don't be. You were there for me when I needed a shoulder. It's what friends are for."

Jess took a deep breath and let it out. "Friends, Erin? Is that what we are?"

"What do you mean?"

"Do you kiss all your friends like you kissed me last night?" She paused for half a beat. "Because I don't."

Caught off guard by the turn of the conversation, Erin took a steadying breath of her own before replying. "Yes, we're friends." She paused. "But I also think there's something else between us," she finished softly.

Jess closed her eyes for a couple of moments. Then, she suddenly stood up and walked across the room before turning around to face Erin. "I don't know if that's a good thing."

"Wha—"

"I'm not...a good bet. And you deserve better, Erin."

She cocked an eyebrow. "Better than what, Jess? An intelligent, compassionate, beautiful woman?"

Jess dropped her gaze, looking away. "There are things you don't know about me...and baggage."

Not entirely sure of the source of her current boldness, Erin got up and walked over to stand in front of Jess. "Of course there are things I don't know about you. There are things you don't know about me. And everyone has their own baggage. But the process of discovery is part of the allure." She reached up, gently lifting Jess' chin until their eyes met. "I'm not one to act rashly, without thought. If anything, I tend to overthink things, but something has drawn me to you from the beginning." Erin caressed Jess' cheek. "You said to trust my instincts. My instincts tell me to take a chance." Erin closed the distance between them and kissed Jess.

A soft moan escaped Jess' throat as she parted her lips to allow Erin's gentle exploration. Erin felt Jess' arms wrap around her, holding her close. She melted into the embrace, feeling wonderfully lightheaded. When Jess deepened the kiss, the world spun a little faster for Erin. She moaned into the sensuously passionate kiss. A lack of oxygen finally caused their lips to part. They gazed into each other's eyes as they both caught their breath.

Jess swallowed before speaking. "Erin—"

She lightly placed a finger over Jess' lips, cutting her off. "What do your instincts tell you?"

She waited patiently, but nervously, for Jess to decide. Erin watched the inner struggle in the shadows behind Jess' gray eyes. She could feel it in the tensing of Jess' body. She honestly had no idea what Jess would do: take a chance or retreat.

Finally, Jess' internal debate apparently came to an end. Erin's pulse raced as Jess claimed her lips with her own. It was a breath-stealing, heart-stopping kiss.

The ringing of a cell phone startled both women, causing them to jump and break the kiss. With a steadying breath, Jess let go of Erin and retrieved her phone from the coffee table.

"Morgan...All right, thank you...Tomorrow...Bye." She hung up and looked at Erin, flashing a small, embarrassed smile. "That was Agent Beckley.

They came up dry with the perfume purchase list." She shrugged. "I didn't expect them to find anything. It's not enough to go on, and we have no idea where or how long ago he bought it."

Erin nodded in agreement. "I'm, uh…I'm going to go ahead and make some dinner."

"All right." Jess sat on the couch and grabbed her laptop from the coffee table.

Once in the kitchen, Erin placed her hands on the counter's edge and let her head hang. She took a deep breath and slowly let it out. She could feel her pulse still racing. It was amazing how much Jess affected her. It had been a long time since someone had kissed her like that.

After dinner, Jess convinced Erin to let her do the dishes. She needed the mundane task and the time it gave her alone to think once again about what was happening between her and Erin. She was second-guessing herself, her decision to give in to her feelings. She had deliberately distanced herself from people for a long time, not getting close and not allowing others to get close to her. It was practically instinctual now.

She didn't used to be that way. She had withdrawn somewhat after she and Casper had taken Neil Croskey down, after she'd almost died. Only her partner had ever really known what she was feeling.

But then Toni Jeffers had taken an interest in her. She had looked up to Toni Jeffers 'the agent.' Jeffers was a no-nonsense, take-no-prisoners kind of agent. She faced life entirely on her terms. Toni didn't give a damn what anyone thought about her or her choices. And she left a trail of broken hearts a mile wide in her wake. Toni never misled anyone about her intentions, but everyone seemed to fall for the five-foot-nine, athletic, thirty-year-old brunette. Her dark brown eyes, easy smile, and confident attitude won her many admirers.

Which was precisely why it had taken Toni some real effort to woo Jess. Jess knew Toni's reputation and found it hard to believe the woman was seriously interested in her. Once she finally broke down and accepted a date with the older woman, Jess started hearing the whispers and speculation about how long it would be before she joined the ranks of the brokenhearted. But Toni had surprised everyone. Once she and Jess started dating, she never looked at another man or woman. Because of Toni, Jess knew what happiness was.

Jess hadn't been happy since Toni was killed, and, in truth, she didn't try to be.

But then, out of the blue, there was Erin Little. The petite, brown-eyed blonde was very different from Toni. However, she had that same no-nonsense attitude about work.

Jess smiled as she started drying the dishes. Erin did something no one else had done in years. She made Jess smile and laugh. She reminded Jess she still had the ability to be happy. That was what finally made up Jess' mind. She decided, regardless of how temporary it might be, that she would try to be happy again.

When Erin left Jess in the kitchen washing dishes, she retreated to the living room. She felt unsettled and a little antsy. Instead of sitting, she stood at a window, looking out through a small gap in the drapes. She felt a little like a coward because of the way she had escaped to the kitchen after Jess' cell phone interrupted their kiss. Oh my, what a kiss! She took a deep breath and slowly let it out. She mentally shook her head. One minute, she was uncharacteristically coming on to her partner, urging her to take a chance. The next, she was hiding out in the kitchen.

If kissing Jess and waking in her arms felt so damn right, why did she then retreat and hide from her? What made Erin so nervous? It had nothing to do with Jess being a woman. She'd been down that road before, albeit fifteen years ago. There was no denying that she found Jess attractive and had been drawn to her from the beginning. Erin was impressed with Jess as an agent. She was an excellent investigator and easy to work with. And she *liked* Jess as a person. She was smart, funny, and compassionate; she had a beautiful smile and sparkling eyes; and she made Erin smile and laugh. They had spent a lot of time together on and off duty. Erin recognized, and felt, the gift of the customarily reserved woman opening up to her.

That brought Erin's thoughts to a pause. *She* was usually reserved but had found herself opening up to Jess uncharacteristically. Erin had been experiencing a few things lately that were uncharacteristic. She was enjoying work again; she had been bold and forward with Jess; she preferred time spent with Jess over time spent alone; she was feeling peaceful and happy; and she was feeling like herself again. She was feeling alive again.

Erin closed her eyes and smiled. She was starting a new and fresh chapter in her life. Regardless of what may or may not develop between her and Jess, she would be happy again. She opened her eyes and gazed out of the gap in the drapes at the quiet neighborhood the safe house was in.

She felt more than heard Jess' approach. Jess stood directly behind her, mere centimeters away.

"Here," Jess said softly, holding a mug of coffee in front of her.

"Thank you." Erin took a sip, knowing Jess had prepared it just how she liked it. She felt Jess' body heat across those few centimeters. It wasn't enough, so she leaned back against her. She felt a slight hitch in Jess' breath and then a warm hand came to rest on her waist.

"Just so you know, Erin, there's no pressure, no expectations, and certainly no judgments."

Erin's heart skipped a beat. Jess had apparently sorted out her thoughts and feelings from earlier and was considerately letting Erin know she was safe with her. No pressure to do anything she was uncomfortable with. The ball was in Erin's court now. She set her coffee down on the nearby bookshelf, then turned to face Jess. Still smiling, she took Jess' face in her hands, guiding the other woman's mouth to her own. With Jess' lips millimeters from her own, she spoke. "I may be nervous, but I know what I want." Erin pressed her lips to Jess', kissing her softly at first, then more urgently as they embraced tightly.

After several moments, Jess pulled out of the kiss and smiled. "Unless you tell me 'no,' I'm going to take you to bed and make love to you."

Erin felt her heart skip a couple of beats at Jess' softly spoken words. "Yes," she said before their lips met again.

Chapter Sixteen

JESS TOOK ERIN'S HAND in hers and silently led her to Erin's bedroom, turning off lights on the way. After turning the nightstand light on, she pulled Erin forward and kissed her, holding her close with arms wrapped around her.

As they kissed, Erin slipped her hands under the hem of Jess' t-shirt, sliding them up the smooth, warm skin of her back. She felt the lean muscles of Jess' back flex under her touch. Erin soon trailed her hands back down. She grabbed the hem of the shirt and pulled it up and off Jess, breaking their kiss only long enough to get the material out of the way. Before she could wrap her arms around Jess again, she felt hands removing her shirt. Bras were quickly shed, and they came together, relishing the feel of skin against skin.

Jess trailed kisses down Erin's throat to her pulse point, teasing with lips, breath, and tongue, raising goosebumps and making her quietly moan. She felt her knees start to give, but Jess' strong arms tightened around her, steadied her, and moved her to the bed. Erin lay on the bed, welcoming Jess into her arms. Jess' lips and touch turned her blood into molten heat and gave her chills. Erin gasped and hissed when Jess took a hard nipple into the warmth of her mouth. Erin sank her fingers into silky hair and arched up into her. Jess was moaning as she continued to suck on her nipple.

Erin tried to catch her breath as Jess kissed her way up her chest and throat. As their lips met again, Jess shifted so Erin was lying on her right side. Jess ran her right hand down her side, over her hip, and around to palm Erin's ass, squeezing it. Then her hand slid down the back of her thigh, pulling it up over Jess' thigh as she pressed her thigh against Erin's center. Erin moaned in response to the aching pleasure.

She surged up and pressed Jess onto her back, taking Jess' hands in her own and pinning them to the mattress on either side of Jess' head as she rocked her hips against Jess'. She nibbled on an earlobe before trailing kisses down Jess' neck and throat. Letting go of her hands, Erin palmed Jess' breasts, teasing her erect nipples. She kissed her way down and took a hard nipple into her mouth, reveling in the way Jess whimpered and writhed beneath her.

Hands slid into her hair and took hold, gently yet firmly guiding her up until she once again claimed Jess' lips with her own. As they continued to kiss, Erin felt one of Jess' hands slip between them, unzipping and unsnapping her jeans. Erin felt momentarily bereft when Jess' hand left, but then both of Jess' hands ran down her back and slipped under the waistband of her jeans, slowing inching her jeans and panties down over her ass. Jess' warm hands on her bare ass, caressing and squeezing, made her arch her back and grind her hips against Jess with wanton need. Erin's jeans and panties were removed entirely and discarded, four hands worked in unison to ensure that Jess' jeans and underwear quickly followed.

Their bodies fit together like puzzle pieces. Hands and lips and tongues explored. Erin held tight onto Jess, almost as if she feared the woman would disappear if she let go. Of course she always did whenever Erin awakened from her dreams. A part of her was afraid that even now she was dreaming and would soon wake to find she was alone in bed, having only dreamt about Jess' sublime kisses and electric touch.

"Does this feel like a dream?" Jess whispered in her ear as she gently pushed a couple of fingers inside her. Jess moved her fingers in and out of her with such skill, stimulating all the right places.

"Oh god..." Erin moaned. She realized from Jess' words that she must have given voice to some of her inner thoughts.

Jess kissed her cheek softly before her lips moved to her throat. She teased Erin's pulse point with her lips and tongue as she continued to move her fingers in and out of her. Erin was getting closer and closer to climaxing. Her breathing was labored and her heart was about to pound out of her chest.

Almost with no warning, Erin's body seemed to collapse into itself and explode at the same time, every muscle in her body locking in place and spasming. She cried out Jess' name while clinging to her. Sparks flashed behind her closed eyelids.

Eventually, Erin came back to herself. She lay on her back, gently cradled in Jess' arms as she tried to regulate her breathing and heart rate. Jess lay on her side. She brushed a soft kiss on Erin's jaw, near her ear.

"Thank you," whispered Jess.

"For what?" Erin asked, a bit confused. "You—"

Jess tenderly touched her fingertip to Erin's lips. She spoke softly but clearly. "Thank you for being so open and vulnerable with me. That's a gift."

Her words deeply moved Erin, especially by the sincerity she saw in her eyes. She reached up and caressed Jess' cheek, then kissed her. She shifted onto her side, once again entwining her body with Jess'. She wanted to make

Jess feel as good as Jess had made her feel. She took control of their kiss, gently exploring Jess' lips and mouth.

As Erin kissed Jess, she trailed her hand down Jess' body. Her fingers slid easily between wet folds. Jess reacted immediately. She gasped and arched into her touch. It didn't seem more than a few seconds before Jess cried out from her orgasm. Erin could feel Jess' clit twitching under her fingertips. She was blown away by the sight, sound, and feel of Jess coming—because of *her*. It was the most erotic thing Erin had ever experienced.

Once Jess caught her breath, she pulled Erin into a searing kiss. She surprised her by swiftly rolling her over onto her back. She could feel Jess' wetness against her thigh. They both moaned into the kiss as they rocked against the thigh that each had trapped between their own.

Low groans, quick gasps, loud moans, passionate kisses, questing tongues, grasping hands, arching backs, thrusting hips, and straining muscles brought them to the edge until they both cried out as they experienced powerful orgasms within moments of each other.

Jess rested her forehead on Erin's shoulder as Erin rested her hand on the back of Jess' neck. Neither one could speak because of heavy panting. After a few moments, Jess rolled off Erin and collapsed next to her on her back. Erin grabbed the covers, pulling them up and covering both as she snuggled against Jess' side. She laid her head on Jess' shoulder and sighed contentedly as Jess held her in her arms.

March 7, 2025
Friday

Erin awoke feeling wonderful. She enjoyed the warmth and curves of the body snuggled up against her back, spooning her. Erin was also aroused. Jess' hand was cupping her breast, and her skilled fingers were playing with her hardening nipple. There seemed to be a direct link between her stimulated nipple and her clit—she was already wet. She let out a soft moan. "Mmmm, that feels good," she said.

Jess kissed her shoulder. "I can't seem to keep my hands off you," she replied softly.

"Good." Erin turned her head, seeking Jess' lips. She let out another soft moan as they kissed. She brought her right hand up and covered the one on her breast, intertwining her fingers with Jess'. She then pushed the brunette's hand down, slowly, and through the patch of soft, blonde curls between her thighs.

Jess shifted, gently pulling Erin onto her back. Her fingers, laced with Erin's, discovered Erin's arousal. "Mmmm, you're wet."

Their two hands, fingers still intertwined, caressed Erin's slick folds, teasing her opening, stroking her clit. She was close to coming. Her left hand was buried in Jess' silky hair, holding the dark head to her breast where Jess suckled. Her breath was ragged. She was going to—Erin's moan turned to whimpers when Jess pulled their coupled hands away. She was *so* close! "Oh god. Please, don't stop."

"Shhh, I'm not done." Jess brought their interlaced fingers to her mouth, taking each one into her mouth in turn, and slowly licked and sucked them clean.

When Jess took Erin's finger, wet with her arousal, into her mouth, her eyes flew open. She felt Jess' tongue deftly slide over each finger in turn. Erin thought she could come from the sight and sensation alone.

Fingers clean, Jess shifted to lie on top of Erin. She claimed Erin's mouth in a passionate kiss, sharing with her the hint of taste still on her tongue. She took her time, kissing and caressing Erin, slowly but methodically lavishing loving attention on every part of her body.

Erin had never felt so completely and thoroughly aroused. Every nerve in her body was alight with delicious fire. Her knees drew up and parted of their own accord as Jess' mouth and tongue neared her center. Her hips were already rocking as she felt Jess kiss and lick and tease the insides of her thighs. She almost came the moment she felt a velvety tongue slip between her lips. It felt so good. She was going to come, but she didn't want to. She wanted it to last. But then Jess circled her clit with her tongue, closed her lips around it, and sucked. She came explosively, not recognizing the inarticulate cry as her own.

As Erin lay there gasping for air, Jess remained where she was, placing light kisses around her center and along the insides of her thighs. Jess' gentle caresses and light kisses soothed Erin and calmed her body. Erin reached down her hand and loosely entangled her fingers in Jess' hair. Jess raised her gray eyes and looked up into Erin's eyes, holding her gaze as she again took her into her mouth.

Erin's head slammed back into her pillow and her whole body undulated under Jess' skillful ministration. She was quickly building to another orgasm, this one even more intense. She fisted both her hands in the dark hair of the head between her thighs. Jess slipped a couple of fingers inside her and sucked on her clit. She came hard and loud. Fireworks went off behind her eyelids as she catapulted into pure ecstasy.

Jess was gently cradling Erin when she came back to earth. She slid her hand to Jess' head and pulled her in for a kiss. She hummed at the taste of herself on Jess' lips and tongue, but she really wanted to taste Jess. She pushed Jess onto her back, kissing and licking her way down her body, stopping for a while at her full breasts.

She reveled in every moan, whimper, and gasp of pleasure she elicited from Jess as she caressed, kissed, kneaded, licked, squeezed, and sucked. She settled herself between Jess' thighs and tenderly caressed her, opening her. As a doctor, a pathologist, she was quite familiar with human anatomy. She had also examined several female bodies and done sexual assault kits. But a dead body was nothing like a live woman at the height of arousal. "So beautiful," she said breathlessly before lowering her head and taking Jess in her mouth. She hummed with delight at the taste.

Jess was so wet, and the way she was gasping raggedly for air showed she wasn't going to last for very long. Erin continued to lick her as she pushed two fingers inside her. Jess cried out as she climaxed. Feeling Jess' warm channel squeeze and spasm around her fingers as she came was almost enough to make Erin come again. When Jess' muscles relaxed their grip on her fingers, Erin gently withdrew them, moved up, and took Jess into her arms. She rolled them onto their sides, held Jess, and kissed her forehead. Despite the risen sun, they both drifted to sleep.

When Erin opened her eyes, she found herself still holding Jess. She smiled. Making love with Jess had been wonderful. Fantastic, in fact. But it was a new day, and work was still to be done. With that thought, her head snapped up, and she looked at the clock radio. Damn! It was after ten o'clock. They were very late to work.

"Calm down, Erin," came Jess' soft voice. "We don't have to be in until 1:00."

Erin dropped her head back onto her pillow.

Jess removed her head from Erin's shoulder and laid it on the pillow a few inches from hers. Jess raised her hand from Erin's waist and gently caressed her cheek. "Good morning," she whispered just before leaning in and brushing a light kiss on Erin's lips.

She smiled at the tender kiss. "Good morning," Erin replied before opening her eyes again. She shifted onto her side so they were facing each other. She tightened her arm around Jess' shoulders and slid her left arm around Jess' waist. It felt so good to hold Jess' naked body to her own. "This is nice."

Jess smiled. "Yeah, it is."

The two lay in each other's arms, simply enjoying the comfort and peacefulness. But then it was time to get up.

After parting to prepare for their day, the women put on their clothes, badges, and guns, transforming into FBI agents. However, despite the armor of their professional personas, a shared warmth remained in their eyes.

Chapter Seventeen

THE ONE O'CLOCK MEETING AD Taylor had called was meant to bring everyone up to date with the investigation. It included some round-tabling and exchanges of ideas.

During a discussion of the possible earlier crimes Jess had 'traced' by regressing The Slasher's MO, her cell phone rang. She quietly answered it.

"Morgan."

Erin watched Jess' face become cold and hard as she discreetly left the bullpen and entered her office, closing the door. When she was able to slip away from the discussion, Erin followed. With a tap announcing her presence, she opened the door and joined her partner.

Jess hung up and looked at her. "I just received a phone call."

"From The Slasher?"

Jess' expression was answer enough. "At least someone claiming to be him."

"How the hell did he get your cell phone number?"

"I don't know. I had them try to trace the call. I doubt we'll get an exact location, but it may at least give us an idea of where he's calling from."

"What did he say?"

Jess sighed. "Basically, he said I didn't have what it took to catch him and I should just give up and go away." She paused. "Especially if I didn't want anything to happen to my partner," she said with a clouded look.

"You're not going to back off, are you?" Erin asked somewhat confrontationally.

Jess took a slow breath before responding. "I don't want to. I want to get this bastard." She paused half a beat before continuing. "But it might not be a bad idea if you did, Erin. He—"

"No," Erin snapped in anger. "I'm not about to tuck tail and run because of this son of a bitch. I am not going to be scared off by some vague threat." She bristled. Looking at the shadows in Jess' gray eyes, Erin consciously relaxed her body and softened her tone. "I understand your concern, Jess, but I'm not easily intimidated. Stopping people like this is part and parcel of why I'm an agent."

Jess took a deep breath and slowly let it out. "I can't make you quit, but I need you to promise me you'll be careful, Erin, and not take unnecessary risks."

Erin could see what the situation was costing Jess. She wasn't about to walk away from the case, or Jess, but she didn't have to make things harder for her partner. "All right."

The phone on Jess' desk rang. "Morgan…All right…Thanks anyway." She hung up as she wrote something on a notepad. "The phone he used to call me was a prepaid cellphone." She paused a beat. "He wasn't on long enough for them to get a trace." Letting out a huff, Jess said, "I have to let Taylor know."

Erin nodded in agreement and leaned against the desk as Jess left the office. She took a deep breath and let it out. She and Jess were just getting to know each other. It was too soon to be dropping any 'I love you' bombs…wasn't it?

They eventually stopped for the day several hours later and picked up some dinner on the way back to the safe house.

Both women settled in the living room after changing into more comfortable clothes and cleaning up the dinner dishes. After updating her case notes, Erin settled into a chair adjacent to the couch with a book. Jess was working on her laptop, reviewing and reworking her profile of the UNSUB from scratch.

Jess struggled to reconcile her instincts with the facts of their case. She was disturbed about the recent behavior of the UNSUB. Everything in her said her original profile was spot on. She felt it in her bones. But the killer she profiled just didn't jive with the recent sophomoric taunting. Breaking into her hotel room, breaking into Erin's apartment, calling her—it just didn't make sense. The behavior was contrived and nothing like the earlier elegant misdirection he'd accomplished.

Jess reviewed the dates and places of each murder, finding no pattern. The murders were spread out geographically and varied in time between the crimes. Sometimes, he'd go over a month before killing again, yet he'd also killed on consecutive days as well. The last interval between killings was four days, the interval before that thirteen days. Jess wasn't as confident in her regression of his MO, considering recent events. The killings on the West Coast and in the Midwest could have nothing to do with The Slasher, although her instincts told her they did. Other agents were now following those possible leads.

She knew she tended to second-guess herself when things didn't line up the way she thought they should. It was a byproduct of being right many more times than she was wrong. She'd always had such an uncanny ability to profile and interview people. She figured it was a result of her hyper senses and eidetic memory. She could learn a lot about a person by being observant and paying attention to her senses. Erin, for example. She knew Erin suffered from nightmares before they ever shared a bed. She knew that Erin's shampoo had almonds in it and that her favorite perfume was vanilla-based. She knew Erin's heartbeat changed whenever she spoke of her sister, Lauren, increasing speed with guilt and anger. She also knew Erin wasn't actually reading the book she was pretending to be so interested in.

Jess took a deep breath and slowly let it out. She wanted nothing more than to order Erin off the case. That way, she could be sure Erin would be safe. She had tried to get her reassigned when the bastard broke into Erin's apartment, but the director had overridden her. Whether or not anything more than the night they'd shared developed between them, Jess cared about Erin a lot. She couldn't stand the idea of her getting hurt.

Focusing on her profile once more, Jess knew these kinds of cases were usually only solved because of hard, disciplined work. Or dumb luck. Relying on dumb luck was not something any good agent would do. Of course no one would turn down a little luck if it happened to cross their path, not even Jess. In the meantime, she still needed to finish reworking her profile.

Jess rubbed her face and let out a slow breath. She looked over at the chair and Erin. The paperback book she had been reading was on the floor, having dropped when she fell asleep. Jess took the opportunity to openly observe the woman who had surprised her so. Erin was a beautiful woman, inside as well as outside.

"Erin?"

Erin didn't react at all to Jess' voice.

Jess looked at her watch and saw how late it was. "No wonder you fell asleep." She smiled. "You're going to regret sleeping in that chair if you stay there all night," she said softly.

She stood up and moved to stand next to the chair. She started to wake Erin but stopped herself. Instead, she gently slipped her arms under the sleeping woman and lifted. Erin's only reaction was to roll her head onto Jess' shoulder. Jess carried her precious cargo into Erin's bedroom and carefully laid her on the bed. She pulled the covers over her and bent to drop a tender kiss on her temple. "Good night, beautiful."

March 8, 2025
Saturday

When Erin woke up in the morning, she was surprised to find herself in bed. She didn't remember moving from the chair in the living room. She was also surprised that she was still in her jeans and t-shirt. She must have been exhausted not to remember going to bed and not changing into her pajamas when she did so. She grabbed her stuff and headed to the bathroom for a shower.

She went into the living room, clean, fully awake, and dressed. Somehow, Erin wasn't surprised to find Jess still on the couch, apparently having worked through the night. She almost started to chide her partner but stopped. Jess was an excellent agent and an outstanding profiler. The director wouldn't turn to her on the horrible cases if that weren't true. She was a grown woman, and Jess didn't need Erin to tell her what she should and shouldn't do to accomplish what she needed to do.

Erin went into the kitchen and made some hot tea. After pouring two cups, she returned to the living room. She set one of the cups down on the coffee table and sat in the chair she'd occupied the evening before. "How is it going?" she asked gently.

Jess looked up. "It's frustrating, but it's going." She picked up the cup of tea and took a sip. "Thank you."

"You're welcome."

"Did you sleep well?" she asked with a small smile.

"Mm-hmm. I must have been really out of it last night. I don't even remember going to bed, and I slept in my clothes."

Erin thought she saw Jess hiding a smirk as she took another sip of tea. She put the cup down. "Well, I'll get ready. I won't be long."

Before Jess even got up, her phone rang. "Morgan...What?" She closed her eyes and sighed. "Yeah, thanks." She hung up. "You need to pack a bag."

"Not another one?"

"Yeah. Miami."

Arriving in Miami around two o'clock, Erin and Jess rented a car and drove to the local field office. They met with Special Agent Roger Colson. While Erin went to perform the autopsy, Jess went to the crime scene.

Even though Jess suspected she wouldn't find any relevant clues, she took her time and carefully examined the scene. She went through each room of the victim's apartment, carefully noting everything. She then left to meet up with Erin.

Erin was in the middle of the autopsy when Jess arrived.

"How is it going, Erin?"

"So far, nothing we haven't seen before. But I'm only about halfway done."

Jess nodded and sat on a stool next to a counter. She opened her briefcase and took out a notepad. She began writing.

"What about you? Did you find anything at the scene, any sign of lover boy?"

"No sign of him, but he wouldn't have been romancing Elizabeth Timmons."

Erin looked up and across the bay at her. "Oh? Why do you say that?"

"Elizabeth was gay, so our UNSUB wouldn't have gotten anywhere romancing her." Jess explained in response to her partner's raised eyebrow. "There was a single lambda earring in her jewelry box, a Playboy under the corner of her mattress, and the second pillow on her bed smelled of a perfume different from her own."

Erin smiled. "Very observant of you." She continued the autopsy as Jess concentrated on her notepad.

It was after eight o'clock when Erin and Jess got to their hotel rooms. Erin knocked on the door adjoining Jess' room.

"Come in."

"What do you want to do for dinner, Jess?"

"We can go out to get something. I want to check out a club tonight anyway. I found a matchbook in Elizabeth's car. Maybe we can find someone who saw something, like a new guy hanging around her."

"But you said she was gay."

Jess smirked. "That doesn't mean she didn't have male friends. And it's a club for men and women."

"In that case, let me change clothes."

"Yeah. I'm looking forward to getting out of this suit," Jess said.

Erin returned to her room and changed. She chose a pair of black slacks, a blue button-down shirt, a black vest (to hide the weapon at the small of her back), and of course, high heels. When she returned to Jess' room, she was pleasantly surprised at her partner's outfit for the night.

Jess was dressed in a pair of form-fitting black leather pants, a crisp, white, oxford shirt with the sleeves rolled up past her forearms, and a pair of black boots. At first blush, one would think Jess' outfit more than a bit "butch." But as Erin took in her partner's presence and movements as she moved around her room, Erin realized there was no mistaking how graceful and feminine Jess was. And she definitely liked the way the leather pants fit the woman's ass.

She licked her suddenly dry lips before speaking. "Where's your weapon?"

Jess smirked. "I have my backup weapon inside my boot."

Chapter Eighteen

AFTER DINNER, ERIN AND Jess went to the Crystal Club. It was a large club with three dance floors and five bars and was very popular with both men and women. There was also a significant attendance by straight people even though the Crystal Club was a gay bar.

The two agents made their way to one of the bars. Jess ordered a ginger ale for herself and a club soda for Erin. They then split and unobtrusively began to question the employees of the club, showing them a picture of the victim, Elizabeth Timmons.

When Erin spoke to a bartender at the second bar, a patron overheard their conversation and spoke up. "Are you talking about Beth?"

Erin showed the picture to the patron.

"Yeah, I know her."

"What about anyone she was spending time with?"

The woman shook her head. "I didn't know her well. I just saw her around a lot, but not here. She hung out at the Black Diamond."

"The Black Diamond?"

"Yeah, it's strictly a women's bar, in Ft. Lauderdale."

"Thank you."

Erin passed the information on to Jess when they met back up.

"I talked to a couple of people who recognized her as well," said Jess. "They also said the place she frequented was the Black Diamond. Our guy obviously wouldn't have been seen there since it's a women's bar, but we might find someone who knew her well."

"Do you want to go now?"

Jess looked at her watch, a stunned look clearly on her face. "Not this late," she said, surprised. She took a deep breath and slowly let it out as she looked around the club before looking at Erin. "Do you want a drink?" she asked with a small smile.

Erin returned her smile. "Sure."

"What do you want?"

"Rum and Coke."

"With lime?"

"Please."

Jess flagged down a bartender. "Whisky sour and a rum and coke, please."

"Bacardi?"

"Do you have Charbay?"

The bartender smiled with approval. "Yes." He retrieved the bottle of premium rum and fixed their drinks.

Erin and Jess picked up their drinks.

"Cheers," Erin said with a light tap of her glass against Jess' before taking a sip.

"Cheers."

"Mmmm, this is good."

After a couple of drinks, both women had completely relaxed from the day and were enjoying the music.

Jess tapped Erin on the shoulder. "How about a dance?" she asked.

Jess' full smile was enough to speed up Erin's pulse. She answered the question with a smile of her own. Jess took her hand in her own and led Erin out onto the nearest dance floor. Almost immediately, the upbeat music changed to a slow ballad.

Gazing into sparkling gray eyes, Erin felt Jess' arms slide around her waist and gently pull her close. She slipped her arms around Jess' neck, the fingers of her right hand tenderly teasing the hair at the nape of Jess' neck. They moved to the gentle rhythm of the music, the people and world around them slowly fading from their awareness. The air stilled. Their lips met in a light brush, barely felt. Then again. Jess' tongue gently teased Erin's lips, so she parted them to grant her entrance. Erin was sure her heart was beating loud enough to be heard over the music. Goosebumps ran up and down her arms and spine.

When the music changed again to a more rapid beat, the two made their way off the dance floor and out the door. The inside of the car was silent on the drive back to their hotel, though Jess held Erin's hand in her own, resting it on her thigh. It took all of Erin's self-control to keep her hand simply resting on Jess' thigh, but she didn't want to distract Jess from driving and risk causing an accident.

Jess unlocked the door to her room at the hotel, and Erin pushed her inside, kicking the door shut behind her. She immediately started pulling on Jess' shirt, untucking it from her leather pants, as their mouths met in a passionate kiss. She slid her hand under the shirt, found Jess' bra clasp, and unhooked it.

Both shirts and bras quickly landed on the floor and the women landed on the bed. Four hands worked at removing leather pants as both toed off their footwear. The holster from Jess' leg and the one at the small of Erin's back clunked to the floor. Erin pinned Jess' body to the bed with her own, exploring with hands, lips, and tongue. She rejoiced at the cries that escaped Jess when she came. Erin kissed, licked, and nipped her way back up her lover's body until claiming Jess' mouth in a deep kiss, sharing her taste with her.

Jess maneuvered her hands between them and undid Erin's pants. Once they were gone, she rolled Erin over and proceeded to worship her, relinquishing her place between Erin's thighs only after Erin begged her to. Jess moved up and laid her head over Erin's heart, closing her eyes and quickly falling asleep to the sound of her heartbeat.

Erin gently stroked her fingers through dark, silky hair. She noted Jess' even breaths, showing she'd fallen asleep. It was no wonder, really. Jess had been going for two days without any sleep the night before. Erin tightened her arms around Jess and kissed the top of her head. "Where have you been all my life?" she whispered. She closed her eyes and drifted to sleep, utterly at peace.

Outside, a lone figure sat in a dark sedan in the shadows of the night.

March 9, 2025
Sunday

Jess ran. It felt so good to stretch and work her muscles. She was smiling, thinking about the night before with her partner. A palpable shift in the air occurred when she and Erin consciously decided to end the workday and have a couple of drinks to relax at the Crystal Club. Agent Morgan and Agent Little said goodbye, and the rest of the night was spent as Jess and Erin. Erin had felt so good in her arms as they danced. And their lovemaking had been passionate.

Jess felt privileged to see Erin so open and unreserved. The professionally dispassionate agent belied the passionate woman within. And Erin was a good influence on Jess. She didn't let her ignore her physical needs, such as food and sleep, at least not too much. She also brought a kind of balance to her emotions. Somehow, despite the frustration and disappointment with the case, Erin's presence had lifted Jess' dark mood. Jess, the persistently tough and serious agent, was smiling and *laughing*.

Jess was falling for Erin. It scared her and excited her. A smile graced her lips as she continued to run.

He was glad he'd stayed the night. The sight of Morgan leaving the hotel and going for a run rewarded him. He very carefully followed her in the car, driving and parking ahead of her as needed to stay inconspicuous. He fingered the gun, with silencer attached, in his lap. He could take her down so easily. She'd never see it coming. So much for the highly vaunted Supervisory Special Agent Jessica Morgan.

He hefted the weapon, held it in his right hand, ready to shoot. He watched in the rearview mirror as she approached. She had a stupid smile on her face. Well, he would wipe that smile away in just a few more seconds.

Erin woke up and looked at the clock. She frowned. Jess had left over two hours ago and had not yet returned. She got up, retrieved her cell phone, and dialed Jess' phone. All she got was Jess' voicemail. Why wasn't Jess answering her phone? Erin gathered her clothes and went to her room through the adjoining doorway. She started a pot of coffee and took a quick shower. Once dressed, she tried Jess' cell again. Still no answer.

Erin frowned. Jess probably just decided on a long run. After all, she'd said it had been weeks since she'd gone running. Even Erin didn't count laps in a gym as really running. Jess probably just lost track of the time. That sometimes happened to Erin when she ran. But that didn't settle the worry skittering along her nerves. And it didn't explain why her partner didn't answer her phone. She jumped when her cell rang.

"Little."

"Agent Little? This is Nurse Lisa Jackson. I'm calling from Miami Memorial to inform you that your partner, Agent Morgan, is here in the E.R."

Erin's heart dropped to her feet. "What happened?"

Everything had happened so fast. As far as Jess was concerned, the ambulance couldn't get to her soon enough. Too much blood covered her hands from trying to staunch the flow. Finally, the ambulance arrived. Jess explained what had happened as the EMTs quickly and efficiently worked.

In the back of the ambulance, Jess closed her eyes and took a few slow, even breaths, trying to slow her heart rate. The ride to the hospital seemed to take forever. The E.R. was a typical scene of controlled chaos. It wasn't the first time she'd experienced such a scene.

"Agent Morgan?"

"Yes."

"Hi. I'm Detective Singer with Miami-Dade P.D. Can you tell me what happened?"

"I was on a run. Everything happened so quickly. I heard a loud screech, which made me look just in time to see the truck and the car collide. I don't know who had the right of way or who was at fault, but it was a bad accident. It took me a couple of moments to react. I ran over and checked on the driver of the truck. He was conscious but a bit woozy. I helped him out because of the pervasive smell of gasoline. Once I had him sitting down, someone else stayed with him. That's when I went to the car. The driver was unconscious. It was a struggle to get the door open. When I got to him, it was obvious the wound in his leg would be fatal if the bleeding wasn't controlled. I got him out of the car and applied pressure. I got a bystander to give me his belt so I could place a tourniquet. When I fumbled with my phone, someone said they'd already called 9-1-1 and requested an ambulance."

"And your arm?" Singer asked with a gesture at the blood-soaked bandaging on her arm.

Jess shook her head. "I caught it on some metal getting the driver out of the car." She shrugged. "Nothing to worry about. I heal quickly. Why did M.D.P.D. send a detective to ask about a traffic accident?"

Det. Singer smiled. "I got the call as an accident with an injured federal officer."

"Ah." She nodded in understanding.

"Well, I'm glad you're going to be all right, Agent Morgan."

"Thank you. I hope the driver of the car will be okay." She reached for her phone, but the nurse stopped her.

"I'm sorry, Agent Morgan, but you can't use your cellphone in the E.R., and you need to leave it off."

Jess nodded in acknowledgment. "All right. But is there any way I can call my partner? I've been gone longer than expected and she doesn't know what happened."

"If you give me her number, I'll give her a call and let her know you're here."

Jess gave the nurse, Lisa, Erin's name, and cell number.

Someone pulled the curtain aside and a gray-haired doctor approached. "I'm Dr. Lev Weiss."

"Agent Jessica Morgan."

"Well, let's take a look at your arm."

Erin parked in the E.R. parking lot. Upon entering, she flashed her credentials and asked about her partner. A nurse took her back to where Jess was sitting on a gurney. Her arm was bandaged and there was quite a bit of blood on her tank top. "Jess?"

Jess turned and gave her a small smile. "Hey, Erin."

"Are you all right?"

"Yeah."

"What happened?"

"I was on my run and witnessed an MVA. Had to pull the drivers out and start first aid on one of them." She paused. "I just hope he makes it."

Dr. Weiss returned at that moment. "He will, thanks to your quick thinking. If you hadn't used a tourniquet, he would have bled out from the injury to his femoral artery. Good job, Agent Morgan."

Jess merely nodded.

"Here's your paperwork and a prescription for antibiotics."

"Thank you." Jess signed her discharge papers.

He watched as Little walked from her car to the E.R. entrance. With her white-blonde hair, she was hard to miss. He wasn't happy. He'd been ready to pull the trigger, but the loud screeching of brakes caused him to look. The next thing he knew, Morgan was pulling the drivers out of their vehicles, and too many people were around.

But he could be a patient man.

He perked up when Little exited the E.R. with Morgan. Little was steadying Morgan. She helped Morgan into the car's passenger side before getting in the driver's seat. He saw Little lean over and kiss Morgan on the lips.

Suddenly, he was glad he hadn't killed Morgan. Yet.

Jess swayed slightly when she stood up.

Erin grabbed her arm. "Are you all right?"

"Yeah." She shook her head. "Just a little woozy. They gave me an injection."

"Well, let's get you back to the hotel." Erin kept her hand on Jess' back, ensuring she didn't get too dizzy. After getting Jess into the car, she entered the driver's side. Before starting the car, Erin looked over at her partner. "I was worried about you."

Jess looked at Erin. "Sorry. I meant to get back at a reasonable time."

Erin reached up and cupped Jess' cheek. "It's all right. I'm just glad you're okay." She leaned over and placed a gentle kiss on her lips. Jess was smiling when she pulled back. Erin ran her thumb across Jess' lips before leaning back into her seat. "Rest."

Jess closed her eyes and rested her head against the window.

At the hotel, Erin got Jess stripped and back into bed. She was out like a light. Erin then ran out to a pharmacy and got her antibiotic prescription filled, thankful her lover was not seriously injured.

She never noticed the dark sedan that followed her.

Chapter Nineteen

WHEN JESS WOKE UP, she saw her partner sitting in the chair, reading her notepad. "So what do you think?"

Erin looked up at the sound of Jess' voice and smiled. "Hey. How do you feel?"

"All right. Sorry I conked out on you."

"Don't be. Drugs will do that," she said with an amused smile.

"So what do you think?" Jess asked again with a nod at the notepad.

"I'm a little confused. You seem to be describing two different people in this profile."

Jess sighed. "I know. Or at least two very different facets of the UNSUB."

"Do you think he's got a split personality?"

"I don't want to go that far at this point. It's not unheard of, so I can't rule it out, but it's rare in serial killers. I've seen these behaviors before, just not in the same suspect at the same time."

"If he does have a split personality, would he be aware of it?"

"It's possible that a personality is aware of the other or others. It's also possible this bastard is just smart and is playing with us. Either way, I'm getting very tired of investigating the deaths of young women." She sat up, the sheet falling to reveal her naked form. "I'm going to take a shower and get dressed. Then we can go." She stood up, grabbed some things from a suitcase, and went into the bathroom.

Erin had been unable to take her eyes off the lovely form of her partner when she sat up and walked to the bathroom. She knew that form intimately and wanted to explore it some more in the future. A ringing cell phone interrupted her thoughts—Jess' phone.

"Jess, your phone is ringing," she called out.

"Will you answer it for me?" Jess called back as Erin heard the shower turn on.

"Okay."

"Hello."

"Agent Morgan?"

"No, this is Agent Little, her partner. Agent Morgan is unavailable now. Can I take a message?"

"Hi, this is Alan Stillwell. I'm one of the techs that tried to trace a call Agent Morgan received from an UNSUB yesterday."

"Okay."

"Anyway, he made another call on that phone a few minutes ago. We still couldn't pin down his location because he wasn't on the line long enough, but we were able to find out what city he's in. He's in Miami, Florida."

"All right, Alan, we appreciate all your efforts."

"You're welcome, Agent Little. We'll keep trying."

She ended the call.

Jess was back in the room following her shower. She was wrapped in a typically short hotel towel. God, the more Erin saw of Jess, the more time she spent with her, the more she wanted her! She couldn't find her voice until after Jess had pulled on a pair of slacks and slipped into a button-down shirt. She finally broke the silence.

"Alan Stillwell called while you were in the shower."

Jess looked at her as she buttoned her shirt. "The tech guy who tried to trace that call yesterday. What did he have to say?"

"A call was placed from that phone a few minutes ago. He said it originated from here in Miami."

Jess nodded. "That's not surprising."

Having finished dressing, Jess indicated she was ready to get on with their day, but since Erin insisted that they eat first, they left to have brunch.

The two agents spent the rest of the morning and all afternoon talking with and interviewing family and friends of Elizabeth Timmons. None of her family seemed to have a clue that Elizabeth was gay. Only one of the dozen or so friends they spoke with seemed aware, and she didn't know any specifics, just that she suspected. She'd never actually talked to Elizabeth about it, waiting until Elizabeth brought it up, which hadn't happened yet.

At dinner, Erin and Jess discussed their day.

"Well, it doesn't appear Elizabeth had come out yet. There's a whole part of this young woman's life that her family and friends didn't even know about."

Erin frowned. "That must have been sad and lonely for her."

Jess nodded. "Unfortunately, it's a reality for many gays and lesbians, even today. Hopefully, we'll find someone at the Black Diamond tonight who knew her and may be able to provide us with a lead."

Erin looked at Jess, debating whether to ask the question or not. Jess must have noticed her expression.

"What is it, Erin?"

"I guess I was just wondering. Did your family know about you?"

Jess smiled. "I was fifteen when I came out, so my parents were already gone, but my grandfather knew." Amusement lit up her eyes. "At my graduation from Oxford, he talked to many young women, trying to set me up." She chuckled. "He wasn't successful, but the old bugger did end up with quite a few phone numbers for himself."

Erin smiled at the amusement and affection in her lover's tone. "He sounds like a special man."

"He was." Jess nodded. "He would've liked you," she said with a smile. "What about you? Does your family know?"

"Yes and no. The only person I discussed anything with was my sister, Lauren. She was openly bisexual, but my family, which is military and very Catholic, did *not* discuss it." She paused. "Although, I'm sure my mother knows there was something between my college roommate and me," she said thoughtfully.

Jess nodded in understanding.

Erin focused her gaze back on her lover. She wanted to make sure Jess knew exactly where she stood. "Even though I haven't slept with a woman in a long time, I'm not confused or experimenting with you, Jess."

Jess smiled. "Erin, I may not have known you for very long, but I do know you're an intelligent and strong-willed woman, and I doubt anyone would accuse you of not knowing what you want or of acting capriciously." Her smile morphed into a mischievous smirk and a spark lit her gray eyes. "And it was obvious it wasn't your first time with a woman when we made love."

Erin blushed but smiled.

They returned to the hotel to change clothes before going to the Black Diamond club.

"What are you going to wear tonight, Jess?"

"Probably just a pair of jeans and a shirt."

"Why don't you wear your leather pants again tonight?" she suggested lightly.

A dark eyebrow quirked.

She smiled demurely. "I like the way they look."

Jess smiled, pleased. "All right. I'll wear them. But…"

"But what?"

Gray eyes sparkled. "But I expect you to return the favor at some point."

"But I don't have a pair of leather pants."

"You can do something about that." With a smirk, Jess gently pushed Erin into her room to get ready. "See you in a few."

Dressed pretty much as they had been the previous night, the two agents drove north to Ft. Lauderdale.

At the Black Diamond, the rather large, muscular, middle-aged doorwoman stopped them at the entrance. "Cops. What can I do for you?" she asked challengingly.

Jess smiled. "Feds, actually." She flashed her badge. "We're not here to bother anyone. Just to ask about this young lady." She showed the picture of Elizabeth to the woman. "We're told she frequented this club."

The woman looked at the photo. "What'd she do?"

"Nothing. She was killed. We're investigating her murder."

"Oh hell. Her name was Beth, and she was a good kid."

"Do you know if she was seeing anyone particular? Someone who could tell us more about her?"

The doorwoman nodded. "You'll want to speak to Kate. Ask for her at the bar."

"Thank you…"

"Daphne."

"Thank you, Daphne." Jess pulled out her wallet to pay the cover charge, but Daphne waved it away. "Don't worry about it. Just find whoever killed Beth."

Jess didn't miss the tears that were welling in Daphne's eyes. "We intend to," she said, conveying reassurance and her commitment to catch the UNSUB—another promise made.

When they entered the bar, Jess was somewhat surprised at the interior. There was a long hardwood bar on the right side of the room. On the left was a huge stone hearth fireplace with a fire burning in it. Large, stuffed, leather armchairs were arranged in a semicircle facing the fireplace, set in pairs, with a small, round table for drinks for each pair. A baby grand piano sat idle in the back left corner. There were over twenty women present. They walked up to the bar.

"Welcome to the Black Diamond. What can I get for you, ladies?" the green-eyed blonde behind the bar asked.

"We need to speak to Kate. Could you direct us to her, please?" Erin asked.

"Can I tell her what it's regarding?"

Erin flashed her badge. "It's a personal matter."

The blonde nodded. "Okay. I'll get her."

The blonde picked up the phone behind the bar and made a quick call.

A couple of minutes later, a door in the back corner opened, admitting an attractive brunette and the sounds of typically loud dance music and revelry of a club. The brunette was five-foot-eight, brown-eyed, svelte, and had an air of authority. She looked like she was in her late twenties. She approached the agents. "I'm Kate Rossini. What can I do for you, Officers?"

"I'm FBI Supervisory Special Agent Erin Little, and this is my partner, Supervisory Special Agent Jessica Morgan. Is there somewhere we can speak privately?" Erin asked.

"Sure, come on back to my office." Kate led the way through a locked door in the back wall, which emptied into a long corridor. They passed a small, unused kitchen on the right, then came to Kate's office on the left. "Have a seat." She sat down behind her desk. "Now, what can I do for you?"

Jess handed the picture of Elizabeth to her. Jess didn't miss the quiet intake of air.

"Beth. What's happened?" she asked, trepidation belied by her forced calm.

"I'm afraid Beth was killed two nights ago. We're investigating her murder," Erin said gently.

Kate closed her eyes and her chin began to tremble. A few tears escaped from the corners of her eyes. "Beth and I..." She couldn't continue.

Jess stood and walked around the desk. Crouching next to Kate, she placed her hand over Kate's hand that was shaking in her lap. "I understand, Kate. If you can't do this right now, it's all right. I know what you're feeling—I have been there. I promise you that Agent Little and I are dedicated to finding and catching the person who did this, but we need your help. We can come back tomorrow if you prefer."

Rossini swallowed and opened her eyes. She looked down into Jess' eyes and held them as if looking for something or judging her. Apparently satisfied, she gave a slight nod as she wiped away her tears, even though more followed. "What do you need?" she asked softly.

Jess gently squeezed the woman's hand before letting go and moving back to her chair. "What can you tell us about Elizabeth's social circle? Had she made any new friends recently?"

"Not that I know of. We didn't spend as much time together as I'd liked. And she was in the closet. She said her family wouldn't understand, and she wasn't ready to tell them."

"That can be hard on a relationship."

"She was worth it."

"How did you meet?" Jess asked.

"Here, at the bar. One of my bartenders was out sick, so I was working on the other side."

"The other side?" Erin asked.

"The other side of the bar is the club side—DJ, dancing, pool tables, your typical bar scene. She looked a little overwhelmed sitting at the bar, sipping her drink. We struck up a conversation, and when one of my other bartenders made it in, Beth and I continued talking in the wine bar. We started having nice talks every time she came to the Black Diamond. We became friends, eventually lovers."

"Weren't you concerned that you hadn't heard from her for a couple of days?"

"No. I usually don't during the week. She's—she was very driven and committed to her studies. She was close to getting her PhD in Molecular Biology, so we limited our time together to the weekends, but she had a test tomorrow she had to study for, so we…" Her shaky voice trailed off as she wiped at her tears again.

"All right. Thank you," Jess said. "If you think of anything that might help us, do not hesitate to call either of us." She stood and handed Kate her card. Erin followed suit.

Taking the cards, Kate nodded, once again wiping her tears.

Erin started to say something, but Jess silently urged her out of the office. Erin looked at her and asked, "Why did you stop me from saying anything?"

"Because you were about to ask her if she was all right. She's not," Jess said without reproof but with the certainty of experience.

They arrived back in the wine bar. "Do you want to stay and have a drink?" Erin asked.

"No." Jess wanted to get out of the bar. But she did recognize the desire in her partner and herself to bring the workday to a close and transition to some personal time. "But I wouldn't mind going for a walk." She smiled. "I understand they have some beautiful beaches here."

"That's right. You have a thing for tropical beaches." Erin smiled. "A walk sounds nice."

When they stepped out of the bar, Jess approached Daphne again. "I think it would be a good idea if someone made sure Kate got home safe tonight, maybe stay with her so she's not alone."

Daphne nodded. "I'll see to it."

Jess gave her a nod and then turned back to Erin. They got in the car and drove back to Miami. Jess pulled the car into a parking lot at a small beach, where they got out of the car. Holding hands, they walked along the sand.

"Are you all right in your heels walking in this sand?" Jess asked.

Erin chuckled. "I can walk anywhere in heels."

With a clear sky and a three-quarter moon above, there was plenty of light.

"So you like tropical beaches and walks in the moonlight," Erin said lightly.

Jess laughed. "Sorry, I don't mean to be such a cliché."

Erin squeezed her hand and stopped, pulling Jess to a stop. Jess turned to face Erin, who reached up with her other hand and brushed some hair back from Jess' face. "I don't mind cliché, especially where you and moonlight are concerned." As Erin pressed her lips to Jess' and sighed, Jess responded. They held each other loosely and kissed gently, savoring the softness and emotional connection.

After a few minutes, Jess pulled back, her heart pounding and legs feeling a bit rubbery. "I need...I think I need to sit down." She sat down in the sand, facing the ocean.

Erin knelt next to her. "Are you all right?"

Jess smiled. "Yeah. You just kind of blew me away." She reached up, cupped Erin's cheek, and pulled her into a deep kiss. Wrapping her arms around Erin, she pulled her lover to her as she lay back in the sand.

Sometime later, the two women were sitting up watching the waves. Erin was sitting between Jess' legs, leaning back against her. She rested her hands over the arms wrapped around her waist.

They talked, sharing some of their histories and finding more and more things they held in common: enjoyment of moonlight and beaches, medical school experiences, and a love of seafood among them. Erin spoke of her relationship with her father and his lack of support for her decision to join the Bureau. Jess spoke of her relationship with her grandfather and the immense feeling of loss at his passing. They talked about the last five or six years of work subsuming everything else in their lives and resulting in the loss of a part of themselves.

Eventually, they rose and walked back to the car, arm-in-arm.

In Erin's hotel room, they undressed each other and came together under the sheets, connecting on more than just a physical level.

Erin lifted her head from Jess' chest and gazed down into shining gray eyes. "Jess…"

"What?" Jess prompted when Erin didn't continue.

How much could she risk of herself? She gazed into her lover's eyes and found the answer. "I'm falling for you."

A soft smile graced Jess' lips. She reached up, brushed back some of Erin's hair, and caressed her cheek. "I've already fallen for you."

Erin felt her heart swell and tears filled her eyes. She kissed Jess, gently, thoroughly. Laying her head on her lover's shoulder, Erin closed her eyes. Finally, she knew what real happiness felt like. She slept peacefully in her lover's arms.

Chapter Twenty

March 10, 2025
Monday

THE PHONE WAS RINGING. She'd let the answering machine get it. No, it was a cell phone. She'd let voicemail get it. She growled when her human pillow shifted out from under her. She opened her eyes and blearily saw her lover retrieve the offending noisemaker.

"Morgan."

It was amazing how the woman could visibly transform into Agent Morgan, even naked. Erin sat up, holding the sheet to herself.

Jess sat in the chair. "Why?...I see...Tell me, why now?" Her jaw tightened and she flashed a glance at Erin. "You know I can't do that...Why not this morning?...Where?...I'll find it." She hung up and dialed the airline, making reservations on the four o'clock flight to Atlanta that afternoon.

"We're going to Atlanta?" Erin asked when Jess was done.

Jess sighed. "The son of a bitch wants to talk. He wants me to meet him at a bar in Atlanta: Doc's Saloon."

Erin gave Jess a skeptical look. "Sounds like a very fine establishment," she replied sarcastically.

Jess let out a huff. "Probably a biker bar." She rubbed her hands over her face. "What time is it?"

Erin looked at the clock radio. "Four-twenty-three. Come back to bed and get some more sleep."

Jess moved and sat on the side of the bed. She leaned in and kissed Erin. "Believe me, I'd love to, but I have some work I need to do." She kissed Erin again. "The thought of crawling back under the covers and snuggling with you is so very tempting," she said, standing. "Get some more sleep, Erin. It's probably going to be a long day."

Jess picked up her stuff and went into her room. After slipping on her robe, she sat at the small table and turned on her laptop. She wanted to do some research. She needed to find out where Doc's Saloon was and, if possible, what kind of establishment it was. She also wanted to research apps that could distort and disguise a person's voice. The voice on the phone didn't sound electronic, but it did sound as if it had been altered somehow. It wasn't noticeable *per se*, but there was *something* just enough off that it didn't sound quite right. Someone without her more acute senses probably would not notice the difference.

Jess found several apps that could be used to alter the voice, but she couldn't find any way to tell what app the caller was using.

She sent an email letting AD Taylor and Director Cavanaugh know about her contact with the UNSUB. She also placed a couple of phone calls.

It turned out that Doc's Saloon was not a biker bar, but from the history of police calls to the location, it was definitely a rough place. She also returned a call to the tech department when she saw a missed call from them on her phone. It was too early for Alan Stillwell to be in, but a young man named Pete Hartman verified that the call she'd received had been placed from Atlanta.

She and Erin would spend the day at the University of Miami, speaking with Elizabeth's professors and fellow students. Then they were going to fly up to Atlanta.

Jess rubbed her face and put her laptop aside after completing the tasks she'd set for herself. She looked at the clock. It was about forty minutes before Erin's alarm would go off. Or she could wake Erin up herself. Jess smiled. It was amazing how much Erin had changed her in a little over three weeks. Before this case, she wouldn't have considered setting work aside for a few minutes to spend some personal time with someone. She shook her head. It was time to act, not think.

Jess returned to Erin's room. She stood next to the bed for a moment, gazing down at the beautiful woman. Erin looked so peaceful. Jess shed her robe and slipped into the bed next to her partner, her lover.

Jess tenderly brushed some hair back from Erin's face. She lowered her head and kissed soft lips. Erin smiled into the kiss as she awakened. She moved her arms up around Jess' shoulders, pulling her close. Erin opened her eyes and looked up into her eyes.

"Good morning," said Erin.

"Good morning." Jess ducked her head and started nuzzling Erin's throat and neck.

"Mmmm, is it time to get up?"

"Not yet. I hope you don't mind me waking you a little early," she replied softly. She latched onto Erin's pulse point, teasing it with her lips and tongue.

Erin's breath caught in her throat as Jess gently explored with her hands. "Not...at all."

Content and satisfied, the two women were holding one another in quiet lassitude when the alarm clock finally announced it was time to get up. They parted to shower and dress in their respective rooms.

Jess was closing her briefcase when Erin entered her room. "Ready to go?" Jess asked.

Erin nodded. But she set her things down next to the door and turned to Jess. "Just one thing."

"What?"

Erin leaned in and kissed her partner lightly. "Thank you for my wake-up call, Agent Morgan," she said with a soft smile. She was rewarded with a beautiful smile.

"You're welcome, Agent Little." Playfulness shone in gray eyes. "Just trying to be a good partner."

They shared another kiss, then went to check out of the hotel.

Erin and Jess spent the morning and a good portion of the afternoon at the University of Miami, interviewing Elizabeth's fellow students and her professors. They were both frustrated and disappointed as they left for the airport. No one knew of any new person in the young woman's life. No one stood out. No one didn't belong.

Jess sat down in her airplane seat with a sigh, and Erin settled beside her. She patted her partner's arm. "We will catch him, Jess."

"I know. I'm just afraid of how many more women will die before we do."

Erin was going to express her concerns about the meeting in Atlanta, but Jess had closed her eyes and was soon napping.

In Atlanta, they rented a car and checked into a hotel. It was over takeout in Jess' room that Erin finally confronted her partner.

"Just what exactly are your plans for this meeting tonight?"

"What do you mean?" Jess asked.

Erin got the distinct impression that Jess would rather not discuss the meeting. Erin didn't think meeting with the UNSUB was a good idea, at least not without a dozen or so agents already staked out in the meeting place and ready to take him down.

"I mean, just what exactly are we going to do? What if he doesn't show up? What if he *does*? What kind of backup are we going to have?"

Jess put down her plastic fork and pushed the remnants of her meal away. "Not we. Me."

"What?" Erin asked, not sure she'd heard correctly.

"We are not going. I am."

Erin was so angry she couldn't see straight or sit still. "Are you stupid? Not only can you not go alone, but we should make arrangements to have a dozen agents in place before we get there. We should coordinate with local law enforcement and set a perimeter with roadblocks in case he gets out of the bar. HRT should be on standby. This is a serial killer who's killed dozens of women. And you want to just saunter in alone and have a chat? That's not what we do! We don't put our lives in danger like that. You will not put your life in danger like that. Not like that! And you know damn well there's no way you're going anywhere near that bar without me by your side. Partners don't do that. Partners don't leave you hanging out to dry. Partners always cover you and have your back. So tell me just how the hell you think this is going to happen?" she growled as she stopped pacing and faced Jess. "Well? Are you going to say something?" Erin demanded.

"He said he wouldn't show if I didn't go alone." Before Erin could go off again, Jess continued. "And he said he'll kill you on sight, Erin. It's not a vague threat anymore. It's an explicit threat against your life."

"I'm *not* quitting this case!"

"I'm not asking you to."

Jess' quiet response took some wind out of Erin's sails. She sat down on the end of the bed.

"I am asking you to trust me."

Erin ran a hand across her eyes and tried to rein in her ire. She reminded herself that Jess wasn't an unreasonable person. Jess had always been professional and respectful to her. The least she could do was hear her partner out. "All right. Talk to me, Jess."

Jess nodded. "Okay. First, please remember that this isn't my first time at the rodeo. I'm an experienced agent with a history of dealing with these cases."

Erin nodded.

"I'm going to Doc's Saloon tonight, but I won't be alone, and neither will you."

"What do you mean?"

"I made a call early this morning to a local detective I've worked with before. He's going to be at the bar." She looked at her watch. "In fact, he should already be there. And his partner will be with you."

"With me?"

"I'm not naïve enough to discount the possibility that this is just a ruse to get me out of the way so he can come after you, Erin."

"Or it could be an attempt to isolate you so he can kill you, Jess."

Jess nodded. "That is a possibility, although I honestly don't think it's the most likely."

"Why not?"

"None of his threats have been directed at me, only you." She paused. "Erin, I know you don't like it, but you have to let me go without you."

"Damn it, Jess. You made me promise to be careful and not take unnecessary risks." She stood up, walked back to the table, and knelt beside her lover. She took Jess' hand in her own. "I need you to make me the same promise, Jess. I don't want anything to happen to you. Please do not take any unnecessary risks."

Jess looked down into Erin's eyes. "I promise." Leaning down, she kissed her. With her hands on Erin's shoulders, Jess stood up, pulling Erin up.

Erin pulled out of the kiss and gazed into Jess' shining gray eyes. "What time do you have to leave?"

Jess glanced at the clock. "Bobby's partner should be here in a couple of hours. I won't leave until he gets here."

"Good." Erin claimed Jess' lips with her own in a passionate kiss. She pushed Jess onto the bed, pinning her.

Jess looked through the peephole when she heard a knock on her hotel room door.

"Agent Morgan? It's Detective Gene Franco, Bobby Marinelli's partner." He held his shield up.

Jess opened the door. "Come on in, Detective."

"Just call me Frank," he replied as they shook hands.

Jess introduced the detective to her partner. She then grabbed her weapon and slipped it into the holster at the small of her back.

"Bobby's been at Doc's for about two hours. He said a couple of fights had already broken out the last time he checked in with me, so keep your eyes open, Agent Morgan."

"Will do." She turned to Erin. "I'll see you later." And then she was gone.

Chapter Twenty-One

AS JESS WALKED INTO Doc's Saloon, her senses were on high alert. She knew what a risk she was taking, but she honestly didn't think The Slasher would try to kill her. Even his earlier invasion into her hotel room had been timed to ensure she wasn't present. And he'd followed her, as evidenced by the break-in at Erin's apartment, giving him ample opportunity to kill her. No, his goal didn't appear to be to kill her.

She'd dealt with his kind before. They wanted a foil to parry against, to test and prove their superiority. She had been that foil on more than one occasion.

However, she wasn't dumb enough to dismiss the possibility of a trap for herself or Erin. When The Slasher told her to come to Atlanta, she'd called an old contact there. Bobby Marinelli was a detective on the Atlanta police department's night shift. He was a good detective with several years' experience in undercover work and the homicide division. In a worst-case scenario, he was someone she knew could more than handle himself and back her up.

Jess spotted Bobby almost immediately. His five-foot-nine, lanky frame, unshaven and unkempt appearance belied the man's sharp intelligence and unexpected strength. The brown-eyed man was doing a good impression of a sleepy drunk, conveniently sitting in a spot that allowed his field of vision to cover the entire room. Neither one acknowledged the other beyond making fleeting eye contact.

Jess went to the bar and ordered a Jack Daniels. She didn't care for the amber liquid, but Doc's wasn't where one ordered ginger ale, and she could nurse the whiskey for quite some time.

Jess had been sitting at a table for over an hour. She'd had to fend off some unwanted advances and had been called several choice names. Finally, a man sat down at her table who didn't look like he would try to hit on her. He looked her up and down before speaking.

"You're Morgan."

"And you're not the person who called me," she said with certainty.

He smirked. "No. But he sent me."

She arched an eyebrow. "I was told to be here to meet with *him*."

"There's something he wants me to give you."

"What?"

He looked around. "Not here."

"Well, I'm not about to go anywhere with you."

"You misunderstand. I just mean not right here." He jerked a thumb toward the back of the bar. "There's a room in the back, more private."

Jess weighed her options. The man in front of her was large, at least six feet tall and 250 pounds. And he was not fat. But she also knew she could take him if it came down to it. She gave a slight nod. "All right." As she stood, she made an inconspicuous gesture with her hand, signaling Bobby to stay put but to keep his eyes open. She didn't have to look to know Bobby was watching. She followed the "Hulk" to the back of the bar.

As soon as Jess stepped through the door, a heavy object came down on the back of her head. When she came to, she was tied to a wooden chair with her hands tied behind the back. Her feet were also tied to the legs of the chair. Suddenly, cold water was thrown in her face. She sputtered a little and raised her head. She was rewarded with a fist to her left cheek. She tasted blood where the inside of her cheek was cut. And she was dizzy.

"Hey! I said not to do anything until she woke up!"

"She is awake," said the Hulk.

Footsteps marked the approach of a second man. "Well, well. What have we here?"

Jess glared at the second man.

"You are a feisty one, aren't you? Well, that's why we're here."

"I'm gonna love teaching you a lesson or two, bitch." Hulk smirked just before he smashed the side of her face again.

Jess spat some blood onto his shoes. She then looked back up at the second man. He was clearly "the brains" of the duo, but that also made him the more dangerous one. "Look, if I'm supposed to be learning something here, wouldn't it be better if I knew what the hell the lesson was?"

She received a blow to the opposite cheek for her impertinence.

"Gag her," ordered Brains. He walked away as Hulk gagged her.

Even with Jess' strength, it was difficult to break the bindings on her wrists without good leverage. But since it was evident that these two wanted to beat her rather than kill her, she knew she could last long enough for Bobby to realize something was wrong.

Erin waited precisely ten minutes after Jess left. She then tucked her weapon at the small of her back, slipped on her blazer, and headed to the door.

"Um, Agent Little? Where are you going?"

She gave Det. Franco a determined look. "To back up my partner. You can either stay here or come with me." She opened the door and walked out of the hotel room.

Det. Franco was on her heels, doing his best to stop her, but finally gave up when it became clear that he could find no way to sway Erin from her course of action. He told her he'd drive his car so she wouldn't have to hail a cab. He did get her to agree to wear one of the Kevlar vests in his trunk. She also agreed to go along with his plan to park two blocks down from the bar so they weren't so obvious in the parking lot. He assured Erin that his partner would call him if a problem occurred that he and Jess couldn't handle.

They'd been sitting in the car for quite a long time when Frank's phone rang. "Franco…Bobby?…Bobby?" He slapped his phone shut.

"What's going on?" Erin demanded.

Instead of answering her directly, Frank picked up the mike to his radio and called in, requesting backup. Since he wasn't starting the car and getting them to the bar, Erin opened her door and started to get out to cover the two blocks on foot. Frank caught her arm barely in time to keep her in the car as he turned the key in the ignition. As far as Erin was concerned, they couldn't get there fast enough. Pulling up short of the bar's front door, they both jumped out of the car.

Frank reached to open the door of the bar, but before he could, a body came crashing out of a painted-over window. Erin and Frank exchanged a look and headed inside with determination. What greeted them was one of the biggest and roughest melees Erin had ever encountered. When Frank spotted his partner unconscious on the floor, they pushed and shoved their way to Bobby. Erin knelt to check him out. He was alive and his pulse was strong, but he had a bleeding wound on the back of his head.

"He should be all right. He's bleeding, but it's not a bad wound. Head wounds always bleed a lot," she reassured Frank.

Frank took off his overshirt, folded it up, and pressed it against Bobby's head wound. Erin stood up to try to find her partner. "Where's Jess?"

Bobby came to. "Back…"

"What?" Frank asked.

"Jessica…backroom…"

Erin tried to work her way to the back of the bar, but the fighting around her also threatened to engulf her. She found an overturned chair, set it upright, stood on top of it, and fired three quick shots into the ceiling. The noise level dropped dramatically, and nearly every head in the place turned toward her.

"Everyone settle down, sit down, and shut up!" Several objections started, but she fired another shot. "*Now!*"

The battlers, for the most part, obeyed. She looked at Bobby and Frank, who indicated they would take charge of the room. She quickly made her way to the back of the bar. Even in the most remote way, she was not prepared for what she found when she entered the backroom.

Jess realized that something had gone wrong. Bobby wasn't coming. It was up to her to deal with the situation she was in. Despite the blows she'd taken to her face and body, she continued to try to break the bindings holding her arms and hands behind the back of the chair. Finally, they gave. Jess didn't waste any time. She surged up, surprising both men. Her features shifted in an instant. She kicked her legs free as she ripped off her gag. A solid and well-placed punch knocked out Brains. That left Hulk.

The change in Jess' features may have stunned Hulk, but he quickly recovered. He met her with a fist to her face, but it wasn't enough to stop her. She lunged at Hulk, but he met her lunge, grabbing one of her arms and yanking it behind her with all his strength. Jess let out a yell when her arm was twisted and her shoulder dislocated. It also caused her already high adrenaline levels to spike even higher. With a roar, she spun, landing a punch to his jaw that she followed up with physically shoving him into the wall with her own body. She grabbed his throat with her right hand, lifted, and squeezed. Suddenly, the door flew open.

Erin froze as she took in the appearance of her partner. Jess' face was bruised, she had blood running from the corner of her left eye and below her broken nose, her left arm hung uselessly at her side, and her wrists were chafed raw from being tied up. All that was a shock, but they weren't what gave her pause. What rooted Erin to the spot was Jess' no longer gray, but depthless black eyes and fangs. And she was holding a 250-pound man a few inches off the floor with one hand around his throat.

Erin's arrival apparently distracted Jess, and the large man took advantage. He broke the grip Jess had on his throat and threw a hard right to her body, following it up with a left to her head.

All three heard the snap of ribs breaking and the forceful expulsion of air from Jess' lungs. The blow to her head clearly stunned her, and Jess dropped to her knees. As the man raised a broken chair leg, preparing to bring it down on Jess' head, Erin was finally spurred into action.

"FBI! Freeze!"

He didn't.

She pulled the trigger. The bullet struck him in the chest, knocking him back. He didn't go down. With a yell, he still attempted to attack Jess. A second bullet ended his life.

Jess was on the floor. Erin moved toward her. Pain was written in her features. The gray eyes she recognized were the ones that looked up at Erin. Before she could say anything, Bobby and Frank appeared in the room.

"Fuck!" growled Bobby, while Frank stepped out and called for a couple of paramedics who'd just arrived. Bobby knelt next to Jess while Erin checked the unconscious man on the floor. "Take it easy, Jessica. You're going to be okay."

Erin sat down on a couple of stacked boxes. She didn't know what to think or say. Did she really see what she thought she did? Could Jess really be a monster in disguise? What did it all mean?

Chapter Twenty-Two

ONCE JESS COULD CATCH her breath and answer the medics' questions, she was helped up from the floor and, at her insistence, walked out of the backroom, through the bar, and out to one of the ambulances.

Bobby went with her, still holding a cloth to the back of his head. "I'm sorry, Jessica. I should have moved sooner. I knew something was wrong because you were gone too long. When I tried to get to you, I got blindsided."

Jess sat on the gurney in the back of the ambulance as the medic checked her out more closely and prepared her for transport.

"It's not your fault, Bobby."

"Did you at least find out what you needed to?"

She let out a sigh. "The guy I'm after wasn't here, but apparently I was being taught a lesson, punished."

"For what?"

"They wouldn't say." She winced when the medic gently examined her nose.

"Sorry," the paramedic apologized.

"I still have to question the second one in the morning," Jess finished.

"I'm going to put you on some oxygen and start an I.V., Agent Morgan," the medic said. "Then we'll get you both to the hospital."

When Erin finally arrived at the hospital, she flashed her credentials. She inquired about Jess' condition but didn't go back to see her. She took a seat in the waiting room.

Frank went back to check on his partner. He, of course, found Bobby with Jess. After ensuring they would both be okay, he left and returned to the precinct to help process the three dozen or so people arrested at the bar.

Erin sat in the E.R. waiting room, trying to sort out her thoughts and feelings. What the hell had she seen? What was Jess? What did it mean for their partnership?

What did it mean for them on a personal level?

Jess had to fight with the attending physician, but she vehemently refused to be admitted into the hospital for observation.

"Agent Morgan, you have a concussion, your ribs are broken, and your shoulder was dislocated."

"All of which you can't do a damn thing about at this point."

"Agent—"

"I'm also a doctor. I know you can't make me stay, and I'm not going to. So go get the damn paperwork I need to sign so I can get out of here."

The paperwork was brought, and she signed herself out against medical advice.

Erin stood when Jess and Bobby walked out together. "They're not keeping you overnight?"

"I'm fine."

Jess' reply received a highly arched eyebrow. Erin clearly didn't believe her. Erin exchanged a questioning look with Bobby, but Jess just sighed and walked out the door.

"Det. Franco brought me in your car," Erin said to Bobby. "It's over here." She took the lead.

Bobby helped Jess into the back seat and got into the driver's seat. "We need to stop on the way back to the hotel," he informed Erin. Erin nodded, and Bobby pulled out of the parking lot.

When the car stopped, Jess looked out the window to see where they were. "What are we doing here?"

"You know why we're here," replied Bobby.

"Forget it, Bobby. I just want to go back to the hotel."

At Jess' irritated tone, Erin turned slightly to look at her.

Bobby turned around to look at Jess. "I didn't say anything about want. This about need, Jessica, and you damn well know it," he snapped, not giving an inch.

Jess glared at him. "I don't—"

"I know."

When she didn't reply, he opened the door and exited the car.

Erin frowned but stayed silent. Jess knew that it was over as soon as Erin had seen her at the bar. Erin had seen something Toni never had. She'd seen her other half. She closed her eyes and mourned what was not to be.

Bobby returned to the car after only a few short minutes. He lightly tossed a small, white paper bag to Jess in the back seat. They exchanged a look before he turned back. "Now we can go to the hotel."

At the hotel, Bobby helped Jess up to her room. Erin watched silently as Jess stiffly walked into the bathroom with the paper bag in her hand and closed the door. She was clearly in pain. When Jess exited the bathroom a minute or so later, she threw the paper bag at Bobby. He caught it and, with a nod, left without a word.

Jess began to unbutton her shirt with her right hand. She carefully shrugged it off, exposing her bound left arm and ribs. She then undid her jeans and managed to push them down and off. She didn't bother with pajamas as she moved to the bed. The visible damage, the bruising, on Jess' body transfixed Erin, evidence of the brutality she'd withstood. Erin was startled a little at the sound of her partner's voice.

"If you don't mind, turn off the light on your way out, please. I'll be sleeping in late." Jess was lying under the sheet, her eyes already closed.

Silently, Erin turned off the light and retreated through the connecting door to her room, locking it behind herself.

She didn't know what to think about what had happened, what she'd seen. She didn't know what to think about Jess or how she acted. Who and what was Jess? What exactly did Erin see? How could Jess' eyes change from gray to black? How could she have fangs? How could what Erin saw be real? Jess had been upset in the car, but Erin didn't know what to say. She didn't know how to break the silence. A distance was between them now, a gulf.

Erin tossed and turned the rest of the night, sleeping poorly and having disturbing dreams. She dreamt of eyes black as night and sharp fangs...and blood. She dreamt of monsters and being caught in quicksand, unable to escape. She dreamt of eyes sparkling gray and full of warmth and understanding. She dreamt of happiness and passionate lovemaking.

March 11, 2025

Tuesday

Since it had been after three o'clock in the morning by the time they'd finished at the hospital and returned to the hotel, it was a little after ten o'clock when Erin woke. She awoke to find herself clutching the second pillow and wondering why it wasn't Jess she was holding.

Jess. Everything from the night before, including the dreams, came flooding into her mind. She didn't know what she had seen meant, but she knew she had to find out.

Erin got up, showered, and dressed. Having braced herself for the coming conversation, she unlocked the adjoining door and padded into her partner's room. She was not prepared for what awaited her.

Nothing.

Jess was gone, as was her luggage. Erin was livid. "Fuck!" She whirled around to leave the room, but something caught her eye. A folded, white piece of paper was taped to the door adjoining their rooms. It had her name on it. She took it down and opened it. It was in Jess' handwriting.

> Erin,
> I've cleared it with the director—you do not need
> to continue this case with me or stay on the
> taskforce. You're free to do as you please and
> have your choice of assignments in any division,
> at any location you want. Good luck with whatever
> you choose.
> With my highest regards,
> SSA Jessica Morgan

Erin stalked back into her room, the note crumpled in her fist. She was so angry that she was having trouble thinking clearly. She closed her eyes and counted to ten, trying to calm herself. She pulled out her cell phone and called Jess. Not surprisingly, Erin got her voicemail. She was too angry to leave a message. Erin went to her nightstand and picked up the business card Det. Bobby Marinelli had given her. She dialed his number.

"Marinelli." He sounded half asleep.

"Det. Marinelli, it's Agent Little. I need to speak with you."

"Umm...all right." He gave her directions to his place.

Erin knocked on the detective's door. The door opened and she stepped into a rather dark apartment. Blinds and heavy drapery covered all the windows. The only light in the living room came from a floor lamp beside the couch.

"Come on in, Agent Little."

"Thank you. I appreciate you meeting with me."

"Would you like something to drink? Coffee?"

"Coffee would be great."

"Come on into the kitchen." Bobby led Erin into the kitchen and started a pot of coffee as she sat at the kitchen table. He sat down across from her. "Now, what can I do for you?"

"How long have you known Agent Morgan?"

"Let's see, the Stevenson case was in 2017, so about eight years." He gave her a hard look. "Is something wrong?"

"I'm trying to figure out what's going on, what's happened." She took a breath and let it out. "What was all that about in the car between you and Jess? What was in that paper bag?"

"I think that's something you should ask her. It's not my place to tell you."

"I would, except she's gone," Erin snapped.

Bobby sighed. "I didn't expect that, but it's still not my place to tell you."

"What *can* you tell me?"

"I can tell you that Jessica is the best damn cop I've ever seen, even if she is Fed. She has great instincts and cares about the job, the cases, the victims. I'd work with her anytime, anywhere. She saved my life back in 2017." He got up and poured two cups of the freshly made coffee. He set a cup down in front of Erin before retaking his seat. "Jessica is as good a person as they come. I was pleased she called me for help. Although, in the end, I didn't turn out to be much help," he said regretfully. He lightly touched a hand to the back of his head. "I got blindsided."

"It can happen to anyone."

"You said Jessica was gone. Did she indicate where she went?"

"No. She was gone when I got up. She just left me a note saying I didn't need to continue to work with her, that I was free to do whatever I wanted."

"And what if what you want is to continue to work with her?" He paused for a couple of beats. "Or do you?"

Erin looked down into her cup of coffee, feeling a little ashamed. "I don't know," she said softly. "I need to know what's going on before I can determine that."

"Then you need to talk to Jessica."

"Yeah. But she left."

Bobby let out a snort. "Well, I can tell you she did *not* walk out on the case. And I don't imagine it would be all that hard for you as an FBI agent to find her."

After a few seconds of silence, Erin put her cup on the table and thanked Bobby for his time. She then left.

Bobby poured the remnants of the coffee down the drain. He opened the refrigerator, pulled out a container of blood, and put it in the microwave to warm it up. "What in the hell are you up to, Jessica?" After the microwave dinged, he took out the blood and started to drink it. It would be hours before the sun set and it was safe for him to go out, but he could make a call. He dialed Jessica's number.

"Hello, Bobby. Isn't it a bit sunny for a creature of the night like you?" she quipped.

"Up yours, half-breed. What the hell did you do, Jessica?"

"What do you mean?"

"I mean, you disappeared without telling your partner where you were going."

"I told you: she saw me, Bobby."

"So?"

"So it was best for me to continue working the case without her. I gave her a glowing and well-deserved review and ensured she has her pick of assignments."

"What if she still wants to work with you?"

"I highly doubt that."

"Why?"

"Because most people don't take it too well when someone they've gotten involved with has deceived them. And I can tell you that Erin is not a woman who takes kindly to being lied to or misled."

"Involved wi—Damn, Jessica."

"Yeah, well..."

"Where are you now?"

"Why?" she asked suspiciously.

"Keep your knickers on. Erin was just here asking questions about you." Jess sighed. "What did you tell her?"

"Well, I didn't tell her you're a half-breed. But you need to sit down and talk to the woman. You owe her that, Jessica."

Chapter Twenty-Three

AFTER JESS HAD HEARD Erin lock the door between their rooms, she'd made a decision. She knew she couldn't bear the rejection. She had opened up to someone for the first time in years, but she'd ruined it. It wasn't Erin's fault. Jess was the one who had deceived her, the one who hadn't told Erin about herself.

But then, how does one go about telling someone her kind of secret? Not even her parents had known. Only her grandfather knew. He was the one who explained to her what was going on when she realized she was different from everyone else. He was the one who explained to her what she was, who she was, and what she needed to do.

Her family gave her privilege, her heritage gave her power, and her grandfather taught her the responsibilities required of her. One of those responsibilities was not to inflict herself upon an innocent person. Actions had consequences. She'd set the alarm to wake her up at six o'clock so she could make some phone calls and travel arrangements.

When Jess had gotten up, she'd felt better physically, but she really should have had more time to recover. Her ribs were no longer broken, but they were still sore. At least her shoulder only had a twinge, and only faint bruising remained on her face. She would be good as new with another pint of blood and some more sleep.

After making her phone calls and travel arrangements for the day, she went to the local precinct to interview the "brains" of the previous night's escapades. His name was Bill Simon. Simon was little more than a low-level criminal. Her interrogation of the man produced only the confession that he'd been hired by phone to "teach some uppity bitch" a lesson. He'd received a picture of her and three thousand dollars in an envelope delivered to his mailbox with no postage. For a mere five hundred dollars, he hired the Hulk, Jerry Brunson, to do the actual beating because he didn't like to get his hands dirty and Brunson enjoyed beating women.

Not expecting to get anything more from him, Jess turned over the follow-up to the locals. She then caught the ten o'clock flight back down to Miami. Since she was on her own dime, she'd made a reservation at the Faena Luxury Hotel.

A discreet symbol on the concierge desk (visible only to those of a particular breed) let her know that she wouldn't have to leave the hotel to obtain the pint of blood she required. She placed her order and retired to her room. Not ten minutes after she arrived in her room, there was a knock on the door. She took delivery of her order. Even though it wasn't even one o'clock in the afternoon, she drank the warm, thick liquid and then went to bed.

Jess got up at six o'clock, feeling pretty good. She changed into some shorts and a tank top and went for a run. She showered and changed at the hotel at half past seven, went to dinner, and drove up to Ft. Lauderdale.

Jess was on downtime for a couple of days because of what had happened. She hadn't told the director just how badly she'd been hurt since she knew she'd be fully recovered in a short time. What was unusual for her, though, was going out for the evening just to be herself and relax. She had liked the Black Diamond wine bar when she and Erin went there during the investigation. So on this Tuesday night, she headed to the Black Diamond.

Daphne, the doorwoman, recognized Jess. "Good evening, Agent Morgan."

Jess smiled. "Good evening, Daphne. And tonight, it's just Jess."

"Any luck with finding Beth's killer?"

"I can't discuss the case, but don't worry, we'll get him."

Daphne nodded. She waved Jess' money away when she tried to pay the cover charge. "I told you, no charge for you."

"I'm not working tonight, Daphne."

"Just go in. Kate wouldn't want me to charge you."

"How is Kate?"

Daphne sighed. "Hurting. But she's a strong woman. She'll be okay."

"She's not in, is she?"

"No. Although she would have been if we hadn't all threatened to walk out on her if she did."

Jess nodded. "She'll need some time to mourn, but she'll also need to keep busy. Don't be too hard on her if she needs to work."

The older woman recognized the sound of experience of in Jess' voice. "Don't worry. We'll take good care of Kate. Have a nice evening, Jess."

"Thank you, Daphne."

Jess entered the bar. There was a different bartender on duty, and only eight customers were present. She went to the bar, ordered a glass of wine, and sat in one of the leather armchairs.

After a couple of glasses of wine, Jess wandered to the bar's back corner to the baby grand piano. While at Oxford, she worked part-time at a quiet little pub called The Squire where she played the piano. It had been a much more innocent time in her life. It had been a long time since Jess sat down to play the piano because no matter how she tried, her emotions always came out in the music. If she was angry, so was the music; if she was happy, so was the music; if she was melancholy, so was the music. She placed her fingers on the keys, caressing them, but not yet applying any pressure.

"Go on."

Jess looked up at the softly spoken words.

"Go on and play something," Daphne gently encouraged her.

"Taking a break?"

"No. I was just filling in for Barb, who was running late. I'm not working tonight." Daphne sat on one of the stools placed around the piano. "Play something," she said with a smile.

Jess let out a slow breath, caressed the keys momentarily, and started playing. Her eyes drifted shut as the melancholy notes mingled, formed a coherent union, and wrapped themselves around her. Jess wasn't sure how long the music had carried her, but when she opened her eyes again, five or six other women were also sitting on the stools around the piano. She felt her face color and dropped her gaze as she let her hands fall away from the ivory.

"No, don't stop."

"That was beautiful!"

"Please, play some more."

"Yeah."

"Play some more."

Jess looked at Daphne, who was smiling.

"I think you'd better play some more before they get rowdy," Daphne said with a smirk.

Jess played the baby grand piano for over two hours. The women commented on the beauty of the music, though not the melancholy woven within it. Finally, she took a break. She grabbed the latest glass of wine that had been purchased for her and moved back to one of the leather armchairs. Daphne sat in its companion, sipping mineral water.

"You play beautifully, Jess. But I have to ask: Why so blue?"

Jess sighed. "Just things catching up with me, I guess."

"Things?"

Jess had had enough wine to loosen her tongue more than usual. "I'm tired of investigating the murders of young women; tired of crawling around in the minds of the sick and evil bastards that rape, murder, and molest; tired of trying to catch monsters after they've wreaked havoc in the lives of innocents..." she trailed off. "Tired of being afraid and alone...and not being happy," she said softly.

Daphne placed her hand on Jess' forearm and squeezed it. "I can't imagine a beautiful woman like you ever having to be alone...if she didn't want to be."

"I don't want to be, not anymore." She took another sip of wine. "I miss her," she said, thinking of Toni and Erin.

"What happened?"

Jess' mind played out the scene of Toni's murder and Erin locking the door. Right at that precise moment, she wasn't sure which hurt more. She let out a sigh. "Bad things happened."

Daphne didn't press Jess for more details, but she did keep her company throughout the evening.

Around two o'clock, Jess decided it was time to go. She had long since surrendered the keys to her rental car. She turned to Daphne. "Time to call a cab."

Daphne smirked. "Where are you staying?"

"The Faena Hotel in Miami Beach."

Daphne stood up and offered a hand to Jess. "Come on. I'll drive you." She helped Jess up, who wavered just slightly. The bartender tossed Jess' keys to Daphne when she asked for them. Daphne got Jess into the passenger's seat of the car and then got behind the wheel.

"How old are you, Jess?"

Jess, gazing out the window, missed the question. "What?"

"I asked how old you are."

"Ah. Just turned thirty-three a couple of weeks ago."

"Regardless of what's happened in your life, you're still young enough to set yourself on the path you want to follow."

Jess frowned. "You sound as if you think you're too old to do that for yourself."

Daphne chuckled. "It gets a little hard when you're in your fifties."

"Fifties? I'd have thought forty, forty-two tops."

"Thank you. And I'm not complaining about my life. I don't have many regrets."

When they arrived at the Faena, Daphne insisted on seeing Jess up to her room.

"I'm not that drunk, you know," said Jess.

"I know," Daphne replied with a smile. "Besides, I wouldn't mind a look at Miami's most luxurious 5-star hotel. I hear it's pretty posh."

"The suite I have is nice. It has a soaking tub and a separate marble shower," Jess said as they walked inside.

"Suite? And the feds pay to put you up in a place like this?"

"No. I'm here on my own dime."

When they neared the door to Jess' suite, she heard something from inside. She froze instantly and tried to concentrate through the effects of the wine. "Daphne," she said softly, "Move to the side of the door and don't make a sound." Jess reached down and retrieved her backup weapon from her boot.

Daphne's eyes got large. "What's going on?" she whispered.

"I don't know yet. But stay put." Jess cringed at the snick of the electronic lock releasing. As quietly as possible, she slipped into the dark interior, her eyes shifting so she could see.

"We need to talk."

Jess spun around and aimed her weapon at the source of the voice. She quickly pulled up though. "Bloody *hell*, Erin! I could have shot you!"

Erin turned on the lamp on the table next to the end of the couch she was sitting on. "Nice room."

"It's okay, Daphne," Jess called out. "Come on in."

The older woman peeked around the door and then entered. "Is everything all right?"

"Yeah." Jess replaced her weapon in the holster inside her boot. "Everything's fine. Daphne, you remember Agent Little? Agent Little, this Daphne Grayson, from the Black Diamond."

"I remember."

"Hi."

"Well, I'll be on my way, Jess. You have my number if you need anything while you're in town."

"Wait." Jess walked out into the hallway with Daphne. She insisted on giving the woman money for the long Uber ride back to Ft. Lauderdale. "It's the least I can do, Daphne. Thank you for everything tonight."

"It was my pleasure, Jess."

Erin had been surprised to see Daphne, the doorwoman, enter Jess' suite. But then a lot of things surprised her, especially where Jess was concerned. She could hear them speaking quietly outside the suite in the hallway but couldn't hear what they were saying. Finally, Jess came back in.

"We need to talk, Jess."

"Perhaps. But not tonight." She cut Erin off before she could say anything. "Because I've either had too much to drink or not nearly enough to do this tonight." She closed her eyes. Jess took the keycard from her back pocket and dropped it on the desk. "You're welcome to the room. I'll see you in the morning." With that, she turned for the door.

"Jess, wait!" Erin got up and moved a couple of steps toward her.

Jess looked over her shoulder. "What?" she replied a little snappishly.

Erin wasn't sure what to say. When she didn't speak, Jess continued to the door. "I need...I need to know what's going on, Jess. I saw...what I saw..." She trailed off, at a loss.

Jess turned around and looked at her. "What you saw was *this*!" Her eyes transformed into fathomless obsidian, her teeth elongated into fangs, and an aura of power radiated from her. Jess stepped toward her and stopped when Erin took an instinctive step backward, away from her. Jess shook her head. "I'll see you tomorrow." With that, Jess turned and walked out of the suite.

Erin stood, without moving, for a full minute after Jess' exit. She couldn't believe the transformation that had taken place right before her eyes. She saw it. She watched it happen. But, ever the scientist, her mind struggled to find a rational explanation. Even transformed, Erin couldn't miss the hurt in her partner's eyes when she took an involuntary step back from her. Or the melancholy that settled around Jess like a cloak as she turned and left. And that hurt.

Finally, Erin went into the bedroom. She retrieved a t-shirt from Jess' suitcase, bringing it to her face and inhaling her scent. She stripped, put on the t-shirt, and crawled into bed.

When Erin had finished talking with Det. Bobby Marinelli, she'd returned to the hotel and placed some phone calls to find out where Jess had gone.

She'd called headquarters and spoken to AD Taylor and then the director. Director Cavanaugh congratulated her on the glowing review she'd received from Jess. He then asked her what assignment she wanted. When she expressed her desire to stay on the taskforce, he expressed his concern over the threat against her life. Erin reassured him she didn't want to leave the case, and he finally agreed. However, since he wasn't aware of any issues between the two agents, he didn't tell Erin where Jess was, and she felt it was best not to ask him.

Erin ended up calling her old partner and asking for a favor. She hadn't talked to Special Agent George Sheffield in a long time. She'd saved his ass, which was why he was now working in personnel and close to retirement, rather than six feet under.

"Sheffield."

"Hey, George. It's me."

"Long time no talk, Tiny."

She rolled her eyes. "It has been a while. How's the family?"

He let out a snort. "The wife left me last year, and the kids haven't spoken to me since, even though they're sending me to the poor house with college tuition."

"Sorry to hear that. Listen, George, I need a favor."

"See? That's the problem with all you women. You always want something."

"You owe me, George."

"Yeah, yeah. I know. What can I do for you?"

"I need to pull a file on an agent, and I need you to keep it between you and me."

"What are you up to, Tiny?"

"Nothing nefarious. Just trying to get to know my new partner a little better."

He just made a grunt that vaguely sounded like "Name?"

"Her name is SSA Jessica Morgan."

"Okay, I got it: Jessica Renee Morgan. What do you need to know?"

"She's got a Bureau credit card. What activity has there been on it in the last twenty-four hours?"

"There hasn't been any."

"Damn," she muttered lowly. "Then pull a credit report and check her personal credit cards."

"Now wait a minute, Tiny. What are you getting into here? Do you have any idea who this Morgan works for? I'm looking at her file, and the name on her reviews for the last few years is Cavanaugh, as in Director Louis Cavanaugh!"

"I'm aware. Just do it, George."

"All right," he said with a sigh. "Okay, no activity on her personal cards either. But hold on. Another file is linked to Morgan's."

"What do you mean?"

"I'm not sure. I've never seen this before. It's buried in her personal info, but there's a link to another file. The link brings up a file under the name of Lady Essington. Let's see. It's not really a file, just a name and a few miscellaneous pieces of information. There is an active credit card account though. It was used to book a room at the Faena in Miami Beach tonight."

"Okay. Thanks."

"Stay out of trouble, Tiny."

"You too, George."

━━▶

And now, she was lying in bed in Jess' room, unable to sleep and still unsure what was happening. She saw Jess change right before her eyes. But her rational, scientific mind was having trouble wrapping itself around the obvious explanation. She didn't believe in the existence of vampires. But what other explanation was there for what she'd seen?

She rolled over again, pounding her pillow in a vain attempt to relax enough to sleep.

Chapter Twenty-Four

March 12, 2025
Wednesday

WHEN JESS WOKE UP in the morning, she wasn't looking forward to the day. Erin's presence in her hotel room threw her, primarily since she'd used the Essington account to pay for it. Very few people knew about her familial ties. But Erin was an excellent investigator, and she really shouldn't put anything past the woman. She rubbed her hands over her face and shook her head.

Jess realized that she didn't have a change of clothes. Her bag was in the suite she'd left Erin in. She didn't want to walk through the hotel hallways in just one of the provided robes, so she put on her clothes from the night before.

Time to face the music.

When Erin heard the knock on the door, she looked through the peephole. Tugging on the bottom of the t-shirt in an effort to cover herself more effectively, she turned the doorknob. As soon as the door opened, she retreated to the bathroom to get one of the robes. She came back out, securing the robe around herself.

"Where's your stuff?" Jess asked.

Erin blushed. "In the car."

Jess picked up the phone and called down to the concierge desk. She requested they send someone up to get Erin's car keys and retrieve her luggage. In three minutes, there was a knock on the door. Erin tossed the keys to Jess, who opened the door and gave them to the bellhop.

"The car is..." Jess turned back to look at Erin.

"A dark blue Mercury Sable," she provided.

"Not a problem. I'll take care of it, Lady Essington."

"Thank you." Jess closed the door. She sighed when she turned around again. She gestured toward the bedroom. "Would you mind if I got a change of clothes so I can shower? I feel grungy in last night's clothes."

"No. Of course not."

Jess walked into the bedroom and got some stuff from her bag. When she returned to the living room and headed for the door, Erin stopped her.

"You don't have to leave, Jess. You can shower here. This is your room, after all."

Jess visibly hesitated.

"It's not like you'll use all the hot water," Erin quipped, trying to lighten the heaviness in the air between them. "Go on, Jess, take your shower."

Jess returned to the bedroom with a quiet sigh and entered the bathroom.

Erin sat down on the couch when she heard the shower start. She felt nervous, and confused, and angry. She wanted answers but didn't know what she would do with them once she got them. She went to the door when she heard a knock. Answering the door, she found the bellhop with her bags. "Wait a moment," she said as she moved to get her purse to tip him.

"No need, ma'am. Have a good day." He left, closing the door behind him.

Erin took her bags into the bedroom. She didn't notice the shower had stopped, so she was surprised when Jess came out of the bathroom, wrapped in a towel. She stood silently, unable to move. She couldn't take her eyes off Jess. Gone were any traces of the beating she'd taken. Even the gash on her left arm that she'd gotten rescuing the driver from the accident was gone. She was in perfect condition.

Erin shook her head. "Sorry," she murmured when she realized she'd been staring.

Jess simply finished dressing and retreated to the living room.

Erin took a long shower. She was putting off the coming conversation, and she knew it. She demanded that they talk but was also scared of what the result might be. Finally, she turned off the water, stepped out, and dried herself. Jess was nowhere in sight when she entered the bedroom. She quickly dressed and went out to the living room. She was afraid Jess had disappeared again, but she spotted her out on the balcony. She took only two steps toward the balcony before Jess turned around and looked at her through the open sliding glass door.

"What did you want to talk about?" Jess asked flatly.

Erin's jaw dropped. "What did I—How the hell can you even ask me that?" she snapped. "You *know* what we need to talk about!"

With a sigh, Jess came back inside. She walked over to the mini-bar and took out a cold bottle of water. She spoke after taking a drink. "I'm just not sure what you want to accomplish, Erin. I can't change what's happened or who I am."

"Well, for one, you could tell me why the hell you ditched me yesterday in Atlanta. I expected better from you! I expected some consideration from you."

"Consideration? Why the hell do you think I left? I left out of consideration for you!"

"I don't count being unceremoniously dropped from the case consideration. An impersonal note from you, and it's a done deal? I don't think so!"

"I didn't just get you dropped from the case. I got you your choice of assignment, anywhere in the damn country. I did what I thought was best for you."

"Any assignment except working on the task force to stop this killer! And who are you to decide what's best for me? Don't you think that should be up to me?"

"What the bloody hell do you want from me?"

"I want to know what the hell is going on, and I want to know what you are."

Jess turned away, flinching at the "what" in Erin's demand. She'd expected it, but it hurt more than she'd anticipated. Her eyes watered until she curbed in her feelings and erected another wall around her heart. Her face was an expressionless mask when she turned back around. "Come on, Erin. You're a smart woman. Do you really need me to spell it out for you? I'm a bona fide monster! I'm half vampire!"

"But vampires aren't real."

"*Ha*!" Jess barked bitterly. "Then I guess I don't exist!" she snapped as her features shifted.

Erin recoiled, taking a step backward.

"And *that's* why I left! You're afraid of me."

"I'm not afraid of you!"

Jess marched toward Erin, following her as she retreated until Erin's back hit the wall. Jess planted her hands on the wall, boxing Erin in. Jess glared at her before dipping her head and sniffing the side of Erin's neck then raised her head and looked into her eyes again. "Perhaps you should be. After all, I do need blood now and then," she growled. Then she forcefully shoved herself back from the wall and Erin, turning and walking away. Her features were back to normal when she turned back around. There was bitterness in her voice when she spoke. "Don't worry, I've never taken human blood, and I'm not about to start with you."

Erin flared with anger. "Then what the hell was that about?"

"Making a point. You can't help but recoil from me. Fear, revulsion, disgust—it doesn't matter why. Forcing us to work together won't do either of us any good. Being partners was only temporary anyway."

"Well, for your information, I spoke to the director—I'm still on the taskforce. I'm not a quitter."

"So you're still on the taskforce. Great. Last I heard, they were headquartered in DC. I suggest you join them."

"And what about us?"

"What about us? It was great while it lasted."

Erin felt hurt and betrayed by Jess' dismissive words. But she was more angry than anything else. So enraged that she saw red. She turned, stalked into the bedroom, grabbed her bags, and marched out of the suite, slamming the door behind her.

She drove to the airport and caught the first flight she could find back to Washington.

On the plane, Erin laid her head back, closing her eyes. She fought to hold back her tears: tears of anger, tears of frustration, and tears of a broken heart. What had she been trying to accomplish by confronting Jess? Get the woman to admit she was something other than human? Well, she'd done that. Get Jess to tell her why she ditched her? That, too, was accomplished. Determine where they stood personally? Well, she got that answer as well, didn't she? But then, what did she expect? Jess had warned her that she wasn't a good bet. But Erin had still pressed, encouraging Jess to take a chance on what she felt between them.

Erin drifted to sleep even as her thoughts of Jess continued.

Since it was still early afternoon when Erin landed at Reagan National Airport, she returned to the office. At the end of the day, she drove to the safe house. When she closed the door behind herself, it struck her just how empty the place felt. She went to her room and changed. Then, she started a load of laundry. After she finished the laundry and ate a lonely dinner for one, she decided to retire for the night.

Without thinking about it, she bypassed her bedroom and went into the bedroom Jess had used. She abruptly stopped when she realized just how empty the room was. Jess' things were gone. Someone had packed up and removed them. She pulled the covers back and lay down, pulling the covers up and clutching the second pillow to herself. She could make out the faint scent of Jess. Silent tears soaked into the pillow as she drifted to sleep.

Outside a dark sedan drove past the house and turned at the corner, parking three blocks away. A lone figure made his way back in the shadows. He watched the house from the cover of a hedge. He couldn't keep from smiling as the lights were turned off and he donned his night vision goggles.

Jess stood still, breathing heavily as Erin walked out and slammed the door. Her breaths soon turned to quiet sobs. She dropped to her knees and cried. It hurt so much. But it would have been worse and hurt so much more to have to work beside Erin and see the revulsion in her eyes.

Jess allowed herself fifteen minutes to mourn. After that, she clamped down on her feelings, erected walls around her heart, and focused on the job, just as she had done for the last six years.

"What's done is done. Back to work, Jess," she told herself out loud.

She retrieved her laptop and opened some files. Unless something new turned up in the case, she would return to Washington the next day. In the meantime, even though she was on downtime, she would immerse herself anew in the case files.

Some hours later, Jess was surprised when her hotel phone rang. She wasn't expecting any calls and certainly not on the hotel phone. "Morgan."

"Good evening, Jess. It's Daphne."

"Hey, Daphne. What's up?"

"I was wondering what your dinner plans were."

"Uh, I was just going to order something from room service."

"You're off work and you're in Miami Beach. I can think of much better places to have dinner than your hotel room. I'll pick you up in an hour."

Daphne hung up before Jess could respond, but she didn't miss the good humor in the older woman's voice. And Daphne did have a point. She'd probably benefit from a nice dinner out, knowing she'd likely not bother with dinner if she stayed in her room.

Jess was ready when Daphne arrived.

"How much longer are you going to be in Miami Beach?" Daphne asked over after-dinner drinks.

"I'm going back to DC tomorrow."

"Does that mean you're giving up on Beth's case?"

"No. Of course not." She paused. "This is the only case I'm working, but the answers aren't to be found here."

"Beth's case is related to another," she concluded thoughtfully.

"I really can't discuss it with you, Daphne, but rest assured, I'm doing everything I can to find the person who killed Beth."

Daphne nodded. "Fair enough." She took a sip of her drink. "Where's your partner, that cute little blonde?"

Only Jess' years of experience allowed her to keep her features schooled in an impassive mask. "Agent Little and I were only temporary partners. She's from another division."

Daphne smirked. "I wasn't talking about your work, *Agent Morgan*. I saw the way you two looked at each other. There's more than just work between the two of you," she finished confidently.

"I'm not sure what you think you saw, Daphne, but Agent Little and I are not together," Jess replied evenly.

It was apparent that Daphne didn't believe her.

Chapter Twenty-Five

March 13, 2025
Thursday

IT WAS ALREADY AFTER midnight when Jess got back to her hotel room. Daphne hadn't pressed her further about Erin, but she hadn't been far from Jess' thoughts all night. Once she was back in her room alone, she packed, showered, and went to bed. She was awake for a long time before finally drifting to sleep.

Jess dreamt of soft brown eyes, platinum blonde hair, soft kisses, and passionate lovemaking. And she dreamed of gunshots, blood pooling, and the ghostly pale face of Erin.

Jess came awake with a yell. "No!" She struggled for air and was covered in a cold sweat. After several gasping breaths, she looked at the clock radio on the nightstand: five o'clock. After that dream, there was no way she would get any more sleep. She placed her feet on the floor and stood up. Might as well start the day.

Jess called the airport and rearranged her flight to an earlier one. A quick shower, a change of clothes, and she was good to go.

Upon landing in Washington, DC, at ten o'clock, she drove to Headquarters. She received a few nods from the agents in the bullpen as she passed through to her office, where she found her luggage from the safe house stowed in the corner. She would worry about where she would be staying later. She picked up a couple of folders from her desk and started to read.

It was after one o'clock when a figure appeared in her office doorway. "Welcome back."

Jess looked up and saw AD Taylor as he entered. "Thanks."

"I understand your 'meeting' didn't go so well." He paused for a beat as he sat down. "Agent Little told me things got a little out of hand. You could have been really hurt, Morgan, or killed."

"It was a calculated risk, one worth taking. Besides, killing me wasn't the point. Teaching me a lesson was."

Taylor reserved his judgment on the matter. "What was the lesson?"

She shook her head. "They didn't say, but I suspect it was to demonstrate that our guy can get to anyone he wants to, whenever he wants."

"What did you find out about the men who attacked you?"

"Bill Simon was contacted by phone and hired for three thousand dollars to 'teach me a lesson.' He received payment via his mailbox, though the envelope containing the money and a picture of me wasn't sent through the mail. In turn, he hired Jerry Brunson, the dead guy, for five hundred dollars. Brunson had a penchant for and a history of beating up women. He had a record of domestic abuse and assaults. Brunson wasn't very imaginative. He was a follower."

"What about the guy in custody?"

"Simon is small time—a few cons, receiving stolen goods, and the like. Anything that made him money without getting his hands too dirty. Of the two, he was the brains of the outfit, but that's not saying much. And, unfortunately, since he had no direct contact with our guy, he's pretty much a dead end. I ordered the money he had left from the three thousand to be checked for prints and see if the serial numbers could be traced. I'm not holding my breath though."

"Do you care to tell me why I received a call from the director telling me Agent Little was off the taskforce and then another call telling me she was back on? Or why she came back before you did?"

Jess carefully measured her words and tone. "A direct, explicit threat was made against Agent Little's life. Given the circumstances, I felt it was best not to risk her further by having her continue working the case. The director agreed. I understand that Agent Little expressed a strong desire to remain on the taskforce anyway. She successfully convinced the director to allow her to do so. However, I do not see the need for her to accompany me in the field in light of the threat against her. So she returned. I was on enforced downtime and chose to take my personal time elsewhere until my return here today."

"I see." He stood up. "Well, we're getting some new blood. Six more agents have been assigned. They'll be here tomorrow. If nothing takes you out of town, I'd like you to bring them up to speed."

"All right."

Jess worked in her office until late evening. She then left and checked into a hotel, using the Essington account to prevent anyone from tracking her.

➤━

March 14, 2025
Friday

When Jess arrived, Erin was sitting at a desk and talking on the phone. Jess entered her office and closed the door. After a few minutes, Jess reappeared, only to head into Taylor's office.

Erin felt her stomach tighten and her breath catch a little when Jess arrived that morning. She hadn't seen Jess since she'd left her in Miami Beach two days earlier. However, she had dreamt of her extensively. She had spent time trying to reconcile her feelings about the beautiful woman.

As a scientist, Erin had always been driven to find answers and explanations, so she had been trying to come to terms with the reality of what Jess was, something she had no reference for, other than supernatural fiction books and movies. She had so many questions and needed answers.

She had allowed Jess to get close to her. Erin hadn't opened her heart in longer than she cared to remember. Because she had opened her heart and taken such a risk on a personal level, her need for answers was intensified. She needed to talk to Jess again.

Erin couldn't take her eyes off Jess when she exited Taylor's office and headed to the elevators.

Jess' desk phone rang. It was Taylor, who asked her to come to his office. Once there, they discussed the imminent arrival of the six new agents. When the call came that the new agents had arrived, she headed to the elevators and went down to escort them up to the taskforce bullpen.

Once she brought the new arrivals up, she gathered them in a corner of the bullpen and brought the group up to speed with the visual aid of the whiteboards containing the photographs and facts of the victims. Most agents that were already part of the task force joined the group of new agents to listen to Jess' briefing. She covered everything that had happened in the case, including her encounter at Doc's Saloon in Atlanta. Jess then took some questions, answering them to the best of her ability.

"Each of you were added to the taskforce because of your individual abilities. I *want* to hear your ideas, thoughts, and theories. You are the ones with fresh eyes. If you have questions or ideas, my door is open, and if I'm not available, Assistant Director Taylor is." With a nod, Jess dismissed the assembled group. She turned and started toward her office.

"Agent Morgan."

She turned back to the sandy-haired agent who called her name. "In my office." Once they both entered her office, she closed the door and turned to him. A smile lit up her face. "God, it's good to see you, John."

They hugged and held each other closely.

"It's been a long time, Jessica. Too long."

They let go and kissed before fully parting and sitting in the chairs at the worktable.

"So how long have you been back with the Bureau?" John Casper asked.

"About three years."

His green eyes widened.

"I'm sorry I haven't been in touch with you, John." She paused for half a beat. "I haven't been in touch with anyone from back then. And I'm never in one place too long since I work on a case-by-case basis for the director."

"Where did you go, Jessica? It was like you dropped off the face of the earth after we arrested Conrad."

She let out a sigh. "I went back to England, stayed at my grandfather's place, and basically had an emotional meltdown," she said with a rueful half-smile. "Finally, with the help of an old friend, I got off my ass and decided to go to medical school."

"Really? So you're a doctor now?"

"I've never practiced. Before graduation, Lou came to me and asked me to come back to the Bureau. It took some serious negotiating, but I eventually agreed. So instead of taking a residency, I came back to the Bureau. Been hopping all over the country ever since." She got up and retrieved a couple of bottles of cold water from the small refrigerator. "What about you, John? How are Jennie and Jeremy?" she asked as she retook her seat and handed him one of the bottles.

"Uh, Jennie and I divorced."

"Oh, John, I didn't know. I'm sorry."

John shrugged. "You know things were rocky between us for a long time. She had a hard time dealing with the job." His green eyes twinkled when he smiled. "I've got Jeremy's latest school picture." He pulled out his wallet and handed it to her.

"My god! He's gotten so big!"

"Well, he was only five years old the last time you saw him. He's eleven now."

"He looks like he's fourteen."

"And he's as tall as a fourteen-year-old. He keeps growing the way he has been, and he'll be taller than me in no time."

Jess shook her head. "I remember holding him the day he was born." She smiled at her good friend and former partner. "I also remember the look on your face when you finally got to the hospital and walked into Jennie's room. It's the first time I saw you cry. The only other time was when Toni was killed."

"You know I loved Toni, Jessica. You two were family. I've really missed you."

She nodded. "I've missed you too. Where have you been keeping yourself?"

"San Diego. I took a post working narcotics after you left. And I was supposed to report to the Cyber Crime Division in Norfolk today, but I was tapped for this taskforce. They said I wouldn't start with Cyber until after this case was solved. I heard some other new agents mention similar stories this morning."

A knock on her door interrupted them. She got up and answered it. One of the mailroom interns stood there with a bouquet in a vase.

"This arrived for you, Agent Morgan. Security cleared it."

Jess carefully took the vase to avoid leaving undue fingerprints on it. "Thank you." The intern left as Jess set the flowers on her desk.

John Casper smiled. "So whose heart have you captured and has sent you flowers?"

She frowned. "I don't know." But she had a suspicion. She pulled out some gloves and put them on before removing the attached envelope. She carefully lifted the flap of the envelope and removed the card within.

> Roses are red, violets are blue.
> I enjoyed Atlanta. How about you?

With a scowl, Jessica dropped the envelope and note into an evidence bag. She approached the doorway and called for AD Taylor, who was talking to an agent in the bullpen. He walked into her office.

Jessica showed him the note. "He's toying with us again. This just arrived with these flowers," she said with a nod at the vase on her desk. "I highly doubt he wrote the note—the handwriting is feminine. But we may be able to trace something through the florist." She wrote down the florist information from the card stock and handed it to Taylor. "I'll take the note and flowers down to the lab so they can check for fingerprints."

"All right."

Taylor and John followed her out of the office.

"Barker, Little, check this out," Taylor instructed as he handed the information to Little.

"Yes, sir." Little frowned, her eyes following Jessica as she carried the vase of flowers and evidence bag in gloved hands to the elevators.

Taylor turned to John. "I understand you used to be partners with Morgan."

"Almost six years."

The assistant director nodded. "Then you won't mind keeping an eye on her. This son of a bitch has made things personal with her. Since there seems to be some friction between her and Little, you're her backup, Casper."

"Yes, sir." John clenched his jaw in consternation. He'd been there the last time a suspect made things personal with Jessica. It had nearly destroyed her. And despite not hearing from her in the previous six years, he still cared about her just as much as ever.

John was waiting for Jess when she returned to her office. She opened a file and pulled out pictures of the messages written in blood on her wall and Erin's wall. She also set a photocopy of the note from the flowers on the table. "What do you think about this guy, John? Because I've been struggling with the profile."

John took his time looking over the notes. "Let me see your profile."

She gave him a printout of her original profile and the revised profile after the notes and phone calls started.

John carefully read the profiles. "He's changed the rules of the game. But I don't know why the sudden taunting. You're right. It doesn't fit with your original profile. Of course that may be the very reason for it: an effort to throw you off your game." He paused. "What kind of flowers did he send you?"

"According to one of the lab techs, they were rhododendrons."

John went to the computer on Jess' desk and did a quick online search. He turned back to her. "The symbolization of rhododendrons is 'beware' or 'caution.'"

Jess let out a snort. "Like hiring a couple of guys to beat me up and teach me a lesson isn't enough of a warning?"

The two agents spent the day discussing and dissecting the case. Jess enjoyed the easy give and take she and her old partner had. John Casper was a great agent, and she loved him like a big brother. He had been her partner, dearest friend, and staunchest ally when they were both in the Behavior Analysis Unit.

But the truth was, she missed Erin. However, she couldn't dwell on what she couldn't have.

Jess and John finally decided to call it a day. He was going to check into his hotel, and then they would meet for dinner. She opened the door, and they both stepped out of the office.

"Thanks for your help, John."

"My pleasure. I'll see you later, Jessica."

They shared an easy smile, then he turned and left. Jess turned to reenter her office.

Chapter Twenty-Six

ERIN AND AGENT BARKER tracked down the florist shop that had delivered the flowers to Jess. They spoke to the owner and verified someone had paid cash when placing the order in person. They went to the shop to obtain the security camera videotape. Back in the bullpen, they reviewed the tape. The person who'd placed the order was just a teenager, probably not even out of high school yet, clearly not The Slasher himself.

On a hunch, Erin called the tech department to see if any more calls had been placed by the phone number they were interested in. Alan Stillwell verified there hadn't been any more activity since the call from Atlanta several days earlier.

She sat at the desk and stared at the closed door of Jess' office. One new addition to the taskforce had been in there all day with Jess. And, quite frankly, it hurt that she wasn't the one with Jess. Being closed out by Jess hurt more than she could have imagined.

If they were going to talk about things again, apparently, it would be up to Erin to initiate the discussion. She had done a lot of thinking since leaving Miami Beach. Just as the thought of remaining an agent at the DC field office, and consequently Holton's partner, had become overwhelmingly unbearable, so had the idea of not clearing the air with Jess.

Erin decided to confront a problem head-on. She stood and approached Jess. "Jess."

Jess looked over her shoulder.

"Would you have dinner with me?"

"I already have plans," she replied and retreated into her office, closing the door.

Erin was angry at Jess' dismissive attitude. So much for it being easy. She silently counted to ten, took a deep breath, and pushed open Jess' office door without knocking. She quickly closed it behind herself and spoke before Jess could react to her intrusion. "Look, I get that you don't want to work with me, but I'll be damned if I'll let you simply dismiss me as if nothing ever happened between us. I thought we were friends, Jess," she said accusatorily.

Jess took a couple of moments before she responded. Her voice was even and modulated when she spoke. "I'm not dismissing you. I *do* have plans tonight. I'm meeting John for dinner. It's been six years since I've seen him. We have a lot to catch up on."

"John Casper? Your old partner?"

"Yes. I may be a number of things, but I'm not a liar." She stood and picked up her briefcase and coat. "Now, I have to go and meet John. I'll see you tomorrow." She left.

Alone in the elevator, Jess punched the wall. Seeing Erin every day was going to be hell.

Jess drove on automatic pilot to a restaurant that she and John used to frequent. They spent a pleasant night talking and filling each other in about the last six years. Jess' phone chirped. She had a text message.

> Have him in my sights. If u
> let on its me ill kill him

Jess kept her face impassive.

"What is it, Jessica? Something about the case?"

"Uh, no. Just a friend," she replied, looking around. Another chirp.

> Don't look4 me. Excuse
> yourself so we can talk

Jess looked up at her companion. "John, could you excuse me, please? I need to make a personal phone call."

"Sure."

Jess got up from the table, and her phone rang as soon as she stepped into the hallway leading to the bathrooms. "What do you want?" she growled.

"Did you like the flowers?"

"I repeat, *what* do you want?"

"I see you aren't too much worse for wear after Atlanta."

"You didn't hire very competent people. One is dead, and the other is in custody. I would have expected better from you. I would think someone like you could find someone capable of carrying out simple orders."

"Don't test me!"

"Or what? You'll have someone try to beat me up again?"

"Or I could take out your dinner companion right now!"

"You aren't that stupid."

"Perhaps you're right. I could always pay a visit to the lovely Agent Little. After all, she must be lonely in the house all by herself."

"What house?" she asked, dread filling her.

"Even you aren't that stupid. I'm talking about the house at 703 Tribeca Ave. The house Agent Little is in. The house I can see right now. She looks quite lovely in her blue silk pajamas."

"You s—" She was cut off when he hung up on her. Jess slammed her hand against the wall and marched back into the dining room. "John, we have to go. Now."

John's expression let her know he recognized her tone of voice and didn't question her. Jess wanted to drive since she knew where the house was, so they rushed to her car.

"Call Taylor and tell him we may have a problem. Have him contact Agent Little and the agents watching the safe house. Tell them our UNSUB might be there."

As Jess sped through the streets of DC, John called AD Taylor. They were almost at the house when his phone rang. He wasn't on the phone for long.

"Taylor says all he gets is Erin's voicemail."

"What about the agents watching the house?"

"No answer from any of them. He said backup is on the way."

"Fuck! We're almost there."

Jess brought the car to a stop a block from the house. She saw the first vehicle that contained an agent on watch. Jess and John got out of the car with their weapons already drawn. She was the first to reach the vehicle. One look told her the agent was down. She opened the door and checked his pulse.

He was alive but unconscious.

"He's out cold."

"Where are the others?" John asked.

"Another car, closer to the house. Then there are two agents in the house behind the safe house."

"Check the other car. I'll check on the others."

With a nod, they split to their individual tasks. Jess quickly moved through the shadows and found the second car. That agent, too, was unconscious. All her senses were on high alert, but she didn't see or hear anything suspicious.

She knew she had to get to Erin to ensure she was all right. Jess stealthily made her way to the house. She felt exposed on the porch at the front door, so she decided on the best way to limit her time there. She gripped the doorknob and, using her strength, forced it to turn despite being locked. She cringed at the noise but quickly slipped inside.

Jess left the foyer and entered the well-lit living room. Erin was sitting on the couch, laptop on her lap, head laid back: asleep, unconscious, or dead. She silently moved to the couch and was relieved to note the blonde was breathing.

"Erin," she prompted softly. She reached out and placed a gentle hand on Erin's shoulder. "Erin."

"What?" Erin exclaimed as she abruptly awoke.

"Are you all right?"

"What are you doing here?"

"Taylor couldn't get a hold of you. You didn't answer your cell."

"My battery died. It's charging. And I was online," she replied, powering down her computer.

Jess' head snapped up when she heard something at the back door. "Stay here, and stay away from the windows," she ordered as she crept further into the house and to the back door. John was the only thing she saw. She unlocked the door and let him in.

"Both agents in the house are unconscious, but their pulses are strong. I called Taylor and told him to send a couple of ambulances to check them out," he reported as they returned to the living room. "How's Agent Little?"

"She was asleep on the couch."

"What the hell is going on?" Erin demanded when Jess returned with John.

"I received a call," Jess replied as she moved to a window and carefully peeked out.

Before Erin could ask more questions, John spoke. "The agents in the house in the back and the two out front in the cars are all unconscious."

"What?"

Jess turned to look at Erin and moved from the window. "I received a text message and then a call while John and I were talking after dinner. First, he led me to believe he was at our location. But then he clarified that he knew where the safe house was and that you were here alone." She looked pointedly at Erin's blue pajamas. "He complimented you on your attire. We called Taylor, and he said he couldn't reach you or the agents on watch—"

Something she saw cut Jess off: a targeting laser moving along the wall toward Erin. "Look out!" She threw herself at Erin, knocking her down as the window broke and the impacts of silenced rounds hit various items in the room.

John was the first to move afterward. "Stay here! I'll check it out."

"John. He's using a targeting laser," Jess shouted as a warning as he headed out the back of the house in an attempt to circle around the shooter.

Erin started to get up, but Jess forcibly held her in place. "Stay down," she growled.

"Damn it, Jess, let me up."

"No. Not until it's clear."

Sirens were soon heard, and police cars with flashing lights skidded to a halt in front of the house. Unmarked FBI cars were right behind them. Jess still wouldn't let Erin move until AD Taylor entered through the front door. "Morgan! Casper!"

"In here," responded Jess.

Taylor stepped into the living room. "Where's Agent Little?"

Jess let Erin up from where she was on the floor behind the sofa.

"Here, sir."

"Are you all right?"

"Yes. I'm fine."

"Where's Agent Casper?"

Jess answered, "He went after the shooter." She continued before he said anything more. "The agents out front are unconscious. And from the sweet odor, I'd say he used chloroform on them. John checked on the ones in the house. They're also unconscious, but I don't know how they were knocked out."

More sirens could be heard, and AD Taylor looked outside. "The ambulances are here now. They can check the agents out." He pinned Erin with a look that said she had no choice. "Go pack. You're being moved."

Clearly, she didn't like it, but under the circumstances...Erin retreated to her bedroom to pack.

John returned and entered through the front door. "Sorry, Jessica, I didn't find him."

She shook her head. "I don't think anyone could have. He put planning into this. His phone call to me, chloroform for the agents out front, whatever he used on the agents in the back, silencer for his weapon, laser sight. It's all part of his plan."

"Well, thank god he missed," John replied.

Jess frowned. "That may have been part of the plan as well."

"What do you mean?" Taylor asked.

"He could have taken Erin out while she was asleep on the couch. He'd already taken care of the guards. But he texted me and called me. He told us where he was and that Erin was vulnerable. He gave us the time to get here."

"Then maybe he was actually after you instead of me," Erin remarked as she returned to the living room with packed bags.

Jess sighed. "A possibility, but I doubt it. He's had more than ample opportunity to kill me. Even when he hired a couple of thugs to beat me up, it was to deliver a message, not to kill me. He also used the threat of killing John to control my actions at the restaurant. No, I don't think he wants to kill me. But hurt me? By hurting someone I care about? Yeah, that I do believe is part of the game."

Her old partner gave her a concerned look. "He knows your buttons and is pushing them, Jessica."

She shot him a perturbed look that made it clear he wasn't telling her anything she didn't already know.

"Well, either way, we need to get you two out of here." Taylor looked at John. "Actually, I'd say the three of you."

"What?"

"This UNSUB has successfully murdered at least thirty women that we know of; he's been leading the Bureau on wild goose chases; he leaves clues that mean nothing and doesn't leave clues that do; he took out four trained agents tonight. And now you are the second agent he's directly threatened, Agent Casper." He glared at Jess and spoke before she could object. "And you are the one he's seen fit to spar with. So I want the three of you somewhere safe. Even if that means I have to plant you in a conference room at FBI headquarters with sleeping bags!"

Jess closed her eyes in frustration. She knew the director. Under the circumstances, he'd back up Taylor's orders. She ran a hand over her face and let out a sigh. "All right. But we don't have to stay at headquarters. I'll make arrangements. I need to make a couple of phone calls." She took out her phone and left the living room to give herself some privacy.

"MacRusso."

"Hey, Mac. It's me."

"What's up, Jess?"

"I need you to take care of some things for me."

"That's why you pay me. Shoot."

Jess told her lawyer, Lindsey MacRusso, what she needed and ended the call.

Jess rejoined the others in the living room. "I've made some arrangements. I expect a call back shortly letting me know everything has been taken care of."

Taylor nodded. "It'll be a little bit before you can leave anyway. I've made some plans for getting you out of here, but it will take some time to implement."

Chapter Twenty-Seven

"SO TELL ME. WHERE will you be staying?" Ben asked.

"I don't—" Morgan's phone ringing cut her off. "Morgan…All right. Thanks, Mac." She hung up. "Sorry," she said in apology for the interruption. "I don't think it's a good idea to say where we'll be. But it is very secure. There's no way he'll be able to get anywhere near us without us knowing. All we need to do is get out of here without being followed."

At that moment, two more agents arrived, both brunette women wearing red wigs.

"I think I can help with that," he was pleased to say.

The red wigs were removed and given to Erin and Jess. A third wig, a blonde one, was produced, and one of the recent arrivals put it on.

"You may want to exchange clothes to sell this better," he said.

With a nod, Jess asked her decoy to follow her back to one of the bedrooms. Erin led the other decoy to the bedroom she'd used. Once the clothes were swapped, the four women returned to the living room. With wigs in place, they all checked each other out. Agent Casper traded coats with a male agent as well.

"Well, it won't pass close inspection, but it should be enough to throw someone off the trail long enough for you to get away," Ben pronounced. "Okay, you know what to do," he said, addressing the decoys.

"Yes, sir."

The three decoys and a fourth agent to drive exited the house. They were noisier than necessary and obvious in their intentions to head to FBI headquarters.

Quite a bit later, after the ambulances, police cruisers, and extra agents left, Jess, Erin, John, and Ben silently slipped away unnoticed.

"Okay, Morgan, where to?" Ben asked from behind the steering wheel.

"To Dulles Airport, the cargo hangars."

Ben wasn't sure how he felt about sending these three agents off to who knew where and without knowing where they were going. However, Director Cavanaugh had made it clear to him on more than one occasion that SSA Morgan was to get his complete cooperation, and he was to do everything in his power to keep her safe. He just hoped letting them go to some secret location would fulfill the second as well as the first of those mandates.

March 15, 2025
Saturday

After one o'clock in the morning, the private chartered jet took off, with Erin, Jess, and John on board. About two and a half hours later, the plane landed in Key West. As soon as they exited, they were taken to the helipad where a helicopter waited to take them on their journey's final leg. After a short twenty-five-mile ride, the helicopter landed on a private island. A man was waiting for them when they disembarked.

"Lady Essington?"

Jess stepped forward. "Yes."

He held his hand out. "I'm Greg Titan. Lindsey MacRusso called me."

"Thank you for making the arrangements so quickly."

"My pleasure. Since you rode the helicopter out here, I brought the boat, so it's here for your use. Likewise, a car is parked in the lot on Summerland Key. Here are the keys to the car, boat, and house." He handed her the items. "I didn't know what you would and wouldn't want, but I did stock the kitchen. And here's my number," he said, giving her a business card. "If you need anything—provisions, the helicopter, anything—call me, day or night."

"Thank you."

He walked to the helicopter and got in. It took off, returning to Key West.

Jess turned and looked at her companions. "Well, let's take a look at our new accommodations."

Erin and John exchanged a look and followed her into the three-story house.

The building was unusual, open-air verandahs surrounding two octagonal structures linked together. On the first floor was a large anteroom and a staircase leading up to the living quarters. The second floor had the laundry room and three bedrooms, each with a full bathroom. The third floor consisted of the fully equipped kitchen, a spacious great room with a fourteen-foot beamed ceiling and a wet bar, and the dining room, which offered a spectacular view of the ocean and surrounding islands. Also, just off the kitchen there was a workstation with internet access.

It was after four o'clock in the morning, and all three agents had been going since early morning of the day before. By tacit agreement, they each retreated into a bedroom and went to sleep.

When Erin woke up later that day, she smelled eggs and bacon. She opted for a fast shower, dressed in jeans and a t-shirt, and joined Jess and Agent Casper on the third floor. She found Jess cooking at the stove and Casper sitting on the verandah.

"I know it's lunchtime, but I opted to cook breakfast. How many eggs do you want?" Jess asked without turning around.

"Two. Scrambled, please."

"Coming right up. There's some juice in the refrigerator, and if you want some coffee, it's in the cupboard above the coffeemaker."

"Thanks." Erin moved to the counter and opened the cupboard with the coffee in it. She silently started a pot in the coffeemaker. Erin turned, leaning her hip against the counter, and watched Jess as she cooked the late breakfast. "Can I ask you a question, Jess?"

"Do I have a choice?" Jess quipped, her trepidation coloring her voice with irritation.

Erin sighed sadly and looked away. "Never mind," she said softly.

Jess dropped her head and took a slow breath. "No. I'm sorry. What did you want to ask?"

"What's up with the name Essington? I mean, you used it in Miami and now here. Is it a cover identity?"

"No. It's who she is," came Casper's voice from the open doorway to the verandah.

"I don't understand."

"Our Jessica comes from nobility. She is Lady Essington," he said with an amused smile.

Erin saw Jess blush as she plated everyone's breakfast and carried the plates to the verandah. She sat down and started buttering her toast. Erin and Casper joined her at the table.

"So your name is really Jessica Essington?"

"No. My name is Jessica Morgan, but my grandfather, Geoffrey Morgan, was the Earl of Essington. My mother was Lady Elizabeth Rodier." Jess looked at Casper, who was grinning like a fool. "Shut up, John."

"What? I didn't say anything."

"No, but you're thinking it."

He snickered and took a bite of his eggs.

"But you said you were Lady Essington, not Lady Morgan," Erin pointed out.

Jess quietly sighed. "As my grandfather's sole living heir, I inherited his title and estate."

"I thought titles were handed down through male heirs."

"Most are, but not all."

"Well, you *are* full of surprises, aren't you?"

Jess just started eating her breakfast.

"Where exactly are we?" Erin asked, changing the subject.

"This is a privately owned island that the owners used to rent out. They're friends of a friend and agreed to let us use it. The only way here is by helicopter or boat, so there's no way The Slasher can get here without us knowing it. But we're only a few minutes from the airport by helicopter, and with our phones and the internet access here, we can still work the case," Jess answered.

After breakfast, Jess gathered the dishes and returned to the kitchen. Erin followed and volunteered to wash the dishes.

"No need. It's John's turn."

"What?"

"It's a tradition. Whoever does the dishes gets to cook the next meal. And John said he wanted to cook dinner."

"That's right! We're having grilled steaks tonight," Casper said enthusiastically as he joined them.

Jess turned and pinned him with a look, arching an eyebrow. "You are not grilling my steak, John. I prefer my steak not to be burnt."

"I do *not* burn steaks. I prefer them cooked. But you, if you stuck a steak with a fork and it mooed, you'd say it was cooked just right."

Jess' eyebrow arched higher. "Whatever. You are not cooking my steak, John." She glanced at Erin. "And if you hope to enjoy yours, you won't let him cook your steak either." With that, Jess turned to go downstairs to her bedroom to change clothes. "I'm going for a swim before getting to work."

It wasn't a large pool, but it was enough to let Jess stretch her muscles and to think. She wasn't sure how she felt about Erin knowing about her family background. But since she'd found her in Miami under the name Essington, it wasn't exactly a secret. However, very few people in the FBI knew—John, the director, and now Erin. Toni had known, of course, but not until they'd been together for a while.

Jess finished her swim, returned to the house, changed out of her swimsuit, and went to the computer workstation off the kitchen. Once online she checked her email and some reports.

"Anything interesting?" John asked from behind her.

"I was right about chloroform being used on the agents in the cars. The agents in the house were knocked out with chloral hydrate. It was found on their pizza at near overdose levels. They were lucky."

"Where did the pizza come from?"

"Pizza King. They're interviewing all the employees who worked last night and looking for the delivery driver."

"Looking for the driver?"

"The driver apparently didn't go home last night. He hasn't been seen since leaving work."

"Do you think he's dead?"

"It's possible. But it wouldn't fit with the MO. I think it's more likely that our guy hired, bribed, or possibly duped the delivery person."

John grabbed a chair from the kitchen table and set it next to Jess, facing her. "Jessica."

Jess heard her old partner's tone of voice. She looked at him. "What?"

He reached out and took one of her hands in his. "It's been six years, but I still know you, Jessica. What's wrong?"

She frowned. "You mean other than working a case trying to catch a man that's killed possibly as many as a hundred women?"

"I'm not talking about work. Or at least, not the case." He looked into her eyes intently. "What's going on between you and Erin?"

She should have expected it. John had been her partner and best friend for years. And despite her lack of communication with him for the last six years, he still knew her better than just about anyone, even if there were a few things he *didn't* know. But it didn't mean she wanted to have this conversation. "Nothing."

"Bullshit nothing. Come on, Jessica, talk to me."

She rubbed her hands over her face and leaned back in the chair with a sigh. "It's personal, John. Just let it go. Please."

"It's affecting the job."

She gave him a sharp look and snapped, "Don't you think I know that? Why do you think she was at that safe house alone? I tried to walk away."

"From what? The case?"

"Of course not." She paused for a very long moment. "From Erin," she said in a whisper.

"What happened, Jessica?" he asked gently.

She couldn't meet his eyes. "I screwed up, John. Big time. I-I let her get close. Too close."

"And?"

"And it didn't work out. What more do you want?" She abruptly stood up, pushing her chair back. "I'm going for a walk."

It was dark out, and Jess hadn't returned to the house yet. The island was less than five hundred feet long and three hundred feet wide, so there weren't many places to hide or get lost. However, John also knew from experience that Jessica needed time alone, particularly when sorting out her feelings. He also knew, from experience, that she could retreat into herself too far if left alone for too long. While preparing dinner, he decided to give her until after he and Erin ate dinner and talked. Then he would retrieve Jessica from her self-imposed isolation.

"Only two steaks?"

Little's voice brought John out of his thoughts. He glanced at the grill where two steaks were cooking. "No use grilling Jessica's if she's not going to join us."

"What do you mean?"

John nodded to the woods surrounding the house and clearing. "She's out there somewhere, has been almost all day." He took one of the steaks off the grill and put it on a plate. He handed the plate to Little. "Here you go, one steak medium rare."

"Thank you."

"Go on in. I'll be right behind you."

Little went into the house and up to the dining room. Bringing his steak and aluminum wrapped potatoes for them, John joined her a few moments later and found she had poured the iced tea and set out salad and dressing.

"Mmmm, this is good."

John smiled. "Contrary to what Jessica would have you believe, I know how to grill a steak without burning it." He chuckled. "But I will admit to charring a few in the past."

After eating most of his meal, John decided to sound out Little. "So how long have you been on the taskforce, Agent Little?"

"About a month and a half. And you can call me Erin."

"And you've been working with Jessica the entire time?"

"No. She joined the taskforce a month ago."

"But you've been working closely together."

Little nodded.

"So what happened?"

Little suddenly looked uncomfortable. "What do you mean?"

John pinned her with a look. "Something is happening between you and Jessica, and I know it's personal. Normally, I wouldn't poke my nose into it, but it's got Jessica so twisted up in knots that it's affecting her ability to do her job." He pointed his fork at the blonde. "Fix it, Agent Little."

She frowned. "Jess has made it quite clear she doesn't want to work with me anymore. She had me removed from the case."

"Yet you're still here," he pointed out.

"I told the director I wanted to stay on the taskforce."

"So you didn't give up and pushed to get what you wanted. Right?"

She nodded.

"Then you should do the same thing with Jessica." He paused. "That is if you want to work things out," he said easily. His tone hardened as he said, "But if you don't want to work things out with her, leave. Walk away and let Jessica get over whatever happened. Because no matter what happened, she doesn't deserve to be toyed with." John abruptly got up, placing his plate, glass, and silverware in the sink before going to his bedroom. It amazed him how protective he felt for Jessica. How much time had passed since he'd last seen her didn't matter. They had been through so much together as partners. He would always consider her family.

Chapter Twenty-Eight

ERIN WAS A BIT taken aback by John's attitude. It was, after all, Jess who had ditched her and left an impersonal note ending their professional and personal relationship. And she *had* tried to get Jess to talk to her, more than once. She took a deep breath and let it out slowly while trying to defuse her ire. She then thought about John's apparent care and protectiveness for Jess, even after not seeing her in almost six years. Quite frankly, it impressed her.

Erin got up and put her dishes in the sink. She started the water and added some dishwashing soap. She absentmindedly washed the dishes as she considered her next move. Almost before she knew it, she'd finished the dishes. As she put the last glass in the drainer, she smiled, with realization that she was on the hook for their next meal since she did the dishes. Folding the hand towel after drying her hands, she took a deep breath and let it out. It was time.

Erin walked down the stairs to the first floor and then outside. She looked around the area and headed out to find Jess. A glance over her shoulder confirmed John was watching from a second-story window.

Erin found Jess sitting at the end of the dock. Without waiting for an invitation, she sat down next to her. "You've been out here a long time."

"Been thinking."

"Yeah. Same here," she replied softly. "Look, Jess, you don't have to talk to me, but I'd appreciate it if you'd hear me out."

Jess nodded.

"I'm sorry for the way I reacted. I was surprised and caught off guard. I'm a scientist. I need to be able to understand things and have them make sense. Finding out you're...Well, it threw me."

"I can see how it would," Jess conceded.

"Jess, I was thrown off balance, but I was never afraid of you. You may be part..." she still couldn't say it without hesitating, "vampire, but I know you're not a monster. I know you're one of the good guys."

Jess simply nodded.

After a few seconds of silence, Erin spoke again. "I want...I want things to be okay between us, Jess. I want to be friends again."

Jess took a deep breath and slowly let it out. "I'm sorry for the way I handled things. I shouldn't have taken off like I did. I felt it was the right thing to do at the time."

"Why?" Erin asked without reproach, not wanting Jess to shut her out now that she was finally talking to her.

"Because I knew you wouldn't be pleased about being lied to and misled, especially since we got so close. I couldn't imagine you wanting to work with me after that, so I got you released from having to do so."

"What did you lie about?"

Jess looked at Erin in disbelief. "It was the lie of omission. I didn't tell you what I am." She looked away and back over the dark water under the almost moonless night.

Erin thought about it. "How *do* you tell someone that you're part vampire?"

"As a rule, I don't." Jess smirked. "Although, I admit a few perps have seen my other half. It's helped a few times during interrogations."

Erin had a sudden insight. "That's why you wanted the camera turned off when you were with Conrad."

Jess smiled. "I confess it was rather satisfying to wipe that arrogant sneer off his face."

Erin couldn't help but smile at the image of the brutal serial killer suddenly finding himself alone with a pissed off vampire. She let out a chuckle. "I'll bet."

They sat in silence for a few minutes.

"I know you have questions, Erin. Ask them."

Erin was silent. She wasn't sure what to ask first. She had wanted answers, but now that she was getting them, she wasn't so sure.

Jess looked at her, irritation starting to show in her eyes. "Ask."

"I've read there's a word used to call half—"

Jess cut her off with a derisive snort. "Yeah, dhamphir. That's a made-up word used by humans in books and movies. We do not use it. I'm a half-breed."

"Okay." That was a tender point, so Erin tried a different topic. "How old are you? Seventy-five? A hundred? Two hundred?"

"I'm younger than you. I just turned thirty-three."

"When was your birthday?"

"February twenty-third."

"That was my birthday! Why didn't you say anything?"

Jess shrugged. After a few seconds, she prompted Erin. "I know that's not the question you want to ask."

"I'm unsure how to ask, or even if I should."

"Well, I suggest you ask while I'm willing to answer," she snapped. "This is not an experience I'm particularly looking forward to repeating."

Erin took a deep breath and dived in. "What about blood?"

Jess took a slow breath. "I've never taken human blood. And I don't drink blood unless I need to."

"How often do you need blood?"

"Not often, but if I go too long without it, I can get rundown and sick. I also need it to heal when I'm injured."

Erin looked at Jess with realization. "That's what was in the paper bag that Det. Marinelli gave you on the way back from the hospital."

Jess nodded. "Yes. It was a pint of pig's blood."

"You mean you can just go into a drug store and buy a pint of pig's blood?"

"Only businesses that cater to a certain clientele. And not just pig's blood."

"A certain clientele?"

"Vampires, and half-breeds like me, are in every part of society, Erin. From boardrooms to hospitals to law enforcement to skid row. In that sense, we aren't any different from anyone else."

"How did Marinelli know?"

She looked at Erin. "Bobby is a vampire."

Erin's eyes widened. After a few moments, she dared another question. "Do I want to know where the blood comes from?"

Jess pinned Erin with a hard look. "I don't know. Do you?"

Erin hesitated. Did she really want to know? What would it change? But she was afraid that the opportunity would be lost if she didn't get the answer now. She gave a slight nod.

"Cow and pig's blood obviously come from livestock. Human blood is voluntarily donated. It's available prepackaged or fresh from a donor."

"By donor you mean..." Erin felt a little queasy.

"I mean, there are some humans who volunteer to let vampires feed on them." Jess shook her head. "Some of them get addicted to it."

"Addicted? Why?"

"Because of the way it makes them feel. They say it feels good. Unfortunately, if they get together with an undisciplined or unscrupulous vampire, it can have a deadly cost. But most vampires are careful, particularly since feeding directly from a human can have consequences."

"What do you mean?"

"They say human blood is like no other. For some, it's like a drug. For others, it can become a physical life-and-death need which no other kind of blood can satisfy. They can literally starve to death on cow or pig's blood. For some, feeding directly from a human can create an unbreakable bond, affecting both human and vampire for the rest of their lives. They all say nothing compares to human blood, especially for healing."

"But you've never…"

"No. I've never had human blood." Jess took a deep breath and let it out. "I'm tired. I'm going to go to bed." She stood up and walked back up the pier, leaving Erin alone.

After Jess had left, Erin sat at the end of the pier for several minutes. She had gotten some answers from Jess, but she wasn't sure what it had accomplished. At least Jess was talking to her again, even if it was clear Jess had been uncomfortable with their conversation. She finally got up and made her way back to the house. After taking a long, hot bath, she put on her pajamas and slipped into bed.

March 16, 2025
Sunday

When Erin woke up in the morning, she headed to the third floor. She found Jess in the great room, where she had put the pictures of the victims and crime scenes on the walls. She also put up photos of the messages in blood from The Slasher. Jess was completely focused on the case files with pen and notepad in hand.

Erin went into the kitchen and started preparing breakfast. John soon joined her. They exchanged a few pleasantries while she continued cooking breakfast. When it was time to eat, Erin called for Jess to join them. Since Jess didn't reply, Erin left the kitchen and entered the great room.

Jess stood next to a wall, peering at crime scene pictures. Case files were scattered on and around the coffee table in front of the couch, as were several balled-up pieces of paper.

"Jess?"

John appeared by Erin's side.

"Jess?" Erin tried again.

"Leave her be," he said gently. "It's best to let her work when she gets like this."

"She needs to eat. She hasn't had anything since breakfast yesterday."

"Trust me, she won't starve, but she may break the case open." John gently pulled Erin back to the kitchen.

After Erin and John finished breakfast, they went into the great room. Even though John had spent a day with Jess going over things, he was still new to the case, so he and Erin went through the files and discussed the details of each victim and crime scene.

The day passed uneventfully. As did the next.

March 18, 2025
Tuesday

Jess' cell phone woke her on Tuesday morning. "Morgan."

"It's Ben Taylor."

"What is it?"

"We got another one."

Jess closed her eyes and clenched her jaw. "Where?"

"Boston."

"All right. We'll be there." She ended the call and then arranged for the helicopter to take them to the airport. She then woke up the other two agents.

By the time the three of them were dressed and ready, the helicopter was arriving.

They landed in Boston at Logan International Airport at half past one in the afternoon. An agent from the local office was waiting for them as they disembarked.

"Agent Morgan?"

Jess stepped forward and took the agent's hand. "Hi. I'm SSA Morgan. This is SSA Little and SSA Casper."

"Special Agent Sean Travis. The ASAC sent me to take you to the crime scene."

"Let's go."

Less than half an hour into the autopsy, John showed up at the morgue.

"How's it going?" he asked Erin.

She looked up. "No surprises so far. Where's Jess?"

"She's still at the crime scene." Seeing her questioning look, he said, "She wanted some time alone to look around and get a feel for the victim's home."

"You left her alone?"

John nodded. "It's not the first time she's wanted some time alone to get the feel of a crime scene. And, as she pointed out, the threats haven't been made against her. They've been made against you."

Erin was angry. "But she was set up in Atlanta!" She snapped her gloves off and walked over to retrieve her phone.

"She wasn't hurt, though, because she arranged for backup. Jessica knows how to handle herself. She's been working alone for the last three years."

Erin merely glared at him as she dialed. It was clear that Jess hadn't told John about the severe beating she'd taken in Atlanta. As the phone rang in her ear, she paused in thought. How could Jess tell anyone how severe the beating had been since she showed no signs of it? Erin figured that meant John didn't know about Jess'...condition? Heritage? She still wasn't sure what name to call it.

Jess answered her phone. "Morgan."

"Jess, it's me. What are you doing?"

"Just taking a look around the victim's place."

"Alone?"

"Yes. Why?"

"Why? Jess, you promised me you wouldn't take any unnecessary risks."

"And I'm not."

"You shouldn't be there alone. Not after what happened in Atlanta."

"You're the one that was shot at the other night. Atlanta wasn't about taking my life but teaching me a lesson. I'm fine, Erin. Don't go anywhere without John."

Erin's retort was cut off by Jess hanging up on her. Erin put her phone down and returned to the autopsy table. She was too angry to attempt even minimal conversation with John.

Jess went through the victim's home, taking note of small details like family pictures, perfumes on her dresser, frozen dinners in her freezer, and appointments in her organizer. She felt something important was to be found, some vital clue, if only she would recognize it. After a couple of hours, she finally left Sheila Cousins' house.

A Bureau car had been left for her, so she drove to the victim's place of work. It was a small but upscale real estate office.

"May I help you?" the receptionist/office manager asked when Jess entered.

"Yes. I was wondering if I could speak with someone about Sheila Cousins. I'm Supervisory Special Agent Jessica Morgan with the FBI."

"Oh." The woman was thrown. "I can't believe she's dead. Sheila was such a sweet person. Everyone loved her."

"Did you know her well?"

"About as well as anyone here, I guess."

"Can I get your name?"

"Oh, I'm sorry. I'm Monica Reed."

"Thank you. Was Sheila seeing anyone, Monica, or did she get any personal visitors here?"

"I don't think she was seeing anyone, and Sheila was very professional. She only had clients come in to see her. Most of the time, though, she would meet with clients at the properties she was showing."

"Was she a busy agent?"

"Oh yes. Sheila is…was our top agent." She gestured to some plaques on the wall behind Jess.

Several of the accomplishment plaques had Sheila Cousins' name engraved on them. "Would it be possible for me to look at her desk and computer?"

"Of course. Let me show you to her office."

Monica led Jess to Sheila's office and then left her alone. Sheila Cousins was very organized. Everything seemed to have a place and be in its place. She turned on Sheila's computer and opened the calendar and other files. The victim was meticulous and organized. Every appointment she ever had with a prospective client appeared to be listed and cross-referenced. Almost every minute of each day was accounted for. Something caught Jess' eye. Sheila had had several meetings with a new client over the last week. Even more interesting was that the same name appeared in her personal calendar at home.

Russell Schiff.

Rare Vintage

It had been eleven days since the murder in Miami, so The Slasher had the time to come to Boston and pose as Russell Schiff. If it was him. Either way, Russell Schiff needed to be checked out.

Chapter Twenty-Nine

"AGENTS MORGAN, CASPER, LITTLE?"

"I'm Agent Casper." He gestured to Erin, who had changed back into her clothes after finishing the autopsy. "This is Agent Little. What can we do for you?"

"I'm Agent Lessing. The ASAC sent me to take you to your accommodations while you're here in Boston. Where's Agent Morgan?"

"She's not here right now. She'll join us later," John answered.

The young agent nodded and led John and Erin out to the car. Lessing drove them to the Holiday Inn Express on Boston Street. Lessing flashed his badge and spoke to the front desk manager. The manager, Melissa O'Rourke, checked them into the rooms the local field office reserved.

Lessing turned to John and Erin and held out the room keys. "Here you go. If you need anything, don't hesitate to call the field office."

"Thank you," John said as he took the keys from Lessing.

"Have good evening, Agent Casper, Agent Little." He turned and left.

"Agent Little?" Miss O'Rourke asked.

"Yes?"

"I have something for you." She retrieved an envelope and handed it to Erin.

"What's that?" John asked.

"I don't know." Erin opened the envelope and took out the note contained within.

> Sorry I missed you. Perhaps
> we'll connect in Boston.
> T.S.

John saw the expression on Erin's face. "What's wrong?"

She turned the note so he could read it.

"Damn," he said. "Who the hell knew we would be at this hotel?"

"Someone at the Boston field office made the arrangements, but it should not have been general knowledge under the circumstances. You and I didn't even know where we'd be staying."

"Well, somehow, our UNSUB does." John opened his phone and called Jess. "Jessica, it's me. We've got a problem…The local office arranged for us to stay at a hotel. There was a note waiting for Erin when we got here. He knows we're here…All right…We'll wait for your call." He hung up and looked at Erin. "Jessica didn't know about the arrangements either. She's going to make some calls and get back to us. In the meantime, we're *not* going to check in here." He spoke to Miss O'Rourke and canceled their rooms.

When Jess left the real estate office, she called the Boston field office and gave them Russell Schiff's name so they could start checking him out. She made a second call and then drove to Eli Compton's home.

Dr. Eli Compton was a psychology professor at Harvard, and Jess had been his teaching assistant. She knew of no one better than Dr. Compton at delving into a mind, especially a disturbed mind. She knocked on his front door and smiled when he answered.

"Jessica!"

"Hi, Dr. Compton."

"Now, now, you know to call me Eli unless you want me to call you Dr. Morgan," the gray-haired man said as they shook hands. "Come in, come in."

Jess followed the older man into the house. They sat down in the living room.

"Can I get you something to drink, Jessica?"

"No, thank you."

"What can I do for you? You were a bit mysterious on the phone."

"I want to pick your brain," she replied with a smile.

They hadn't been talking for very long when Jess' phone rang.

"Excuse me." She answered her phone. John called to let her know about the problem at the hotel. She looked at her old professor when she hung up. "The suspect left a note at the hotel the FBI made arrangements with for our stay."

"You've got a leak."

She nodded. "*I* didn't even know where we were going to be staying. Please excuse me while I make a couple of phone calls."

"Take your time. I'll put on a pot of tea." Dr. Compton got up and retreated to the kitchen.

Jess called the local field office and asked to speak to the Special Agent in Charge. She questioned him about the arrangements. He indicated his ASAC had handled them, so she spoke to ASAC Agent Cooper, who said he'd received a call from AD Taylor about arranging secure accommodations. He'd contacted the hotel without using their names. That was why Agent Lessing took them to the hotel and spoke with the desk manager.

"Well, we won't stay at the hotel since our UNSUB already knows about it."

"What can I do to help, Agent Morgan? Assistant Director Taylor made it clear you were to be afforded every courtesy and that your safety and the other agents' safety were a high priority."

"Just make sure everyone keeps their mouths shut and there aren't leaks about the case. I'll make other arrangements for our stay here. Thank you." Jess hung up and called AD Taylor. She then discovered that he had never contacted the Boston field office. Something was *very* wrong.

"Why don't you stay at my place, Jessica?" Dr. Compton proposed when he returned from the kitchen.

"We wouldn't want to impose."

"Nonsense. Besides, I'm talking about my condo. I've lived here in this house for less than a month. The townhouse is unoccupied."

"Where is it?"

"It's on Concord Avenue. It's Harvard faculty housing. I bought it when they were built in eighty-seven. Since I'm retiring after this year, I'm putting it up for sale. Consider it yours for however long you're here in Boston."

"That's very kind of you, Doc—Eli. Thank you." Jess called John back and let him know where they'd be staying. He assured her he would get Erin and himself there without any problems.

After Jess was done with her phone call, she and Dr. Compton continued discussing her profile of the UNSUB.

John and Erin made their way out of a service entrance in the back of the hotel and took a cab to the address Jess had given them. Just as promised, a key was hidden away in a compartment of a brick, one of several bricks that lined the small walkway to the door. John ushered Erin in after unlocking the door.

John and Erin changed into casual clothes and sat at the kitchen table, going over the results of the autopsy and the information they'd received from the local agents about the victim.

But Erin wasn't happy with the situation. She all but slammed a folder down on the table, stood up, and started to pace in the kitchen. "Doesn't it bother you that Jess is out there alone while we're holed up in this townhouse like a couple of timid mice?"

John leaned back in his chair. "First off, I trust Jessica implicitly. She was my partner for six years and never let me down. Her exceptional observational skills and insightfulness saved my life more than once. She's gone above and beyond more times than I can count. She's more than earned my respect, trust, and loyalty. And second, I don't consider being prudent acting like a timid mouse. We've received direct threats against you, and it's obvious that The Slasher knows you're here in Boston, as evidenced by the note at the hotel."

"I don't need to be babysat and coddled!"

"Perhaps not. But Jessica does need to know you're safe. Look at this from her point of view for a minute. Her entire career at the Bureau has been about going after the worst of the worst, the real monsters. She's taken them on and won a hell of a lot more times than any other profiler. She never let them intimidate her or scare her off. She almost lost her life to one, but even that didn't stop her. The only thing that got to her was the murder of someone she loved. It broke her, and it made her run. She resigned from the Bureau and cut off contact with everyone in her life. She could have chosen to withdraw completely from life. It's not as if she ever has to work another day in her life. But even after everything she'd been through, she still wanted to help people and make a difference, so she went to medical school. But instead of becoming a doctor, she came back to the Bureau. She's worked alone ever since, not getting too close to anyone, not allowing anyone close to her, not letting herself care too much about anyone except the victims." John paused and waited until Erin returned his gaze. "Not until you."

Erin started to say something, but John held up a hand, stopping her.

"I don't know exactly what has and hasn't happened between you, and I don't need to. But I know that she let you get close and cares a great deal about you. Having someone hurt, or worse, because of her or her work is Jessica's greatest fear and nightmare. One she's already had to live through once. It nearly destroyed her. Imagine what it would do to her to go through it again."

Erin sat back down with a silent sigh. "I talked to her on the island like you asked, but she still hasn't been very open with me. I'm beginning to think a way to make things right between us doesn't exist."

"I doubt that. It's obvious she still cares, or else it wouldn't affect her as much as it is." He paused for a moment. "Let me offer you a piece of unsolicited, friendly advice. When it comes to Jessica, patience and persistence pay off." At Erin's confused look, John continued. "Toni had to ask her out several times before she finally agreed, and several more times before she agreed to a second time."

Erin looked at John. "Why are you telling me this?"

"I don't know you well, but Jessica has good instincts about people. If she let you get close, it's because she saw something special in you. If you want her...it'll be up to you to pursue her. Jessica won't. She will deny what she wants if she believes it's in the best interest of someone else."

"In other words—"

"It's totally up to you. You need to decide what you want and whether to pursue it or not."

Erin let out a heavy sigh. Now, she just had to decide what she wanted with Jess, if anything. She jumped slightly when John's phone rang.

"Casper...No, we haven't...We?" John asked. He looked at his phone and then put it away. "Jess said she's bringing dinner and that they'll be here shortly."

"And she didn't say who was coming with her, I take it."

"No."

"Hey, guys. Food's here!" Jess called out. She appeared in the kitchen with a gray-haired man on her heels. "John, Erin, this is Dr. Eli Compton. Dr. Compton, this is Agent John Casper and Agent Erin Little. We're working the case together."

"Please, call me Eli," Compton said as he shook hands with the other agents.

Jess emptied the bags and set out several different selections of Chinese food.

"There should be some plates in the cupboard to the right of the sink, Jessica," Compton told her.

Soon, the dishes were filled with food, and everyone was enjoying their meal.

"Eli's the one who volunteered this place for us to stay. It's his condo," Jess informed Erin and John.

"Thank you for your hospitality, Dr. Compton," said John.

"I told you, call me Eli. I hear Dr. Compton, and I think I'm in class," he replied with a smile.

"What do you teach?" Erin asked.

He looked at Jess. "You didn't tell them?"

She shook her head.

"I teach psychology here at Harvard. Jessica was my TA when she was here." He grinned. "In a way, I was sorry to see her graduate. She was the best TA I ever had."

Jess snorted. "That's just because you had me grade all the papers from the grad students."

He grinned. "I did enjoy watching them try to argue with you. You were never intimidated and rebutted their arguments point by point."

Jess shrugged. "Right was right, and wrong was wrong."

They finished dinner and cleared away the dishes.

"Now, let me see this note from the hotel," Compton said.

Erin arched an eyebrow in question and looked at Jess.

"It's okay, Erin. I asked for Eli's help. He taught me everything I know about profiling, and there's no one better at getting inside someone's mind than he is."

Erin retrieved the note and handed it to the professor.

"Well, he didn't write this," the professor said almost immediately. "The handwriting is too neat. Either he had someone else write it for him, or someone wrote this while taking a message."

John nodded. "We spoke to the desk clerk at the hotel who took the message over the phone. Unfortunately, there wasn't anything else he could tell us."

"What do you think about this message and the others, Doc—" Erin cut herself off at the corrective but lighthearted look she received. "I mean Eli," she finished with a smile.

"The author of the messages is...puerile. He's selfish, egocentric, and unhappy unless he's the center of attention. He would say, 'If I can't have you, no one can,' and eventually follow through on that threat."

"How does that fit with the murders?" John asked.

Compton shook his head. "It doesn't. The killer is sophisticated and meticulous. He doesn't leave behind clues unless he chooses to. He's very socially adaptable since he's engaged women of varying backgrounds and socioeconomic levels."

Erin jumped in. "Couldn't he have targeted the women at random and not have any contact with them prior to the actual murder?"

"He most likely does pick them randomly, but he definitely interacts with them before killing them. He's shown familiarity with their residences, meaning he'd been inside their homes at least once. And based on the frequency of the murders and the geographical distance between them, I'd say he earns their trust quickly. I'd say he's quite charming and just about 'sweeps them off their feet.' Money isn't an issue for him. So he's from money, either his family's or his own. If he's working, it's for himself." Compton looked at Jess. "I shouldn't be telling you anything you don't already know, Jessica. You are exceptionally gifted at profiling. You always have been. I didn't teach you all that much. You're a natural."

Jess sighed. "There's just something about this one that doesn't feel right. Something that I can't figure out."

"How do you reconcile the author of the messages with the killer?" John asked.

"They are two distinct personalities," Compton said without hesitation.

"Are they two different people?"

"*That* is the question. I don't know. It very well could be two different people or simply two different personalities of one person. I don't know. And you won't know until you catch him."

"What does your gut tell you, Eli?" As his former student, Jess earnestly looked at her former professor, hoping for some insight into the UNSUB, a conclusion different from the one she had come to on her own.

"He's made this a personal thing between you. He's taunting you. Eventually, he will make you pay, and I'm afraid he knows enough about you to know how to hurt you the most."

Chapter Thirty

AFTER DR. COMPTON LEFT the townhouse, Jess changed out of her suit. She grabbed her laptop and settled on the living room couch. John joined her.

"I can hear the gears turning in your head, Jessica. What are you thinking?"

She sighed. "I'm just wondering what the best move would be."

"What do you mean?"

"This guy has focused on me as his foil to test himself against, and as a target to be played with. It might be a good idea to remove myself from the equation. Walk away and let someone else get this guy."

"What? You've never backed down or walked away from a case. Why start now?"

"*Because* I've never backed down or walked away. He may be counting on that. And I don't know how much good I'm doing since, as you pointed out, he knows my buttons and pushes them. I'm not being proactive. I'm only reacting to him."

"Well, you can be proactive without walking away, Jessica."

"How?"

"By changing the game, by not waiting to react to him, by making him react to you." He paused. "When you figure out how to do that, you'll be that much closer to catching him."

"And what if it's not just him? What if there are two of them?"

"We'll cross that bridge when we get to it. Just concentrate on what you know. Know what the game is and change it." With that, he patted her leg and left her alone.

March 19, 2025
Wednesday

Jess stayed up late into the night. As a result, she fell asleep on the couch. The smell of breakfast cooking woke her up. She went into the kitchen to find John making breakfast.

"Hey, John," she said while yawning.

"Morning. What time did you finally fall asleep?"

"I don't know. But I feel like I've gotten two or three hours of sleep."

"Sit down." John set a plate in front of her and poured some juice.

Jess quirked and eyebrow. "Where the hell did this food come from?" she mock-teased him.

John smiled. "I went out and got it at the drive-thru," he joked. At her confused look he said, "I felt like making breakfast."

Jess looked at him and frowned. "Who the hell are you, and where's the John Casper I know?"

He laughed. "After Jennie left me, I had to fend for myself. I also like to cook for Jeremy when he's with me."

Erin soon joined them, and they all enjoyed the breakfast John cooked.

Starting the workday, the three agents drove to the Boston field office. Jess set John and Erin on the trail of Russell Schiff, the name in Sheila Cousins' work and personal calendars, while she started making some phone calls.

Jess quickly found out that the pizza delivery driver had finally been located. He was a twenty-one-year-old named George Linz. He was found coming back into the country after having spent some time in Mexico. Someone who flashed a badge and claimed to be an FBI agent when he exited his vehicle stopped Linz, according to his statement. He demanded to inspect the pizza before Linz delivered it to the agents in the house. Afterward, the man who stopped him gave him a big tip for his inconvenience.

After leaving work that night, Linz stopped at a convenience store and bought scratch-off lottery tickets. He won several hundred dollars and, on a lark, decided to take off for some fun in the sun in Mexico, which he did without telling anyone. Unfortunately, Linz could not describe the alleged agent that stopped him because the man had worn a coat with a hood that obscured his face.

She then called Alan Stillwell at Headquarters to verify no any further activity occurred on the suspicious phone number since the texts and call she received the past Friday. For the rest of her day, Jess interviewed the family, friends, and coworkers of Sheila Cousins.

March 20, 2025
Thursday

It was three o'clock in the morning when her phone woke her. "Morgan."

"How do you like Boston?"

Instead of replying, Jess followed John's advice and changed the game. She hung up on the caller.

He called back. "Don't you fu—"

She hung up again.

The phone rang again. "Listen! I'm not going to play your fucking game so you might as well quit calling," she said before he could react. She hung up and turned off her phone.

A dark figure stared at his phone in dismay and anger. "You fucking bitch!"

When Jess got up later, she turned her cell phone on and checked her messages. Several messages from the UNSUB were full of angry ranting and name-calling. Part of her felt pleased she had ruffled his feathers by refusing to talk to him. But the other part of her was concerned about his response.

Jess joined John and Erin for breakfast.

"How are things going with tracking down this Russell Schiff?" she asked.

John answered. "He doesn't have a Massachusetts driver's license. No address, no accounts, nothing that can be traced to him."

"Have you tried neighboring states?"

He nodded. "New York, Vermont, New Hampshire, Connecticut, Rhode Island. I also checked Maine and New Jersey. There's a Russell Schiff in New York, but he's eighty-seven years old and has been in a nursing home for four years."

"Is there any reason for us to stay here in Boston?"

"I'm afraid not. We can continue to work on the case via computer and phone. The local agents are handling any local interviews. They'll report if they come across anything."

Jess nodded. "I spoke to Taylor. He's sending some agents to follow up our investigations here."

After breakfast, the agents packed up and headed to the airport. They had an hour and a half layover in Atlanta. Jess turned her cell phone on while waiting for their flight from Atlanta to Key West to board. She wasn't surprised to have a few more messages from the UNSUB. He was still angry. Then she got to the last message he left. He *asked* her to call him.

Jess moved a few steps away to place the call. "What do you want?" she asked as soon as he answered.

"You really shouldn't ignore me!"

She hung up. She wasn't surprised when her phone almost immediately rang. "What?"

"Godda—"

She again hung up. Once again, her phone rang. "If you can't keep a civil tongue in your head, we have nothing to discuss." She hung up and turned off her phone as she followed John and Erin up the jetway to the plane.

After landing in Key West, the helicopter took the agents back out to the private key. They changed into casual clothes, and all three agents quietly worked. When Jess didn't answer her ringing phone, Erin picked it up from the coffee table.

"It's him," said Erin after seeing the number on the phone.

"I know."

"Aren't you going to answer it?"

"Nope. I already told him at three o'clock this morning, and again while we were in Atlanta, that I wasn't going to play his game, and he needed to keep a civil tongue in his head. He can wait until I'm ready to talk to him."

John looked up and caught her eye. He smiled. "Good girl."

"I don't understand. Don't we want to talk to him?" Erin asked.

"Jessica has changed the game by refusing to talk to him on his schedule. The UNSUB is now reacting to her instead of the other way around. She's taken some of the control away from him."

"But doesn't that risk he'll kill sooner rather than later?"

Jess nodded. "It's a possibility. But as long as he's pissed at me, and thinking about me, he's more likely to make a mistake since he's emotional. I've got to keep him off balance."

It wasn't long before Erin received a call from Alan, the tech guy. The calls originated in Boston. They were ahead of him for once, and he was the one playing catch up.

Jess took a break later in the afternoon and went for a walk. She ended up down at the pier again. For the first time in a long time, she felt better about their chances of catching the killer. She always believed they'd eventually catch him, but somehow, it felt like the odds were finally on their side. And all it took was changing the game. She wondered why the hell she hadn't thought of it herself. She shook her head. What mattered was that someone thought of it. She could feel it in her bones—something in the case would break, and soon.

It felt so good, feeling the warmth of the sunshine, and the water looked so blue. Jess gave in to temptation. She took off her clothes and lowered herself into the water. She began swimming. It felt good to stretch her muscles and push her body. The private key didn't have much room for running, and there wasn't any workout equipment. So swimming was the best way to exercise. She felt her body respond positively to the exercise, and her mind cleared as she concentrated on her strong strokes.

After Erin had signed off the internet at the workstation, she walked out onto the verandah off the great room. She leaned on her hands on the railing and took a deep breath. She'd almost forgotten how much she enjoyed the water. Both of her brothers had followed Brigadier General Gregory Little Sr. into the Army and spent several years in the deserts of the Middle East. But Erin could never survive in that environment. She loved the sea, had always loved it since reading Jules Verne's *20,000 Leagues Under the Sea*. As a kid, she had dreamed of joining Captain Nemo's crew (much to the chagrin of her father) and living under the sea while solving the mysteries of the *Nautilus*.

Even though the Army kept her father away for long periods of deployment, they had been close. Of course that didn't mean they didn't ever have any conflict. Her father had not approved of her decision to join the FBI after graduating from medical school. She was glad they had reconciled before he died a few years ago.

Erin took another deep breath, taking in the salt air. "I could definitely get used to this."

"The ocean or the private island?"

Erin turned to see John standing in the doorway. She smiled. "In truth, both."

John stepped out onto the verandah and joined Erin at the railing. "I shouldn't be surprised Jessica chose this location as a safe house. She's always liked the water."

"She did say a tropical beach was her preference for a vacation."

"Yep. Every vacation she took when we were partners was to a beach somewhere: the Caribbean, the Mediterranean, the South Pacific. Toni even taught her how to sail and SCUBA dive."

Erin couldn't help but mentally smirk at the idea of a half-breed vampire who relished the beach and other sunny activities.

John looked over at Erin. "Jessica took a break a few minutes ago. Why don't you go see what she's up to?" he said, nodding to the tree line.

Erin silently turned and left. She exited the house and walked to the path that led to the pier. When Erin got to the dock, she stopped and observed the woman who had turned her life upside-down. Jess was sitting on the end of the dock, knees drawn up and arms around her knees. Her face was turned upward toward the sun. She looked so peaceful.

Erin was about to walk out onto the pier when Jess stood up. She was transfixed as the beautiful woman started undressing. Then Jess gracefully dove into the water. She should have left and given Jess her privacy, but she couldn't take her eyes off her athletic body as it cut through clear, blue water. Erin knew that body intimately, but not as well as she'd like.

Watching Jess, without her knowledge, made Erin feel like a voyeur, but she still hid behind a tree as the brunette finished her swim and returned to the pier. She watched Jess pull herself out of the water and lay down on her back to dry off in the sun. Eventually, she pulled herself away and returned to the house.

While Jess was drying in the sun, her mind was busy. She was reviewing every detail of the case. Changing the game and making the UNSUB react to her was good. But what could she do to take further control?

Once she was dry, Jess put her clothes back on and returned to the house. She ate a quiet, late dinner with Erin and John. Then, she retreated to her bedroom.

Sleep evaded Jess for hours. She couldn't shut her brain off. She kept going over all the messages and calls from the UNSUB. Instead of worrying about how they didn't fit the killer's profile, she focused on just that aspect of his personality. It was his weakness. This facet of the UNSUB was much more emotional and less rational, though still organized and manipulative. It was only this part of him that she'd been able to throw off balance. The brilliant and cunning part of him had made no mistakes, or at least none that they'd found. But the emotional part of him had made more than one.

What could she do to take advantage of his weakness? She needed to throw him off his game and do something unexpected. She reached over and snagged her cell phone from the nightstand. She dialed and left a short message.

"Let's talk. Face-to-face, no tricks."

After hanging up, she was finally able to go to sleep.

Surprisingly, Jess' phone rang only a couple of hours later. "Morgan."

"DC warehouse district, one hour."

"No. Tomorrow night."

"Fine," came the irritated agreement.

"What address?"

"I'll contact you when you're in the area. Midnight. Don't be late."

Chapter Thirty-One

March 21, 2025
Friday

JESS WAS THE FIRST one up in the morning. She made herself some breakfast before showering and changing into a business suit. She was writing a note at the kitchen table when John came in.

"Good morning."

"Good morning," she replied.

"Why are you so dressed up this morning?" he asked.

"I'm going back to DC. I have a meeting I have to attend. I was writing you a note to let you know."

The sound of the helicopter could be heard as it approached the island.

"Why is the helicopter coming?" Erin asked as she entered the kitchen.

"I have to go to DC for a meeting. I'm not sure when I'll be back." Jess handed the piece of paper to John. "If you need anything while I'm gone, just call Greg Titan. This is his number." She smiled. "Want me to pick up anything while I'm in DC?" she asked lightheartedly to keep them from suspecting the truth. "Pizza with everything, maybe?"

"Just be careful, Jessica," said John.

"I can't get in too much trouble at headquarters." She picked up her briefcase and headed to the stairs. "I'll see you when I get back."

"Do you think one of us should go with her?" Jess heard Erin ask John, sounding uneasy.

"For a meeting? We should probably thank her for not making us go," he replied.

Once in DC, Jess went to the Hoover building only to pick up a vest. She may have been willing to meet with the UNSUB at midnight in the warehouse district, but she wasn't an idiot.

Jess changed into the clothes she'd packed in her briefcase. After getting something to eat, she headed to the warehouse district. She wanted a chance to look around while it was still afternoon. Besides, he had told her not to be late. He'd said nothing about her being early.

John's cell phone rang around three o'clock that afternoon.

"Casper."

"Let me talk to Agent Morgan," ordered AD Taylor.

"What do you mean? She's not here. She left this morning to go back to DC for a meeting at headquarters."

"What meeting?"

John's stomach tightened with worry. "I don't know. She said she had a meeting. Since she didn't take any of her bags, I assumed she'd be back sometime tonight."

"Well, there was no meeting. No one's seen or heard from her, and I've been trying to reach her for a couple of hours. We've got a possible lead on this Russell Schiff guy from Boston."

"Agent Little and I will be there as soon as possible."

"Fine. And try to contact Morgan. I want her here."

"Yes, sir." John hung up and went out onto the verandah where Erin was working. "We've got a problem."

"What?"

"No one's seen or heard from Jessica. According to AD Taylor, no meeting was scheduled. Taylor wants us back at headquarters. There's a possible lead on Russell Schiff."

Erin was up and moving in an instant. "Call for the chopper. I'll call the airport and get us a flight back," she said as she pulled out her phone and entered the house.

John and Erin were able to catch a flight to Washington via Charlotte, North Carolina. They landed at Dulles and arrived at Headquarters a little before nine o'clock that evening.

Taylor met them as they entered the bullpen and brought them up to date on the new lead.

"We caught a break. Agents have been interviewing all of Sheila Cousins' clients and coworkers. She was at an open house a couple of days before she was killed. We caught a lucky break because the owners had a nanny cam. It recorded everyone who was in the house that day. By reviewing the footage with Cousins' clients and the other agents who were present, we've been able to put a name to all but three people who were there that day—three men." He handed them pictures of the men. "These are the men. Based on interviews and information in Cousins' computer and calendar, we're pretty sure one of these three is Russell Schiff."

Taylor's phone suddenly rang. "Taylor...Great...Good job." He hung up and pointed to one of the pictures John was holding. "That guy is Ronald Blaine." He tapped the other picture John was holding. "And this one is David Yoro."

"So that leaves us with this guy," Erin said, indicating the photo she was holding. "How sure are we this is Schiff?"

"Everyone else has been accounted for, and according to Cousins' calendar and notes, Schiff was there."

"So we possibly have a face to put to the crimes." Erin tacked the photo on one of the boards with pictures of the victims.

"We need to identify this guy. I'm sure Russell Schiff is not his real name if he is The Slasher. We need to find a name to go with this face." John tapped the picture.

"Right. We also need to find Agent Morgan. The director is all over me about her. No one has seen or heard from her. We verified that she took a flight from Key West to here. But there's no record of her renting a car," said Taylor.

"Try running the name Essington," Erin said.

"What?"

"Just try it," she urged.

"All right, I'll have it checked out."

A couple of hours later, Taylor told Erin and John that they received no hits on the name Essington. He then returned to his office.

Erin pulled her phone out and tried to call Jess yet again. Just like the previous half a dozen times, she reached Jess' voicemail. She hung up her phone and looked at John. "Something's wrong."

"You don't know that," John said, obviously trying to convince himself as much as her.

Erin looked at him incredulously. "Jess left the island to go to a meeting. We know there was no meeting—at least not with the FBI. No one has seen or heard from her since she left the island. And she's not picking up her phone. We need to find her."

John let out a sigh. "How?"

Not having an answer, Erin shook her head in frustration. After a few moments, she thought of something. She picked up a desk phone and called the tech department. She spoke to someone and verified a call was placed to Jess' phone from the suspect number in the middle of the night and that it had originated from DC. She hung up and looked at John. "She came here to meet with the UNSUB. She called him two hours before he called her. I think she initiated the meeting." She felt her heart drop to her feet. "Why would she do that?"

"Damn it! I told her to change the game, but I didn't know she'd pull something like this."

"We need to have a trace put on her phone." Erin turned and walked into Taylor's office.

Taylor agreed with Erin and ordered the trace. Unfortunately, they could not trace its location because it wasn't turned on.

▬

Jess looked at her watch. It was almost time. She turned on her phone and waited. She noted the number of messages left, and the incoming call log revealed a Bureau number and Erin's and John's. She shook her head. Jess knew she'd ruffle some feathers handling this the way she did, but she couldn't risk anything happening to Erin or John.

She looked at her watch again. He should be calling her any second. She didn't have to wait long. She received a text with an address. It was all she needed. She turned her phone off and started walking.

▬

March 22, 2025
Saturday

Shortly after midnight, Taylor stood in the doorway of his office. "Casper! Little! Get in here."

The two agents entered his office.

"They traced Agent Morgan's cell phone. She's in the warehouse district. They'll try to narrow it down to a specific address if they can, but in the meantime—"

"We're on it!" John cut him off as he turned to leave the office. Erin was on his heels.

"Wear vests," Taylor called after them.

Erin and John raced to the warehouse district northeast of Gallaudet University, hoping for a more definitive location on Jess. When they arrived, John drove slowly, looking for any sign of Jess. They both jumped when John's phone suddenly rang.

"Casper."

"They've narrowed her location to the fifteen hundred block of Okie Street Northeast."

"Got it." John hung up and told Erin the location.

"That's just around the corner. Turn left on Fenwick, then right on Okie," Erin instructed.

John made the turns and turned off the car's headlights. He coasted to a stop. They exchanged a look before slipping out of the car and into the night. With weapons drawn, they carefully moved to the nearest warehouse. It was mostly empty, but it took several minutes to confirm that no one was there. They made their way to the next warehouse.

Jess stuck to the shadows. With the moon less than a quarter full, it wasn't difficult. Her dark attire and mood helped her blend invisibly into the night. She arrived at the address she'd been given. Just as promised, the side door was unlocked. Jess entered. Crates were piled all over the warehouse, but the center area was clear. As instructed, she moved to the center of the cleared area and waited. Finally, she heard a voice.

"How do I know you came alone?"

She could tell the voice was coming from a device somewhere in the stacks of crates. It was the same voice from the phone calls.

"Don't be an ass," she snapped with irritation. "You undoubtedly watched my approach to the building, and then you waited a few minutes after I arrived to see if anyone followed me. Besides, this was your choice of location, so you obviously scouted it out in advance. Let's say we get on with this."

"What did you want to meet about?"

"I was hoping we could come to a resolution."

"A resolution? A resolution to what?"

"I want to stop the killing. What will it take to get you to stop killing young women?"

"What if I told you I don't know why I kill them?"

"I'd say you're a liar. I'm not here to play games. If that's all you want to do, I'm leaving." Jess turned and took a step toward the exit.

An almost silent shot chipped the concrete a few inches from her feet.

"You don't leave until *I* say so," the disembodied voice said with a growl.

Jess let out an exaggerated sigh. "This is tedious. I wanted to meet with you to talk and find a way out of this." She heard a derisive snort.

"You think you're going play head-shrinker with me, *Doctor* Morgan? You think you can *help* me?" he replied mockingly. "You can't even help yourself. You certainly couldn't help Agent Jeffers, and you won't be able to help Agent Little!"

Despite her desire not to, Jess couldn't hide her reaction to his baiting. The son of a bitch really did know how to push her buttons. Her hands curled into tight fists, her whole body began to tremble angrily, and she clenched her jaw, grinding her teeth. "You sick bastard."

Jess suddenly burst into motion, running for the stacks of crates, bullets striking the floor in her footsteps, but not nearly as close as they could have been. He was still playing with her.

From the sound of Jessica's voice, John figured he was closer to her than Erin, who was on the other side of the warehouse. He also heard a man's voice, but not from the same location. It was coming from a radio.

A couple more turns in the stacks, and he spotted his partner. "Jessica," he whispered.

When she turned her head to look at him, anger burned in her glare. He was taken aback.

Jessica suddenly burst into motion, running toward him, bullets striking the floor in her footsteps. She marched past him, anger rolling off her in waves.

"Jessica, what the hell is going on?" he whispered as he followed her.

She ignored him and retrieved a radio hidden in the stacks.

Jess had determined where the device he was using was located. She glared at John, then moved through the stacks to the walkie-talkie. She picked it up. "If you have anything to say, come out of the shadows and face me. Or are you too much of a coward to face a woman when she knows what you really are?"

"And what's that?"

"Scared. Scared to be yourself, so you put on a fake personality like most people put on clothes. A fake personality you know a woman will like. But you don't do it for her. No. Everything you do is for you, about you. You probably can only come when you masturbate. I bet you don't even know how to make love to a woman. And you certainly don't know how to please a woman, how to make her come. But then you don't care about them enough to try, do you?"

"Stop it!"

"Why? Hitting too close to home?" Jess walked out of the stacks back into the cleared area. "I already know you don't have sex with your victims. You do terrible things to them, but you don't have sex with them. Is that why you kill them? Because after you sweep them off their feet, they want to take things to the next level, they want to have sex? But you can't, can you? You're impotent when you're with a woman, aren't you? How much porn do you watch? Jerking off to porn is the only way you can get off, isn't it?"

"Stop!"

Jess smiled. The stress level in his voice was increasing. She was getting to him. "You have your dick in your hand right now, don't you? You're trying to get your puny, flaccid dick hard right now to prove I'm wrong. But you can't. You can't get hard without watching some trashy porno movie. You can't get it up with a real woman."

"Stop!"

"You don't know what it's like to have a woman love you, do you? You don't know what it's like to be wanted by a woman, not as yourself. Only by playing a part can you get them interested in you. But you're all talk and no action. You can't deliver when it counts. You can't give yourself to anyone because you're too selfish, too self-centered…because you're an egomaniac."

"That's not true!"

"You'll never know what it's like to hold a woman and have her open, vulnerable, and passionate. You'll never know what it's like to look into her eyes and see love shining in them just for you. You'll never know what it's like to give her so much pleasure she cries out to God. You'll never know what it's like to touch her so deeply that you touch her soul. You'll never know what it's like to hear your name on her lips in passion. You'll never know what it's like for her to love you."

"She *will* love me!"

"No, she won't. She'll never love you, because you can't be what she desires, what she needs, what she deserves."

"*Nooo!*"

Jess miscalculated. She had found his most vulnerable button and pushed it a little too hard.

Jess went down, a look of surprise on her face.

Chapter Thirty-Two

ERIN EASED HER WAY through the stacks and toward the sound of Jess' voice. Erin could hear a man's voice, but she couldn't see him anywhere. His voice sounded like it was coming through a radio. She finally came to a cleared area and was relieved to see Jess standing there. Then she heard the man's voice coming over a radio on the other side of the area.

"You think you're going play head-shrinker with me, *Doctor* Morgan? You think you can *help* me?" he replied mockingly. "You can't even help yourself! You certainly couldn't help Agent Jeffers, and you won't be able to help Agent Little!"

"You sick bastard."

It infuriated Erin to hear the suspect use Toni and her against Jess.

Jess suddenly burst into motion, running for the stacks of crates, bullets striking the floor in her footsteps.

Erin tried to get a look in the direction the shots had come from without exposing herself. She listened as Jess continued to talk to the suspect. A frisson of foreboding set her heart racing when Jess stepped out of the stacks, back into the clear area, and back into the field of fire. She also felt proud of how well Jess handled the suspect, pushed his buttons, and kept him off balance.

"*Nooo!*"

"Jess!" She felt her heart stop when Jess went down.

He was surprised she'd called and left the message asking him to call her, especially after she had refused to talk to him. He thought it was the perfect opportunity to go to the next step of his plan. But then she refused to meet him until the next night.

No matter. She would be showing up soon. He'd stayed in his spot all through the night and the next day. No one was going to get anything past him or set him up. He was too smart for that. And that bitch would find out she wasn't good enough.

He looked at his watch. It was time. He turned on his phone and texted Morgan. He told her which warehouse to visit, then turned off his phone. He watched her enter and made her wait a few minutes. He wasn't stupid. He waited to make sure she was alone. Finally, he activated the cellular walkie-talkie he'd set up with another prepaid phone.

"How do I know you came alone?"

He didn't like her attitude. When she turned to go, he let loose a few shots, letting her know *he* was in control. She wouldn't leave if he didn't want her to, and he wasn't done with her yet. He relished her visible reaction to his taunting at the mention of Jeffers and Little. He had the upper hand. This was *his* game, and she would have to play by his rules.

He was caught a little off guard when Morgan suddenly dashed for the stacks. He was sure he could take her out, but he didn't want to, at least not yet. She needed to be taught a few lessons first. He followed her footsteps with his almost silent shots.

After a few moments, he heard her voice again, coming directly over his radio. She had found it and was now holding it. That was when she started. First, she called him a coward. Then, she accused him of not knowing how to love a woman, how to please a woman. How dare she?

"Stop it!" he ordered.

She taunted him, even stepped back out into the clearing. He could take her out so easily. The fucking bitch deserved it! He *wasn't* impotent! He unzipped his pants and took out his dick. He wasn't impotent. He'd prove it. He started rubbing himself.

"Stop!"

He realized he'd closed his eyes. He opened them to see that cunt smiling. Smiling! Fuck! How did she know he was jerking off? How could she know? His dick *wasn't* puny. He *could* get hard without watching porn. Damn it! Why wasn't he getting hard? He moved his hand faster, squeezing and pulling. She was still smiling.

"Stop!"

That fucking cunt dared to tell him he couldn't deliver. Well, he'd show her. He was going to deliver a lesson she'd never forget. Damn it, his dick was still limp. He spat on his hand and tried to rub himself faster. Fuck her! He was not an egomaniac.

"That's not true!"

He was having trouble keeping his weapon aimed at her as he continued to try to make his dick hard. Tears...must be from the dust. Tears blurred his vision. He closed his eyes and tried to picture his favorite object of lust. He was *not* impotent! If he could keep the right pictures in his mind.

"You'll never know what it's like for her to love you."

"She *will* love me!"

"No, she won't. She'll never love you, because you can't be what she desires, what she needs, what she deserves."

"*Nooo*!" He let go of his flaccid dick and wiped the tears from his eyes. He aimed and fired. Fucking bitch!

Jess went down, a look of surprise on her face. John heard Erin's yell, but she was on the far side of the area, too far to get to Jess. He would have to get Jess out himself. As the shots kept coming, John moved out from behind a crate and started returning fire in the direction he thought the shots were coming from. He didn't get far. He was hit in the shoulder. The force of the impact spun him around, and he hit his head on a crate on the way down. He was nearly knocked out and was struggling to stay conscious.

"Jess!" Erin felt her heart stop. Her partner, the woman she lo—.

Jess was down, and shots were still being fired. John was hit next. A round slammed into his shoulder, spinning him around. He hit his head on the way down and was knocked out.

Erin shoved a new magazine into her weapon and watched for movement. Finally, she saw it. The suspect was a dark mass, moving his gun back and forth between the fallen bodies of the downed agents. He was waiting for either of them to move to take another shot. Erin couldn't get a shot at him without fully exposing herself.

"Erin..."

She looked at Jess. Her eyes were open, and she was looking right at Erin. "Don't move, Jess." She looked back up in the shadows. There was sudden movement from the shooter as he detected motion from John. Erin made her move. She stepped from behind cover, fully exposing herself, and rapidly fired three times. Her target went down, his weapon dropping from his hands.

"John! Are you okay?" she called across the room.

"Yeah," he called back. "I'm hit, but the vest caught it. I've got him covered. Check on Jessica."

Erin rushed to Jess, dropping to her side. "Jess?" She set her weapon down and ripped open Jess' shirt to reveal a bulletproof vest with a bullet embedded in the place over her heart, but blood was pooling next to Jess. Erin pulled the vest away and found the bullet wound. A bullet had hit her in the side, missing the Kevlar. She pulled her jacket off, folded it, and pressed it against the wound, putting pressure on it. She pulled out her cell and called for help.

"9-1-1. What's your emergency?"

"Yes. I'm FBI Agent Erin Little, badge number JTT0441614. I need two ambulances at 1550 Okie Street Northeast. I've got two agents down. Repeat, two agents down. Hurry! Send backup."

"Ambulances are on the way, Agent Little. ETA six minutes. Backup ETA three minutes."

Erin hung up. "Jess? Jess!"

Jess' eyes opened again, and she slowly moved her head to look up at Erin. Her eyes were dull. "Cold…" she said.

"You have to fight, Jess!" Tears ran down Erin's face. "Help's coming. It's almost here. Hang on, Jess. Just a few minutes."

"S-Sorry…" Her eyes drifted shut.

"*Jess*! Damn it, *fight*!" They could hear the sirens closing in on them.

Jess' eyelids fluttered and then opened. "Too late…"

The problem with being a doctor was recognizing when someone was dying and knowing it was too late for medical intervention. The pool of Jess' blood was too big. The rattle in her lungs portended her final breaths. Erin leaned down and got in Jess' face. "Damn it, Jess, I just found you, and I am *not* going to lose you. You can make it. You can survive if you take my blood."

"No."

"Yes."

"I can't…told you…consequences…"

"I know. Now do it, before it's too late." She slipped her hand under Jess' head and lifted it, pressing Jess' face to her throat. "Please! I love you, and I need you."

Erin felt the initial stab of two sharp fangs breaking her skin, but then there was no pain at all. She felt like she was floating. Time slowed. She became aware of each beat of her heart, the movement of air in and out of her lungs with each breath, the blood flowing through her veins, flowing from her and into the woman she loved. She could sense strength returning to Jess' body, her heartbeat, and their hearts beating as one. She had no idea how long it lasted, but she knew the instant Jess stopped because time snapped back to normal. Erin gently eased Jess' head back down. Erin looked into fathomless, obsidian eyes and saw two gleaming fangs between her parted lips, but she saw no monster, only love.

"Are you…You're going to be okay, right?" Erin tenderly brushed Jess' hair away from her face.

Jess closed her eyes. "Yes." When she opened her eyes, they were once again gray and held the spark of life within them instead of the flatness of death.

Two squad cars screeched to a halt. The police, under John's direction, checked on the shooter. He was alive but unconscious.

Only minutes later, Erin was riding in the first ambulance with Jess on the way to the hospital, never once letting go of her hand.

Officer Kyle Noble and his partner cautiously rushed in. They found the three agents in question. The male agent immediately directed them to the shooter's position. While Agent Casper kept his weapon pointed at the shooter, Noble and his partner made their way up the ladder to the gantry. With weapons drawn, they approached the suspect but relaxed when they determined he was unconscious. Once the shooter was securely cuffed, Noble looked down at the man and shook his head. The bastard had his dick hanging out. Why would the guy have his limp dick hanging out while shooting at FBI agents?

When AD Taylor arrived, Agent Morgan was already on the way to the hospital. Agent Little had gone with her. He walked up to the second ambulance as the paramedics finished preparing the shooter for transport. He looked down at the unconscious man. "You fucking prick. You're going to wish you were dead by the time I'm done with you." He noticed the man's penis was out. "You sick fuck." He assigned an agent to ride to the hospital with him. "You make sure he stays cuffed no matter what. Don't let him out of your sight, and I want to know about anything he says if he comes to."

"Yes, sir."

The second ambulance left.

Agent Casper was sitting in the back of a third ambulance. His vest had prevented one bullet from penetrating, but another did hit his arm. It wasn't as bad as it could have been.

"What the hell happened?" Taylor asked.

"He shot Agent Morgan. I got clipped when I tried to get to her. Then Agent Little nailed his ass. She called for backup and ambulances. The police arrived and took him into custody. Little went with Morgan in the first ambulance."

"How bad was Morgan hit?"

Casper shook his head. "She didn't look good. She lost a lot of blood." He paused. "She was wearing a vest, so I don't know where she was hit." He suddenly winced as the EMT examining his ribs pressed on a particularly tender spot.

"You're going to need x-rays, sir, to make sure you haven't cracked or broken anything," said the EMT.

"I'm fine."

Taylor nodded to the paramedic. "Take him."

Chapter Thirty-Three

EVEN THOUGH JESS HAD told her she'd be okay, Erin couldn't help being worried sick as the ambulance rushed to the hospital. Jess had closed her eyes before the ambulance arrived and hadn't yet opened them again, no matter how hard Erin squeezed her hand.

She had seen how well Jess could heal after drinking some blood, but the beating she'd taken in Atlanta wasn't as severe as the gunshot wound that she had in her side. Jess had lost so much blood, and the rattle as she breathed indicated lung damage. After what seemed like much too long, the ambulance finally arrived at the hospital. Jess was rushed into a trauma bay, and Erin was told to remain in the waiting room. A few minutes later, another ambulance arrived, bringing in the shooter.

"Agent Little?"

Erin was sipping bitter vending machine coffee while pacing and startled slightly when she heard her name. She turned and looked at the worried face of the director.

"Sir."

"How's Jessica?"

"I don't know, sir. She was wearing a vest, but a bullet caught her in the side, missing the Kevlar. She's lost a lot of blood but seemed to have a good pulse."

The director took out his handkerchief. He reached out and dabbed it against the side of Erin's neck at her collar. "You're bleeding."

Erin immediately raised her hand, holding the handkerchief in place as the director withdrew his hand.

"You should have that looked at."

Thinking quickly, she said, "I'm fine, sir. It's just a nick from debris, probably a cement chip." She pulled the handkerchief away and looked at it. "See? Just a couple of drops." She held it out for the director to take back, but he waved her off.

"Keep it."

She buttoned the top button on her shirt, closing the collar.

They waited a few more minutes before Dr. Thomas came out to speak with them.

"Agent Morgan is being prepped for surgery to remove a bullet. It appears to have entered her side, injuring her lung and damaging her liver. The liver was the source of most of her blood loss. Somehow, the bleeding seems to have lessened on its own, so while it's a concern, it's not our greatest concern."

"What is?" Erin asked.

"The location of the bullet, it's lodged against her spine."

Erin's heart dropped. "Cord damage?"

"We don't know yet and won't know until afterward."

"I want your best surgeon working on her," Director Cavanaugh declared.

"You have her. Dr. Kerry Kelvin is the best on the coast."

"Good." He paused for a beat. "What about the gunman?"

"He's also on his way to surgery, but I wasn't on the team that worked on him. I'll have Dr. Mendez come and talk to you about him."

"Thank you."

The doctor left.

It was only a minute or so before Dr. Mendez came out to talk to the director. "How can I help you?"

"Tell me about the shooter."

"He sustained three gunshot wounds: one in his left shoulder and one in his arm. The third bullet hit his head in a grazing strike, creating a gouge about two inches long above his left ear but not entering the skull. He's been taken up to surgery."

"Did he say anything?"

"He was unconscious when brought in, but he did come to. However, he was combative and uncooperative, so we were forced to sedate him."

"What did he say? Did he tell you his name?"

"No. All he did was rant about some woman in very profane terms. Unless there are some unexpected complications, he should be fine."

"Thank you," said the director.

Dr. Mendez left.

Erin and the director went up to the surgical waiting room. After a while, John joined them. He'd been seen in the ER and had his left arm bandaged and in a sling.

"Any news on Jessica?" he asked.

Erin shook her head.

He sat beside her and put his right hand over one of hers, squeezing it. "She's been through much worse and come out okay. She'll be all right."

Erin wanted to believe that, but she wouldn't until she saw it herself. She suspected Jess hadn't taken nearly as much blood as she needed to heal. She stood and walked to the windows. She gazed out but didn't really see anything.

She closed her eyes and recalled what she felt when Jess bit her. It wasn't anything like she had expected. The pain had lasted only a moment, barely a fraction of a second. Then she felt...well, she began to understand how some people could get addicted to it. Even now, just thinking about it, she was feeling the peacefulness and the arousal that had filled her during those moments? Seconds? Minutes?

Erin opened her eyes and took a slow, deep breath. She finally knew what she wanted, what she needed. She was in love with Jess. She needed Jess in her life, and if Jess occasionally needed blood, she would willingly give it.

Erin gasped as suddenly a feeling of...of...No word described what she felt, but she knew something was wrong with Jess. She knew it with unquestionable certainty. She turned and marched through the doors that led to the surgical floor. With the air of authority and determination surrounding her, no one questioned her presence as she marched to her destination.

Erin opened the door to the observation room above an operating room. It was the right one, because she could see Jess on the table below. The doctors and nurses were working on her, trying to get her heartbeat back. Finally, they did. She watched until that indescribable feeling was gone, until she knew Jess was stable. Only then did she leave the observation room.

John sat quietly with his head back against the wall and his eyes closed. The painkillers he'd been given had kicked in.

AD Taylor arrived and approached the director. He had some bad news for him.

"*What*? Are you sure?"

"There's no doubt. It's him, sir. We have the disposable phone he used, the gun he used, and his wallet. I don't have ballistics yet, but I'd be surprised if it didn't match what we took out of the wall at the safe house."

"Son of a bitch! I want that bastard's ass. Make sure guards are on him twenty-four/seven. As soon as the doctors say it's safe to move him, I want him locked up. I want you to interrogate him personally. No one else gets near him."

"Yes, sir." Taylor paused. "Any word on Agent Morgan?"

"Not yet. They said the bullet is lodged against her spine."

"Damn."

"Taylor, no mistakes on this. He tried to kill a couple of my agents, and he's screwed with this investigation. I want him put away with no chance he'll get off."

With a nod, Taylor left.

Erin came back to the waiting room and sat down next to John.

"Any news about Jessica?" he asked.

She shook her head. "Anything going on here?"

"Taylor came and spoke to the director. I didn't hear their conversation, but the director was really pissed."

It was a long five hours later before Jess' surgeon came out.

"Who's here for Jessica Morgan?" she asked.

All three people in the waiting room stood up, although John was a little slower than the others.

"We are," said the director. He made the introductions.

"Does Agent Morgan have any family present?" Dr. Kelvin asked.

"She doesn't have any family. How is she?" said the director.

"Lucky to be alive. The bullet entered her side, injuring both her liver and her lung. It then lodged in an intervertebral disc." She shook her head. "The amount of bleeding was remarkably little considering the damage path."

"But you got the bullet out, right?"

"Yes." She handed him a small plastic container with the retrieved slug. "I'm sure you want this."

"Thank you."

Erin couldn't take it anymore. "What about her spine? Was there any cord damage? Any loss of function?" she asked.

"Due to the trauma, there's some swelling in the area. We've got her on a steroidal anti-inflammatory to treat it. We won't know for sure whether she'll experience any loss of function until the inflammation goes down."

"Can we see her?" Erin asked.

"She's in recovery right now. Once they move her to the ICU, you can visit her, one at a time. I'll have someone let you know when you can see her."

"Thank you, Doctor," said the director.

Dr. Kelvin left the waiting room.

The director looked at John. "How are you feeling?"

"I'm okay, just a little tired."

"After we see Jessica, I want you to go get some sleep." His tone made it clear it was an order.

John nodded. The truth was, he desperately needed some sleep. It was almost seven o'clock in the morning, and he was having difficulty staying awake.

"What about the suspect? We need to interview him when he comes to," Erin pointed out.

"He will be interrogated, but I'm afraid you can't be a part of it, Agent Little."

"Why not? I've been working this case with Jess for over a month."

"Because the shooter at the warehouse was Agent Derek Holton. You're not to go near him or talk to him, Agent Little."

"What?" Erin was shocked. "He can't be The Slasher."

"I don't believe he is, but he *is* the shooter."

"I don't understand. He idolizes her. He wants to be like her," said Erin.

"I have no idea what's prompted his behavior, but he's messed with this investigation. He's had you concentrating on identifying him rather than the real Slasher. Who knows how many of the deaths could have been prevented if he hadn't had you following false leads." The director growled. "He'll be lucky if I don't find a way to charge him with at least a couple of the murders as a result."

"Excuse me."

They all turned toward the nurse who had entered. She let them know they could see Jessica one at a time.

The director went in first. Then John.

Erin looked at the director before going in to see Jess. "I'm going to stay with Jess, so she won't be alone when she wakes up."

He nodded. "Very well." He gave her his private number. "Call me to let me know how she's doing."

"Yes, sir."

Jess looked so pale and was as still as death. The only movement was her chest's slight rise and fall as she breathed. She didn't look like she should. She didn't look like herself. The air of determination and drive that usually clung to her were absent. Also missing were the worry lines that subtly wizened her face. She looked…young and innocent.

Erin looked at the readouts on the monitors. Her heart rate and blood pressure should be higher. She moved to Jess' bed and took her hand into one of her own. Erin reached up and tenderly brushed some hair from her forehead.

"Jess…" A lump in her throat made it hard to speak. She swallowed and tried again. "Jess, I need you to be all right." A couple of tears ran down her cheeks. "Come back to me, Jess. I love you."

Erin pulled the chair closer to the bed. She sat down and held onto Jess' hand, unable to let go of that lifeline.

She woke up a few hours later as a nurse checked Jess' vitals.

The nurse smiled at her. "Good morning."

"Morning."

"I'm Ruth."

"Agent Little—Erin." She looked at Jess' face.

"She hasn't woken up yet, but all of her vitals have been stable," Ruth said, trying to reassure her.

Chapter Thirty-Four

IT WAS FOUR O'CLOCK in the afternoon when Dr. Kelvin came to check on Jess. Erin, who had been resting in the chair next to the bed, still holding her hand, immediately opened her eyes.

The doctor uncovered the end of the bed and Jess' feet. She ran the handle of a mallet along the bottom of Jess' feet to see which way they curled. Kelvin then pushed the covers up further and slipped a hand behind a knee, lifting it slightly. She then tapped below the kneecap with the mallet to test the reflex arc. She repeated the action with the other knee.

Kelvin smiled. "She has normal reflexes, an excellent sign," she said before leaving.

"Thank god."

John came to check on Jess around seven o'clock. "Hi."

"Hey. How are you doing?" Erin asked.

"I'm fine."

"You look better that you did this morning, well-rested."

John nodded. "It's amazing what twelve hours of sleep will do." He looked at Jess. "How is she doing?"

"According to the surgeon, she has good reflexes, so the swelling around her spine has gone down, and she's not paralyzed."

"Thank goodness." He gazed at the Erin for a moment. "How are you doing?"

She was surprised at how her eyes immediately watered. "I'm relieved she's not paralyzed, but I'm worried she hasn't woken up yet." She paused. "And I'm angry as hell she went off on her own and got shot in the first place."

"Yet you're still here," he pointed out gently.

She nodded. "Because even though I met her only five weeks ago, I've fallen in love with her." She wiped her eyes. "I'm here because I want her in my life."

"You mean that?" came softly from the bed, accompanied by a light squeeze on Erin's hand.

"Jess!" Erin jumped up to her feet and looked down at her.

John moved to the foot of the bed and smiled. "Welcome back, partner."

Jess tried to swallow. "Thanks."

Erin poured some water into a cup and put a straw into it. She held it so Jess could carefully take a sip. "Just a sip."

"Thank you." She gazed up into Erin's eyes. "Did you mean it? Even after everything, do you really want me in your life?" she asked softly.

Erin nodded and took Jess' hand in her own again. "Yes, I do. I love you."

This time, it was Jess' eyes that watered. "I love you too."

Erin bent down and tenderly kissed Jess' lips.

John cleared his throat while smiling widely. It wasn't until a second person cleared their throat that Erin stood up, blushing.

"It's nice to see you awake, Agent Morgan," said Dr. Kelvin. "If you'll excuse us, I need to examine my patient," she said, addressing Erin and John.

"Right. I'll be going. I'll stop by tomorrow, Jessica," said John.

"Thanks for being here, John."

"Of course, kiddo." He turned to go.

"I'll wait outside," Erin said, squeezing Jess' hand.

Dr. Kelvin nodded, but Jess stopped her.

"No. You can stay, Erin." Jess didn't let go of her hand.

Erin looked at the doctor.

"If it's all right with her, it's all right with me."

When Erin and Jess were once again alone, Erin sat on the edge of the bed. "I love you, Jess, but I am angry with you. You should not have gone off alone to meet him."

"It was the only way."

"No, it wasn't. You could have trusted me to have your back."

"It wasn't a matter of trust, Erin. I do trust you, more than you know."

"Then why?"

"Because it was the only way I could be sure you and John were safe, especially you," she said softly. "The Slasher never threatened my life, only yours and John's." Jess must have seen something in Erin's expression. "What is it?"

"It wasn't The Slasher."

"What?"

"The caller, the one who left the messages, he wasn't The Slasher."

Jess closed her eyes and sighed. "I was afraid of that. His behavior didn't fit the profile." She opened her eyes. "Who was he?"

Erin looked away, feeling betrayed and heartsick.

Jess carefully reached up and, with her hand on Erin's cheek, turned her head back to look in her eyes. "Hey, what's wrong?"

"It was Holton. He's the one behind the break-ins, the messages in blood, the threats, the calls: he did it all. He's the one who tried to kill you."

Jess gently tugged until Erin leaned down and Jess could wrap her arms around her. "Oh, Erin, I'm so sorry."

Erin finally let a few tears go. "I never knew he could do something like this. I should have…He was my partner. I trained him. I should have known it was him. I should have seen it. I'm so sorry, Jess. I should have—"

"Shhh. You don't have anything to feel guilty about. It's not your fault, Erin. It's not your fault." Jess held Erin until she stopped crying. When Erin sat back up, Jess looked into her eyes. "I'm sorry you have to deal with this. Have you spoken to him?"

Erin shook her head. "The director ordered me to stay away from him. They moved him to prison a few hours ago."

Jess finally convinced Erin to go home and get some sleep in her own bed. After Erin left, Jess made a few phone calls. One to Lindsey MacRusso. She asked Mac to arrange for all their stuff on the private key in Florida to be transported to DC. John's things were to be sent to his hotel room, Erin's stuff to her apartment, and Jess' things to her office.

Her second call was to a place that made deliveries. She would be all right, but if she didn't have some more blood, her recovery would be too slow. She'd wasted enough time dealing with Holton. She needed to return to work and find The Slasher. She arranged for a delivery first thing in the morning.

Her third call was to the director. Erin had already let him know how Jess was doing, but Jess wanted to talk to him about Holton.

"What's going to happen to Holton?"

"He's going down. And there's nothing you can say to me that will change my mind. Knowing what he's done, I'm surprised he passed the psych test to enter the Bureau."

"Well, on the surface, he's a war hero and a cop. And don't forget, Holton has a degree in psychology. He knows all the right answers to give. Are you going to have him psychologically evaluated?"

"After everything he's done, I don't think I have a choice. But I'll be damned if I let him get off because he's crazy."

"Calm down, Lou. Remember, sane is a legal term, not a medical one. All they have to demonstrate is that he knows right from wrong."

"I'll have someone see him tomorrow. And now, you should be getting some rest. You've been through a lot, Jessica. You need to take care of yourself."

"I need to find out who The Slasher is and stop him!"

"You're not getting anywhere near the case until a doctor says you can," he retorted.

"I *am* a doctor, and no one knows my body and what I'm capable of more than I do."

"Be that as it may, no work without a doctor's clearance. That's final."

"Yes, sir."

She hung up. She was angry. She was angry at being sidetracked by Holton's interference in the investigation, angry with herself for miscalculating and getting shot, and angry with The Slasher for killing so many young women.

March 23, 2025
Sunday

Erin woke up early the next morning. She dressed and headed to the hospital. She discovered Jess had been moved from the ICU to a private room when she arrived.

The head of Jess' bed was elevated, so she was sitting up when Erin entered her room. Erin walked over and kissed her. "Good morning."

"It is now. Good morning," Jess replied, returning her smile.

"How do you feel?" Erin asked as she sat on the side of the bed.

"Not bad, considering."

A knock interested them, and a woman stood in the open doorway. "Jessica Morgan?"

"Come in."

"You requested a delivery?" she asked somewhat hesitantly, glancing at Erin.

"Yes, thank you," Jess replied, holding her hand for the brown paper bag.

The woman handed over the bag and made her exit.

Erin made an educated guess as to what was in the bag. "That's blood, isn't it?"

Feeling ashamed, Jess dropped her eyes and gave a small nod.

Erin reached out and gently lifted Jess' chin with her fingers so she could look her in the eyes. "Hey, you don't have anything to be ashamed about." She waited until she sensed Jess relax before continuing. "But I do want to talk to you about it."

Another small nod.

Erin took the paper bag and set it on the rolling bed table. She then took Jess' hand in hers. "First, I have a couple of questions."

"Okay."

"At the warehouse, when you took my blood, you didn't take as much as you needed, did you?"

"No," she answered softly.

"Why not?" Erin asked gently.

"I took what I thought was enough to tide me over until I got to the hospital."

"But it wasn't enough to guarantee you'd live."

"No."

"I need to know why, Jess. I told you to take my blood because I love you and I didn't want you to die. So why didn't you take what you truly needed?"

"You have to understand, Erin, I've never had human blood before, not even donated blood. My whole life, it was drummed into me that I should never take human blood, especially directly. There can be consequences, and I don't want anything to happen to you."

"From what you told me, two things could happen to me. One is that I might become addicted to your feeding."

Jess nodded.

"But that doesn't mean I *will*. The second was something about a bond that could develop between us?"

Jess nodded again.

"What did you mean by that?"

"Sometimes a bond forms between the vampire and human, a kind of connection, an empathy for each other."

"I don't see the problem, Jess."

"What?"

"You need blood to heal." She gestured to the paper bag. "And that will not help you as much as my blood will."

"Erin—"

"I love you, Jess, which means I want what's best for you. That pig's blood isn't." Erin cradled Jess' face in both hands, gently pulling her into a kiss. When she felt Jess' lips part slightly, she slipped her tongue into her mouth and gently explored it. Erin broke the kiss and then guided Jess' lips to her neck. "Please, Jess," she whispered.

Erin's eyes closed at the momentary pain that gave way to the peace and arousal that permeated her entire being. A low moan escaped her lips as she felt their hearts beat as one. Time seemed to bend and stretch. When Jess stopped, time snapped back into place. Erin felt Jess' tongue and lips lightly teasing the pulse point at the base of her neck. She sank her fingers in dark, silky hair, pulled Jess' head back and claimed her mouth in a deep, passionate kiss. She tasted a faint coppery tang on Jess' tongue, but it wasn't unpleasant.

When their lips parted, Erin gazed into fathomless obsidian eyes. They exchanged breaths as they panted. Erin rested her forehead against Jess', closed her eyes, and drew in a slow, deep breath.

Jess tenderly took Erin's face in her hands and placed a chaste kiss on her cheek. "I love you, Erin. And when I get out of here, I'll show you how much." She leaned back against the bed, obviously sleepy. "Just give me a few hours of sleep, and I'll be ready to get out of here." Her eyes drifted shut.

Erin stood up. She kissed Jess' forehead. "I need to go to work, but I'll be back. Sleep well." She lowered the head of the bed.

Before leaving, Erin used the bathroom. She was surprised when she checked her appearance in the mirror. The first bite mark was gone entirely, and the new bite mark was already well on the way to healing. She had two minor, inconspicuous marks already scabbed over. Her shirt collar easily hid them.

When she stepped back into the room, Erin stopped and gazed at Jess sleeping in the hospital bed. She didn't know why Jess had come into her life, but she was infinitely grateful. She grabbed the paper bag containing the pig's blood, which she dropped into a biological waste receptacle on the way out.

Chapter Thirty-Five

ERIN WAS SURPRISED WHEN John arrived at work about half an hour after she did. She arched an eyebrow at him. "What are you doing here?"

"We still have work to do. We need to identify our Mr. Russell Schiff," he replied, pointing at the picture on one of the boards.

"You should be resting. You were shot."

"My arm is fine. I'm taking Motrin and keeping my arm in the sling. I'm right-handed anyway."

Erin shook her head. "You sound like Jess."

"Oh?"

"Yeah. I went by to see her this morning, and she said she'd be ready to leave the hospital later today. Then she fell asleep," she finished with amusement.

"I wouldn't bet against her, Erin. She survived an attack by Neil Croskey that would have killed anyone else, and she was out of the hospital in record time."

"She almost died during surgery yesterday, John."

John started to argue the point but stopped when her words sank in. "What the hell do you mean she almost died during surgery?"

Erin closed her eyes momentarily as the painful memory played in her mind. "When I went into the surgical area, I watched Jess' surgery from an observation room. They were struggling to get her heart going again. I stayed until they stabilized her."

John reached out and squeezed Erin's shoulder. "She's all right, Erin."

She nodded.

"Casper, Little, come into my office."

The two agents went into AD Taylor's office. "I've got an assignment for you." He eyed John. "Are you sure you're up for it, Casper?"

"I'm fine, sir. As I told Agent Little, I'm right-handed anyway."

"Take Barker, Kennedy, and Jackson, and go to Philadelphia. We may have a lead on this Russell Schiff guy."

Both John and Erin perked up.

"Little, you're to report to the director upstairs. He's waiting to speak with you."

"Yes, sir."

They both left Taylor's office.

"I'll call and let you know if we come up with anything in Philadelphia, Erin."

"All right."

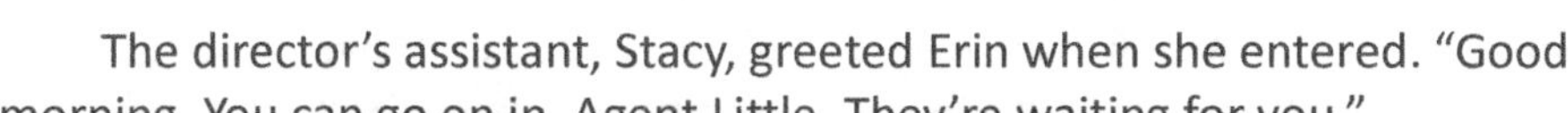

The director's assistant, Stacy, greeted Erin when she entered. "Good morning. You can go on in, Agent Little. They're waiting for you."

"Thank you." Erin was surprised when she entered and found SAC Ken Takashima and another man with the director.

"Agent Little, come in. Have a seat."

"Director, Agent Takashima," she greeted them both as she sat.

"This is Dr. Carl Harkin. He's the psychiatrist who's going to be examining Holton. He and I want to talk with you to get some background," the director explained.

"Yes, sir."

Erin's phone rang around half past one in the afternoon. "Little."

"Agent Little, this is Dr. Harkin."

"What can I do for you, Doctor?"

"I'm here at the prison to evaluate Mr. Holton. He's been extremely disruptive and uncooperative here. However, he says he will cooperate if he can see you. Would you consider coming and talking with him? I've already cleared it with the director, but it is completely up to you."

Erin pinched the bridge of her nose. Did she want to talk to Holton? It had been almost a month since she'd last seen him on her birthday. For three weeks, he had tormented Jess with his notes and messages, he tried to kill Jess, and he shot at *her* at the safe house.

"All right, Doctor. I'll be there as soon as I can."

After Erin passed through the rigorous security of the DC Correctional Center, Dr. Harkin was waiting for her. He took her into the empty visitation room. Glass windows separated visitation stalls from the prisoners. They would have to communicate via one of the telephones built into a stall.

"I did arrange to meet with Mr. Holton in a private room, but he attacked me. So they will only allow him visitation this way," the doctor explained. "He's been so disruptive they've placed him in solitary confinement."

Holton's appearance surprised Erin when he was led in, in shackles. He still had a bandage around his head, covering the gouge above his left ear, and his left arm was in a sling. He had a cut above one eyebrow, a swollen, black eye, a split lip, and visible bruises on his face. The guard pushed him down into the chair on his side of the window.

With trepidation, Erin picked up the handset on her side.

Holton gave Erin a cocky smirk as he picked up the phone. "Hey, Little."

"Holton."

"I haven't seen or talked to you in almost a month, Erin. Is that all you've got to say?"

"And you're a liar. You saw me just fine last Friday when you were taking shots at me."

"I wasn't shooting at *you*. I was trying to shoot Morgan."

"Why?"

"Why? *Why*? She's incompetent! She's supposed to be the best. If she were really that good, she would have found the UNSUB by now. But all she's done is come in and taken you from me and put your life at risk. If it weren't for *her*, we'd still be partners."

"Holton, *you* are the only one who has put my life at risk during this case."

"But I would never hurt you, Erin. Our partnership is special. *You* are special."

"Bullshit! If I were at all special to you, you wouldn't have done any of the things you've done these past few weeks."

"You don't understand. I did everything for you."

"No. You did it for yourself."

"Erin, you don't understand."

"You're right, I don't. I don't understand at all."

"I love you, Erin! Don't you see? *I'm* the one you should be with. I would never let you down. I would never let someone like Conrad get near you the way she let him kill Agent Jeffers. I would protect you. She doesn't deserve you, Erin. She doesn't even know you. I do. I love you. I've always loved you."

She couldn't believe he had the nerve to claim he loved her after everything he'd done. "No, Derek. You don't love me. You don't know the meaning of love." She slammed the receiver down, stood up, and walked out. She never wanted to lay eyes on him again.

Erin was too upset to return to the office, so she simply drove. She was mad at herself for not knowing that he was messing with the case. She kept going over everything that had happened, trying to find that *something* she missed that would have told her Holton was capable of such bullshit.

Without conscious planning, before she realized it, Erin was pulling into her mother's driveway. She got out and walked to the front door.

As soon as her mother opened the door, she seemed to know that something was very wrong. "Erin? What's wrong? Why didn't you use your key?"

Suddenly, tears spilled down her face. Her mother reached out, pulled Erin into her arms, and held her. After a minute, her mom let go of Erin, slipped her arm around her waist, and led her into the living room. They sat down on the couch together.

Erin snagged a tissue from the box on the end table and wiped her eyes as she sniffed.

"What's wrong, Erin?" her mom asked gently.

"I just left the DC Correctional Center…where I visited Holton."

"What? Derek is in prison?"

"He's spent the last three weeks interfering with our investigation, and he tried to kill Jess the other night."

"Are you sure?"

"Yes, Mom. He shot Jess and John Casper, another agent. He was arrested at the scene after I shot him."

"Why?"

"Because he's a selfish bastard," she snapped angrily. "Jess almost died in my arms, Mom." Tears began rolling down her cheeks again. "And they almost lost her during surgery to remove the bullet from where it lodged in her spine."

"Is she okay?" Erin's mother had liked Jess the night they all had dinner together.

"She will be, thank god. John's okay. He was shot in the arm." Erin shook her head. "I just don't understand how he can do such hateful things and then turn around and tell me he did it because he's in love with me."

"He what?"

"He said he loved me. But he doesn't know the meaning of the word."

"What's going to happen to Derek?"

"I don't know, Mom. He shot two agents, made terroristic threats, and interfered with a federal investigation, which may have contributed to the deaths of more than one victim." She wiped her eyes again.

"Could he be sick?"

Erin shrugged. "I know he doesn't regret what he did. He was proud of himself today. A psychiatrist is evaluating him, but if he knows right from wrong, it won't make a difference. That's what's required to be legally sane." She paused. "I've disliked people before but never really hated anyone." She looked at her mother. "Right now, I hate him, Mom. I hate him and never want to lay eyes on him again. I hope they lock him up for the rest of his life and throw away the key."

Her mother put her arm around Erin's shoulders and pulled her close. Erin laid her head on her mom's shoulder.

"Why don't you stay here tonight?" her mom asked after a few moments of silence.

Erin sat up straight. "I can't. I have to go back to the hospital to see Jess. I promised her I'd be back tonight. She doesn't have any family, Mom. No brothers or sisters, and both of her parents are gone. She's all alone."

Her mom put her hand over Erin's and squeezed it. "Then go be with her. And when she gets out of the hospital, bring her here."

Erin looked at her mother in surprise.

"Everyone needs someone to care about them. I like her, and she can stay here while she gets better."

"I'll make the offer, but don't be surprised if she doesn't take you up on it."

"Well, either way, both of you need to come for dinner at the very least."

Erin smiled. "That I can arrange."

"Good."

Erin's phone rang. "Little."

"Hey, it's me, John."

"What's going on? Have you found our Mr. Schiff?"

"I'm in Boston. And I think we've got an excellent lead on this guy. Someone recognized his face but didn't know where from. What he *did* remember was that this guy was wearing a brass rat."

"A what?"

"A brass rat. It's a class ring from MIT."

"So you're—"

"Headed over to MIT now. Yeah. I'll go through every single yearbook personally if I have to. We'll find him, Erin. Tell Jessica we'll find him."

"I'll tell her. Let me know if you need me to come up to Boston."

"I've got some agents with me. Just take care of Jessica, make sure she doesn't push herself too hard."

She let out a soft chuckle. "I'll do my best, but I suspect you know more about how difficult that can be than I do."

"She can be a bit determined," he said, amusement in his voice. "Take care. Bye."

"Bye."

When Erin arrived at the hospital that evening, she was surprised to find Jess sitting up and awake. She smiled. "Hey."

Jess held out her hand. "Come here."

Erin took it in hers and sat on the side of the bed. "How do you feel?"

"I'm fine." They kissed lightly, and then Jess leaned back against the elevated head of her bed. "What's going on with the case?"

"John and some other agents are following up some leads. He said the suspect was seen wearing a 'brass rat.'"

"He went to MIT," she said with a smile. "Somehow, I'm not surprised. I'm sure Russell Schiff is an alias though."

"Undoubtedly. John will go through the class yearbooks and hopefully find his real name."

Jess frowned. "How?"

Erin closed her eyes for a moment and nodded. "That's right, you don't know."

"Know what?"

"We've got a picture of him."

"How?"

"Sheila Cousins was at an open house a couple of days before she was killed. The house owners had a nanny cam that recorded everyone that day.

According to Sheila's records, Schiff was there. By interviewing her associates, clients, and other real estate agents, we've identified everyone except one man."

"Schiff."

"Yeah. Hopefully, we'll have his real name tomorrow."

"I need to get out of here," Jess said as she reached for the nurse call button and hit it.

"What you need to do, Jess, is rest."

"I'm fine, Erin."

"No, you're not. Despite the blood you've had, I know you're not fully healed. I can see it in your eyes."

The nurse entered. "What can I help you with, Agent Morgan?"

"I need to see Dr. Kelvin."

"She's left for the day."

"Then I need to see whoever can discharge me."

"I'm afraid that's not going to happen tonight. Dr. Kelvin will be in to see you tomorrow." The nurse left.

"Damn it! I should just get dressed and leave."

"Jess, *no*. You almost died yesterday. You've had major surgery. You need to rest and heal."

Jess was frustrated. "Erin, I've healed as much as I can while I'm in here. I can't heal completely because there'd be too many questions. We're getting close to this UNSUB. I can feel it. I need to get out of here."

"Do you trust John?"

"What?"

"Do you trust John?"

"Yes."

"Do you trust me?"

Jess' expression softened. "Yes, I do."

"Then trust us to work the case."

Jess closed her eyes and took a slow, deep breath. After letting it out, she opened her eyes. "I do trust you to work the case. I just—"

"You just want to finish what you started," Erin said understandingly.

"Yeah."

"Spending another night here in the hospital won't hurt you." She squeezed Jess' hand. "I saw Mom today. She said I should bring you to her house when you get out of here. She wants to look after you while you recuperate." She smiled and continued before Jess said anything. "I told her you'd probably decline the offer. But she insisted we both come to dinner, and I said yes."

Jess gave her a small smile. "I like your mom."

Erin stayed and talked with Jess until the nurse kicked her out for the night. She then went home to her apartment. She took a long, hot shower before crawling into bed. Despite the stress and emotional exhaustion of the day, she had trouble sleeping. She knew Jess would be all right, but it wouldn't feel real until she could hold her in her arms. Also, conversations with and images of Holton raced through her mind. Erin couldn't help but think she could have done *something* to prevent what had happened. Why didn't she see it coming?

Chapter Thirty-Six

March 24, 2025
Monday

JOHN AND BARKER CAME marching into the bullpen just after one o'clock. John walked up to the whiteboard with Schiff's picture, grabbed a black marker, and wrote something under the photo.

Hugh Charles Schilling

He turned around and faced the bullpen. "We have a name to go with the face!"

Taylor came out of his office at the commotion. He looked at the name on the board. "What do we know about him?"

"Hugh Schilling was a gifted student. He graduated from MIT with PhDs in both Aeronautical Engineering and Mechanical Engineering at the age of nineteen. He was raised in Manhattan, NY, and attended Hunter College Elementary School in Manhattan, then Hunter College High School where he graduated at age twelve."

"So the profile was spot on," someone commented.

"So far, yes." John turned to Taylor. "Kennedy and Jackson are in New York, interviewing his family and friends. But I understand that Schilling hasn't lived in New York for some time. He's a trust-fund baby. When he turned twenty-one, he got five million from a trust fund. He received the remainder of the trust fund at age thirty—sixty-five million. He supposedly has property in eight or nine states, including Florida, South Carolina, California, Wyoming, and Texas."

Erin returned to the hospital after she got off work. Dr. Kelvin was talking to Jess when she arrived.

"Quite frankly, I didn't expect results like this. You heal remarkably fast. I've only seen a recovery like this a couple of times before. However, you are *not* completely healed and need to remember that. I'm hesitant to release you without someone to keep an eye on you for at least a couple of days."

"Jess can come home with me," Erin offered as she moved further into the room and stood at the foot of the bed. "I'm a doctor, and I can keep an eye on her."

Kelvin looked at Erin in silence for a few moments but finally relented. "All right." She pinned Jess with a stern look. "But you are *not* cleared to return to field duty, Agent Morgan. Office work only." She looked at Erin again. "Keep an eye on her, especially in the office. If she pushes too hard, too fast, she will end up back in here."

"I will."

Dr. Kelvin left to fill out the appropriate paperwork.

Erin sat on the side of the bed.

"Thanks, Erin. I don't really have to stay with you. I'll be fine."

She smiled. "Oh, but you do. I promised you a home-cooked meal, remember?" She reached out and caressed Jess' cheek. "And it's for my benefit as much as yours. I'll feel better being with you where I can see you and know you're okay."

Jess reached up and took Erin's hand in her own. She kissed her palm and smiled. "I'm all yours."

Jess was soon checked out of the hospital. On the way to Erin's apartment, Jess asked her to stop at a particular drug store.

Erin pulled into the parking lot and turned to Jess. "Is this so you can buy some blood?"

"Yes."

"I thought we already discussed this."

Jess reached over and squeezed Erin's hand. "We did. But it's too soon for you to give any more. I need some blood and some sleep, and I'll be completely healed. Okay?"

Erin nodded. "All right."

Jess stiffly got out of the car and went inside. She returned in only a few minutes.

While Erin fixed some spaghetti and a fresh salad, Jess changed into sweats. She drank the blood and threw the container in the trash. She then went to the living room and stretched out on Erin's couch. It only seemed like a couple of minutes before Erin woke her, telling her dinner was ready.

They enjoyed the simple meal and the normality of quiet domesticity together at the end of the day. Afterward, they dealt with the dishes quickly, and they retired to the living room. Erin joined Jess on the couch and encouraged her to lie down with her head on Erin's lap. As they watched some old movie on the television, Jess enjoyed how Erin absentmindedly carded her fingers through her hair. They decided to turn in early.

When they slipped into bed, Erin took Jess into her arms as she laid her head on her right shoulder.

"Mmmm, this feels nice," Jess said softly.

"Yes, it does." Erin kissed her forehead.

Both women closed their eyes and drifted into a peaceful sleep.

March 25, 2025
Tuesday

When Jess woke up, she took a long, slow, deep breath. It felt good to be completely healthy again. She had little patience for injury.

She listened to the heart beating beneath her ear. She reveled in the feeling of being held by Erin. She was thankful Erin had forgiven her. She'd come so close to ruining a second chance at happiness. And now she didn't have to worry about Erin discovering her secret because she already knew it.

Jess drew in another deep breath. The scent of Erin was intoxicating. She moved her head from Erin's chest to her shoulder. She carefully unbuttoned her satin pajama top and slipped her right hand inside to tenderly cup Erin's left breast. Erin made a quiet noise in the back of her throat, but didn't wake. Jess began to gently massage the flesh under her palm. She felt Erin's nipple harden.

Jess leaned over and teased Erin's nipple with her lips and tongue. As Erin slowly woke, she buried her fingers in Jess' hair and arched up into her, pushing her breast into Jess' mouth.

"Mmmm." She moaned softly.

Jess gently sucked and licked for a minute or so before trailing open-mouth kisses to Erin's pulse point, where she suckled and teased. Then she shifted up and claimed Erin's lips with a deep kiss, as Erin wrapped her arms around Jess' neck tightly. When the kiss finally broke, Jess kissed her way back down to her breasts. As she kissed and licked down Erin's torso, she removed Erin's pajama bottoms and panties. Finally, Jess lowered her head and took Erin into her mouth, her arms wrapped around Erin's thighs.

Erin cried out as Jess took her to the precipice, but she stretched out her torture. Only after taking her to the precipice a third time did Jess finally send Erin flying off of it. Jess moved up and took the gasping woman in her arms. She rolled them onto their sides and kissed Erin's forehead. Erin laid her head on Jess' shoulder and melted into her embrace, as she recovered from her mind-blowing orgasm.

"If I get addicted to anything, it'll be your lovemaking," she said with a very satisfied smile.

Jess smiled and kissed her forehead again. "I'm already addicted to you. You taste so good."

Erin tilted her head back so she could kiss Jess on the lips. The alarm clock sounded, and Erin quickly rolled over to slap her hand down on the offending noisemaker before rolling back into Jess' embrace. "It's a good thing I set the alarm early."

Chuckling, Jess pulled back so she could look into Erin's eyes. She raised her right hand and gently cupped her cheek before kissing her tenderly. "I'm sorry," she whispered as their lips parted.

"For what?"

"For being scared and pushing you away. I didn't mean to hurt you."

Erin tightened an arm around Jess. "What matters is that we're here now." She paused. "Just don't ever do that again. Okay? I can take a lot of things but not being shut out. Promise me, no matter what, we'll talk things through."

Jess nodded. "I promise," she replied softly. She took a breath and slowly let it out. "No one, except my grandfather, has ever known about my other half. Not even Toni or my parents."

"What about Bobby Marinelli?"

Jess gazed into Erin's soft brown eyes. "No one that matters," she said softly. "And I didn't tell Bobby. He recognized me for what I am, like I recognized him," she said with a small smile.

"Wait a minute. How could your parents not know?"

Taking a deep breath, Jess shifted onto her back and stared at the ceiling. "My mother was on vacation in Europe when a vampire seduced her. My grandfather intervened when he realized what was happening. He ensured she returned home to her husband, Philippe Rodier, in Vancouver. He had been too busy with work to take a vacation. Anyway, I was born about nine months later. I don't think either of them realized," she finished with a shrug.

"But growing up, they didn't know?"

Jess shook her head. "My mother was already gone when I began to notice things. And I had stopped going home for the summers from boarding school. My grandfather was the one I turned to. He came to visit me at school regularly. He explained it all to me. I was seven."

Leaning up on her elbow, Erin gently nudged with her left hand to get Jess to meet her eyes. "You don't have to carry the secret alone anymore, Jess." She lowered her mouth to Jess' and gently conveyed her feelings through her kiss.

As their kiss heated up, Erin shifted on top of Jess, straddling her hips. Her hands palmed Jess' breasts through the thin cotton of her tank top. When Jess moved to remove her tank top, Erin helped her. She kissed her way to a breast and took an erect nipple into her mouth. Jess' skin broke out with goosebumps. Erin moved to her other breast and sucked, replacing her lips with her fingers on the abandoned one. Erin was driving her crazy with her lips and tongue. Her breasts felt heavy, and her nipples ached from arousal. She took Erin's head between her hands and pulled her up for a deep, passionate kiss. Jess broke the kiss and her head slammed back into the pillow as slender, deft fingers slid over her clit. She was so wet. Her heart clenched painfully, just for a moment, as the thought of how close she'd come to losing Erin ran through her mind.

"I love you, Jess," Erin murmured as she slipped two fingers inside her slick heat.

Jess opened her eyes and gazed up into the eyes of the woman who'd captured her heart and was now taking command of her body. "I love you too."

Erin curled her fingers inside her. Jess' eyes snapped shut, and she sucked in a gasp as her body arched up into Erin. Erin kissed and nipped her way down Jess' body until she settled between her well-muscled thighs. Still moving her fingers in and out of Jess, she began to lick and suck. Jess sank her fingers into soft, blonde tresses as she writhed and moaned under Erin's loving attention. She cried out, her orgasm slamming into her. Erin held on, not stopping. She curled her fingers and continued to pump in and out of her. Somehow, Jess' orgasm intensified.

"Fuck!" She couldn't take anymore. She begged Erin to stop.

Erin smiled down at Jess, satisfaction shining in her eyes, as Jess looked up at her through hooded eyes.

"That was incredible."

Erin brought her fingers to her mouth and licked them clean while glancing at the clock. "We still have some time before we have to get up." She quickly moved to reset the alarm and then held Jess, who was content to lie limp and blissful in her arms.

Twenty minutes later, the alarm once again sounded, waking both women.

"Do we have to get up?" Jess asked.

"This time, I'm afraid we do," Erin answered as she turned off the alarm. She got out of bed and smiled, taking in the view of her naked lover. "I'm going to take a shower. You can join me if you want."

Jess opened her eyes and smirked at her. "You, wet and slick under the water? If I do, we'll never get out of here. Go. I'll wait my turn."

Erin felt Jess' sparkling gray eyes on her as she turned and headed to the bathroom. Under the shower's hot water, Erin thought about how different Jess was from her previous lovers, and not because she was half-vampire or a woman. It was because of how Jess made her feel, physically and emotionally. She had never been a prude, but she felt so comfortable and uninhibited with Jess. She looked forward to exploring all kinds of pleasures with her. Erin had never truly let go with her previous lovers. She always felt she had to maintain control over herself and any relationship.

As she soaped her body, her left hand unconsciously caressed and teased her nipples. Her eyes closed. God, she felt so free, so happy, so *alive*! A soft moan passed her lips as the fingers of her right hand slid through soft blonde curls and into a wetness that had nothing to do with the water. Her eyes drifted shut.

Jess' heavy breathing registered before the fact that the shower door was open. She opened her eyes and felt her heart skip a few beats. Jess' eyes were black, fathomless pools of animalistic arousal. There was a predatory air about Jess, and she was the lucky prey. She almost climaxed on the spot. With a very soft growl, Jess took Erin in her arms and kissed her, hard. Erin sank her fingers in dark hair and returned the kiss with equal fervor. When she felt Jess' fingers enter and fill her, she tore her mouth from Jess' and moaned. "Oh god...Jess...fuck me!"

She was lifted and pressed against the steam-warmed tiles of the shower wall. She wrapped her legs around Jess' waist and met her every thrust. Her fingernails left crescent-shaped marks on Jess' back and shoulders. A primal cry was ripped from her throat as she came with Jess' name on her lips. The climax was so intense she collapsed into Jess' embrace, lacking the strength even to keep her eyes open, much less hold her head up.

She was barely aware of Jess gently cleaning her, drying her off, and carrying her into the bedroom.

The next thing Erin knew, she was waking up, lying on her bed.

"Hey."

Erin opened her eyes to the soft voice.

Jess, already dressed for work, sat on the side of the bed next to her. Jess tenderly caressed her cheek. "Time to get up and get ready for work," Jess said with a smile.

Chapter Thirty-Seven

ERIN AND JESS WERE only a few minutes late to the office. When they entered the bullpen, most of the agents present made it a point to ask Jess how she was and to say they were glad to see she was okay.

Before she got to her office, AD Taylor came out of his office, with John following behind him. "All right, everyone, listen up. Agent Casper will bring us up to date on our investigation into Hugh Charles Schilling."

Jess looked at Erin. "Who the hell is Hugh Charles Schilling?"

"Our Russell Schiff. We think he's The Slasher."

After John briefed everyone on the investigation into Hugh Charles Schilling, Jess wanted to immediately get after the guy. But before she could formulate a plan, AD Taylor pulled her into his office, closing the door behind her.

"Before you say anything, the director has given me strict orders. You are on desk duty."

Jess opened her mouth to protest, but Taylor cut her off.

"And if you have a problem with that, you can just go home. Those are the director's exact words," he said as he crossed his arms. "So what's it going to be?"

Jess knew she couldn't fight it. To prove she was fit for field duty would do nothing but cause way too many questions. With a nod, she said, "I'll be in my office."

Jess sat down at her desk and turned on the computer. Something about this Hugh Charles Schilling was nagging at the back of her mind. She started to research everything she could find on him.

Jess jumped when she felt a hand on her shoulder.

"Easy, it's just me, Jessica," said John. "What are you working on?" he asked as he pulled over a chair from the worktable and sat next to Jess.

Jess let out a sigh. "Just digging into Schilling, seeing what I can find." She shook her head. "There's something..."

"What?"

"I don't know. There's something niggling at the back of my mind, but I can't put my finger on it."

"I'm sure it'll come to you. I know how your mind works," he said with an easy smile.

Jess rubbed her hand over her face and let out a frustrated growl. "I think I've been doing this too damn long."

"Why do you say that?"

Jess looked at her old partner. "Holton. It's one thing when we're trying to deal with the UNSUBs, but for one of our own to sidetrack us? I didn't see it coming, John, not from one of our own agents."

"I wish I could say I was surprised."

"How the hell did he get away with it, John? He was part of the task force and working with a partner. Yet he was in Miami, Atlanta, and Boston. How was he able to get away without anyone knowing?"

"From what I understand, he and the agent he was partnered with, Coleman, didn't get along all that well. Coleman would send Holton off to run errands just to keep him busy and out of his hair all day and didn't care if Holton checked in with him at all."

Jess shook her head and sighed. "Coleman made it easy for Holton to do whatever he wanted."

"Yeah."

She pressed the heels of her hands against her eyes. "I'm so tired of these sick bastards and trying to crawl around in their minds. I'm sick of the rapes and murders and molestations of innocent victims. I don't know how much longer I can do this, John." She angrily wiped away tears that threatened to spill.

John reached out and took one of Jess' hands in his. "Look at me, Jessica." He waited until she did. "You are very good at what you do, but you are *not* the only profiler in the Bureau. It's not up to you to solve all the crimes. The Bureau survived without you. If doing what you're doing is too much for you, you should do something else. Organized Crime, Cyber Crimes, White Collar, Counterterrorism, you name it, any division in the Bureau would be thrilled to get you. Not to mention you'd make a hell of an instructor."

"My thoughts exactly."

Both agents jumped at the voice that came from the doorway.

"Sir." John gave the man a nod of respect.

"Director," Jess said in greeting.

"Give us some privacy, please."

"Yes, sir," John said. He stepped out of the office and closed the door behind himself.

Jess looked at the man who had personally asked her to return to the Bureau almost three years previously. He sat on the chair John had vacated.

"I wanted to come down to see how you were doing, returning so quickly after the shooting. But I think we need to talk about more than that, don't you?" he said kindly. "I know I'm the one who came to you and asked you to return to the Bureau. And you've performed even beyond my expectations." He paused, gathering his thoughts and carefully choosing his words. "You are an extraordinary profiler, and you've given so much of yourself to the Bureau. But don't push yourself so much that you burn out. I know what you went through and why you walked away." He dropped his eyes as he remembered the tragic events. "We all loved Toni." He looked back up and into her eyes. "Don't let this work suck the life out of you. You've worked the worst of the worst for almost nine years now. I think it's time to ease that load."

The fact that Jess stayed quiet was more telling than anything she could have actually said at that point.

"I know I've been pushing to get you to Quantico as an instructor, but that's not your only option. John's right. Any division would be thrilled to have you. There are also some SAC positions opening up soon."

Jess finally spoke. "I appreciate that, Lou. And before this case, I would have told you flat out that I didn't want to do anything else." She sighed. "But I do think I at least need a break. Let's talk about it after we get this guy."

"All right. In the meantime, think about what you'd like to do."

"I will."

He patted her shoulder as he stood up and then left.

"Son of a bitch!"

The agents near Jess' office were looking at her in surprise when she exited her office. With a folder in hand, she marched into AD Taylor's office and plopped the folder onto his desk.

"I knew there was something about this guy. I *know* this bastard."

"What?"

"Hugh Charles Schilling. We were both in Boston when I was at Harvard and he was at MIT. There aren't that many twelve- and thirteen-year-olds that are in college. Harvard and MIT had some social gatherings for their younger students. I met this guy. We were the same age. His family is old money...like mine. He was pimply-faced and wore glasses, but this is him."

"Obviously, his skin has cleared up, and he either switched to contacts or had Lasik. What do you remember about him?"

"Brilliant. Of course he'd have to be to enter MIT at age twelve. But he was smart in more than just science and engineering. He was good with people, always seemed to know how to get along with anyone when he chose to be around others. He was charming even then."

"Did you spend much time around him?"

"No. He didn't really interest me." Jess smiled mentally as she remembered who *interested* her then. She officially came out a few years later, when she was fifteen. "But from what I remember about him, he'll have thought out every possibility and devised at least three ways of dealing with those possibilities." She paused. "John said Schilling has property in eight or nine states."

"Yeah, we're trying to get search warrants for all his places. I want to hit all of them simultaneously, so he doesn't get tipped off."

"Do me a favor and don't execute them without talking to me. I'm going to try to narrow down our best options."

"All right. Let me know what you come up with."

Jess ruled out Schilling's apartment on Fifth Ave in New York, his house in Palm Springs, CA, his condo on Hilton Head Island in South Carolina, his condo in South Beach, FL, and his horse ranch outside Dallas. She concentrated on his place in Jackson Hole Valley in Wyoming. About an hour of focused digging led her to believe that wasn't where they'd find their quarry either. Then she stumbled onto something by accident.

Jess left her office and headed to seek help from someone in the White-Collar Crime Division. She spoke to Section Chief Harrison, who introduced her to Agent Rod Michaels.

"What can I do for you, Agent Morgan?"

"Harrison says you're the best and fastest at sorting through financials, shell companies, and such. I'm trying to find a piece of property I think is hidden by a financial Rubik's cube."

"Let me see what you have."

Jess handed the file to Michaels.

He glanced through it. "Give me a few hours to dig through this and see what I can come up with."

"All right. Here's my number," she said, handing him her card. "I'll call you as soon as I find something."

"Thanks."

When Jess returned to the bullpen, Erin intercepted her on the way to her office. She gently grabbed Jess' arm.

"Come on. You haven't eaten all day. Let's go grab a late lunch."

Part of Jess wanted to decline, but it was only a tiny part. She smiled. "Okay."

They decided on a quiet, small restaurant close to the office. They chose a private booth in the back, away from prying eyes.

After the waiter left with their orders, Erin looked at Jess. "Are you sure a salad is all you want to eat?"

Jess smiled. "Yes. I'm not very hungry and it will tide me over until dinner." She smirked, and her gray eyes sparkled with mischievousness. "Besides, what I had for breakfast was quite delicious."

Erin felt the heat from her blush coloring her face. She lowered her gaze with a small, coy smile expressing her satisfaction and pleasure. Jess' comment did bring up a topic she wanted to discuss. "About that…"

Jess' expression changed from one of amusement to attentiveness. "What is it, Erin?" she asked gently.

Erin looked back up into warm and caring eyes. "What exactly happened this morning? I mean…" She searched for the words.

Jess reached out and put her hand over Erin's on the table. "I know what you mean, Erin." She took a deep breath and let it out. "I felt you this morning. In the shower when you…Well, I felt it, viscerally." She paused for a couple of beats. "I guess we now know I was affected by taking your blood."

Erin turned her hand under Jess' so she could clasp it. She squeezed her hand and nodded slightly. "I was too." At Jess' questioning look, she explained. "When you were in surgery, your heart stopped." Erin closed her eyes as they watered, and a lump formed in her throat. She swallowed around the lump and opened her eyes. "I was in the waiting room, and I *knew* something was wrong. I had to find you. I found the O.R. you were in and watched from the observation theater. Once they got your heart started and stabilized you, the feeling went away."

Jess squeezed Erin's hand and was about to say something, but their waiter reappeared at that moment with their order.

The rest of their lunchtime was spent eating and avoiding any heavy topics.

Chapter Thirty-Eight

IT WAS ABOUT FOUR o'clock in the afternoon when Jess' phone rang.
"Morgan."

"Agent Morgan, it's Rod Michaels. I think I've got what you were looking for."

"Great. I'll be right there."

She rushed out of her office and went to see him.

"What do you have?" Jess asked when she arrived at Michaels' desk.

"This." He laid out a copy of a deed he'd printed out. "It's not under his name; it's been hidden behind a couple of shell companies and a holding company. As were these." He started laying out invoices for her to see. "He's used a shell game to hide everything related to this property." He pointed at one invoice. "This generator could supply electricity for a small house." He pointed to another. "This is for the rental of excavation equipment. And here is a satellite dish. Whatever is there, it appears he's taken steps to make it self-sufficient, no need for public utilities that could leave a paper trail."

Jess gathered the papers and put them in the folder she'd given him. "Great work. Thank you."

Arriving back in the bullpen, Jess went in to see AD Taylor.

"I think I know where he's at, or at least where he spends quite a bit of time." She handed him the folder. "It's the only piece of property he's bothered to hide. This is where we need to concentrate our greatest efforts when executing the search warrants."

Taylor nodded and then walked to the doorway of his office. "Little, Casper," he called.

Both agents stood and walked over to him.

"You two are going to Carbondale, Illinois. Get there tonight because we need to move on this tomorrow. Morgan's got the details."

Jess briefed Erin and John in her office.

"This is the only piece of property he's tried to hide. But you have to understand something: Schilling is smart and not just book smart. If this is his sanctuary, he'll have thought about all the possible avenues of approach and will have more than one exit strategy. This is the guy of my original profile. He's dangerous."

Erin called to arrange for their flight. While she was occupied with that, John and Jess spoke quietly.

"Are you sure you're up to this, John, with your arm?"

"I'm fine. It wasn't a bad wound, and it's only my left arm. I've been good and have been resting it for the last few days. Besides, we'll have plenty of backup with the locals. Don't worry. We'll get this guy, Jessica."

"I should be going, but the director's grounded me, put me on desk duty."

"And rightly so. You're concerned about my arm, but *you* almost died. Quite frankly, I wouldn't have let you back to work at all yet."

Jess nodded, but everything in her chafed at being deskbound.

Erin hung up. "Okay. We're on a seven o'clock flight out of Dulles and should land a little after eight local time. We'll fly into St. Louis and then have a two-hour drive to Carbondale."

John looked at his watch. "We should get going then."

"Just give me a couple of minutes," Erin said. "I'll be right back."

When Erin stepped out of the office, Jess pinned John with a hard look. "You make sure nothing happens to her, John. Or else you and I are going to have a problem."

He knew she was deadly serious but didn't take any offense. He was happy for her. John smiled and pulled her into a one-armed hug. "I'll protect her with my life," he whispered in her ear before kissing her temple.

John's quiet promise touched her heart, suddenly causing tears to sting the backs of her eyes. Damn, her emotions were so out of control. She'd kept a tight control of her emotions for six years. But then she met, and fell for Erin. Now she had a real chance of being happy again. Hell, she *was* happy!

"Thanks, John."

"You deserve to be happy, Jessica."

Jess pulled back and looked up into his eyes. "I am."

Erin reentered the office as John and Jess let go of each other.

With a look at both women, John excused himself. "I'll, uh, I'll wait by the elevators." He left, closing the office door behind him.

"Do I want to know what that was about?" Erin asked.

Jess smiled. "Just being reminded of why John's such a good friend." Her expression changed to a serious one, as she moved to stand directly in front of Erin. "The director won't let me go with you. And to prove I'm field-ready would cause way too many questions."

Erin nodded in understanding.

"Promise me you'll be careful, Erin."

"I will be."

"This guy is smart. You need to be prepared for the unexpected. Make sure you wear protection, and—"

With a smile, Erin laid a finger across Jess' lips, silencing her. Then she kissed her. Jess' arms wrapped around her, and they deepened the kiss. When oxygen became an urgent need for both, they broke the kiss, resting their foreheads together momentarily.

"I hate that I'm not going with you," Jess said as she pulled back. "I know that you can handle yourself, but..."

"I know. Now you know how I felt when you took off to the warehouse."

Jess dropped her head, feeling remorseful. "I'm sorry."

Erin cupped Jess' cheek and lifted her face. "Like I said, just don't do it again."

Jess nodded.

Erin reached into her pocket and handed Jess her apartment keys. "Stay at my place while I'm gone." Jess started to object, but she cut her off. "There's no reason for you to stay at a hotel, Jess." She smiled. "And I like the thought of you sleeping in my bed."

Jess smiled. "Call me when you land. Hopefully I'll have an update and more information for you."

"I will."

Jess turned the key in the lock. Part of her felt like an intruder, entering Erin's apartment without her. But a part of her felt like she was coming home.

Home. She hadn't had a home in a long time. She didn't count the manor in England she'd inherited from her grandfather, even if that's where she retreated when she quit the Bureau. No, this was the first time she felt anything close to "home" in six years.

Jess had already eaten while at work, so she headed to the bedroom to undress. After a long, hot shower, she fell into bed, curled around Erin's pillow and, breathing her scent, fell asleep.

"Thank you." John's voice broke the comfortable silence in the car, surprising Erin. She looked over at him from the passenger seat.

"What for?"

John looked at the beautiful platinum blonde. Jessica always did have great taste in women. "Thank you for not giving up on Jessica. Thanks for loving her and making her happy."

Erin's heart warmed, and she smiled. "My pleasure. Loving her is the easiest thing I've ever done."

John pointed out the windshield. "Ah, here we are. That's the sheriff's office." He pulled into the parking lot at 1001 Mulberry Street and parked in front of the two-story, glass-front building. John turned off the car engine and looked at his watch. Almost a quarter to midnight—Washington time anyway. He quickly set it back an hour. "Hopefully, we won't be going after him first thing in the morning. It's going to be a long night."

"Let's go."

They approached a window in the sheriff's office, behind which sat a woman wearing a blue polo shirt with an embroidered department insignia on the left chest. Erin and John both flashed their credentials.

"We need to speak with someone in charge, please," John said.

"Sgt. Thomas is here, but you'll want to see the sheriff. I'll call him."

"Thank you."

Only fifteen minutes later, Sheriff Ted Shipley pulled into the department parking lot at the back of the building. He entered through the back door and came to the front to see why the feds were in *his* county.

Shipley took in the appearance of the male agent—six-foot, sandy hair, green eyes, early forties—but the female agent almost made him do a double take. The petite, platinum blonde with brown eyes was gorgeous! He was so taken with her that he nearly missed what she said.

"Oh, sure. We can go back to the conference room. Follow me." He led them through the locked door and down a hallway. They passed the dispatch office, a couple of rooms, and a stairway leading up to the second floor. They turned right down another long corridor and entered the second room on the right. The sheriff had called it the conference room, but it obviously doubled as a break room.

Once in the conference room, the blonde agent laid out the reason for their presence. As soon as Shipley realized how serious the situation was, he interrupted her.

"Before you go any further, Agent Little, please let me get my people together so you don't have to go over everything twice."

She nodded, and he stepped out of the room.

Shortly after, Erin addressed the sheriff; his lieutenant, Eric Brown; the on-duty sergeant, Noah Thomas; a couple of detectives; and several uniformed deputies.

When a map was put up on the wall, John and Erin began to recognize how difficult things were going to be.

Schilling's property was several miles southwest of Murphysboro on a heavily wooded bluff above the Mississippi River. The only access was a dirt road.

"You're not going to get a car up that road," one of the deputies said.

The sheriff nodded in agreement. "We'll have to use the ATVs." He looked at the agents. "How sure are you something's up there to find? Because I know of only one house up there, and they're a nice couple."

"According to the deed and land plot, he owns twelve acres. He could have a place hundreds of feet back into the woods," John answered.

"Look, this guy is smart. He has two PhDs in engineering. We know he rented excavation equipment, purchased a satellite dish, and a large generator that could easily power a small home. He tried to hide the existence of this place and kept it completely off the grid," Erin pointed out. "We're executing search warrants on all his properties simultaneously tomorrow. But we believe this is our best bet. This is his refuge, and even if he's not there, we should be able to gather important intelligence and evidence." She paused for a beat. "But you should also know that we have an arrest warrant if he is there. We consider him very dangerous. He's a suspect in the brutal murders of over thirty women, possibly as many as a hundred. And he has been practically perfect in leaving no clues or forensics. The only clues he left behind he'd left deliberately as red herrings. Do *not* underestimate this man."

"What time is the warrant to be served?"

"Three o'clock."

John gave the sheriff a folder with background on the suspect, a couple of stills taken from the nanny cam footage, Jess' profile, and some information on the murders. The sheriff made copies and distributed them to the personnel participating in the operation with harshly worded warnings of *dire* consequences for any leaks.

The mood in the sheriff's station was one of excitement. Cases like this didn't come along but once in a blue moon. However, as the detectives and deputies reviewed the file, the mood transformed into simmering anger and quiet determination. They were going after an absolute monster, a monster who had chosen to make their community his roosting place.

Outside, the clouds thickened, and rain started falling. It was as if Nature herself was reflecting the same mood as those preparing for what was to come.

Chapter Thirty-Nine

March 26, 2025
Wednesday

IT WAS AFTER THREE o'clock in the morning when Erin and John checked into their hotel in Carbondale. Erin took a quick shower before putting on her pajamas. She slipped into bed, exhausted, but sleep didn't come.

So much had happened in the last six weeks. For almost a year, she had worked with and mentored Holton. She had ended that partnership and felt guilty about it because she'd asked for the transfer without telling him. But then she found out what he had been doing.

Erin rolled over and punched her pillow. She should have seen it coming! How did her life get so far off track? She'd gotten so wrapped up in work that nothing else had mattered. Hell, she's put the job ahead of her own family. Lauren was gone because of…No, she couldn't go down that road right now. Her eyes watered. Before she was even aware of her actions, she had picked up her cellphone from the nightstand and dialed.

Her tears finally broke free and flowed down her cheeks when she heard the sleepy voice on the other end. "Jess?"

▬■

Jess reached and snagged her cell phone from the nightstand. "Morgan."

"Jess?"

She came fully awake in a split second. Something was wrong with Erin. "Erin? What's wrong?" She heard a sniff before Erin answered.

"I just…" Why had she called Jess? She knew Jess was sleeping. It was after four o'clock in the morning in DC. "I'm sorry, I shouldn't have called."

"No. You did the right thing. Can you tell me what's wrong?" Jess asked, her voice soft.

Erin sighed. "I couldn't sleep. I can't stop thinking about things."

"What things?"

"Holton, my sister, the job, this case, Schilling…everything."

"Talk to me about it," Jess said.

"Honestly, I don't want to talk about it. I don't want to *think* about it."

"Okay. So we'll talk about something else."

"What?"

"Tell me about the last place you went for vacation."

"Vacation? What's that?"

Jess chuckled. "All right. I won't give you a hard time about not taking vacation since I'm hardly in a position to criticize anyone about that. Tell me about where you would go if you could take a vacation anywhere in the world you wanted."

Erin slid down onto her back. "Hmm, I'm not sure. At one time, I would have said the Netherlands."

"Why?"

"My family's Dutch."

"Really? I never would have guessed," Jess lightly teased.

Erin couldn't help but smile. "Oh yes. I even inherited a Dutch stubbornness to go with my blonde hair."

"You don't say." They both chuckled. "Well, if the Netherlands isn't your choice now, what is?"

"I think somewhere on the water and warm. I've always loved the water."

"Do you like sailing?"

"Oh, definitely!"

"SCUBA diving?"

"I learned one summer when I was a teenager. There was a class on the base through the community center. It's been many years since I've gone on a dive though—probably not since my freshman year in college."

"Okay, somewhere on the water. How about the Caribbean? Or the South Pacific?"

Erin hummed in thought. "Either would be nice."

"Somewhere secluded or around other vacationers?"

A smile crept into Erin's voice. "Depends. Am I on this vacation with someone?"

"Yes, if you want."

"Then I would say somewhere secluded."

"Done."

"What?"

"When we close this case, let's take a vacation, Erin. You and me, somewhere on a secluded beach."

"That would be wonderful."

"Is that a yes?"

"Yes, it's a yes. I'd love to go on vacation with you." She yawned twice.

"Can you sleep now, Erin?"

"Mm-hmm..." She was already falling asleep.

"Good night, love."

"Night..."

Rain. It had been raining for hours. And, from the rolling, dark gray clouds, it appeared it would be raining for some time.

Erin sighed as she thought about what one of the deputies had said about their destination. No car would take them up to that bluff. ATVs were going to be the mode of transportation. It was going to be a rough, muddy, wet ride. There had been no question about dressing casually.

Erin looked over the assembled group. The detectives and deputies from the previous night's shift had come in early to execute the operation. She easily picked up on the determined atmosphere and was infinitely grateful for the serious attitude and lack of territorial posturing. The man they were going after was a monster in every sense of the word. And she had examined and autopsied more than enough young women to be intimately familiar with his "work."

A female deputy, Ashlee Stratton, according to her nametag, tapped Erin on the shoulder. "Here you go, Agent Little. Use my spare vest. It'll fit you better than those," she said with a nod toward the ones Sgt. Thomas was handing to John and a male deputy.

"Thank you." Erin immediately slipped it on and adjusted the straps for a snug fit. Then her phone rang. "Little."

"Hey, Erin, it's me."

"What's up, Jess?"

"I've got some more information on Schilling. He spent a year in Carbondale teaching at the college, Southern Illinois University, only he used the name Brian Adams. That time corresponds to when he was setting up his place."

"The place is up on a bluff, Jess, overlooking the Mississippi. Once we turn off the main road, the cars will only go to the base of the bluff. From there, it's a dirt road. And with the rain we're having, it will be muddy as hell. The sheriff has arranged for us to go up on ATVs."

"Damn. He could hear those coming from a distance. You're not going to have the element of surprise, Erin. If he is there, he will be ready for you."

"Maybe the rain will mask the ATVs."

"Maybe, but don't count on it. You know how good he is, so be careful."

"I will, Jess. We're about to leave to be ready on time. I'll call you later."

"All right."

A caravan left the sheriff's office, led by Sheriff Shipley in his department SUV. Riding with him were Sgt. Thomas and Lt. Brown. John and Erin followed in their rental car. Behind them were three patrol cars with a detective and a uniformed deputy in each one. In total were nine locals and two federal officers, all serving a search warrant and arresting one man.

The sheriff pulled off Route 3 onto a muddy, loose gravel road. Less than half a mile later, he pulled to the edge of the road and waited as the other vehicles followed suit. Deputy Norwood was already there since he'd driven the truck and trailer that delivered the four red ATVs. He had unloaded them, and one already looked pretty muddy. John and Erin got out of the car and joined the sheriff. It was raining so hard they were soaked through within seconds.

"I checked out the road ahead, Sheriff. Not even your SUV is going to make it up to the bluff. This rain has washed out most of it. It's nothing but mud," Andrew Norwood reported.

Shipley looked back at the assembled group. They had twelve people and only four ATVs to get everyone to the suspect's property. It was going to take more than one trip. The first group was prepared to go in only a few minutes. Erin had been assigned to ride with Deputy Stratton.

Ashlee Stratton looked over her shoulder at Erin. "You're going to want to hold on, Agent Little." When Erin placed her hands on Stratton's waist, the deputy grabbed them and pulled Erin's arms completely around her waist. "I mean, hold on tight. This is going to be a tricky ride."

Despite the cold rain, Erin felt a little warmer snugged up behind the five-foot-seven deputy. And when Stratton started up the muddy road, she felt the ATV slip and slide through the deep mud, causing Erin to hold on tighter.

Once they got up to the top of the bluff, the ATVs drivers let off their passengers and returned to the bottom for the four remaining people. Finally, they were all once again assembled. Since no one knew precisely where Schilling's cabin was, they passed the entrance of his property twice before someone realized it. Schilling's driveway was little more than a mud footpath. It was mostly grown over, so the ATVs slowly went ahead of those on foot to widen the path slightly. Over six hundred feet off the road, they finally came to a cabin in a small clearing.

"I'll be damned. I had no idea this was even here," the sheriff muttered as he signaled for his people to circle the area, sticking close to the tree line so they remained out of sight.

Despite everyone being alert and moving carefully, one of the detectives missed a tripwire and sprung a trap. A piece of rebar shot up and hit him just to the side of his heart. Had he not been wearing Kevlar, the metal bar would have easily impaled him. As it was, he went down hard and had trouble breathing.

Erin rushed to him. "Don't move. Take small, easy breaths."

The sheriff knelt in the mud next to Det. Whitten and supported his head. "You're going to be all right, Charlie."

Erin pulled open the man's jacket, vest, and then shirt. A bruise was already starting to blossom on his chest. She carefully checked the area. "I don't think you've broken any ribs, Detective."

"Why can't he breathe?" Shipley asked as the man struggled to get a decent amount of air into his lungs.

"It knocked the wind out of him and then his chest muscles tightened up from the shock of the impact." She looked down at the detective. "Relax, Detective, slow, calm, easy breaths."

The man closed his eyes as he tried to breathe slowly. The tenseness in his face eased as he got more oxygen into his lungs. When he opened his eyes, he gave Erin a nod.

"That's it," she said. "You may have cracked a rib and bruised your lung, so you're going to need to be checked out at the hospital."

"Does he need to be evacuated immediately?" the sheriff asked with concern.

"No. But he should rest until we do leave."

Charlie nodded. "Go on. I'll be all right," he assured the sheriff.

"Let's get you moved somewhere a little drier first," Erin suggested. She and the sheriff helped the detective up and over to sit against a tree.

Whitten was still wet and muddy, but the trees at least blocked some of the rain. Erin was worried about him being chilled, but before she could say anything, the sheriff called to one of the deputies.

"Stratton, get one of the first aid kits."

"On it!" Ashlee replied. She carefully hurried to the nearest ATV, retrieved a first-aid kit, and brought it to Erin. "Here you go, Agent Little."

"Thank you." Erin removed a space blanket from the kit and tore open its packaging. She quickly had it unfolded and, with Stratton's help, wrapped it around the injured detective.

The sheriff keyed his radio. "Okay, people, tighten up. We move in pairs. Watch where you step and where your partner steps."

Chapter Forty

JESS WAS BESIDE HERSELF. She couldn't sit, she couldn't eat, she couldn't keep her heart from racing, and she couldn't think clearly. Erin and John were out there without her watching their backs. Jess chafed at being stuck in the office. It went against everything she was to sit back and be passive. She wanted to be *out there*, catching the sick bastard.

It was one thing to come into a case, profile an UNSUB, and then move onto the next case. However, profiling the UNSUB and then working on the case until its conclusion was another story. She wanted to help! But she was not doing anyone much good at the moment. Since she couldn't concentrate enough to dig through Schilling's past, she took each piece of the puzzle agents had gathered and wrote them on a list to help order her thoughts.

- Dark brown hair and brown eyes, 5'11", right-handed
- Graduated from Hunter College High School in 2004 at age 12
- Attended MIT, graduated in 2011 at age 19 with 2 engineering PhDs
- Worked at Boeing from 2011-2013 until he quit without notice
- Nothing for the last half of 2013 or all of 2014
- In 2015, at age of 23, entered Los Angeles police academy and resigned only one week shy of completing the 6-month training program (What happened?)
- Fall of 2016 through spring of 2018, taught at Southern Illinois University in Carbondale using the name of Brian Adams
- Purchased property in the area December of 2017 – invoices for equipment rentals and purchases through summer of 2019 indicate still in area even though no longer teaching
- 2022 receives balance of trust fund – 65 million. Drops off face of the earth, no sign of Hugh Charles Schilling.
- Used name Joel ?? with Andrea Nicks (Annapolis)

- Used name Russell Schiff with Sheila Cousins (Boston)
- Used name Thomas Weeks with Andrea Bishop (Richmond)

Schilling changed names and identities as easily as most people changed their clothes. They already had four aliases for him and were probably only scratching the surface. His picture was being shown to the families and friends of all their known victims to see what other names he'd used. An icon on her computer started blinking, letting her know she had a new email. She opened it and read its contents. She then added another item to her list.

- Used name Jerry Tyler with Elizabeth Timmons (Miami)

She closed her eyes while trying to focus her thoughts. Then the phone on her desk rang. She quickly picked it up.

"Morgan."

"Agent Morgan?"

"Yes?"

"This is Chief Bud Calhoun from Midway, Georgia. I don't know if you remember me."

Jess pinched the bridge of her nose. "I remember you, Chief. What can I do for you?"

"It's about this picture I received."

"What about it?"

"I know this guy. His name's Ben Lufkin. He applied for a job in my department. Unfortunately, we didn't have the budget to add anyone. He had great credentials, worked for Chicago PD."

Jess perked up. "Did you check his references, Chief?"

"Of course. Spoke to his old lieutenant, Pete Sawyer. Sawyer couldn't say enough about him. What's going on, Agent Morgan? You think this is the guy you've been looking for? I did check him out, you know."

"Thanks for calling, Chief." Jess hung up and added to her list.

- Used name Ben Lufkin with Dawn Browning (Midway)

Jess got on the phone and called the Chicago field office. She spoke with Agent Harry Sabine. "Agent Sabine, I need you to get down to Chicago PD and show the picture I just emailed you to Lt. Pete Sawyer. I need to know if that picture is of the same man who worked for him, Ben Lufkin. And verify if he spoke to a Chief Bud Calhoun from Midway, GA."

"All right, Agent Morgan. I'll call you as soon as I get any information."

"You have my cell number."

After the call ended, Jess left her office and went into AD Taylor's office. "Maybe we should distribute Schilling's picture much more widely."

"Why?"

"Well, he attended LAPD's police academy but resigned one week shy of graduation even though he was at the top of his class. No explanation was given. He also applied for a job as a cop in a small town in Georgia under a different name, claiming to have worked for the Chicago PD." Before Taylor could ask her, she said, "I've got an agent going to talk to someone and show his picture to verify it's the same guy."

"I know the director wanted to keep a lid on this, which is why we're executing all the search warrants simultaneously." Taylor looked at his watch. "Which should be in about twenty minutes. Let's see how things go after that. If necessary, we'll open the investigation up wider, okay?"

Jess nodded. It was always a balancing act, figuring out how much information to keep confidential and how much to release in a case like this.

Taylor frowned. "Why would someone with engineering degrees from MIT want to be a cop?"

"I'm not sure that's what he wanted."

"What do you mean?"

"Well, it could have just been research for him. A way to discover how cops think and what they look for." She shrugged. "We won't know until we find out more or can ask him."

Jess walked out of Taylor's office. She had to get outside for some air. Erin and the others were about to serve the warrant at Schilling's cabin. She didn't know whether she wanted Schilling to be there or not. Erin and John would be safer if he weren't there, but he'd still be on the loose. If he was there, they'd be able to arrest him, but he could hurt them, or worse.

She was on the elevator when her cell phone rang. She waited until the doors opened and stepped out to answer it. The elevators at the Hoover building were notorious for wreaking havoc on reception. "Morgan."

"Jessica? It's Stacy."

"What can I do for you?"

"The director would like to see you."

"Now?"

"Yes."
"Okay."

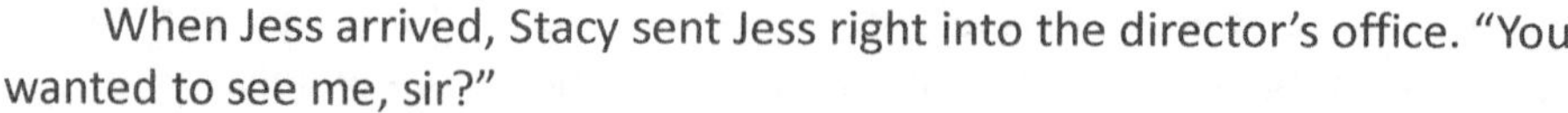

When Jess arrived, Stacy sent Jess right into the director's office. "You wanted to see me, sir?"

"You know Holton has been evaluated for these last three days."

Jess nodded as she sat down.

"Dr. Harkin has submitted his report." The director held a folder out to Jess. "Look at it and let me know what you think."

Jess took the folder and opened it up. She didn't know Dr. Carl Harkin but had heard good things about him. She began to read. She couldn't help but shake her head at what Holton had said and done as she turned the pages. She read a relevant passage out loud. "Axis 1 diagnosis: Delusional Disorder...Expresses an idea or belief with unusual persistence or force; that idea exerts undue influence on his life; despite his profound conviction there is a quality of secretiveness and suspicion when he is questioned about it; no matter how unlikely these strange things are happening to him, he accepts them unquestioningly; is oversensitive about the belief; any attempt to contradict the belief arouses inappropriately strong irritability and open hostility; he is emotionally overinvested in the idea and it has overwhelmed other elements of his psyche."

She flipped the page and continued. "Axis 2 diagnosis: Narcissistic Personality Disorder with significant Paranoid tendencies...Subject has grandiose sense of self-importance; is preoccupied with fantasies of ideal love, particularly revolving around his partner Agent Little; believes that he is 'special' and unique; has a sense of entitlement; is interpersonally exploitative; and shows arrogant behaviors and attitude. Subject believes that others are exploiting and deceiving him; is preoccupied with unjustified doubts about the loyalty and trustworthiness of associates; is extremely reluctant to confide in others because of unwarranted fear that the information will be used maliciously against him; and persistently bears grudges."

With a sigh, Jess closed the folder. "The bastard is bloody nuts."

The director sighed. "So should he stay in prison or go to a mental institution?"

Jess let out a rueful huff. "Lou, I'm not exactly dispassionate and unbiased here. He threatened my partner and my previous partner. He drugged four other agents, took shots at Erin, and shot me and John. I'd like to see the asshole put away for fucking life—in either setting." She stopped to take a deep breath and contain her anger. "The bottom line is that while he is a very disturbed person, he's legally sane since he acted with malice and forethought and could appreciate the wrongfulness of his acts." She sighed. "However, that said, I can imagine a lawyer trying to argue the insanity defense. A judge and/or jury will undoubtedly have to make that call."

"But you think he's sane."

"Legally? Yes."

"Well, he's been charged with hindering an investigation, terroristic threats, aggravated assault, and attempted murder."

"He's already been arraigned?"

"Yes. He was denied bail and sent to the Chesapeake Detention Facility to await his trial."

Jess nodded. "Good."

In the elevator on the way back down to the bullpen, Jess looked at her watch. It was past time for the search warrants to be executed. Well past! Why hadn't she heard from Erin or John yet? She wanted to call Erin to find out what had happened and ensure she was okay. But a call at an inopportune moment could get an agent killed. She suddenly understood the urge to smoke. She all but growled with frustration. She jumped when her phone rang.

"Morgan."

"Agent Morgan, this is Agent Sabine."

"Yes?"

"I spoke to Lt. Sawyer at Chicago P.D. The man in the picture is not Ben Lufkin. Lufkin is blonde and has blue eyes."

"Does Sawyer know where Lufkin is?"

"That's just the thing. Lufkin quit the department without notice. Just called in and said he was done and not coming back in. When he got the chance, Sawyer went to Lufkin's house to see him and make sure everything was okay, but his house had been cleared out, and the neighbors hadn't seen him or his wife for days. No one has seen or heard from either of them, not even their families. Sawyer had been relieved to get the call from Chief Calhoun. It was the first anyone had heard anything about Lufkin."

Jess closed her eyes. The bastard must have killed them. "All right, Agent Sabine. Thank you for your help." She hung up. "Fuck!"

Chapter Forty-One

WITH ONE MAN ALREADY injured, everyone was in an even higher state of alert. They slowly approached the cabin. Erin and John went up on the small porch. Standing to the side of the door, John knocked on it with the butt of his gun. "Hugh Schilling! We have a warrant for your arrest and to search these premises!"

He knocked a second time, but there was still no response. Erin positioned herself at an angle to the door to cover John when he kicked it open.

It was dark inside, too dark to see if anyone was present.

John and Erin very carefully made their way inside the cabin. All their senses were on high alert. They let the sheriff know it was clear once they determined it was empty of human life.

Shipley decided to leave a couple of deputies, Ashlee Stratton and Ryan Whitcomb, to keep an eye out and provide backup for the agents in case the suspect showed up. Also, the other two deputies, Justin Travers and Andrew Norwood, would wait at the base of the bluff where the cars were parked. He and the others were going to get Det. Whitten to the hospital. They were then going to brief the day shift about the operation and familiarize them with the information on the suspect. The sheriff was determined not to let the suspect slip through their fingers if he was within his jurisdiction.

The weather had worsened outside. Lightning and thunder now accompanied the rain. Even so, Erin heard something. She strained to place the sound. It seemed to be coming from behind a wall.

"John, come here."

John walked over.

"Do you hear that?"

He listened intently for a few moments. "Sounds like a generator or something."

They began to look for any sign of a door on the wall. Moving aside a tapestry, John found it.

"Here." But the way to open the door was not apparent. There was no doorknob, only almost indiscernible cracks showing the panel's location.

Erin started looking around and knocked something aside on the shelf attached to the wall a couple of feet from the door. Suddenly, the panel pulled back, withdrawing from the wall, and slid aside on the other side of the wall. They exchanged looks.

"I thought that kind of shit only happened in movies," John quietly said in an ironic tone. She gave him a one-shouldered shrug in answer.

With weapons and flashlights raised, they carefully entered the room, splitting and moving along opposite sides. Once sure it was clear, John found a light switch. The contents of the room took them both aback.

In the corner was a generator that was quietly running. There appeared to be a pipe of some kind attached to it that led to a wall and presumably vented the exhaust somewhere outside. Next to the generator was a bank of batteries of some sort. As they watched, a dial indicating the charge level reached the fully charged mark, and the generator cut off.

Then they turned their attention to a wine rack built into one wall. It was full of what appeared to be wine bottles. Erin pulled on a latex glove and removed a random bottle.

"Oh my god," she said.

"What is it?" John asked.

She read the label to him. "Katherine Horne; Seattle, Washington; June 2013." Erin held the bottle up so John could see the contents: blood. She put it back and pulled a few others at random. "Sonya Copeland; Abilene, Texas; November 2018. Melody Adams; De Soto, Illinois; April 2015. Annie Jensen; Branchville, South Carolina; September 2022." She paused and stared at the rack. "These are his victims."

John was stunned. "There must be close to a hundred of them."

"It looks like they started in 2013. He's been killing for at least twelve years."

Jess was in her office, standing at the window and staring at nothing. It had been over two hours since the warrants were executed. She still hadn't heard from Erin or John. She just about jumped out of her skin when her cell phone sounded.

"Morgan."

"Jess, it's me."

Jess audibly let out a breath she felt she'd been holding in for hours. "Thank god! Is everything okay? It's been a couple of hours since the warrants were served."

"We were behind schedule because we ran into some difficulty. It's nothing but thick mud up here due to the heavy rain falling since before dawn. And we missed the entrance to the property twice before someone finally saw it." She let out a small sigh. "He's not here, Jess, but we did find something."

"What?"

Erin told her about the generator and battery setup. Then she told her about the wine rack filled with bottles of blood.

Jess sat down heavily in a chair at the worktable. "Fuck."

"Hey! What's going on out there?"

"Erin? What's wrong?" Jess' heart stopped when the call was suddenly disconnected.

John and Erin rushed out of the room to see what the commotion was. Deputy Stratton and Deputy Whitcomb were wrestling with a mud-covered man at the side of the cabin. Ashlee Stratton ended up taking a punch to the jaw before she and Whitcomb got the slippery man cuffed and subdued. Both deputies were covered in mud.

"I was looking around the area and found what appeared to be a hidden storm cellar," Stratton reported to the agents. "Inside was a storage area and him."

John stepped off the small porch and approached the subdued man on his knees. He took out a handkerchief and wiped away most of the mud caking his face. John turned back to Erin. "It's him," he said coldly, disdainfully.

"Read him his rights," Erin told the deputies. She didn't want anything to interfere with the successful prosecution of the man. She lifted her phone to her ear, but it was dead. The battery had died. "Shit." She noticed Stratton was tenderly touching her jaw where she'd been hit. "Come here, Stratton. Let me look at that."

"I'm fine, Agent Little."

"I'm a doctor, so why don't I decide that?" Erin said with just enough authority to get the young woman moving.

Stratton came up on the porch and let Erin check her out.

"When we return, make sure you put some ice on it to keep the swelling from getting too bad. You'll have quite the bruise, but that's all."

"Thank you."

Erin stepped back inside with John. "John, can I borrow your phone? My battery died while I was on the phone with Jess."

"I'm surprised she hasn't—" His phone rang, cutting him off. John didn't even answer when he saw who the caller was. With a smile, he handed his phone to Erin.

Erin answered it. "Jess, it's me. Everything's all right," she assured her lover.

"What the hell happened?"

"The battery on my phone died." She smiled. "And we've got Schilling in custody," she said with satisfaction.

"What? I thought you said he wasn't there."

"One of the deputies found a hidden bunker. He was hiding in it with his supplies." She heard Jess let out a sigh. She could picture Jess sinking into a chair and a huge weight lifting from her shoulders. "We did it, Jess. We got him," she said softly.

"Yeah. Finally."

Erin didn't miss the heavy emotion in Jess' voice. "Are you okay, Jess?"

"Yeah. I'll tell Taylor and the director. I'll let you know how they want to handle transport."

"All right. I'll talk to you later then."

"Bye."

"Bye."

Jess hung up her phone and slumped in her desk chair. A painful lump quickly formed in her throat, and the backs of her eyes stung. It had been a rough case and an emotional roller coaster. Staying and working the case through had not been her usual routine during the last three years. But knowing Schilling was in custody was so satisfying and a huge relief. The release of so much tension from the last six weeks was almost painful.

Finally, she wiped her moist eyes, stood up, and left her office. She walked into AD Taylor's office. "We got him," she said without preamble.

"What?"

"Erin and John have Schilling in custody. We got him."

The big man looked as stunned as Jess felt. Of course they had all hoped for it, but they had tried to keep their hopes from getting too high. The man was wealthy, a chameleon, and could have easily escaped to another country without extradition. Taylor stood up and came out from behind his desk. He gave Jess a comradely hug, which she returned. When he let go of her, he gave her a congratulatory slap on the back.

"Let's go tell them," he said, nodding on the way out his doorway toward the bullpen.

Jess nodded in agreement. It was after five o'clock, but since their job wasn't a nine-to-five job, just about everyone from the taskforce not already in the field or due in for the night shift was present.

"Ladies, gentlemen, I'd like your attention, please," Taylor called out. He waited while those on the phone either put the other party on hold or ended their calls. When he had everyone's attention, he turned things over to Jess. "Agent Morgan has an announcement."

All eyes shifted to her. "Hugh Charles Schilling is in custody! Agents Little and Casper found him at his property in Illinois."

A collective cheer went up. Taylor allowed it to continue for a few seconds before calming things down. "All right, people, job well-done, but it's not over yet. We all know we must dot every 'i' and cross every 't'. There are still avenues of investigation for us to follow before we close the case."

Another cheer went up as Jess and Taylor walked toward the elevators. They would head up to the director's office to tell him in person.

Stacy apparently knew something was up when Taylor and Jess arrived at the director's office. "He's on a phone call right now. I'll let him know you're here as soon as he's done," she said.

"Thanks, Stacy," said Jess.

The two took seats in the outer office. About five minutes later, Stacy picked up her desk phone and spoke quietly. After hanging up, she smiled at the pair and said, "He'll see you now."

Jess and Taylor walked into the director's office.

"What can I do for you two?"

Taylor smiled. "It's what we can do for you."

At the director's confused look, Jess explained. "We got him."

His face lit up. "What? Where?"

"Casper and Little found him in Illinois and have him in custody," answered Taylor.

The director leaned back in his chair and took a deep breath. "How sure are we it's him?"

Jess grimaced. "Little said they found a secret room at his cabin. In it was a wine rack with about a hundred bottles, each labeled with a name and location and filled with blood."

"Jesus." He sighed. "All right, we need everything to be done perfectly."

Taylor nodded. "I already reminded everyone that we need to dot the 'i's and cross the 't's. We're not done until all avenues of the investigation are completed."

"If I may make a suggestion?" Jess asked.

"Of course."

"Fly a forensics team in from St. Louis. Have them take control of the scene, and use one of the Bureau's jets to pick him up and fly him back, avoiding a commercial flight."

The director looked up at Jess, obviously thinking. Jess was sure he knew what was going through her mind. He took his time before responding. Finally, he spoke. "All right." He looked at Taylor. "Make the arrangements for the forensics team."

"Yes, sir." Taylor left since the director's tone had made it clear he was being dismissed.

Jess suspected what the director wanted to talk about. She sat down in one of the chairs and looked him in the eyes. "I'm fine, Lou."

"Less than five days ago, you were shot. Two days ago, you were still in the hospital."

"So you're saying I can't go out on the plane to get him."

He sighed heavily. She could practically hear the gears in Lou's head turning. Finally, he spoke. "I'm going to ask you a question, Jessica, and I trust you to answer honestly."

Jess frowned. "You know I will."

He nodded. "I know you'll be honest with me. I need you to be honest with yourself." When she nodded, he continued. "Are you really up to going out there?"

"Yes, I am."

After a couple of beats, he nodded. "All right. I'll clear the use of a Gulfstream. I'll let you know when it's ready. In the meantime, let John and Erin know what's happening."

"I will." She stood up and turned to go but paused at the doorway, turning back. "Thank you, Lou."

Chapter Forty-Two

TRAVERS AND NORWOOD ARRIVED on one of the ATVs. The four deputies placed Schilling in the transport shackles, which consisted of a leather belt and chain around his waist, cuffs, and leg shackles connected to the belt with chains. They set him down on his ass in the mud, keeping him under close guard. With his feet restricted to only about eighteen inches of movement, he wouldn't be going anywhere quickly or gracefully.

With the prisoner appropriately subdued, two of the deputies began shuttling the ATVs back down the bluff since the forensics team would need them to come up. When they were done, one ATV remained at the top so the two deputies staying to secure the area would have a way back down.

John answered his ringing phone. "Casper…Hey, Jessica…Good, good…Okay, I'll tell Erin…Anything else?…Okay. Bye." He moved over to where Erin was writing down the name, date, and town on each wine bottle label in her notepad. "Jessica called. She said the director's approved using a Gulfstream to transport Schilling back."

"Good. I really wasn't looking forward to transporting him on a commercial flight. Did she say when the plane would arrive?"

"No, she doesn't know yet, but I'd be surprised if it's before morning." John glanced at his watch. "Are you about ready to head down?"

Erin sighed. "Yes. Though I'm not exactly looking forward to trudging down in all that mud."

Noticing how quiet it was, John smiled. "Well, at least the rain has finally stopped."

Just as the group was about to leave, a helicopter flew overhead. The forensics team was already arriving since St. Louis was only about seventy-five miles from their location by air. The helicopter was going to land in a field just across Route 3 from the turnoff for Happy Hollow Road. Since the team was already there, the sheriff decided only one deputy, Deputy Norwood, needed to remain in the cabin.

Because of the shackles and the slippery mud, two deputies would have to hold onto the prisoner, one on each arm, which left the third deputy and the agents to cover them. It was going to be a long walk down. With Stratton on one arm and Whitcomb on the other, the group started down.

Their progress was slow and slippery as they made their way back. It was over a mile to the cars. Besides dealing with the mud, lots of large, uneven rocks littered the path. Not a single person escaped landing in the mud at least once or getting scratched or dinged on the rocks. However, it was Stratton and Whitcomb who had it the hardest. With the transport shackles, the prisoner often couldn't keep his footing. They spent the walk either picking him up or being pulled down with him. In the meantime, the ATVs, carrying the forensics personnel, passed them on their way up.

A motley group arrived at the cars at the base of the bluff. The deputies muscled the struggling, though still silent, prisoner into the back seat of one of the department cruisers. Travers grabbed a rain poncho from his trunk and placed it on the driver's seat of his cruiser to keep from messing it up. Since they were almost as muddy as the prisoner, Stratton and Whitcomb decided to ride back to the department together, so only one of the cruisers got messed up. They were so muddy that their ponchos wouldn't make a difference, so they loaned them to John and Erin to protect their rental car seats.

"Thank you for the poncho," Erin said.

"No problem, ma'am," replied Stratton.

"But why didn't you wear your rain ponchos today?"

Ashlee smiled. "They aren't safe to wear on the ATVs. They could get caught."

Erin nodded. "I see your point. We'll follow you back to the office."

Only a couple of miles down the road, John and Erin exchanged a surprised look when they saw Schilling's feet suddenly come through the back driver's side window. The patrol car quickly pulled over onto the side of the road. John pulled up behind them. By the time he and Erin got out of their vehicle and approached the patrol car, Deputy Stratton and Deputy Whitcomb had managed to remove the kicking and flailing man from the back seat. Despite getting kicked a couple of times, the deputies reconnected the chain to the shackles to the back of the belt and shorten it, effectively hogtying him and preventing any further kicking. They picked him up and put him in the back seat on his stomach.

Both cars were soon on their way down the road again.

The deputies pulled up into the sally port at the sheriff's department. The outer door was lowered, and Whitcomb went inside to enlist the aid of a couple of the jailers. The prisoner was taken in, strip-searched, and made to shower. Once clean, he was given a black and white striped jumpsuit and placed in an isolation cell. He would stay in the cell until the feds transported him back to DC.

While the jailers got Schilling settled, John and Erin took care of the paperwork. That done, they finally returned to the hotel to clean up and to change clothes. They met for a late dinner before returning to their respective rooms. Erin plugged in her dead cell phone to charge.

Erin's cell phone woke her up.

"Little."

"Hey, it's me."

Erin smiled. "Hey, Jess."

"Sorry if I woke you."

"No, no. I'm glad you called. Any word on the plane?" she asked, taking care of business first.

Jess smiled. "You'll be able to fly back tomorrow."

"Good."

"How was your day?"

"Could have been worse. I'm afraid I got mud in places I didn't know I had," she said with some mirth. "I took a shower before dinner and a long bath before going to bed. I'm still not sure I got it all."

"Really? Well, perhaps someone should make sure."

Erin's eyebrow arched in reflex. "And just who would you recommend for the job?" she said playfully.

"Hmm, good question." Jess' tone changed from playful to seductive. "I'm available for the job."

Erin's heart fluttered, and she felt warmed. "If only you were. I wish you were here."

"Erin?"

"Yes?"

"Close your eyes and listen to my voice." She paused for a beat. "Are your eyes closed?"

Eyes closed, Erin smiled. "Yes, they are," she answered softly.

"Good. Imagine me there, sitting next to you on the edge of the bed. I reach down and oh so tenderly caress your cheek with the back of my fingers. As your breath slightly quickens, I lean down and kiss your other cheek softly. I take a deep breath, taking in your scent. I kiss along your jawline until I get to your ear. Then I say softly into your ear, 'I love you.' I pull back to look into your soft, brown eyes before claiming your lips in a long, sensuous, deep kiss."

Erin's breathing hitched. A small whimper escaped her throat as she pictured, and felt, Jess with her. "God, Jess...I wish you were here!"

"Erin?"

"Hmm?"

"Open your door."

Erin frowned. "What?"

"Get out of bed and open your door." Jess hung up.

Erin unhooked the chain and opened the door to see Jess standing in front of her with a beautiful, seductive smile. She shot her hand out, grabbed Jess by the arm, and quickly pulled her inside. Kicking the door shut, she shoved Jess up against the wall and kissed her hungrily. Jess dropped her bag and wrapped her arms around Erin, holding her close, as she returned her kiss with equal fervor.

After a minute or so, Jess reached down with her left arm and scooped Erin's legs up. As they continued to kiss, she carried Erin to the bed and lowered her down on it. She lay down on top of her, but Erin quickly rolled Jess onto her back, as she kissed and nuzzled Jess' neck and throat.

Erin's deft hands made quick work of Jess' clothes. Her pajamas quickly followed them onto the floor. When Jess attempted to roll her over again, Erin put her hands on Jess' shoulders and pressed down as she lifted her head to look down at her. "Not this time," Erin said.

She quickly had her fingers inside Jess, moving and stimulating all those special places. Jess let out a moan, which Erin swallowed as she reclaimed her mouth with a passionate kiss. When Erin trailed kisses down to her breasts, Jess sunk her hands in Erin's hair. Every nerve in her body was alive. Erin could tell from the way Jess' warm channel clenched at her fingers that her lover was close to coming. She settled her full weight against Jess and nipped at her earlobe. "That's it. Come for me, Jess. Come for me because you're mine."

Erin's hotly whispered words, especially those of possessiveness, seemed like gasoline on fire. Jess came hard, a primal cry escaping her as her orgasm rocked her body, her arms and legs clenching onto Erin. Lying on top of Jess as she came was a thrill ride. Her body writhed and bucked, threatening to dislodge Erin. She held on and drew out Jess' orgasm as long as she could. Finally, Jess collapsed onto the mattress as her oxygen-starved body gasped for air. Erin gently withdrew her fingers, cleaned them with her tongue, and pulled Jess to her as she rolled to the side. She tenderly caressed a cheek as she gazed into the face of her lover, her lover who had fainted.

When Jess came to, she settled into Erin's embrace. "I love you, Erin," she whispered.

Erin tightened her arms around her lover and kissed Jess' forehead tenderly. "I love you too, Jess."

Jess took a slow, deep breath. "Guess I passed out."

Her lips curled into a smile where they rested against Jess' forehead.

Jess pulled back just enough to be able to look at Erin. "Feeling proud of ourselves, are we?"

Erin blushed but didn't even try to contain her smile or amusement. "Actually…"

Jess chuckled lightly as she laid her head back on Erin's shoulder. "You should be. That's never happened to me before."

Erin answered with a squeeze of her arms. "Well, I guess we're even then, since it never happened to me before yesterday morning in the shower."

Jess shifted to lean on her elbow and looked down at her. "Do you have any idea what you do to me?"

Erin gazed intently into sparkling gray eyes. "I hope it's half of what you do to me." She took Jess' hand and placed it over her heart, covering it with her own. "I feel alive with you, Jess."

Jess lowered her head and gently captured Erin's mouth with her own. Erin spent the better part of the next hour letting her lover worship her.

Chapter Forty-Three

March 27, 2025
Thursday

ERIN AWOKE AND FOUND herself spooning Jess. Yes, she loved being held by Jess, but it felt just as good to hold the younger woman as well. Whether in Jess' arms or Jess in hers, being with her was the way things were supposed to be. She knew it with a certainty that came from her soul. "I love you, Jess," she whispered before kissing her shoulder.

Jess woke up in time to hear Erin's softly whispered words. She pressed back against her. "I love you too," she sleepily replied. "Is it time to get up yet?"

She glanced over her shoulder at the clock radio. "Not yet."

"Good, because I don't want to move."

She nuzzled Jess' neck.

"Mmmm…" Jess smiled.

"Do you want to go back to sleep?"

Jess let out an amused chuckle. "Like that's going to happen, especially with you fondling my breast."

She stopped squeezing the breast in her hand. "I can stop."

Jess shifted, turning in Erin's arms to face her. "Not unless you want to."

Erin looked deep into her sparkling gray eyes. "I don't want to stop. I like touching you," she replied as her hand traveled down Jess' side and rested on her hip.

Leaning into Erin, Jess whispered, "And I like the way you touch me," before their lips met in a kiss. She moaned as Erin's hands sought out and found all the places that made her groan and whimper.

When the alarm went off, the two women got up. Erin quirked an eyebrow as she watched Jess pull on her clothes from the night before.

Jess smiled when she saw her expression. "I'm going to go to my room and take a shower." With a deliberate look at Erin's state of undress, she said, "Because if I don't, I doubt either of us will be ready on time." She picked up her bag. "I'll meet you and John in the restaurant."

With a soft chuckle, Erin returned her smile. "You're probably right. See you shortly." She turned and entered the bathroom.

John was clearly surprised to see Jessica enter the restaurant. He stood up as she approached the table and hugged her before they both sat down. "What are you doing here?"

"I came on the transport plane. I thought I would take a crack at Schilling on the way back, see if I can get him to talk."

"He's been pretty combative and uncooperative." He paused for a beat. "And does the director know you're here?" he asked suspiciously.

"That is a good question," Erin said as she arrived.

Jess smiled at both her companions. "Yes, I have the director's permission to be here. I just wish the plane could have been ready sooner than it was."

"When do you want to pick up Schilling and fly out?" John asked.

"Doesn't really matter. All you need to do is drop me and the pilots off at the airport on the way so we're ready for you when you pick up Schilling."

"What airport?"

"Southern Illinois. I'm sure you've seen the sign. It's about halfway between here and Murphysboro on Route 13."

"Oh yeah."

Jess looked up and saw the two pilots enter. She waved them over. She made the introductions all around. Agent Marks and Agent Denison joined them for breakfast, and after all the agents checked out of the hotel, they left.

Schilling changed into the orange jumpsuit federal prisoners had to wear, and the local guards placed him into transport shackles the feds provided. Once John took care of all the necessary paperwork, two deputies, with Schilling in the back of the patrol car, followed John and Erin to the airport.

A strategy had been worked out at breakfast. Even though Schilling had been combative and uncooperative, he had been completely silent, refusing to speak a single word. Jess would use their common background to try to break through his silence and get him talking. Also, they would emphasize Jess' position in the Bureau as the Director's personal troubleshooter. In addition, John would play the uncouth and disgruntled coworker, giving Schilling and Jess a common source of irritation and reinforce their shared "upper-class upbringing." Erin would also make her irritation with John obvious.

Jess was not on the plane when they arrived. She waited in the terminal, watching. John placed Schilling in a seat inside the aircraft and secured his seatbelt.

John turned to Erin. "Any sign of her yet?"

"Not yet."

"I still don't see why we have to wait for her," he said in irritation.

"She's here at the request of the director himself."

John waved his hand dismissively. "Well, if we've got to sit around on our asses waiting for her, I'm going to have something to drink. You want something?" he asked as he passed her into the small galley.

"No, thank you."

The copilot, Denison, was pouring himself a cup of fresh coffee in the galley.

John stuck his head back out. "There's fresh coffee if you want it, Little."

"No, thank you."

John returned with a glass filled with contents that looked like scotch.

Erin gave him a disdainful look. "You know better than that, Casper."

He again waved her off dismissively. John gave Schilling a sneer. "Oh, do you want a cup of coffee or a cigarette while we wait?"

The pilot, Agent Marks, came back. "She's here, so we'll take off in just a few minutes."

"Thank you," Erin replied. She shot a dirty look at John, who quickly downed his drink.

Both Erin and John stood when Jess entered the plane.

"Welcome aboard, ma'am. It's a pleasure having you aboard. I'm Agent Marks, your pilot. Agent Denison is my copilot today. If you need anything, please don't hesitate to let us know," the pilot greeted Jess before closing the hatch behind her. "If you'll make yourself comfortable, we'll take off in only a few minutes. Unfortunately, we do not have a flight attendant for this flight. However, once we are at altitude, you may help yourself to the refreshments available in the galley."

"Thank you."

Marks returned to the cockpit. Erin and John each introduced themselves and shook her hand in turn.

Once the plane reached altitude, Jess released her seatbelt and approached Schilling. She looked him in the eyes and gave him a nod of respect. "Hugh, it's good to see you again."

He looked up at her in confusion. "Excuse me?"

"You may not remember me, but we met about twenty years ago at one of the socials MIT and Harvard held for their youngest students. I'm Jessica Morgan. My father was Philippe Rodier."

He frowned in thought for a few moments, but then a look of recognition came over his face. "Oh yes, the Rodiers of Vancouver. My family owns some stock in Rodier International."

She nodded. "That's right, and my accountant would be glad to hear that," she said with a small smile.

"I do remember you. Didn't you leave Harvard in '07 to take a Rhodes scholarship?"

She nodded. "Yes. I graduated in '07. I took the Rhodes scholarship to pursue a degree in Theology and Religious Studies," she replied, surprised he'd remembered.

He cocked his head to the side. "You didn't come to very many of the socials."

She smiled softly. "No, I didn't."

He smiled roguishly. "As I recall, you were quite taken with a certain Vanessa Turner."

Jess arched an eyebrow and smirked. "As were you, I believe."

Schilling laughed. "True! Great minds do think alike, don't they?"

After a shared laugh, Jess gestured to a small table toward the back of the cabin. "Let's sit back here where we can have a bit of privacy."

Because of the transport shackles, Schilling struggled to undo his seatbelt and to stand.

"Hold on, Hugh." Jess called to John, "Agent Casper, come undo these shackles."

"I don't think that's a good idea, ma'am."

"I didn't ask you if it was a good idea, Agent. I gave you an order. Where's he going to go? We're on a plane several thousand feet in the air. All three of us are armed. He'll still be cuffed. There's no need for the shackles."

"You don't understand, ma'am. The prisoner has been violent and uncooperative while in custody. He kicked out a sheriff's patrol car window and had to be hobbled as a result."

Jess looked at Schilling in surprise. "Did you really?"

Schilling looked embarrassed and sheepish. He silently nodded.

She looked him in the eyes. "Will you give me your word you won't try anything, Hugh?"

"I give you my word, Jessica," he said solemnly.

"All right." She looked at John. "Remove the shackles."

"Ma'am—"

"Agent Casper, either remove the shackles or give me the key so I can. We have no car windows for the man to kick out, and he has given me his word not to try anything in any event."

John made a show of reluctantly following her orders. That done, Jess and Schilling moved to the small table, sitting opposite each other.

"Hugh, I'm sure you understand that I must ask you some questions."

He nodded. "I know."

"Before we get started, would you like something to drink?"

"He offered me some coffee and said I could have a cigarette."

"Well, that was rude of him, since you don't smoke or drink coffee," she said with a smirk. She leaned to the side to look around Schilling. "Casper, get us some tea," she called out.

"There's some fresh coffee in the galley," he replied.

Jess stood up and marched over to John. "Agent Casper, I do not know what your problem is, but I've had enough of your insolence. And don't think I haven't noticed the alcohol on your breath. When we land, you will surrender your badge and weapon and consider yourself on suspension until further notice. Now, get your ass in the galley and get us some tea: two cups, hot, and one empty cup, please."

As John went into the galley, Jess returned to her seat. "I'm sorry, Hugh. You know how hard it is to find quality help."

He sighed and nodded in agreement.

Erin watched everything silently, an almost imperceptible smile playing on her lips as she pretended to read.

John returned with two cups of hot tea and an empty cup.

"Is there any lemon?" Jess asked.

"Uh, no."

She exchanged a look of disappointment with Schilling. "Sorry, Hugh."

He shrugged as if to say he wasn't surprised. When Jess carefully placed her teabag in the empty cup between them, he gave her a surprised look.

"What? You didn't think I would squeeze the bag, did you, releasing the tannic acid into my tea?"

He smiled as he removed his teabag and placed it in the cup. "I shouldn't have doubted someone of your breeding and intelligence."

Several moments were spent in silence, sipping their tea. Jess knew exactly what she wanted to do. Even though they had a lot of evidence to prove Hugh Charles Schilling was The Slasher, she wanted a confession so they could lock him up, throw away the key, and not worry about him getting off due to any technicality. Finally, she broke the silence.

"Did they inform you of your rights, Hugh?"

He waved his hand dismissively. "I know my rights."

"Are you willing to talk to me then?"

He nodded.

Jess reached into her jacket pocket and withdrew a digital recorder. She pushed record and set it on the table. "This is Supervisory Special Agent Jessica R. Morgan, badge number JTT0440703, interviewing Mr. Hugh Charles Schilling. Today is Thursday, March 27, 2025. Mr. Schilling has been advised of his rights and is voluntarily answering questions without a lawyer present." She looked at him. "Would you please verify that, Hugh, for the record?"

"Of course. This is Hugh Charles Schilling. I know my rights and am willing to answer any questions Jessica Morgan poses to me." He paused. "But *only* her," he said and smiled. "How's that?"

"That's fine, Hugh." She paused for two or three beats. "When was the first time you killed, Hugh?"

"Animal or human?"

Not expecting him to be so forthcoming, Jess fought to keep her expression impassive. "Animal."

"When I was seven. I hated the neighbor's dog. It was an annoying, yippy, little thing. One day, I'd just had enough of its incessant yip-yapping. I snapped its neck. There was something so satisfying about it."

"What did you do with the body?"

"Tossed it on their back porch," he replied with a nonchalant shrug.

Jess frowned. "But you grew up in Manhattan, Hugh, on Park Avenue."

"Oh, this was in the summer, in the Hamptons."

"I see. And when was the first time you killed a human?"

Schilling didn't answer. He appeared lost in thought.

"Hugh?"

"Do you remember Calvin Thibodaux? You probably met him at one of the socials that first year. Dirty blonde, blue eyes, horn-rim glasses, lanky."

Jess nodded slowly. "I remember."

"When did you see your first dead body, Jessica?"

"My mother. I was six."

"But that was at the funeral, right?"

"Yes."

"When was the first time you saw a body before it was made to look pretty?" he asked, using finger quotes.

"I was twenty-one."

"Calvin was the first one I saw."

Jess' eyes widened. "Are you saying you killed Calvin?"

"No. He killed himself. I found him. He had hanged himself in the lab the night we were supposed to finish our project for Professor Kensington's class."

"I'm sorry you had to go through that, Hugh."

He shrugged. "No big deal. He was weak, couldn't take the pressure." A second shrug. "I thought it would have been interesting to autopsy the body though."

Hugh had no feelings whatsoever about the suicide of his lab partner. He really was a psychopath. "When did you start killing, Hugh?"

"The first time was in 2013. It was an accident. Kira Norris."

Jess flipped through the names Erin had written down. "I don't see that name as one of the ones labeled on the bottles, Hugh."

"No, it's not. Like I said, it was an accident. The ones on the bottles were planned. They're the ones I savored, each a rare vintage."

The flight to Baltimore-Washington International was an hour and a half. However, at a discreet signal from Jess, Erin got up and went to the cockpit to tell the pilots to circle until further notice. As long as Schilling was talking, Jess would get all she could from him. The Gulfstream could stay in the air for ten hours if necessary.

Chapter Forty-Four

FOR OVER SEVEN HOURS, Schilling sat and told Jess about the women he'd murdered. Finally, Jess gave the signal to have the plane land. When they landed, Jess ushered Schilling out of the plane and into the back of the waiting vehicle—without the shackles. He'd told her he wouldn't try anything, and she believed him, at least as long as she was present. She did not doubt that if she weren't present, Schilling would be completely uncooperative.

As the SUV pulled away from the plane, he turned to her. "Just out of curiosity, it was you who figured out about my refuge, wasn't it?"

She shrugged. "It was the only property you tried to hide, Hugh." She gave him a hard look. "But did you have to rig booby traps? A detective was injured. He could have been killed."

He looked surprised. "I haven't set any of the booby traps in years. Which one tripped?"

"A piece of rebar just about impaled him near his heart. It would have killed him if he hadn't been wearing Kevlar."

Schilling shook his head in thought. "That shouldn't have happened. I swear, Jessica. After the first couple of years and with no sign of anyone knowing where I was, I stopped setting the traps. Hell, the only reason I wasn't inside the cabin when they showed up was because I went to the storage cellar for some soup."

"And what would you have done if you had been in the cabin? I understand you put up quite a fight. And then you kicked out the backseat window of a deputy's car."

Schilling looked genuinely ashamed. "I had always thought that if I were caught, I would just accept it." He shrugged. "But after all these years and no one even coming close to catching me, I guess it took me by surprise and it kind of pissed me off."

"And now?"

Schilling sighed. "I went almost twelve years without anyone even coming close. And I didn't leave any incriminating evidence behind. Not many can say that."

"No, not many can say that."

"Tell me, Jessica, how long have you been after me?" he asked with genuine curiosity.

"I was brought in on the case six weeks ago."

"Six weeks?"

She nodded. "I might have found you sooner, but someone who pretended to be you distracted me."

"Really?"

"It's not important."

"Actually, I was thinking six weeks was damn good considering how careful I was. Well done," he said with a smile.

At the Chesapeake Detention Facility, Jess accompanied Schilling as far through the booking process as she was allowed.

"Jessica."

She turned back when he called out to her.

"It was good to see you again."

"Try to behave, Hugh," she replied with a nod.

He nodded, and she left.

Erin took one look at Jess when she exited the prison and knew she'd reached her limit. She walked up to Jess and wrapped her arms around her. "It's over," she whispered in her ear. Erin tightened her arms around Jess as she felt the woman sag a little. "Come on, let's get out of here."

"Where's John?"

"He headed back to Headquarters." Erin opened the passenger side door for Jess before getting in the driver's seat. She looked over at Jess before starting the car. "John called Taylor when we landed at the airport. The director was with him. We're to take the morning off, then report to the director's office at one o'clock."

"Good."

"I thought that since we were in Baltimore anyway, we could have that dinner with my mom, but I think I'll call her back and cancel."

Reaching out and placing her hand over Erin's, Jess said, "No, don't cancel, Erin. It's early, and I like your mom."

She turned her hand under Jess' and squeezed it. "Are you sure? I know you're beat."

Jess nodded.

When Ellie opened her front door, she hugged Erin. Then she pulled Jess into a warm hug. She exchanged a look with Erin that clearly expressed her concern. Erin nodded, letting her mother know that while she was concerned, Jess would be okay.

With her arm around Jess' waist, Ellie ushered them inside. "You look like you're ready to drop, Jess. Come in and rest while I finish making dinner."

"I'm fine, Mrs. Little."

"Now you know better than that! It's Ellie."

Jess smiled. "Sorry. And I'm just a little tired, Ellie. It's been a long day."

"Do you need some help with dinner, Mom?" Erin asked.

"No, no. You two make yourselves comfortable." Ellie disappeared into the kitchen.

They both sat on the couch.

"Are you sure you're all right, Jess?"

"Yeah. Schilling was just..." Jess trailed off and sighed.

"A sick bastard."

Jess nodded. "A true psychopath. He has absolutely no remorse and no feelings about killing at all. Nothing would have stopped him. And he was perfect, Erin. He didn't leave any evidence behind. By all rights, we shouldn't have caught him. We did only because we got a lucky break with a nanny cam." She let out a slow breath. "I need a break from dealing with these guys." Suddenly, her phone rang.

"Morgan...Just a second." Jess looked at her as she stood up. "Would you excuse me, Erin?"

"Certainly."

After Jess walked outside to take the call, Erin entered the kitchen.

"Erin, are you sure Jess is all right?" Ellie asked.

"Yes. She's just had an extremely long day. She interrogated a psychopathic serial killer for over seven hours straight."

"Oh my."

"Anything I can help you with?"

"Nope. The chicken is in the oven. We need to wait for it to finish cooking." They walked back out to the living room. "Where's Jess?"

"She stepped outside to take a call."

Just then, Jess came back in from outside. "Sorry about that."

"Is everything okay?" Erin asked since Jess looked a little shell-shocked.

"Yeah. That was the director. You know he's been trying to get me to Quantico."

Erin nodded.

"Well, he said that wasn't my only choice. He just offered me my choice of three SAC postings."

"Where?"

"Miami, San Francisco, and London."

Erin's eyes widened. All prime postings, and all some distance from DC. "Wow. Those are all choice postings."

"What exactly is a SAC?" Ellie asked.

"It's a Special Agent in Charge. They command a field office," Erin answered her mother.

"And the FBI has field offices overseas?"

"Well, actually, they're legal attaché offices within American embassies," Jess explained.

Ellie looked at Jess as she sat down. "Would you want to go overseas?"

Jess took a deep breath and let it out slowly. "I think the director offered me London because he knows I have a home there."

"You do?"

"It was my grandfather's."

"Well, it sounds like you have quite a decision to make. Congratulations."

"Thank you, Ellie."

"How soon do you have to give him your decision?" Erin asked.

Jess looked at her lover and smiled. "Not until after I get back from vacation."

"Oh, you're taking a vacation?" Ellie asked.

"Yes." She chuckled. "I think I shocked the director. I haven't taken a vacation in years."

"You sound like my daughter."

"Mom."

"Well, it's true," Ellie quipped.

"Actually, I've invited Erin to go on vacation with me, Ellie."

Ellie looked at her daughter. "Are you going to go?"

Erin felt herself blush. "Yes, I am."

"Good!" Ellie said with a smile. "You're long overdue for a vacation."

After dinner, Erin and Jess drove back to Washington. Despite wanting to talk to Jess about what posting she was considering, Erin recognized Jess' need to decompress from the very stressful day. They made the journey in a comfortable and companionable silence.

As soon as they entered the apartment, Erin reached out and caught Jess' hand, causing her to turn and look at her.

"Why don't you go and get undressed while I start a hot bath for you?"

Touched by the offer, Jess smiled at her. "That would be wonderful. Thank you."

Erin went into the bathroom to start the bath while Jess entered the bedroom and undressed. She slipped on a robe and entered the bathroom, a little surprised not to find Erin present. When the water reached the correct level, she turned off the water and shed her robe. She sighed as she carefully eased herself into the large claw-foot tub, filled with steamy water and bubbles. She closed her eyes and laid her head back. After a couple of minutes, she opened her eyes when she heard Erin's voice.

"Mind if I join you?" Erin was wearing a robe and holding a tray with an opened wine bottle and two glasses.

She smiled widely. "Not at all."

Erin pulled over a small stand and set the tray on it. She then shed her robe and slipped into the tub behind Jess. After pouring two glasses of wine and handing one to Jess, Erin pulled Jess back against her, kissing her temple.

"Mmmm, this is nice. Thank you," said Jess.

"You've had quite a day."

She closed her eyes and allowed herself to settle against Erin fully. "God, to sit there and listen to him recount every one of the murders so dispassionately as if they were nothing..." Jess felt Erin's arms tighten around her.

"They weren't nothing. They were ninety-eight women whose families love and miss them."

"Those are just the ones he planned and took blood from."

"What do you mean?"

"The first one wasn't planned, a woman named Kira Norris. He killed her in his office at Boeing. When he got away with it without any questions, he quit and started planning and executing murders."

"Well, he was flawless."

"Until Claudia Keenan in Chicago. Schilling was sure he'd been spotted. So he followed Ben Lufkin home. It turned out Lufkin was a cop. He made him call into work and quit. Then he killed him, his wife, and two kids. He cleared out their home, making it appear they'd moved. He even had the nerve to use Lufkin's name and give his lieutenant's name as a reference to your pal Chief Bud Calhoun in Midway, Georgia. Lieutenant Sawyer was so relieved to hear from Calhoun that Lufkin was in Georgia that he gave a glowing reference without questioning if it was really him."

"Damn."

"Yeah."

"And he told you about all of them?"

Jess nodded and sighed. "He found me worthy. 'Someone of proper breeding and intelligence,'" she said mockingly. She let out a derisive huff. "All because my 'father' was Philippe Rodier, a misogynistic bastard who could never be described as nice on his best day," she practically growled.

Erin kissed Jess' temple and gave her a gentle squeeze with her arms. "Well, you were certainly a gifted student."

Jess waved her hand dismissively. "Plenty of people could excel scholastically if given the same advantages I had."

"Can I ask you something?"

"Sure."

"Why is your name Morgan if your parents' name was Rodier?"

"Ah, that. Lady Elizabeth was a bit whimsical, to put it politely. And Philippe was a cold-hearted bastard. Sometimes, Elizabeth would go off alone, especially when they traveled on business trips. Often, it was the only way she could gain his attention. When he eventually noticed, he would send someone after her. He did become a little more attentive once he was told she was pregnant with his son. However, on a business trip in the States, Elizabeth again set out on her own and checked into a hotel under her maiden name, Morgan. While out on her excursion, she ended up having some complications and was rushed to the hospital, where she was given an emergency C-section. It was the next day before Philippe realized she'd taken off again. When the family lawyer tracked her down, he'd told Philippe she'd already given birth. He showed up with a large bouquet, which he promptly threw in the trash when presented with his *daughter* instead of the son he had expected. Anyway, Elizabeth had been checked into the hospital under her maiden name, and that's what was put on my birth certificate. When Philippe was asked about changing it, he said only his son would bear his name."

Erin set her wineglass down and wrapped both her arms around Jess. Her heart ached for her lover. "Oh, Jess. I'm so sorry."

Jess shrugged. "It's okay. Morgan was my grandfather's name, and he was a good man, a very good man," she said softly.

After their relaxing bath, Erin and Jess turned in for the night. They curled up together with Erin spooning Jess.

"So which posting do you think you'll take?" Erin finally asked.

Jess smiled as she shifted to roll over and face Erin. "That depends."

"On what?"

"On where you'd like to go."

"What do you mean?"

Jess reached up and caressed Erin's cheek. "Do you really think I'm going anywhere without you? And in case you need that answer spelled out for you, it's 'no.'" Jess leaned in and captured Erin's lips with a tender kiss.

She felt her heart swell at Jess' quiet but firm declaration and skip a beat as Jess kissed her.

Jess pulled back from the kiss and gazed into her eyes. "You still have your choice of postings, Erin. I'll go wherever you want."

"After we came back from the West Coast, I had requested to go back to Quantico once the case was over."

"All right, if that's still what you want, we can go to Quantico."

"The thing is, I don't know if that's what I want. I requested it as a stopgap until I could figure some things out. I don't know where I'd like to go."

"Well, we don't have to decide until after our vacation. And if we still don't know by then, there's nothing wrong with Quantico. It might be nice to have regular hours for a change. We certainly don't have to decide right now."

They drifted to sleep in each other's arms.

Epilogue

March 28, 2025
Friday

ERIN AND JESS SHOWERED and dressed after sleeping in and some languorous lovemaking. They went out for brunch and then drove to the Hoover building. John arrived at the same time, so they rode up together in the elevator. When the three arrived at the director's office, they found AD Taylor waiting in the outer office.

They didn't even get a chance to sit down before Director Cavanaugh opened the door to his inner office and greeted them all. He turned to his assistant. "Hold my calls, Stacy. And bring us some fresh coffee, please," he ordered.

"Yes, sir."

He indicated that they all should have a seat in the sitting area of his office. "Okay, bring me up to date."

Jess started. "As you know, Erin and John apprehended Schilling in Illinois. On the plane back, he freely confessed to every one of the ninety-eight murders represented by the bottles of blood in his cabin. He also confessed to the murder of Kira Norris, his first victim, and Chicago police officer Ben Lufkin, his wife, and their two children," Jess answered.

"Is he sane?"

"He's a true psychopath. He has no remorse whatsoever, but he does know what he did was wrong. However, even though I could record his complete confession, I'm afraid his expensive lawyers could argue his sanity and a judge could decide." She paused for a beat before continuing. "But then again, he could surprise us and simply plead guilty," she finished with a shrug.

There was a knock on the door, and Stacy entered with a tray. She brought a pot of fresh coffee to the sitting area and poured a cup for everyone except Jess. Knowing Jess didn't care for coffee, she handed her a mug of hot tea. Each person took care of adding cream and sugar to their preference.

"Thank you, Stacy," the director said.

"You're welcome, sir." Stacy closed the door behind herself as she left.

The director looked at AD Taylor. "And what of the forensics team? What did they find?"

"The wine bottles full of blood, four bottles of Clive Christian's No. 1 perfume, driver's licenses for over two dozen identities, empty wine bottles, and some trocars with tubing."

Erin's eyes lit up. "That must be how he took their blood and filled the wine bottles."

Jess frowned. "But wouldn't you have found evidence of him having used a trocar during the autopsies?" she asked.

"I don't understand. What is a trocar?" asked John.

"It's a device used in embalming to drain bodily fluids," Jess answered.

"That's not all they're used for. They're also used in laparoscopic surgery, and small ones are used to place intravenous cannulas. And with the knife wounds on the victims, it would have been very easy to destroy any evidence of their use," Erin explained.

"What about the booby traps he had set up at the cabin?" the director asked.

"The one Detective..." Taylor checked his notes, "Whitten was injured by was the only one set at the time."

"Schilling did tell me that he hadn't set any of the traps in years. He said that after the first couple of years with no sign of anyone knowing he was up there, he'd stopped setting the traps altogether," Jess said.

"And you believe him?" John asked.

"Actually, I do."

"The forensics team did say it appeared to have been a malfunction rather than a deliberate act," Taylor agreed.

They continued to discuss the specifics of the case for the next hour or so before the director called the meeting to an end.

"All right, John, you can report to Norfolk for your original assignment. Good work."

"Yes, sir. Thank you." He got up and left, dismissed.

He then looked at Jess and Erin. "And I understand you both have put in for a couple of weeks of vacation before deciding on your next assignments." He waited until they nodded. "Your vacation is approved starting Monday, April 7th."

"Thank you, sir," Erin replied.

Jess nodded.

"In the meantime," he paused, "take next week off. I don't want to see either of your faces around here until April 21st. Now get out of here," he said with a smile.

"Thank you, sir," Jess said with a smile.

Jess and Erin got up and left.

Outside the director's office, Erin turned to Jess. "Did he just give us an additional week of vacation?"

Jess grinned. "He sure did. And I, for one, plan to make good use of it. Come on, let's get out of here."

Once they were in Erin's car, Jess turned to her. "You said a secluded beach somewhere. I know a couple of wonderful places. Let me make some phone calls, and we can be there tomorrow. What do you say, Erin?"

Erin smiled, unable to resist. "I say yes!"

Jess placed her phone calls and received a return phone call. She hung up and smiled at Erin. "It's all set."

"What?"

"A small private villa on the beach in Saint Martin. We fly out of BWI at seven o'clock in the morning, change planes in Charlotte, and land at a quarter past one. A car will be waiting to drive us to the villa. Then we'll fly back the Saturday before we're due back at work at about three in the afternoon with a direct flight to Dulles, landing at half past seven."

Erin and Jess spent the rest of the afternoon getting ready for their vacation. They packed light, knowing they wouldn't be venturing out often. After an early dinner, they showered and turned in since they had to get up early.

Erin laid her head on Jess' shoulder as they settled. "I've never actually gone on vacation with anyone besides my family."

"You haven't?"

"Nope."

"Well, I'm thrilled you've decided to go with me."

Erin pulled back so she could look at Jess. She reached up and caressed her cheek. "I know we've only known each other for a few weeks, but I've never felt this way about anyone, Jess. I know in my heart that I belong with you."

Jess felt her heart skip a beat and then race. She knew that she and Toni had loved each other, but Erin...Erin touched her heart and soul in a way no one ever had.

Erin was gazing directly into her eyes as she continued. "I feel like I was born to love you," she said softly.

Jess was moved by Erin's words, so much so her eyes changed, but only momentarily. Something about Erin pulled at her other half. Something she'd felt even before she had taken Erin's blood, but it had grown stronger since then. More than once, she'd felt an urge to bite Erin when they made love, but not to feed. It was something else. She didn't know what it was, just what it wasn't. It didn't matter though, because she would never hurt Erin. She'd hurt herself before she'd let herself hurt Erin.

Erin rolled Jess onto her back, straddling her hips, and took her face in both hands. "No, Jess. No. Don't ever hold back, not with me."

"You don't understand, Erin."

"Yes, I do. I know that you've never been able to be yourself completely with anyone. But that's exactly what I need from you. I need you to not hold back, Jess. Please. I love you, *all* of you."

Jess held her eyes for a few moments before her eyes once again shifted to black, and she raised her head to claim Erin's lips with her own. She wrapped her arms around Erin and rolled them over so she was on top, deepening the kiss.

Erin broke their kiss long enough to peel Jess' tank top off over her head. She then slipped her hands under the waist of Jess' pajama bottoms and panties and squeezed her ass cheeks. Jess brought her hands up and started unbuttoning Erin's top. She trailed open-mouthed kisses down the slowly exposed skin until she captured an erect nipple and sucked. Erin let out a quiet moan and arched up into her.

She continued to kiss her way down and slid Erin's pajama bottoms and underwear off. Her knees raised and parted as Jess kissed, licked, and nipped her way down her torso. She settled between Erin's thighs and took her in her mouth.

Her head slammed back into the pillow, and her hands slid into Jess' hair. As Jess pushed a couple of fingers into Erin, her body bowed up off the bed. It didn't take long for her to come. She immediately started pulling at Jess, urging her up and wrapping her arms around her. Jess shared Erin's taste on her lips and tongue as they kissed.

Deft hands quickly removed and discarded Jess' pajama bottoms and panties. A foot ran down the back of Jess' thigh and calf. Then a hand slipped in between them, fingertips sliding through the wetness of Jess' arousal and zeroing in on her clit.

Jess' back arched, and she bucked against Erin's hand. She kissed her way down and sucked at Erin's breast, shifting so she was straddling Erin's hips. Erin slid her fingers inside her, making her moan.

Erin urged Jess back up from her breast so that they could kiss again. Jess ran her fingers through Erin's hair. She broke the kiss and pulled back just enough to gaze into her brown eyes.

Wrapping her hand around Jess' neck, Erin pulled Jess down and whispered hotly in her ear, "Don't hold back."

It was as if Erin knew what Jess feared...and craved.

"Don't you dare hold back, Jess. I love *all* of you."

For the first time in Jess' life, she completely gave in to her other side...and another person. She gave in to the urge to bite Erin. She didn't taste blood. She was, however, convinced she was having an out-of-body experience. She felt everything and everywhere and everywhen. She felt Erin. She felt Erin and herself merge, flowing in and out and around each other, becoming one, remaining two, perfectly combined. Stars faded, and still the two of them were together. She came to rest, cradled in Erin's arms where she remained as they slept.

The driver of the car handed Jess a message when they landed on the island the following afternoon. She closed her eyes and rubbed her forehead as the driver loaded their bags in the trunk.

"What's wrong, Jess?" Erin asked as they got in the back seat.

Jess sighed. "There was a screw up at the prison yesterday afternoon, a violation in security protocol. Schilling tried to kill Holton. He stabbed him. Schilling's still in isolation, but Holton was taken to the infirmary." She paused. "He wasn't as hurt as he let on. He escaped last night." Jess looked at Erin. "We can turn around and head back."

"No. He's a fugitive. Let the Bureau and the Marshal Service worry about him. He's not my problem anymore." Erin leaned over and kissed her lover. "My future is with you."

THE END

Acknowledgements

Special thanks to Gin, Ingrid, Jodi, Ashley, and Roxy.

About Dee Rismiller

Dee was born in California and raised in Iowa. After two years in college, she served in the US Navy from 1981 to 1985. Upon leaving the service, she held a couple different jobs, until settling in as a financial fraud investigator in the banking industry. Over the years she's lived in Georgia, Virginia, and Delaware. Currently, Dee is retired, single, and living in Corpus Christi, TX.

Note to Readers

Thank you for reading a book from Desert Palm Press. We appreciate you as a reader and want to ensure you enjoy the reading process. We would like you to consider posting a review on your preferred media sites and/or your blog or website.

For more information on upcoming releases, author interviews, contests, giveaways and more, please sign up for our newsletter and visit us at Desert Palm Press: www.desertpalmpress.com and "Like" us on Facebook: Desert Palm Press.

Bright Blessings